SUMMER'S END

Danielle Steel

A DELL BOOK

Published by
Dell Publishing Co., Inc.
1 Dag Hammarskjold Plaza
New York, New York 10017

Dell ® TM 681510, Dell Publishing Co., Inc.

Printed in the United States of America

To Bill, Beatrix, and Nicholas,
cherished people of my soul

SUMMER'S END

The summer came
  like a whisper
    dancing
  in her hair,
wishing he would
      care
  and dream
  and stop
    the carousel
  until he heard
    her truth
until he brought
  her youth
back
    laughing
      to her eyes,
she wanted him
    to realize
  she loved him
      still
    until
too late . . .
  but time
    would never
      wait,
  would never be . . .
    and she was free
for sand castles
  and dreams,
the summer schemes
  so sweet
    so new,
      so old . . .
the story told,
  the heavens
    blend
the love lives on
    'til
      summer's end.
                d.s.

1

Deanna Duras opened one eye to look at the clock as the first light stole in beneath the shades. It was 6:45. If she got up now, she would still have almost an hour to herself, perhaps more. Quiet moments in which Pilar could not attack, or harass; when there would be no phone calls for Marc-Edouard from Brussels or London or Rome. Moments in which she could breathe and think and be alone. She slipped out quietly from beneath the sheets, glancing at Marc-Edouard, still asleep on the far side of the bed. The very far side. For years now, their bed could have slept three or four, the way she and Marc kept to their sides. It wasn't that they never joined in the middle anymore, they still did . . . sometimes. When he was in town, when he wasn't tired, or didn't come home so very, very late. They still did—once in a while.

Silently she reached into the closet for the long, ivory, silk robe. She looked young and delicate in the early morning light, her dark hair falling softly over her shoulders like a sable shawl. She stooped for a moment looking for her slippers. Gone. Pilar must have them again. Nothing was sacred, not even slippers, least of all Deanna. She smiled to herself as she padded barefoot and silent across the thick carpeting and stole another glance at Marc, still asleep, so peaceful there. When he slept, he still looked terribly young, almost like the man she had met nineteen years before. She watched him as she stood in the doorway, wanting him to stir, to wake, to hold his arms out to her sleepily with a smile, whispering the words of so long ago, *"Reviens, ma chérie.* Come back to bed, *ma Diane. La belle Diane.*

She hadn't been that to him in a thousand years or more. She was simply Deanna to him now, as to everyone else: "Deanna, can you come to dinner on Tuesday? Deanna, did you know that the garage door isn't properly closed? Deanna, the cashmere jacket I just bought in London got badly mauled at the cleaner. Deanna, I'm leaving for Lisbon tonight (Or Paris. Or Rome)." She sometimes wondered if he even remembered the days of *Diane*, the days of late rising and laughter and coffee in her garret, or on her roof as they soaked up the sun in the months before they were married. They had been months of golden dreams, golden hours— the stolen weekends in Acapulco, the four days in Madrid when they had pretended that she was his secretary. Her mind drifted back often to those long-ago times. Early mornings had a way of reminding her of the past.

"*Diane, mon amour,* are you coming back to bed?" Her eyes shone at the remembered words. She had been just eighteen and always anxious to come back to bed. She had been shy but so in love with him. Every hour, every moment had been filled with what she felt. Her paintings had shown it too, they glowed with the luster of her love. She remembered his eyes, as he sat in the studio, watching her, a pile of his own work on his knees, making notes, frowning now and then as he read, then smiling in his irresistible way when he looked up. "*Alors,* Madame Picasso, ready to stop for lunch?"

"In a minute, I'm almost through."

"May I have a look?" He would make as though to peek around the easel, waiting for her to jump up and protest, as she always did, until she saw the teasing in his eyes.

"Stop that! You know you can't see it till I'm through."

"Why not? Are you painting a shocking nude?" Laughter lighting those dazzling blue eyes.

"Perhaps I am, monsieur. Would that upset you very much?"

"Absolutely. You're much too young to paint shocking nudes."

"Am I?" Her big green eyes would open wide, sometimes taken in by the seeming seriousness of his words. He had replaced her father in so many ways. Marc had become the voice of authority, the strength on which she relied. She had been so overwhelmed when her father had died. It had been a godsend when suddenly Marc-Edouard Duras had appeared. She had lived with a series of aunts and uncles after her father's death, none of whom had welcomed Deanna's presence in their midst. And then finally, at the age of eighteen, after a year of vagabonding among her mother's relatives, she had gone off on her own, working in a boutique in the daytime, going to art school at night. It was the art classes that kept her spirit alive. She lived only for that. She had been seventeen when her father died. He had died instantly, crashing in the plane he loved to fly. No plans had ever been made for her future; her father was convinced he was not only invincible but immortal. Deanna's mother had died when she was twelve, and for years there had been no one in her life except Papa. Her mother's relatives in San Francisco were forgotten, shut out, generally ignored by the extravagant and selfish man whom they held responsible for her death. Deanna knew little of what had happened, only that "Mommy died." Mommy died—her father's words on that bleak morning would ring in her ears for a lifetime. The Mommy who had shut herself away from the world, who had hidden in her bedroom and a bottle, promising always "in a minute, dear" when Deanna knocked on her door. The "in a minute, dears" had lasted for ten of her twelve years, leaving Deanna to play alone in corridors or her room, while her father flew his plane and went off suddenly on business trips with friends. For a long time it had been difficult to decide if he had disappeared on trips because her mother drank, or if she drank because Papa was always gone. Whatever the reason, Deanna was alone. Until her mother died. After that there had been considerable discussion about "what in hell to do. For God's sake, I don't know a damned thing about kids, least of all little girls." He had wanted to send her away, to a school, to a "wonderful place where there will be horses and pretty country and lots of new friends." But she had been so distraught that at last he had relented. She didn't want to go to a wonderful place, she wanted to be with him. *He* was a wonderful place, the magic father with the plane, the man who brought her marvelous gifts from faraway places. The man she had bragged about for years and never understood. Now, he was all she had. All she had left, now that the woman behind the bedroom door was gone.

So he kept her. He took her with him when he could, left her with friends when he couldn't, and taught her to enjoy the finer things in life: The Imperial Hotel in Tokyo, the George V in Paris, and The Stork Club in New York, where she had perched on a stool at the bar and not only drank a Shirley Temple but met her as a grown woman. Papa had led a fabulous life. And so had

Deanna, for a while, watching everything, taking it all in, the sleek women, the interesting men, the dancing at El Morocco, the weekend trips to Beverly Hills. He had been a movie star once, a long time ago, a race driver, a pilot during the war, a gambler, a lover, a man with a passion for life and women and anything he could fly. He wanted Deanna to fly too, wanted her to know what it was to watch over the world at ten thousand feet, sailing through clouds and living on dreams. But she had had her own dreams, that were nothing like his. A quiet life, a house where they stayed all the time, a stepmother who did not hide behind "in a minute" or an always locked door. At fourteen she was tired of El Morocco, and at fifteen she was tired of dancing with his friends. At sixteen she had managed to finish school, and desperately wanted to go to Vassar or Smith. Papa insisted it would be a bore. So she painted instead, on sketch pads and canvases she took with her wherever they went. She drew on paper tablecloths in the South of France, and the backs of letters from his friends, having no friends of her own. She drew on anything she could get her hands on. A gallery owner in Venice had told her that she was good, that if she stuck around, he might show her work. He didn't of course. They left Venice after a month, and Florence after two, Rome after six, and Paris after one, then finally came back to the States, where Papa promised her a home, a real one this time, and maybe even a real-live stepmother to go with it. He had met an American actress in Rome—"someone you'll love," he had promised, as he packed a bag for the weekend at her ranch somewhere near L.A.

This time he didn't ask Deanna to come along. This time he wanted to be alone. He left Deanna at the Fairmont in San Francisco, with four hundred dollars in cash and a promise to be back in three days. Instead he was dead in three hours, and Deanna was alone. Forever this time. And back where she had started, with the threat of a "wonderful school."

But this time the threat was short-lived. There was no money left. For a wonderful school or anything else. None. And a mountain of debts that went unpaid. She called the long-forgotten relatives of her mother. They arrived at the hotel and took her to live with them. "Only for a few months, Deanna. You understand. We just can't. You'll have to get a job, and get your own place when you get on your feet." A job. What job? What could she do? Paint? Draw? Dream. What difference did it make now that she knew almost every piece in the Uffizi and the Louvre, that she had spent months in the Jeu de Paume, that she had watched her father run with the bulls in Pamplona, had danced at El Morocco and stayed at the Ritz? Who gave a damn? No one did. In three months she was moved in with a cousin and then with another aunt. "For a while, you understand." She understood it all now, the loneliness, the pain, the seriousness of what her father had done. He had played his life away. He had had a good time. Now she understood what had happened to her mother, and why. For a time she came to hate the man she had loved. He had left her alone, frightened, and unloved.

Providence had come in the form of a letter from France. There had been a small case pending in the French courts, a minor judgment, but her father had won. It was a matter of six or seven thousand dollars. Would she be so kind as to have her attorney contact the French firm? What attorney? She called one from a list she got from one of her aunts, and he referred her to an international firm of lawyers. She had gone to their offices at nine o'clock on a Monday morning, dressed in a little black dress she had bought with her father in France. A little black Dior, with a little black alligator bag he had brought her back from Brazil, and the pearls that were all that her mother had left her. She didn't give a damn about Dior, or Paris, or Rio, or anything else. The promised six or seven thousand dollars was a king's ransom to her. She wanted to give up her job and go to art school day and night. In a few years she'd make a name for herself with her art. But in the meantime maybe she could live on the six thousand for a year. Maybe.

That was all that she wanted, when she walked into the huge wood-paneled office and met Marc-Edouard Duras for the very first time.

"Mademoiselle. . . ." He had never had a case quite like hers. His field was corporate law, complex international business cases, but when the secretary had relayed her call, he had been intrigued. When he saw her, a delicate child-woman with a frightened beautiful face, he was fascinated. She moved with mystifying grace, and the eyes that looked into his were bottomless. He ushered her to a seat on the other side of the desk, and looked very grave. But his eyes danced as they talked their way through the hour. He too loved the Uffizi, he too had once spent days at a time in the Louvre; he had also been to São Paulo and Caracas and Deauville. She found herself sharing her world with him and opening windows and doors that she had thought were sealed forever. And she had explained about her father. She told him the whole dreadful tale, as she sat across from him, with the largest green eyes he had ever seen and a fragility that tore at his heart. He had been almost thirty-two at the time, certainly not old enough to be her father, and his feelings were certainly not paternal. But nonetheless he took her under his wing. Three months later she was his wife. The ceremony was small and held at city hall; the honeymoon was spent at his mother's house in Antibes, followed by two weeks in Paris.

And by then she understood what she had done. She had married a country as well as a man. A way of life. She would have to be perfect, understanding—and silent. She would have to be charming and entertain his clients and friends. She would have to be lonely while he traveled. And she would have to give up the dream of making a name for herself with her art. Marc didn't really approve. In the days when he courted her, he had been amused, but it was not a career he encouraged for his wife. She had become Madame Duras, and to Marc that meant a great deal.

Over the years she gave up a number of dreams, but she had Marc. The man who had saved her from solitude and starvation. The man who had won her gratitude and her heart. The man of impeccable manners and exquisite taste, who rewarded her with security and sable. The man who always wore a mask.

She knew that he loved her, but now he rarely expressed it as he had done before. "Shows of affection are for children," he explained.

But that would come too. They conceived their first child in less than a year. How Marc had wanted that baby! Enough to show her once more how much he loved her. A boy. It would be a boy. Because Marc said so. He was certain, and so was Deanna. She wanted only that. His son. It had to be; it was the one thing that would win her his respect and maybe even his passion for a lifetime. A son. And it was. A tiny baby boy with a whisper in his lungs. The priest was called only moments after the birth and christened him Philippe-Edouard. In four hours the baby was dead.

Marc took her to France for the summer and left her in the care of his mother and aunts. He spent the summer working in London, but he came back on weekends, holding her close and drying her tears, until at last she conceived again. The second baby died too, another boy. And having Marc's child became her obsession. She dreamed only of their son. She even stopped painting. The doctor put her to bed when she became pregnant for the third time. Marc had cases in Milan and Morocco that year, but he called and sent flowers and, when he was at home, sat at her bedside. Once more he promised that she would have his son. This time he was wrong. The long-awaited heir was a girl, but a healthy baby, with a halo of blonde hair and her father's blue eyes. The child of Deanna's dreams. Even Marc resigned himself and quickly fell in love with the tiny blonde girl. They named her Pilar and flew to France to show her to his mother. Madame Duras bemoaned Deanna's failure to produce a son. But Marc didn't care. The baby was his. His child, his flesh. She would speak only French; she would spend every summer in Antibes. Deanna had felt feeble flutterings of fear, but she reveled in the joy of motherhood at last.

Marc spent every spare moment with Pilar, showing her off to his friends. She was always a child of laughter and smiles. Her first words were in French. By the time she was ten, she was more at home in Paris than the States—the books she read, the clothes she wore, the games she played had all been carefully imported by Marc. She knew who she was: a Duras, and where she belonged: in France. At twelve, she went to boarding school in Grenoble. By then the damage was done; Deanna had lost a daughter. Deanna was a foreigner to her now, an object of anger and resentment. It was *her* fault they didn't live in France, *her* fault Pilar couldn't be with her friends. *Her* fault Papa couldn't be in Paris with Grandmère who missed him so much. In the end they had won. Again.

Deanna walked softly down the steps, her bare feet a whisper on the Persian runner Marc had brought back from Iran. Out of habit she glanced into the living room. Nothing was out of place; it never was. The delicate green silk of the couch was smoothed to perfection; the Louis XV chairs stood at attention like soldiers at their posts; the Aubusson rug was as exquisite as ever in its soft celadon greens and faded raspberry-colored flowers. The silver shone; the ashtrays were immaculate; the portraits of Marc's enviable ancestors hung at precisely the right angle; and the curtains framed a perfect view of the Golden Gate Bridge and the bay. There were no sailboats yet at this hour, and for once there was no fog. It was a perfect June day, and she stood for a moment, looking at the water. She was tempted to sit down and simply watch. But it seemed sacrilege to rumple the couch, to tread on the rug, even to breathe in that room. It was easier to simply move on, to her own little world, to the studio at the back of the house where she painted . . . where she fled.

She walked past the dining room without looking in, then soundlessly down a long corridor to the back of the house. A half flight of stairs led to her studio. The dark wood was cold on her feet. The door was stiff, as always. Marc had given up reminding her to have something done about it. He had come to the conclusion that she liked it that way, and he was right. It was difficult to open, and it always slammed rapidly closed, sealing her into her own bright little cocoon. The studio was her own precious world, a burst of music and flowers tenderly tucked away from the stifling sobriety of the rest of the house. No Aubussons here, no silver, no Louis XV. Here, everything was bright and alive—the paints on her palette, the canvases on her easel, the soft yellow of the walls, and the big, comfortable, white chair that embraced her the moment she relinquished herself into its arms. She smiled as she sat down and looked around. She had left a terrible mess the morning before, but it suited her; it was a happy place in which she could work. She flung back the flowered curtains and pushed open the French doors, stepping onto the tiny terrace, the bright tiles like ice beneath her feet.

She often stood here at this hour, sometimes even in the fog, breathing deeply and smiling at the specter of the bridge hanging eerily above an invisible bay, listening to the slow owl hoot of the fog horns. But not this morning. This morning the sun was so bright that she squinted as she stepped outside. It would be a perfect day to go sailing, or disappear to the beach. The very idea made her laugh. Who would tell Margaret what to polish, who would respond to the mail, who would explain to Pilar why she could not go out that night? Pilar. This was the day of Pilar's departure. Cap d'Antibes for the summer, to visit her grandmother and her aunts, uncles, and cousins, all down from Paris. Deanna almost shuddered at the memory. After years of enduring those stifling summers, she had finally said no. The eternal charm of Marc's family had been insufferable, politesse through clenched teeth, the invisible thorns that ripped through one's flesh. Deanna had never won their approval. Marc's mother made no secret of that. Deanna was, after all, an American, and far too young to be a respectable match. Worst of all, she had been the penniless daughter of an extravagant wanderer. It was a marriage that added nothing to Marc's consequence, only to her own. His relatives assumed that was why she had snared him. And they were careful not to mention it—more than twice a year. Eventually Deanna had had enough, and had stopped making the pilgrimage to Antibes for the summer. Now, Pilar went alone, and she loved it. She was one of *them*.

Deanna leaned her elbows on the terrace wall, and propped her chin on the back of one hand. A sigh escaped her unnoticed as she watched a freighter glide slowly into the bay.

"Aren't you cold out here, Mother?" The words were as chilly as the terrace tiles. Pilar had spoken to her as though she were an oddity, standing there in her bathrobe and bare feet. Deanna cast a look at the ship and turned slowly around with a smile.

"Not really. I like it out here. And besides, I couldn't find my slippers." She said it with the same steady smile and looked directly into her daughter's brilliant blue eyes. The girl was everything Deanna was not. Her hair was the palest gold, her eyes an almost iridescent blue, and her skin had the rich glow of youth. She was almost a head taller than her mother, and in almost every possible way, the image of Marc-Edouard. But she did not yet have his aura of power—that would come later. And if she learned her lessons well from her grandmother and aunts, she would learn to mask it almost as viciously as they did. Marc-Edouard was not quite as artful; there was no need to be, he was a man. But the Duras women practiced a far subtler art. There was little Deanna could do to change that now, except perhaps keep Pilar away, but that would be a fruitless venture. Pilar, Marc, the old woman herself, all conspired to keep Pilar in Europe much of the time. And there was more to Pilar's resemblance to her grandmother than mimicry. It was something that ran in her blood. There was nothing Deanna could do, other than accept it. She never ceased to marvel, though, at how acutely painful the disappointment always was. There was never a moment when she didn't care, when it mattered less. It always mattered. She always felt Pilar's loss. Always.

She smiled now and looked down at her daughter's feet. She was wearing the absentee slippers. "I see you've found them." Deanna's words teased, but her eyes wore the pain of a lifetime. Tragedy constantly hidden by jokes.

"Is that supposed to be funny, Mother?" There was already warfare in Pilar's face, at barely seven-thirty in the morning. "I can't find any of my good sweaters, and my black skirt isn't back from your dressmaker." It was an accusation of major importance. Pilar flung back her long, straight, blonde hair and looked angrily at her mother.

Deanna always wondered at Pilar's fury. Teenage rebellion? Or merely that she didn't want to share Marc with Deanna? There was nothing Deanna could do. At least not for the moment. Maybe one day, maybe later, maybe in five years she'd get another chance to win back her daughter and become her friend. It was something she lived for. A hope that refused to die.

"The skirt came back yesterday. It's in the hall closet. The sweaters are already in your suitcase. Margaret packed for you yesterday. Does that solve all your problems?" The words were spoken gently. Pilar would always be the child of her dreams, no matter what, no matter how badly the dreams had been shattered.

"Mother! You're not paying attention!" For a moment Deanna's mind had wandered, and Pilar's eyes blazed at her. "I asked you what you did with my passport."

Deanna's green eyes met Pilar's blue ones and held them for a long moment. She wanted to say something, the right thing. All she said was, "I have your passport. I'll give it to you at the airport."

"I'm perfectly capable of taking care of it myself."

"I'm sure you are." Deanna stepped carefully back into her studio, avoiding the girl's gaze. "Are you going to have breakfast?"

"Later. I have to wash my hair."

"I'll have Margaret bring you a tray."

"Fine." Then she was gone, a bright arrow of youth that had pierced Deanna's heart yet again. It took so little to hurt. The words were all so small, but their emptiness stung her. Surely there had to be more. Surely one did not have children merely to have it end like this? She wondered sometimes if it would have been this way with her sons. Maybe it was just Pilar. Maybe the pull between two countries, and two worlds, was too great for her.

The phone buzzed softly on her desk as she sighed and sat down. It was the house line, no doubt Margaret asking if she wanted her coffee in the studio. When Marc was away, Deanna often ate alone in this room. When he was at home, breakfast with him was a ritual, sometimes the only meal they shared.

"Yes?" Her voice had a soft, smoky quality that always lent gentleness to her words.

"Deanna, I have to call Paris. I won't be downstairs for another fifteen minutes. Please tell Margaret that I want my eggs fried, and not burned to a crisp. Have you got the newspapers up there?"

"No, Margaret must have them waiting for you at the table."

"*Bon. A tout de suite.*"

Not even "good morning," no "how are you? How did you sleep? . . . I love you." Only the papers, the black skirt, the passport, the—Deanna's eyes filled with tears. She wiped them away with the back of her hand. They didn't do it deliberately, they were simply that way. But why didn't they care where *her* black skirt was, where *her* slippers were, how *her* latest painting was coming. She glanced over her shoulder wistfully as she closed the door to her studio behind her. Her day had begun.

Margaret heard her rustling the papers in the dining room and opened the kitchen door with her customary smile. "Morning, Mrs. Duras."

"Good morning, Margaret."

And so it went, as ever, with precision and grace. Orders were given with kindness and a smile; the newspapers were carefully set out in order of importance; the coffee was immediately placed on the table in the delicate Limoges pot that had belonged to Marc's mother; the curtains were pulled back; the weather was observed; and everyone manned his station, donned his mask, and began a new day.

Deanna forgot her earlier thoughts as she glanced at the paper and sipped coffee from the flowered, blue cup, rubbing her feet along the carpet to warm them from the chill of the tile on the terrace. She looked young in the morning, her dark hair loose, her eyes wide, her skin as clear as Pilar's, and her hands as delicate and unlined as they had been twenty years before. She didn't look her thirty-seven years, but more like someone in her late twenties. It was the way she lifted her face when she spoke, the sparkle in her eyes, the smile that appeared like a rainbow that made her seem very young. Later in the day, the consummately conservative style, the carefully knotted hair, and the regal bearing as she moved would make her seem more than her age. But in the morning she was burdened with none of the symbols—she was simply herself.

She heard him coming down the stairs before she heard him speak, calling back gaily to Pilar in French as the girl stood with wet hair on the second-floor landing. It was something about staying out of Nice and making sure she behaved herself in Antibes. Unlike Deanna, Marc would be seeing his daughter again in the course of the summer. He would be back and forth between Paris and San Francisco several times, stopping off in Antibes for a weekend, whenever he could. Old habits were too hard to break, and the lure of his daughter was too great. They had always been friends.

"Bonjour, ma chère."

Ma chère, not *ma chérie.* My dear, not my darling, Deanna observed. The *i* had fallen from the word many years since. "You look pretty this morning."

"Thank you." She looked up with the dawn of a smile, then saw him already studying the papers. The compliment had been a formality more than a truth. The art of the French. She knew it well. "Anything new in Paris?" Her face was once again grave.

"I'll let you know. I'm going over tomorrow. For a while." Something in his tone told her there was more. There always was.

"How long a while?"

He looked at her, amused, and she was reminded once again of all the reasons she had fallen in love with him. Marc was an incredibly handsome man, with a lean, aristocratic face and flashing blue eyes that even Pilar's couldn't match. The gray at his temples barely showed in the still-sandy-blond hair. He still looked young and dynamic, and almost always amused, particularly when he was in the States. He found Americans "amusing": It amused him when he beat them at tennis and squash, at bridge or backgammon, and particularly in the courtroom. He worked the way he played—hard and fast and well, and with extraordinary results. He was a man whom men envied and over whom women fawned. He always won. Winning was his style. Deanna had loved that about him at first. It had been such a victory when he first told her he loved her.

"I asked you how long you'd be away." There was a tiny edge to her voice.

"I'm not sure. A few days. Does it matter?"

"Of course." The edge to her voice.

"Have we something important?" He looked surprised; he had checked the book and hadn't seen anything there. "Well?"

No, nothing important, darling . . . only each other. "No, no, nothing like that. I just wondered."

"I'll let you know. I'll have a better idea after some meetings today. There's a problem apparently on the big shipping case. I may have to go directly to Athens from Paris."

"Again?"

"So it would seem." He went back to the papers until Margaret set his eggs in front of him then glanced at his wife again. "You're taking Pilar to the airport?"

"Of course."

"Please see to it that she's properly dressed. Mother will have a stroke if she gets off the plane again in one of those outrageous costumes."

"Why don't you tell her yourself?" Deanna fixed him with her green eyes.

"I thought that was more your province." He looked unmoved.

"What, discipline or her wardrobe?" Each of them thankless tasks, as they both knew.

"Both, to a degree." She wanted to ask to what degree, but she didn't. To the degree that she was capable of it? Was that what he meant? Marc went on, "I've given her some money for the trip, by the way. So you won't have to."

"How much?"

He glanced up sharply. "I beg your pardon?"

"I asked how much money you gave her for the trip." She said it very quietly.

"Is that important?"

"I think so. Or are discipline and wardrobe my only departments?" The edge of eighteen years of marriage colored her tone now.

"Not necessarily. Don't worry, she has enough."

"That's not what I'm worried about."

"What are you worried about?" His tone was suddenly not pleasant, and her eyes were like steel.

"I don't think she should have too much money for the summer. She doesn't need it."

"She's a very responsible girl."

"But she is not quite sixteen years old, Marc. How much did you give her?"

"A thousand." He said it very quietly, as though he were closing a deal.

"Dollars?" Her eyes flew wide. "That's outrageous!"

"Is it?"

"You know perfectly well it is. And you also know what she'll do with it."

"Amuse herself, I assume. Harmlessly."

"No, she'll buy one of those damn motorcycles she wants so much, and I absolutely refuse to allow that to happen." But Deanna's fury was matched only by her impotence and she knew it. Pilar was going to "them" now, out of Deanna's control. "I don't want her to have that much money."

"Don't be absurd."

"For God's sake, Marc. . . ."

The telephone rang as she began her tirade in earnest. It was for Marc, from Milan. He had no time to listen to her before he left. He had a meeting to attend at nine-thirty. He glanced at his watch. "Stop being so hysterical, Deanna. The child will be in good hands." But that was a whole other discussion right there, and he didn't have time. "I'll see you tonight."

"Will you be home for dinner?"

"I doubt it. I'll have Dominique call."

"Thank you." They were two tiny, frozen words. She watched him close the door. A moment later she heard his Jaguar purr out of the driveway. She had lost another war.

She broached the subject again with Pilar on the way to the airport. "I understand your father gave you quite a lot of money for the summer."

"Here we go. What is it now?"

"You know damn well what it is now. The motorcycle. I'll put it to you very simply, love. You buy one and I'll have you hauled home."

Pilar wanted to taunt her with "how will you know?" but she didn't dare. "O.K., so I won't buy one."

"Or ride one."

"Or ride one." But it was a useless parroting, and Deanna found herself, for the first time in a long time, wanting to scream.

She glanced at her daughter for a moment as she drove and then looked straight ahead again. "Why does it have to be this way? You're leaving for three months. We won't see each other. Couldn't it be pleasant between us today? What's the point of this constant haggling?"

"I didn't start it. You brought up the motorcycle."

"Do you have any idea why? Because I love you, because I give a damn. Because I don't want you killed. Does that make any sense to you?" There was desperation in her voice, and finally anger.

"Yeah, sure."

They rode on in silence to the airport. Deanna felt tears sting her eyes again, but she would not let Pilar see them. She had to be perfect, she had to be strong. The way Marc was, the way all his damned French relatives pretended to be, the way Pilar wanted to be. Deanna left her car with the valet at the curb, and they followed the porter inside, where Pilar checked in. When the clerk handed back her passport and ticket, she turned to her mother.

"You're coming to the gate?" There was more dismay in her voice than encouragement.

"I thought that might be nice. Would you mind?"

"No." Sullen, and angry. A goddamn child. Deanna wanted to slap her. Who was this person? Who had she become? Where had the sunny little girl who loved her gone? They each held tightly to their own thoughts as they walked toward the gate, collecting appreciative glances as they went. They were a striking pair. The dark beauty of Deanna in a beautifully cut, black wool dress, her hair swept into a knot, with a bright red jacket over one arm; Pilar in her youthful blaze of blonde, tall and slender and graceful in a white linen suit that had met with her mother's approval as she came down the stairs. Even her grandmother would approve—unless she found the cut too American. Anything was possible, with Madame Duras.

The plane was already boarding when they arrived, and Deanna had only a moment to hold the girl's hand tightly in her own. "I mean it about the motorcycle, darling. Please. . . ."

"All right, all right." But Pilar was already looking past Deanna, eager to be on the plane.

"I'll call you. And call me, if you have any problems."

"I won't." It was said with the assurance of not-quite-sixteen years.

"I hope not." Deanna's face softened as she looked at her daughter, then pulled her into a hug. "I love you, darling. Have a good time."

"Thanks, Mom." She favored her mother with a brief smile, and a quick wave, as her golden mane flew into the passageway. Deanna suddenly felt leaden. She was gone again. Her baby . . . the little girl with the curly blonde hair, the child who had held her arms out so trustingly each night to be hugged and kissed . . . Pilar. Deanna took a seat in the lounge and waited to see the 747 begin its climb into the sky. At last she rose and walked slowly back to her car. The valet tipped his cap appreciatively at the dollar she handed him and wondered about her as she swung her legs gracefully into the car. She was one hell of a good-looking woman; he couldn't quite guess how old she was; twenty-eight? thirty-two? thirty-five? forty? It was impossible to tell. Her face was young, but the rest of her, the way she moved, the look in her eyes, was so old.

Deanna heard him coming up the stairs as she sat at her dressing table, brushing her hair. It was twenty after ten, and he hadn't called her all day. Dominique, his secretary, had left a message with Margaret at noon: Monsieur Duras would not be home for dinner. Deanna had eaten in the studio while she sketched, but her mind had not been on her work. She had been thinking of Pilar.

She turned and smiled at him as he came into the room. She had actually missed him. The house had been strangely quiet all day. "Hello, darling. That was a long day."

"Very long. And yours?"

"Peaceful. It's too quiet here without Pilar."

"I never thought I'd hear you say that." Marc-Edouard smiled at his wife as he slid into a large blue-velvet chair near the fireplace.

"Neither did I. How were your meetings?"

"Tiresome."

He was not very expansive. She turned in her seat to look at him. "You're still going to Paris tomorrow?" He nodded, and she continued to watch him as he stretched his long legs. He looked no different than he had that morning and seemed almost ready to take on another day. He thrived on the meetings he called "tiresome." He stood up and walked toward her with a smile in his eyes.

"Yes, I'm going to Paris tomorrow. Are you quite sure you don't want to join Pilar and my mother in Cap d'Antibes?"

"Quite sure." Her look was determined. "Why would I want to do that?"

"You said yourself that it was too quiet here. I thought perhaps. . . ." He put his hands on her shoulders as he went to stand behind her for a moment. "I'm going to be gone all summer, Deanna."

Her shoulders stiffened in his hands. "All summer?"

"More or less. The Salco shipping case is too important to leave in anyone else's hands. I'll be commuting back and forth between Paris and Athens all summer. I just can't be here." His accent seemed stronger now when he spoke to her, as though he had already left the States. "It will give me plenty of opportunity to check up on Pilar, which should please you, but not any opportunity to be with you." She wanted to ask him if he really cared, but she didn't ask. "I think the case will take the better part of the summer. About three months."

It sounded like a death sentence to her. "Three months?" Her voice was very small.

"Now you see why I asked if you'd like to go to Cap d'Antibes. Does this change your mind?'

She shook her head slowly. "No. It doesn't. You won't be there either, and I think Pilar needs a break from me. Not to mention . . ." her voice drifted off.

"My mother?" Marc asked. She nodded. "I see. Well then, *ma chère*, you will be here all alone."

Dammit, why didn't he ask her to go with him, to commute between Athens and Paris. For a wild moment Deanna thought of suggesting it to him, but she knew he wouldn't let her go. He liked to be free when he worked. He would never take her along.

"Can you manage alone?" he said now.

"Do I have a choice? Do you mean I could say no and you wouldn't go?" She turned her face up to his.

"You know that's not possible."

"Yes, I do." She was silent for a time and then shrugged with a small smile. "I'll manage."

"I know you will."

How do you know dammit? How do you know? What if I can't? What if I need you? . . . What if . . .

"You're a very good wife, Deanna."

For a brief second she didn't know whether to thank him or slap him. "What does that mean? That I don't complain very much? Maybe I should." Her smile hid what she felt and allowed him to dodge what he chose not to answer.

"No, you shouldn't. You are perfect the way you are."

"*Merci, monsieur.*" She stood up then and turned away so he would not see her face. "Will you pack yourself, or do you want me to pack for you?"

"I'll do it myself. You go to bed. I'll be there in a while."

Deanna watched him dart around his dressing room, then disappear downstairs, to his study, she assumed. She had turned off the lights in the bedroom and was lying very still on her side of the bed when he returned.

"*Tu dors?* Are you asleep?"

"No." Her voice was husky in the dark.

"*Bon.*"

Good? Why? What did it matter if she were asleep or not? Would he talk to her, tell her that he loved her, that he was sorry he was going? He wasn't sorry and they both knew it. This was what he loved to do, gad about the world, plying his trade, enjoying his work and his reputation. He adored it. He slid into bed, and they lay there for a time, awake, pensive, silent.

"Are you angry that I'm going away for so long?"

She shook her head. "No, not angry, sorry. I'll miss you. Very much."

"It will pass quickly." She didn't answer, and he propped himself up on one elbow to study her face in the dark room. "I'm sorry, Deanna."

"So am I." He ran a hand gently across her hair and smiled at her, and she turned her head slowly to look at him.

"You're still very pretty, Deanna. Do you know that? You're even prettier than you were as a girl. Very handsome in fact." But she didn't want to be handsome, she wanted to be his, as she had been so long ago. His *Diane*. "Pilar will be beautiful one day too." He said it with pride.

"She already is." Deanna said it dispassionately, without anger.

"Are you jealous of her?"

He almost seemed to like the idea, and Deanna wondered. Maybe it made him feel important. Or young. But she answered him anyway. Why not? "Yes, sometimes I'm jealous of her. I'd like to be that young again, that free, that sure of what life owes me. At her age it's all so obvious: you deserve the best, you'll get the best. I used to think so too."

"And now, Deanna? Has life paid you its debt?"

"In some ways." Her eyes held a certain sadness as they met his. For the first time in years he was reminded of the eighteen-year-old orphan who had sat across from him in his office wearing the little black Dior dress. He wondered if he had truly made her unhappy, if she really wanted more. But he had given her so much. Jewels, cars, furs, a home. All the things most women wanted. What more could she possibly want? He looked at her for a very long time, his eyes questioning, his face creased with a sudden thought. Was it possible that he really did not understand?

"Deanna . . . ?" He didn't want to ask, but suddenly he had to. There was too much in her eyes. "Are you unhappy?"

She looked at him squarely and wanted to say yes. But she was afraid. She would lose him; he would leave her, and then what? She didn't want to lose Marc. She wanted more of him.

"Are you unhappy?" He repeated the question and looked pained to realize what the answer was. She didn't have to say the words. Suddenly it was clear. Even to him.

"Sometimes I am. And sometimes not. Much of the time I don't give it much thought. I miss . . . I miss the old days though, when we first met, when we were very young." Her voice was very small as she said it.

"We've grown up, Deanna, you can't change that." He leaned

toward her and touched her chin with his hand, as though perhaps he might kiss her. But the hand fell away, as did the thought. "You were such a charming child." He smiled at the memory of what he had felt. "I hated your father for leaving you in that mess."

"So did I. But that was just the way he was. I've made peace with all that."

"Have you?" She nodded. "Are you quite sure?"

"Why shouldn't I?"

"Because I sometimes think you still resent him. I think that's why you continue to paint. Just to prove to yourself that you can still do something on your own, if you ever have to." He looked at her more closely then, his forehead wrinkling into a frown. "You won't ever have to, you know. I'll never leave you in the condition that your father did."

"I'm not worried about that. And you're wrong. I paint because I love it, because it's a part of me." He had never wanted to believe that, that her artwork was part of her soul.

He didn't answer for a time but lay looking up at the ceiling, turning things around in his mind. "Are you terribly cross that I'm going away for the summer?"

"I told you, I'm not. I'll simply paint, relax, read, see some of my friends."

"Will you go out a great deal?" He sounded worried, and she was amused. He was a fine one to ask about that.

"I don't know, silly. I'll let you know if I'm asked. I'm sure there'll be the usual dinner parties, benefits, concerts, that sort of thing." He nodded again, saying nothing. "Marc-Edouard, are you jealous?" There was laughter in her eyes, and then she laughed aloud as he turned to look into her face. "Oh, you are! Don't be silly! After all these years?"

"What better time?"

"Don't be absurd, darling. That's not my style." He knew that was true.

"I know that. But, *on ne sait jamais.* One never knows."

"How can you say something like that?"

"Because I have a beautiful wife, with whom any man in his right mind would be crazy not to fall in love." It was the most elaborate speech he had made to her in years. She showed her surprise. "What? You think I haven't noticed? Deanna, now you are being absurd. You are a young and beautiful woman."

"Good. Then don't go to Greece." She was smiling up at him again, like a very young girl. But he didn't look amused now.

"I have to. You know that."

"All right. Then take me with you." There was an unaccustomed note in her voice, half teasing, half serious. He didn't answer for a long time. "Well? Can I go?"

He shook his head. "No, you can't."

"Well, then I guess you'll just have to be jealous." They hadn't teased like this in years and years. His going away for three months had produced an assortment of very odd feelings. But she didn't want to push him too far. "Seriously, darling, you don't have to worry."

"I hope not."

"Marc! *Arrête!* Stop it!" She leaned forward and reached for his hand, and he let her take it in hers. "I love you . . . do you know that?"

"Yes. Do you know as well that I love you?"

Her eyes grew very serious as they looked into his. "Sometimes I'm not so sure." He was always too busy to show her he loved her, and it wasn't his style. But now something told her that she had hit home, and she was stunned as she watched him. Didn't he know? Didn't he realize what he had done? The wall he had built around himself, surrounded by business and work, gone for days or weeks, and now months, and his only ally Pilar? "I'm sorry, darling. I suppose you do. But sometimes I have to remind myself of it."

"But I do love you. You must know that."

"Deep inside I think I do know." She knew it when she recalled the moments they had shared, the landmarks in a lifetime, which tell the tale. Those were the reasons why she still loved him.

He sighed. "But you need a great deal more. Don't you, my dear?" She nodded, feeling at once young and brave. "You need my time as well as my affection. You need . . . *enfin,* you need what I don't have to give."

"That's not true. You could have the time. We could do some of the things we used to. We could!" She sounded like a plaintive child and hated herself for it. She sounded like the child who had hounded her father to take her along. And she hated needing anyone that much. She had sworn long ago that she never would again. "I'm sorry. I understand." Her eyes lowered and she withdrew.

"Do you understand?" He was watching her very closely.

"Of course."

"Ah, *ma Diane*. . . ." His eyes were troubled as he took her in his arms. She didn't notice; her own were too filled with tears. He had said it at last. "*Ma Diane*. . . ."

2

"You have enough money in the bank for the entire time I'll be gone. But if you need more, call Dominique at the office, and she'll transfer it. I told Sullivan I want him to look in on you at least twice a week. And . . ."

Deanna looked at her husband in surprise. "You told Jim to look in on me? Why?" Jim Sullivan was Marc-Edouard's American partner, and one of the few Americans he truly liked.

"Because I want to make sure that you're well, happy, and have everything you need."

"Thank you, but it seems silly to bother Jim."

"He'll enjoy it. Show him your latest paintings, have him for dinner. I trust him." He looked at his wife with a smile. And she smiled back.

"You can trust me too." In the eighteen years of her marriage, she had never cheated on Marc. She wasn't going to start now.

"I do trust you. I'll call as often as I can. You know where I'll be. If anything comes up, just call. I'll get back to you as soon as possible, if I'm not in." She nodded quietly at his words, and then let out a small sigh. He turned to look at her in the silence of the Jaguar. For a moment there was worry in his eyes. "You'll be all right, Deanna, won't you?"

Her eyes found his. She nodded. "Yes. I'll be fine. But I'll miss you terribly."

He was already looking back at the road. "The time will go

quickly. If you change your mind, you can always join Mother and Pilar in Cap d'Antibes." He smiled at his wife again. "Not that you will."

"No, I won't." She smiled back.

"*Têtue, va.* Stubborn one. Perhaps that's why I love you."

"Is that why? I've often wondered." There was a teasing sparkle in her eyes now as she studied the handsome profile next to her in the car. "You'll take care of yourself, won't you? Don't work too terribly hard." But it was a useless admonition, and they both knew it.

"I won't." He smiled at her tenderly.

"You will."

"I will."

"And you'll enjoy every minute of it." They both knew that was true too. "I hope the Salco case comes out in your favor."

"It will. You can be quite sure of that."

"Marc-Edouard Duras, you are unbearably arrogant. Has anyone told you that yet today?"

"Only the woman I love." He reached for her hand as he took the turnoff for the airport, and she touched his fingers gently with her own. It made her think of the night before and the rare meshing of their bodies that she cherished so much. *Ma Diane. . . .* "I love you, darling." She pulled his hand to her lips and gently kissed the tips of his fingers. "I wish we had more time."

"So do I. We will one of these days."

Yes . . . but when? She carefully put his hand back on the seat and left her fingers intertwined with his.

"When you come back, do you suppose we could go somewhere together, for a holiday?" She watched him, her eyes wide, childlike. She still wanted him, wanted to be with him, to be his. After all these years she still cared. Sometimes it still surprised her how much she did.

"Where would you like to go?"

"Anywhere. Just so we're together." And alone.

He looked at her for a long moment as they pulled up outside the terminal, and for an instant Deanna thought she saw regret in his eyes. "We'll do that. As soon as I get back." Then he seemed to catch his breath. "Deanna, I . . ."

She waited, but he said no more; he only put his arms around her and held her close. She felt her own arms go around him and hold him close. She squeezed her eyes tightly shut. She needed him more than he knew. There were tears sliding slowly down her face. He felt her trembling in his arms and pulled away to look at her with surprise.

"*Tu pleurs?*" You're crying?

"*Un peu.*" A little. He smiled, it had been so long since she had answered him in French. "I wish you didn't have to go." If only he'd stay, if they had some time without Pilar . . .

"So do I." But they both knew that was a lie. He pulled the keys out of the ignition and opened the door, signaling for a porter.

Deanna walked sedately beside him, lost in her own thoughts, until they reached the first-class lounge where he generally hid while waiting for a plane. She settled into a chair next to his and smiled at him. But he was already different, already gone, the moment in the car all but forgotten. He checked the papers in his briefcase and looked at his watch. He had ten minutes left, and he suddenly seemed impatient to leave.

"*Alors,* is there anything we forgot to discuss in the car? Any message for Pilar?"

"Just give her my love. Will you stop there before you go to Athens?"

"No, I'll phone her tonight."

"And me too?" She watched the seconds tick by on the enormous clock on the wall.

"And you too. You're not going out?"

"No, I have some work I want to finish in the studio."

"You should do something amusing, so you don't feel alone."

I won't, I'm used to it. Again, she didn't say the words. "I'll be fine." She crossed one leg over the other, looking down at her lap. She had worn a new lavender silk dress and the purple jade earrings encircled by diamonds that he had brought her from Hong Kong, but he hadn't noticed. His mind was on other things.

"Deanna?"

"Hm?" She looked up to find him standing next to her, his briefcase in his hand and the familiar smile of victory in his eyes. He was off to the wars now, gone again, free. "Is it time to go?" *Already? So soon?* He nodded, and she stood up, dwarfed by his considerable size, but the perfect companion beside him. They were a strikingly good-looking couple. They always had been.

Even Madame Duras, his cold-eyed mother, had acknowledged it
—once.

"You needn't walk me to the gate." He already seemed distracted.

"No, but I'd like to. Is that all right?"

"Of course." He held the door for her, and they stepped back
into the bustle of the terminal, instantly lost among an army of
travelers burdened with suitcases, gifts, and guitars. They arrived
too soon at the gate, and he turned to look down at her with a
smile. "I'll call you tonight."

"I love you."

He didn't answer but bent to kiss the top of her head, then
strode into the passageway to the plane, without a backward look
or a wave. She watched until he disappeared, then slowly turned
and walked away. *I love you.* Her own words echoed in her head.
But he hadn't answered. He was already gone.

She slid into the car waiting at the curb, and with a sigh turned
the key and drove home.

She went quickly upstairs to change her clothes, and was buried
deep in her own thoughts in the studio all afternoon. She
sketched absently, and had just gone out on the terrace at last for
some air, when Margaret knocked softly on the studio door.
Deanna turned in surprise, as the housekeeper hesitantly entered
the room.

"Mrs. Duras . . . I—I'm sorry. . . ." She knew how Deanna
hated to be disturbed there, but now and then she had no choice.
Deanna had disconnected the studio phone.

"Is something wrong?" Deanna looked distracted, standing
there with her hair loose over her shoulders and hands tucked into
the pockets of her jeans.

"No. Mr. Sullivan is downstairs to see you."

"Jim?" And then she remembered Marc-Edouard's promise that
Jim would look in on her. He certainly hadn't lost any time. Always devoted to his associate's subtle commands. "I'll be right
down."

Margaret nodded. She had done the right thing. She knew that
Deanna wouldn't have wanted him upstairs in the studio. She had
shown him into the icelike green living room and offered him a
cup of tea, which he'd declined with a grin. He was as different

from Marc-Edouard as two men could be, and Margaret had always liked him. He was rugged, American, and easygoing, and somewhere in his eyes was always the promise of a rich Irish smile.

Deanna found him standing at the window, looking out at the summer fog drifting in slowly over the bay. It looked like puffs of white cotton being pulled by an invisible string, floating between the spires of the bridge, and hanging in midair over the sailboats.

"Hello, Jim."

"Madam." He executed a small bow and made as though to kiss her hand. But she waved the gesture away with a gurgle of laughter and offered her cheek, which he unceremoniously kissed. "I must admit I prefer that. Kissing hands is an art I've never quite mastered. You never know if they're going to shake with you, or expect to be kissed. Couple of times I damn near got my nose broken by the ones who planned to shake."

She laughed at him and sat down. "You'll have to get Marc to give you lessons. He's a genius at it. It's either the Frenchman in him or a sixth sense. How about a drink?"

"Love it." He lowered his voice to a conspiratorial whisper. "Margaret seemed to think I should have tea."

"How awful."

She was laughing again, and he watched her appreciatively as she opened a small inlaid cabinet and withdrew two glasses and a bottle of Scotch.

"Drinking, Deanna?" He said it casually but he was surprised. He had never seen her drink Scotch. Maybe Marc-Edouard had had a good reason after all for suggesting he come by. But she was already shaking her head.

"I thought I'd have some ice water. Were you worried?" She looked at him with amusement as she returned with his glass.

"A little."

"Don't worry, love. I haven't hit the bottle yet." Her eyes seemed suddenly wistful as she took a sip from her own glass and set it down carefully on a marble table. "But it's going to be a mighty long summer." She sighed and looked up at him with a smile. Gently, he reached over and patted her hand.

"I know. Maybe we can go to the movies sometime."

"You're a sweetheart, but don't you have anything better to do?" She knew he did. He had been divorced for four years and was living with a model who had moved out from New York a few months ago. He adored that type, and they always loved him. Tall, handsome, athletic, with Irish-blue eyes and ebony black hair, barely salted with gray. He was the perfect contrast to Marc-Edouard in every possible way, easygoing when Marc was formal; All-American, unlike Marc's totally European manner; and surprisingly unassuming, in contrast to Marc-Edouard's barely concealed arrogance. It had always struck Deanna as odd that Marc had chosen Jim as his partner, but it had been a wise choice. Marc's own special brilliance was matched by Jim's; their stars just shone differently, and they moved in their own very separate orbits. The Durases rarely saw Jim socially. He was busy with his own life, and his collection of models, now dwindled to one—for the moment. Jim never stayed with one woman long.

"What are you up to these days?"

He smiled at her. "Work, play, the usual. You?"

"Fiddling around in my studio, also the usual." She played it down as she always did.

"What about this summer? Have you made any plans?"

"Not yet, but I will. Maybe I'll go see some friends in Santa Barbara or something."

"God." He made a horrible face, and she laughed.

"What's wrong with that?"

"You'd have to be eighty years old to enjoy that. Why don't you go down to Beverly Hills? Pretend you're a movie star, have lunch at the Polo Lounge, have yourself paged."

"Is that what you do?" She laughed at the idea.

"Of course. Every weekend." He chuckled and set down his empty glass, glancing at his watch. "Never mind. I'll get you organized in no time, but now"—he looked regretful—"I have to run."

"Thank you for stopping by. It was kind of a long afternoon. It's strange with both of them gone."

He nodded appreciatively, suddenly sobered. He remembered the feeling from the time when his wife and their two boys had first moved out. He had thought he'd go nuts, just from the silence.

"I'll call you."

"Good. And Jim"—she looked at him for a long moment—"thanks."

He rumpled her long dark hair, kissed her forehead, and departed, waving at her as he slid into his black Porsche, thinking that Marc was crazy. Deanna Duras was one woman he'd have given almost anything to get his hands on. Of course he was too smart to play with that kind of fire, but he still thought Duras was nuts. Christ, he never even realized what a little beauty she was. Or did he? Jim Sullivan wondered to himself as he drove away, and Deanna softly closed the door.

She glanced at her watch, thinking that it was nice of Jim to come by and wondering how soon Marc would call her. He had promised to call her that night.

But he never did. Instead, there was a telegram in the morning:

Off to Athens. Wrong time to call. All well. Pilar fine.

Marc

Brief and to the point. But why hadn't he called? "Wrong time to call," she read again. *Wrong time. Wrong time. . . .*

The telephone broke into Deanna's thoughts as she read Marc's telegram again. She already knew it by heart.

"Deanna?" The bright voice jarred her out of her reverie. It was Kim Houghton. She lived only a few blocks away, but her life couldn't have been more different. Twice married, twice divorced, eternally independent and merry and free. She had gone to art school with Deanna, but she was a major creative force in advertising now, because she had never been a very good artist. And she was Deanna's only close woman friend.

"Hi, Kim. What's new in your life?"

"Not much. I was in L.A. being nice to one of our new clients. The bastard is already talking about pulling the account. And it's one of mine." She mentioned the name of the national chain of hotels, for which she handled the advertising. "Want to have lunch?"

"I can't. I'm tied up."

"Doing what?" Suspicion crept into her voice. She always knew when Deanna was lying.

"A charity luncheon. I have to go."

"Dump it. I'll be your charity. I need some advice, I'm depressed." Deanna laughed. Kimberly Houghton was never depressed. Even her divorces—two of them—hadn't depressed her. She had rapidly moved on to more fertile terrain. Usually in less than a week. "Come on, love, let's go somewhere for lunch. I need a breather from this place."

"So do I." Deanna looked around the blue silk-and-velvet splendor of her bedroom, trying to fight off a feeling of gloom. For an unguarded moment her voice sagged into the phone.

"What does that mean?" Kim asked.

"It means, you nosy pain in the ass, that Marc is away. Pilar left two days ago, and Marc left yesterday morning."

"Jesus, can't you enjoy it? You don't often get a breather like that, with both of them gone. If I were you I'd run around the living room stark naked and call in all my friends."

"While I was still naked, or after I got dressed?" Deanna threw her legs over the side of the chair and laughed.

"Either way. Listen, in that case, forget about lunch. How about dinner tonight?"

"That's a deal. That way I can do some work in the studio this afternoon."

"I thought you were going to a charity lunch." Deanna could almost see Kim grinning. "Gotcha."

"Go to hell."

"Thank you. Dinner at seven at Trader Vic's?"

"I'll meet you there."

"See ya." She hung up, leaving Deanna with a smile. Thank God for Kim.

"You look gorgeous. New dress?" Kimberly Houghton looked up from her drink when Deanna arrived, and the two women exchanged the smile of old friends. Deanna was indeed looking lovely in a white cashmere dress that clung to all the right places and set off her dark hair and enormous green eyes.

"You don't look so bad either." Kim had the kind of body men loved, rich and generous and full of promise. Her blue eyes danced, and her smile dazzled everyone it took on. She still wore her hair in the short cap of blonde curls she had worn for the last twenty years. She didn't have the startling elegance of Deanna, but she had irresistible warmth and a certain way with clothes. She always looked as though she ought to have ten men at her heels, and she usually did. Or at least one or two. Tonight she was wearing a blue velvet blazer and slacks with red silk shirt, unbuttoned dangerously low to reveal ample cleavage and a single diamond dangling enticingly on a narrow gold chain that fell neatly between her full breasts. An "eye catcher"—as though she needed any help.

Deanna ordered a drink and settled onto the seat, dropping her mink coat on a chair. Kim was neither interested in it nor impressed. She had grown up in that world and had no desires for money or mink, only for independence and good times. She always made sure she had a great deal of both.

"So what's new? Enjoying your freedom?"

"More or less. Actually, this time I'm finding it a little hard to get used to." Deanna sighed and took a sip of her drink.

"Jesus, as much as Marc travels, I'd think you'd be used to it by now. Besides, a little independence is good for you."

"Probably. But he'll be gone for three months. That seems like forever."

"Three months? How did that happen?" Kim's voice suddenly lost its champagne brightness, and a question appeared in her eyes.

"He has a big case going between Paris and Athens. It doesn't make sense for him to come home in between."

"Or for you to go over?"

"Apparently not."

"What does that mean? Did you ask?" It was like answering to a mother. Deanna smiled as she looked at her friend.

"More or less. He's going to be busy, and if I go over I'll be stuck with Madame Duras."

"Screw that." Kim had heard all the early stories of Marc-Edouard's indomitable mother.

"Precisely, though I didn't put it quite that way to Marc. So, voilà, I'm by myself for the summer."

"And hating every minute of it after only two days. Right? Right." She answered her own question. "Why don't you go somewhere?"

"Where?"

"Jesus, Deanna, anywhere. I'm sure Marc wouldn't mind."

"Probably not, but I don't like to travel alone." She had never had to. She had always traveled with her father, and then with Pilar and Marc. "Besides, where would I go? Jim Sullivan said

Santa Barbara would be a bore." She looked forlorn as she said it, and Kimberly laughed.

"He's right. Poor little rich girl. How about Carmel with me, tomorrow? I have to go down to meet with a client over the weekend. You could come along for the ride."

"That's silly, Kim, I'd be in your way." But for a moment, she had liked the idea. She hadn't been to Carmel in years, and it certainly wasn't far away, just a two-hour drive from the city.

"Why would you be in my way? I'm not having an affair with this guy for chrissake, and I'd enjoy the company. By myself, it would be a drag."

"Not for long." She looked pointedly at her friend, and Kim laughed.

"Please, my reputation!" She smiled broadly at Deanna then tilted her head to one side, shaking the halo of soft blonde curls. "Seriously, will you come? I'd love it."

"I'll see."

"No. You'll come. Settled? Settled."

"Kimberly. . . ." Deanna was starting to laugh.

"I'll pick you up at five-thirty." Kim grinned a victorious grin.

3

Kim honked twice as she pulled up in front of the house, and Deanna glanced through her bedroom window before picking up her bag and running down the stairs. She felt like a girl again, off on a weekend adventure with a friend. Even Kim's car didn't look like something a grown-up would drive. It was an ancient MG painted bright red. Deanna appeared in the doorway a moment later, wearing gray slacks and a gray turtleneck sweater, and carrying a large brown leather bag.

"Right on time. How was your day?"

"Ghastly. Don't ask."

"All right. I won't." Instead, they spoke of everything else: Carmel, Deanna's latest painting, Pilar and her friends.

Finally, they lapsed into comfortable silence. They were almost in Carmel when Kimberly glanced over at her friend and saw the wistful look in her eyes.

"Penny for your thoughts."

"Is that all? Hell, they ought to be worth at least five or ten cents." She tried to laugh away her own thoughts, but Kim wasn't fooled.

"All right. I'll give you a dime. But let me guess. Thinking about Marc?"

"Yes." Deanna's voice was quiet as she looked out at the sea.

"Do you really miss him that much?" Their relationship had always puzzled Kim. It had seemed to her at first like a marriage of convenience, yet she knew it was not. Deanna loved him. Maybe too much.

Deanna looked away. "Yes, I miss him that much. Does that seem silly to you?"

"No. Admirable maybe. Something like that."

"Why? Admirable has nothing to do with it."

Kim laughed and shook her head. "Sweetheart, eighteen years with one man looks more than admirable to me. It's goddamn heroic."

Deanna grinned at her friend. "Why heroic? I love him. He's a beautiful, intelligent, witty, charming man." And making love with him the night before his departure had renewed something in her heart.

"Yes. He is." Kim kept her eyes on the road as she said it, but she found herself wondering if there was more. If there was a side of Marc Duras that no one knew, a warm side, a loving side, another dimension to the man of unlimited beauty and charm. A human side that laughed and cried and was real. That would make him a man worth loving, to Kim.

"It's going to be a very long summer." Deanna let out a small sigh. "Tell me about this client of yours. Someone new?"

"Yes. He insisted on having this meeting in Carmel. He lives in San Francisco, but has a house here. He was on his way up from L.A. and thought this would be a more pleasant place to discuss the account."

"How civilized."

"Yes. Very." Kim smiled at Deanna.

It was almost eight o'clock when they pulled up in front of the hotel. Kimberly climbed out of the MG with a shake of her curls and a glance at Deanna, pulling herself out of the car with a groan.

"Think you'll survive? I'll admit, this isn't the smoothest possible chariot for traveling."

"I'll live." Deanna looked around at the familiar surroundings. In the early days of their marriage, she and Marc had often come down to Carmel on weekends. They had wandered in and out of the shops, had cozy, candlelit dinners, and walked for miles on the beach. There was a bittersweet feeling to being here again, this time without him.

The hotel was tiny and quaint, with a French provincial facade and gaily painted window boxes filled with bright flowers. Inside, there were low wooden beams, a large fireplace framed by copper pots, and Wedgwood-blue wallpaper with a tiny white design. It was the kind of hotel Marc would have enjoyed; it looked very French.

Kimberly signed the register at the front desk then handed the pen to Deanna. "I asked for adjoining rooms. O.K. with you?" Deanna nodded, relieved. She liked having a room to herself and hadn't really wanted to share one with Kim.

"That sounds fine." She filled in her name and address on the card, then they followed the porter to their rooms.

Five minutes later Deanna heard a knock at the door.

"Want a Coke, Deanna? I just got two out of the machine down the hall." Kim sprawled her long generous frame across Deanna's bed and held out an icy-cold can.

Deanna took a long sip and then let herself into a chair with a smile and a sigh. "It feels so good to be here. I'm glad I came."

"So am I. It would have been boring without you. Maybe we can even find time for the shops tomorrow when I'm through with business. Or would you rather go back to the city tomorrow afternoon? Do you have plans?"

"Absolutely none. And this is heaven. I may never go back. The house is like a tomb without Marc and Pilar."

Kimberly thought it equally tomblike with them, but she didn't say anything to her friend. She knew that Deanna loved the house and that the security of her family meant a great deal. She had met Deanna at art school, shortly after the death of Deanna's father had left her penniless and alone. She had seen her struggle to make it on the little money she earned at her job. She had been there too when Marc began to court Deanna, and she had seen Deanna come to rely on him more and more, until she felt helpless without him. She had watched Marc sweep her friend under his wing, tenderly, irresistibly, and with the determination of a man who refused to lose. And she had seen Deanna nestle there for almost two decades, safe, protected, hidden, and insistent that she was happy. Perhaps she was. But Kim was never sure.

"Any place special you want to go for dinner?" Kim drained the last of her Coke as she asked.

"The beach." Deanna looked longingly through the window at the sea.

"The Beach? I don't know it." Kim looked vague, and Deanna laughed.

"No, no. It's not a restaurant. I meant I wanted to go for a walk on the beach."

"Now? At this hour?" It was only eight-thirty, and just barely dusk, but Kim was hungry to begin her evening and have a look around. "Why don't you save that until tomorrow after my meeting with the new client?" It was obvious that Kim was not lured by surf and white sands. But Deanna was.

She shook her head resolutely and put down her Coke. "Nope. I can't wait that long. Are you going to change before we go out?" Kim nodded. "Good. Then I'll go for a walk while you dress. I'll just wear what I have on." The cashmere sweater and gray slacks still looked impeccable after the drive.

"Don't get lost on the beach."

"I won't." Deanna smiled sheepishly at Kim. "I feel like a kid. I can't wait to get out and play." *And look at the sunset, and take a deep breath of the sea air . . . and remember the days when Marc and I walked down that beach hand in hand.* "I'll be back in half an hour."

"Don't rush. I'm going to take a nice hot bath. We're in no hurry. We can have dinner at nine-thirty or ten." Kim would make reservations in the staid, Victorian dining room of the Pine Inn.

"See you." Deanna disappeared with a wave and a smile, pulling on her jacket and carrying a scarf in her hand. She knew it would be windy on the beach. When she stepped outside the fog was already rolling in.

She walked along the main street of Carmel, weaving her way between the few straggling tourists who had not yet taken refuge at dinner tables or in their hotels, their children chattering at their heels, their arms filled with booty from the shops, their faces smiling and relaxed. It reminded her of the time she and Marc had come here with Pilar. Pilar had been an exuberant nine, and she had joined them on one of their sunset strolls on the beach, collecting bits of driftwood and shells, running ahead of them and then back to report her discoveries, as Deanna and Marc talked. It seemed an aeon ago. She reached the end of the street and suddenly stopped to look down the endless expanse of alabaster beach. Even Marc had admitted that there was nothing like it in France. The perfectly white sand and the rich swell of waves rolling in toward the shore with sea gulls drifting slowly by. She took a deep breath as she looked at the scene again, watching the tide roll inexorably in. There was a lure to that beach, a lure like none she had ever known. She pocketed the scarf and slipped her shoes off, feeling the rush of sand between her toes as she ran toward the shore, stopping short of the water's edge. The wind ripped through her hair. She closed her eyes and smiled. It was a beautiful place, a world she had left buried in memory for too long. Why had she stayed away for so long? Why hadn't they been back here before? With another deep breath, she set off down the beach, one shoe in each hand, and her feet aching to dance in the sand like a child.

She had walked a long way before she stopped to watch the last rim of gold on the horizon. The sky had turned to mauve and a thick bank of fog was moving in toward the shore. She stood watching it for an interminable time, then walked slowly up toward the dunes where she made a seat for herself amid the tall grass and pulled her knees up under her chin as she looked out to sea. After a moment she rested her head on one knee and closed her eyes, listening to the sea and feeling a rush of joy in her soul.

"It's perfect, isn't it?"

Deanna jumped at the unexpected voice at her side. She opened her eyes to see a tall, dark-haired man standing beside her. For a moment she was frightened, but his smile was so kind that it was impossible to feel threatened while in the warm embrace of those eyes. They were a deep blue-green like the sea. He had the build of a man who might have played football in college. His hair was as dark as Deanna's and ruffled by the wind. He was looking down at her intently.

"I like it best at this time of day," he said.

"So do I." She found it easy to answer him and was surprised that it didn't annoy her when he sat down beside her. "I thought I was alone on the beach." She glanced shyly into his face, and he smiled.

"You probably were. I came up behind you. I'm sorry if I startled you." He looked at her again with that same open smile. "My house is just behind here." He nodded over his shoulder to an area shrouded by wind-contorted trees. "I always come out here in the evenings. And tonight I just got in from a trip. I haven't been here in three weeks. I always realize then how much I love it, how much I need to walk on this beach and look at that." He looked straight ahead, out to sea.

"Do you live here all year 'round?" Deanna found herself conversing with him as though he were an old friend, but he had that way about him, it was impossible to be ill at ease.

"No, I come down on weekends whenever I can. And you?"

"I haven't been here in a long time. I came down with a friend."

"Staying in town?"

She nodded, and then remembering, looked at her watch. "That reminds me, I have to get back. I got carried away by my walk on the beach." It was already nine-thirty and the last light of day had fled as they talked. She stood and looked down at him, smiling. "You're lucky to have this anytime you like."

He nodded in answer, but he wasn't really listening, he was looking intensely at her face, and for the first time since she'd noticed him next to her, Deanna felt an odd rush of warmth in her cheeks and was aware of her embarrassment when he spoke.

"Do you know, you looked like a painting by Andrew Wyeth, sitting there in the wind? I thought that when I first saw you sitting on the dune. Are you familiar with his work?" He had a look of great concentration in his eyes, as though measuring her face and the thickness of her hair. But she was already smiling.

"I know his work very well." It had been her passion when she was a child, before she had discovered that Impressionism was much more her style. "I used to know every piece he had done."

"Every piece?" The sea-colored eyes were suddenly teasing but still warm.

"I thought so."

"Do you know the one of the woman on the beach?" She thought for a moment and shook her head. "Would you like to see it?" He stood next to her, looking like a bright-eyed, much-excited boy, only the manly spread of his shoulders and the few strands of gray in his hair belied the look in his eyes. "Would you?"

"I—I really have to get back. But, thank you. . . ." She trailed off in embarrassment. He didn't seem to be the kind of man one ought to be afraid of, but nevertheless he was only a stranger who had appeared on a beach. It struck her then that she was really a little bit mad to be talking to him at all, standing there alone in the dark. "Really, I can't. Perhaps some other time."

"I understand." The fire dampened a little in his eyes, but the smile was still there. "It's a beautiful piece though, and the woman in it looks a great deal like you."

"Thank you. That's a lovely thing to say." She was wondering how to leave him. He seemed to have no immediate intention of returning to his house.

"May I walk you back up the beach? It's a little too dark now for you to be wandering around on your own." He grinned at her, squinting into the wind. "You might get accosted by a stranger." She laughed in answer and nodded as they walked down the shallow dune back toward the sea. "Tell me, how did you become so fond of Wyeth?"

"I thought he was the greatest American painter I had ever seen. But then," she looked apologetically into his eyes, "I fell in love with all the French Impressionists. And I'm afraid I forgot about him. Not forgot, really, but I fell a little bit out of love."

They walked along comfortably, side by side, the only two people on the beach, with the surf pounding beside them. She laughed suddenly then. It was so incongruous, discussing art with this stranger, walking in the sand in Carmel. What would she tell Kim? Or would she tell Kim at all? For a moment she was inclined to tell no one about her new friend. It was just a moment's encounter at dusk on a quiet beach. What was there to tell?

"Do you always fall out of love that easily?" It was a silly thing to say, the sort of things strangers say to each other for lack of something better. But she smiled.

"Generally not. Only when French Impressionists are involved."

He nodded sagely. "That makes sense. Do you paint?"

"A bit."

"Like the Impressionists?" He seemed to know the answer already, and she nodded. "I'd like to see your work. Is it shown?"

She shook her head, looking out at the waves capped iridescently by the first light of the moon. "No, not anymore. Just once, a long time ago."

"Did you fall out of love with painting too?"

"Never." She looked down at the sand as she spoke and then back at him again. "Painting is my life."

"Then why don't you show?" He seemed puzzled by her reaction, but she only shrugged. They had reached the place where she had walked onto the beach.

"This is where I get off." They stood in the moonlight, looking into each other's eyes. For the madness of one moment she wanted to be held in those strong, comfortable arms, wrapped in his Windbreaker with him. "It was nice talking to you." Her face was strangely serious as she spoke.

"My name is Ben."

She hesitated for a moment. "Deanna."

He held out his hand, shook hers, and then turned away and walked back down the beach. She watched him, the broad shoulders, the strong back, and the wind in his hair. She wanted to shout "Good-bye," but the word would have been lost in the wind. Instead, he turned, and she thought she saw him wave at her once in the dark.

4

"Where the hell have you been?" Kim was waiting for her in the lobby with a look of concern, when Deanna returned. She smoothed her tangled hair back from her face and smiled at her friend. Her cheeks were pink from the wind, her eyes shining. The word *radiant* flashed into Kim's mind as Deanna began a rush of explanation.

"I'm sorry. I walked farther than I thought. It took me ages to get back."

"It sure did. I was beginning to worry."

"I'm sorry." She looked remorseful, and Kim's face softened into a smile.

"All right. But Jesus, let the kid loose on a beach and she vanishes. I thought maybe you'd run into a friend."

"No." She paused for a moment. "I just walked." She had missed it. Her chance to tell Kim about Ben. But what was there to say? That she had met a stranger on the beach with whom she had discussed art? It sounded ridiculous. Childish. Or worse, stupid and improper. And she found that when she thought of it, she wanted to keep the moment to herself. She would never see him again anyway. Why bother to explain?

"Ready for dinner?"

"I certainly am."

They walked the two blocks to the Pine Inn, glancing into shop windows, chatting about friends. Theirs was always an easy exchange, and the silence left Deanna to her own thoughts. She found herself wondering about the unknown Wyeth Ben had suggested he had. Did he really or was it only a poster? Did it matter? She told herself not.

"You're mighty quiet tonight, Deanna," Kim said as they finished their dinner. "Tired?"

"A little."

"Thinking about Marc?"

"Yes." It was the easiest answer.

"Will he call you from Athens?"

"When he can. The time difference makes it difficult." And it made him seem terribly far away. In only two days he already seemed part of another lifetime. Or maybe that was just the effect of being in Carmel. When she was at home, with his clothes and his books or on his side of the bed, he felt much nearer. "What about your client tomorrow? What's he like?"

"I don't know. Never met him. He's an art dealer. The Thompson Galleries. As a matter of fact, I was going to ask you if you wanted to come to the meeting. You might like to see his house. I hear he has a fabulous collection in what he calls his 'cottage.'"

"I don't want to get in your way."

"You won't." Kimberly looked at her reassuringly, and they

paid the check. It was already eleven-thirty and Deanna was glad
to climb into her bed.

When she slept, she dreamed of the stranger named Ben.

The phone rang beside her bed as she lay on her back, sleepily
wondering if she should get up. She had promised to go with Kim,
but she was tempted to go back to sleep. And then take another
walk on the beach. The lure of that bothered her. She knew why
she wanted to go back, and it was a strange, uncomfortable feeling
the way he lingered in her mind. She would probably never see
him again. And what if she did? What then? The phone rang
again, and she reached over to answer it.

"Rise and shine." It was Kim.

"What time is it?"

"Five after nine."

"God. It feels more like seven or eight."

"Well, it isn't, and our meeting's at ten. Get up, and I'll bring
you breakfast."

"Can't I order room service?" Deanna had grown used to traveling with Marc.

"The Ritz this ain't. I'll bring you coffee and a Danish."

Deanna realized suddenly how spoiled she'd become. Not
having Margaret and one of her perfect breakfasts was becoming
a hardship. "All right. That'll be fine. I'll be ready in half an
hour."

She showered and did her hair and slipped into a cashmere
sweater of a rich cornflower blue, which she pulled on over white
slacks. She even managed to look fresh and alive by the time Kim
knocked on her door.

"Jesus, you look gorgeous." Kim handed her a steaming cup of
coffee and a plate.

"So do you. Should I wear something more businesslike? You
look awfully grown-up." Kim was wearing a beige gabardine suit
with a persimmon silk blouse and a very pretty straw hat, and a
little straw bag clutched under her arm. "You look very chic."

"Don't look so surprised." Kim smiled and collapsed in a chair.
"I hope this guy is easy. I don't feel like arguing business on a Sat-
urday morning." She yawned and watched Deanna finish the
coffee in her cup.

"Who am I supposed to be by the way? Your secretary or your chaperone?" Deanna's eyes sparkled over her cup.

"Neither, you jerk. Just my friend."

"Won't he think it a little strange that you bring along your friends?"

"Too bad if he does." Kim yawned again and stood up. "We'd better go."

"Yes, ma'am."

The drive took only five minutes, with Deanna reading the instructions to Kim. The address was on a pretty street, the houses all set back from the road and hidden by trees. But she saw when they got out of the car that it was a small, pleasant house. Not elaborate, and far from pretentious. It had a windswept, natural look to it. A small black foreign car was parked outside, something convenient, not handsome. None of the evidence suggested that the promised art collection would be impressive or rare. But the inside of the house told a different tale, as a small tidy woman in a housekeeper's apron opened the door. She had the look of someone who came once or twice a week, efficient rather than warm.

"Mr. Thompson said to wait for him in his den. He's upstairs on the phone. To London." She added the last words with disapproval, as though she thought it a shocking expense. But not nearly as great an expense, Deanna thought, as the paintings on the walls. She looked at them with awe as they followed the housekeeper to the den. The man had a magnificent collection of English and Early American paintings. None of them were what Deanna would have collected herself, but they were a joy to behold. She wanted to linger so she could study each piece, but the woman in the apron marched them quickly and firmly into the den, glared at them long and hard, muttered, "Sit down," then disappeared back to her chores.

"My God, Kim, did you see what he has on his walls?"

Kimberly grinned, readjusting her hat. "Beautiful stuff, isn't it? Not my cup of tea, but he has some awfully good pieces. Though they're not all really his." Deanna raised an eyebrow in question. "He owns two galleries. One in San Francisco, and one in L.A. I suspect he borrows some of these from his galleries. But what the hell, it's beautiful work."

Deanna nodded in rapid agreement and continued to look around. They were seated in a room with a wide picture window that looked out at the sea. A simple pine desk, two couches, and a chair. Like the exterior of the house and the modest car, it was functional rather than impressive. But the art collection amply made up for that. Even here, he had hung two very fine, perfectly framed black-and-white sketches. She leaned closer to peer at the signatures then turned to look at a painting that hung behind her, the only ornament on a totally bare, white wall. Even as she turned to look, she felt herself gasp. It was the painting. The Wyeth. The woman on the dune, her face partially hidden as she rested it on her knees. And even Deanna could see that the woman was startlingly like her. The length and color of her hair, the shape of her shoulders, even the hint of a smile. She was surrounded by a bleak, damp-looking beach and accompanied only by the passing of one lonely gull.

"Good morning." She heard his voice behind her before she could comment on the painting. Her eyes met his in surprise. "How do you do, I'm Ben Thompson. Miss Houghton?" There was an unspoken question in his eyes, but she quickly shook her head and pointed to Kim, who stepped forward with an extended hand and a smile.

"I'm Kimberly Houghton. And this is my friend, Deanna Duras. We heard so much about your collection that I had to bring her along. She's an amazingly gifted artist herself, though she won't admit it."

"No, I'm not."

"See!" Kim's eyes danced as she took in the good-looking man who stood before them. He looked to be somewhere in his late thirties, and he had extraordinarily beautiful eyes.

Deanna was smiling at them both and shaking her head. "Really. I'm not."

"How do you like my Wyeth?" He said it straight into Deanna's eyes, and she felt a little pull at her heart.

"I . . . it's a very, very fine piece. But you already know that." She found herself blushing when she spoke to him. She wasn't sure what to say. Should she admit having met him before? Should she pretend that there had been no meeting? Would he?

"Do you like it though?" His eyes held hers, and she felt herself grow warm under his gaze.

"Very much." He nodded, pleased. And then she understood. He would say nothing about the night before on the beach. But she found herself smiling as they sat down. It was a strange feeling, having this secret between them, stranger still to know that she had met the "new client" before Kim.

"Ladies, some coffee?" They both nodded, and he stepped into the hall to call to the housekeeper. "One medium, two black." As he came back into the room, he grinned at them. "They'll either all be medium or all black. Mrs. Meacham doesn't approve. Of anything. Coffee. Visitors. Or me. But I can trust her to clean the house when I'm gone. She thinks all this stuff is crap." He waved airily around the room, a gesture encompassing the Wyeth and both sketches as well as the pieces they had seen on their way in. Kim and Deanna both laughed.

When the coffee arrived, all three cups were black. "Perfect. Thank you." He smiled boyishly at the housekeeper as she left the room. "Miss Houghton . . . ?"

"Kimberly, please."

"Okay, Kimberly, you've seen the ads we ran last year?" She nodded. "What did you think?"

"Not enough style. Not the right look. Not aimed at the right marketplace for what you want."

He nodded, but his glance kept wandering back to Deanna, who was still drinking in the Wyeth behind him. His eyes betrayed nothing as he watched her, and his words showed that he knew what he wanted from Kim. He was quick, funny, astute, and very businesslike, and their meeting was over in less than an hour. She promised to give him some fresh ideas within two weeks.

"Will Deanna be consulting on the account?" It was hard to tell if he was teasing. Deanna shook her head rapidly and held up a hand, laughing.

"Good God, no. I have no idea how Kim comes up with any of her wizardly ideas."

"Blood, sweat, and a lot of black coffee." Kimberly grinned.

"What do you paint?" He was looking again at Deanna, with the same gentle eyes she had seen on the beach the night before.

Her voice was very soft as she answered. "Still lifes, young girls. The usual Impressionist themes."

"And mothers with young babies on their knees?" The eyes were always teasing, but unrelentingly kind.

"Only once." She had done a portrait of herself and Pilar. Her mother-in-law had hung it in the Paris apartment and then ignored it for the next dozen years.

"I'd like to see some of your work. Do you show?" Again no betrayal of the night before, and she wondered why.

"No, I don't. I haven't shown in years. I'm not ready."

"Now that's crap, to use your housekeeper's word." Kimberly looked first at Ben Thompson and then at Deanna. "You should show him some of your work."

"Don't be silly." Deanna felt awkward and looked away. No one had seen her work in too many years. Only Marc and Pilar, and now and then Kim. "One day, but not yet. Thank you anyway though." Her smile thanked him for his silence as well as his kindness. It was strange that he too should wish to remain mute about their meeting on the beach.

The conversation drew to a close with the usual amenities and a brief tour of his collection, conducted beneath the buzzardlike gaze of the housekeeper as she swept. Kimberly promised to call him the following week.

There was nothing unusual in his farewell to Deanna. No inappropriate pressure of her hand, no message in his eyes, only the warmth that she had already seen, and the smile he left them as he closed the door.

"What a nice guy," Kim said as she started the little MG. The engine grumbled, then came to life. "He's going to be a pleasure to work with. Don't you think?"

Deanna just nodded. She was lost in her own thoughts until Kim screeched to a halt outside their hotel.

"Why the hell don't you let him see your work?" Deanna's reticence always annoyed Kim. She had been the only one in art school who had really had a notable talent, and the only one who had buried her light under a bushel for almost twenty years. The others had all tried to make it and eventually failed.

"I told you. I'm not ready."

"Bull! If you don't call him yourself, I'm going to give him your number. It's time you did something about that mountain of masterpieces you keep standing around in your studio, facing the wall. That's a crime, Deanna. It just isn't right. Jesus, when you think of the garbage I painted and busted my ass to sell—"

"It wasn't garbage." Deanna looked kindly at her. But they both knew it hadn't been very good. Kim was much better at planning campaigns, headlines, and layouts than she had been at her art.

"It *was* garbage, and I don't even care anymore. I like what I do. But what about you?"

"I like what I do, too."

"And what's that?" Kimberly was becoming frustrated now, and her voice betrayed her feelings. It always wound up that way when they talked about Deanna's work. "What *do* you do?"

"You know what I do. I paint, I take care of Marc and Pilar, I run the house. I keep busy."

"Yes, taking care of everyone else. What about *you?* Wouldn't it do something for you to see your work shown in a gallery, hung somewhere other than your husband's office?"

"It doesn't matter where they're hung." She didn't dare tell Kim that they weren't even there anymore. Marc had hired a new decorator six months before, who had declared her works "weak and depressing" and taken them all down. Marc had brought the canvases home, including a small portrait of Pilar, which now hung in the hall. "What matters to me is painting it, not showing it."

"That's like playing a violin with no strings for chrissake. It doesn't make sense."

"It does to me." She was gentle but firm, and Kim shook her head as they got out of the car.

"Well, I think you're crazy, but I love you anyway." Deanna smiled as they walked back inside the hotel.

The rest of their stay went by too quickly. They browsed in the shops, had dinner once more at the Pine Inn. On Sunday afternoon Deanna took one more walk on the beach. She knew where he lived now, knew it when she glimpsed the house hidden behind the trees. She knew how near she was to the Wyeth. She walked on. She did not see him again, and she was annoyed at herself for even wondering if he'd be on the beach. Why should he be? And what would she say if he were? Thank him for not letting Kimberly know they had met? So what? What did it matter? She knew she'd never see him again.

5

When the phone rang, she was already in her studio, sitting back from the canvas trying to evaluate her morning's work. It was a bowl of tulips dropping their petals on a mahogany table, against a background of blue sky, glimpsed through an open window.

"Deanna?" She was stunned to hear his voice.

"Ben? How did you get my number?" She felt a warm blush rise to her cheeks and was instantly angry at herself for the way she felt. "Kim?"

"Of course. She said that if I didn't show your work, she'd sabotage our account."

"She didn't!" The blush deepened as she laughed.

"No. She just said that you were very good. Tell you what, I'll trade you my Wyeth for one of yours."

"You're crazy. And so is Kim!"

"Why don't you let me judge for myself? Do you suppose I could come by around noon?"

"Today? Now?" She glanced at the clock and shook her head. It was already after eleven. "No!"

"I know. You're not ready. Artists never are." The voice was as gentle as it had been on the beach.

She stared into the phone. "Really. I can't." It was almost a whisper.

"Tomorrow?" Not pushy, but firm.

"Ben, really . . . it's not that. I . . ." She faltered and heard his laugh.

"Please. I'd really love to see your work."

"Why?" She instantly felt stupid for the question.

"Because I like you. And I'd like to see your work. It's as simple as that. Doesn't that make sense?"

"More or less." She didn't know what more to say.

"Are you busy for lunch?"

"No, I'm not." She sighed sadly again.

"Don't sound so forlorn. I promise not to throw darts at your canvases. Honest. Trust me."

Oddly, she did. She trusted him. It was something about the way he spoke, and the look she remembered in his eyes. "I think I do. All right then. Noon."

No one going to the guillotine had ever spoken as resolutely. Ben Thompson smiled to himself as he hung up.

He was there promptly at noon. With a bag of French rolls, a sizable wedge of Brie, and half a dozen peaches, as well as a bottle of white wine.

"Will this do?" he asked as he spread his riches out on her desk.

"Very nicely. But you really shouldn't have come." She looked dismayed as she eyed him over the table. She was wearing jeans and a paint splattered shirt, her hair tied in a loosely woven knot. "I really hate being put on the spot." Her expression was troubled as she watched him, and for a moment he stopped arranging the fruit.

"You're not on the spot, Deanna. I really did want to see your work. But it doesn't matter a damn what I think. Kim says you're good. You know you're good. You told me on the beach that painting was your life. No one can ever play with that. I wouldn't try to." He paused, then went on, more softly, "You saw some of the pieces I love in the cottage in Carmel. That's something I care about. This is something you care about. If you like my Wyeth, it makes me happy, but if you don't it doesn't change a bit of its beauty for me. Nothing I see will change what you do, or how much it matters. No one can ever touch that."

She nodded silently, then slowly walked toward the wall where twenty paintings were propped, hidden and ignored. One by one, she turned them around, saying nothing and looking only at the oils as she turned them. She did not look at him until at last he said, "Stop." She glanced up in surprise and saw him leaning against her desk with a look in his eyes she didn't understand.

"Did you feel anything when you saw the Wyeth?" He was searching her face and holding her eyes.

She nodded. "I felt a great deal."

"What?"

She smiled. "First, surprise, to realize that I was in your house.

But then, a kind of awe, a joy at seeing the painting. I felt pulled by the woman, as though she were someone I knew. I felt everything I think Wyeth wanted to tell me. For a moment, I felt spellbound by his words."

"As I do by yours. Do you have any idea how much you've put in those paintings, or how really beautiful they are? Do you know what it means to be reached out to and pulled at time after time after time, as you turn them around? They're incredible, Deanna. Don't you know how good they are?" He was smiling at her. She felt her heart pound in her chest.

"I love them. But that's because they're mine." She was glowing now. He had given her the ultimate gift, and she knew he meant every word. It had been so long since anyone had seen what she painted—and cared.

"They're not only yours. They are you." He walked closer to one of the canvases and silently stared. It was a painting of a young girl leaning over her bath—Pilar.

"That one is my daughter." She was enjoying it now. She wanted to share more.

"It's a beautiful piece of work. Show me more."

She showed him all of them. When it was over, she almost crowed with pleasure. He liked them, he loved them! He understood her work. She wanted to throw her arms around his neck and laugh.

He was opening the bottle of wine. "You realize what this means, don't you?"

"What?" She was suddenly wary, but not very.

"That I will hound you until you sign with the gallery. How about that?"

She smiled broadly at him, but she shook her head. "I can't."

"Why not?"

"That's not for me." And Marc would have a fit. He would think it commercial and vulgar—though the Thompson gallery had a reputation for anything but vulgarity, and Ben's family had been reputable in the art world for years. She had looked him up when she got back from Carmel. His grandfather had had one of the finest galleries in London, and his father in New York. Ben Thompson had carte blanche in the art world, even at thirty-eight years of age. She had read that too. "Really, Ben, I can't."

"The hell you can't. Listen, don't be stubborn. Come to the

gallery and look around. You'll feel a lot better when you see what's there." He suddenly looked very young as he said it, and she laughed. She knew what was there. She had researched that, as well. Pissarro, Chagall, Cassatt, a very small Renoir, a splendid Monet, some Corots. Also a few carefully hidden Pollocks, a Dali, and a de Kooning that he seldom showed. He had the best. As well as a few well-chosen, unknown, young artists, of whom he wanted her to be one. What more could she ask? But what would she tell Marc? *I had to. He asked me. I wanted . . .*

"No." He just wouldn't understand. And neither would Pilar. She would think it an obnoxious, show-offy thing to do. "You don't understand."

"You're right there." He held out a piece of French bread and Brie. Twenty-two paintings spread around the room. And he had loved them all. She beamed as she took the bread from him.

"I've got thirty more in the attic. And five over at Kim's."

"You're nuts."

"No, I'm not."

He handed her a peach. "Yes, you are. But I won't hold it against you. How about coming to an opening we're having tomorrow night? That won't do any harm, will it? Or are you even afraid to do that?" He was goading her now, and she wasn't sure she liked it.

"Who said I was afraid?" She looked very young as she bit into the juicy peach, then smiled.

"Who had to? Why else would you not want to show?"

"Because it doesn't make sense."

"You don't make sense." But by then they were both laughing and into their third glass of wine. "I like you anyway," he announced. "I'm used to dealing with crazies like you."

"I'm not crazy. Just stubborn."

"And you look exactly like my Wyeth. Did you notice it too?" His eyes pulled at her again. He put down his glass. She hesitated for a moment, then nodded.

"I did."

"Only I can see your eyes." He held them for a long moment, then glanced away. They were precisely the eyes he always knew the woman in the painting would have. "You have beautiful eyes."

"So do you." Her voice was like a soft breeze in the room, and they were both reminded of their walk in Carmel.

He said nothing for a while; he only sat silently, looking at her paintings. "You said that was your daughter. Is that really true?" He looked at her again, wanting to know more.

"Yes. She's almost sixteen. Her name is Pilar. And she is very, very pretty. Much more so than she looks in the painting. I've done several of her." She thought wistfully of the one Marc's decorator had rejected into the hall. "Some of them are quite good." She felt free with him now, free to like her own work.

"Where is she now? Is she here?"

"No." Deanna looked at him for a long moment. "In the South of France. Her . . . my husband is French." She wanted to tell him that Marc was away too, that he was in Greece, but it seemed treasonous. Why would she tell him? What did she want of this man? He had already told her that he liked her work. What more could she ask? She wanted to ask him if he was married. But that seemed wrong too. What did those things matter? He was here for her work. No matter how kind those deep, sea-green eyes were.

"You know"—he looked regretfully at his watch—"I hate to say this, but I have to get to work. I have a meeting at three in the office."

"Three?" Her eyes flew to the clock. It was already two forty-five. "Already? How did the time go so fast?" But they had looked at a great deal of her work. She stood up with a regretful look in her eyes.

"You'll come tomorrow night? To the vernissage?" His eyes told her that he wanted her to come. She wasn't sure why.

"I'll try."

"Please, Deanna. I'd like that." He touched her arm briefly, and then with a last appreciative smile around the room, he stepped outside the studio and loped down the stairs. "I'll find my way out. See you tomorrow!" His words faded as she sank into the comfortable white chair and looked around the room. There were four or five canvases of Pilar, but none of Marc. For one totally frantic moment she couldn't remember his face.

6

Deanna parked the dark blue Jaguar across from the gallery and slowly crossed the street. She still wasn't sure if she should go, if it was wise. If it made sense. What if Kim were there? It would make her feel foolish. What if . . . but then she thought of his eyes and pushed open the heavy glass door.

There were two black-jacketed bartenders standing nearby, alternately pouring Scotch and champagne and a pretty young woman was greeting the guests, who all looked either well heeled or artistic. Deanna saw quickly that it was the show of an older man's work. He stood surrounded by his friends, looking victorious and proud. The paintings were well displayed and had the flavor of Van Gogh. And then she saw Ben. He was standing at the far corner of the room, looking very handsome in a navy blue pin-striped suit. His eyes followed her inside and she saw him smile and gracefully extricate himself from the group where he stood. He was standing next to her in a moment.

"So you came, did you? I'm glad." They stood there for a moment, looking at each other, and she felt herself smile. It was a smile she couldn't have repressed. She was happy to see him again. "Champagne?"

"Thank you." She accepted a glass from the extended hand of one of the bartenders, and Ben took her gently by the elbow.

"There's something I want to show you in my office."

"Etchings?" She felt herself blush. "How horrible, I shouldn't have said that."

"Why not?" He was laughing too. "But no, it's a tiny Renoir I bought last night."

"My God, where did you get it?" She was following him down a long beige-carpeted hall.

"I bought it from a private collection. A wonderful old man. He says he never liked it. Thank God. I got it at an incredible price." He unlocked his office door and stepped rapidly inside. There, propped against the far wall, was a lovely delicate nude in the distinctive style that needed no glance at the signature. "Isn't she pretty?" He eyed the painting like a new child of whom he was unbearably proud, and Deanna smiled at the light in his eyes.

"She's wonderful."

"Thank you." He looked at Deanna very hard then, as though there was something more he wanted to say, but he didn't. Instead, he looked around with a smile that invited her to do the same. There was another Andrew Wyeth above his desk, this one well known.

"I like that one too. But not as well as the other."

"Neither do I." Their thoughts went instantly back to Carmel. The silence was interrupted by a knock on the door. The young woman who had been greeting guests at the entrance was beckoning to Ben from the hall. "Hi, Sally. What's up? Oh, this is Deanna Duras; she's going to be one of our new artists."

Sally's eyes instantly opened wide. She approached with a handshake and a smile. "What good news!"

"Now wait a minute!" Deanna glanced at Ben with an embarrassed smile. "I never said that."

"No, but I'm hoping you will. Sally, tell her how wonderful we are, how we never cheat our artists, never hang paintings the wrong way 'round, never paint mustaches on nudes."

Deanna was laughing now and shaking her head. "In that case, this isn't the gallery for me. I've always wanted to see a mustache on one of my nudes and haven't had the courage to do it myself."

"Let us do it for you." Ben was still smiling as he led them back into the hall and began to question Sally. There had already been three buyers at the show, and she had come back to discuss the price of one of the paintings with him. The artist wanted more.

"I'll tell him we'll make it up on another piece. He already agreed to the price on that one. God bless Gustave—he's given me all my gray hair."

"Not to mention mine." Sally pointed at a virgin-blonde head and disappeared back into the crowd as Ben began to introduce Deanna to the guests. She felt surprisingly at home as she wandered through the gallery, meeting artists and collectors. And she was surprised that she didn't see Kim. She mentioned it to Ben when he joined her.

"Isn't she here? I thought she would be."

"No. Apparently, she's tearing her hair out over a new ad for yogurt. Frankly, I'd just as soon she not get us confused. Better she get the yogurt out of her head before she starts in on art. Wouldn't you say?" Deanna laughed as he handed her another glass of champagne. "You know," he continued, "I enjoyed yesterday enormously. Your work is extraordinarily good. And I'm not going to stop badgering you until you say yes."

Deanna smiled at him over the champagne. Before she could protest, they were interrupted by several more collectors who wanted Ben's ear. He had his hands full with them until almost nine o'clock.

Deanna drifted slowly around the gallery, watching prospective buyers and admiring Gustave's work. She had stopped before one of his paintings when she heard a familiar voice just behind her. She turned in surprise.

"Studying the technique, Deanna?"

"Jim!" She looked into the laughing Irish eyes. "What are you doing here?"

"Don't ask. Collecting culture, I guess." He waved vaguely toward a group of people at the door. "They dragged me here. But only after several stiff drinks."

"An art lover to the core." She wore her usual warm smile, but somewhere within her was an uncomfortable stirring. She hadn't wanted to see Jim Sullivan here. She had come to see Ben . . . or had she? Was she here only to see the gallery? She wasn't really sure, and perhaps Jim would know. Perhaps he'd see something different in her face, in her eyes, in her soul. Almost defensively, she reached for a familiar subject. "Have you heard from Marc?"

He eyed her warily for a moment. "Have you?"

She shook her head. "I got a telegram the day after he left that he hadn't been able to call because it was the wrong time, and then I went to Carmel for the weekend. With Kim," she added quickly and unnecessarily. "He might have tried to call me then. I suppose he's in Athens by now."

Sullivan nodded and gazed back toward his friends. Deanna followed his gaze, and her glance fell immediately on a stunning, chestnut-haired girl gowned in shimmery silver. Jim's model—she had to be.

"He must be," Jim was saying. "Well, love, I've got to run." Almost as an afterthought, as he kissed her cheek, he pulled away to look at her again. "Do you want to join us for dinner?"

Instantly, she was shaking her head. "I—I can't . . . I have to get home . . . really. But thank you." Damn. Why did she feel so uncomfortable? She had nothing to hide. But he hadn't seemed to notice anything different about her. And why should he? What was different?

"You're sure?"

"Positive."

"All right. I'll call you." He kissed her quickly on the cheek and rejoined his friends. A moment later, they were gone. She stared absently after them. He hadn't answered her about whether or not he'd heard from Marc. Instead, he had countered her question with his own, asking her if she had heard from him. She wondered why.

"You look awfully serious, Deanna. Thinking of signing up with us?" There was teasing in Ben's whispered tones, and she turned to him with a smile. She hadn't noticed him come up to her.

"No. But I was thinking that I ought to go home."

"Already? Don't be silly. Besides, you haven't eaten." He looked at her for a moment. "Can I interest you in some dinner? Or would your husband object?"

"Hardly. He's in Greece for the summer." Their eyes met and held. "And dinner would be lovely." Why not? She smiled and forced Jim Sullivan from her mind.

Ben signaled to Sally that he was leaving, and unnoticed by the last stragglers, they passed through the glass door and into the cool summer fog. "Sometimes this reminds me of London," he said. "I used to visit my grandfather there as a child. He was English."

She laughed at the anonymity he assumed. "Yes, I know."

"Did you bring your own car?" Ben asked. She nodded at the dark blue Jaguar. "My, my. I'm impressed. I drive a little German car no one here has ever heard of. It runs on practically no gas and gets me where I want to go. Would you be ashamed to be seen in something so simple, or shall we take yours?" For a moment she was embarrassed to have come in Marc's car, but she always drove it when she went out in the evening. It was a matter of habit.

"I'd much rather go in yours."

"To L'Étoile?" He said it hesitantly, testing the waters.

"I think I'd like some place more like your car. Quiet and simple." He smiled his approval, and she laughed. "I suspect that you have a horror of ostentation, except in art."

"Exactly. Besides, my housekeeper would quit if I showed up one day in a Rolls. She already thinks all that 'crap' on the walls is an outrage. I once hung a beautiful French nude, and she took it down as soon as I left Carmel. I found it wrapped in a sheet when I got back. I had to take it back to the city." She laughed as he unlocked his car and held the door for her.

He took her to a little Italian restaurant tucked into a side street near the bay, and they talked about art through most of the evening. She told him of her years of floating around Europe and the States with her father, devouring the museums wherever they went, and he told her of learning about art from his grandfather and then his father, watching great auctions in London and Paris and New York. "But I never thought I'd go into business."

"Why not?"

"I wanted to do something more interesting. Like ride in rodeos or be a spy. I planned to be a spy at least until I was nine, but my grandfather insisted it wasn't respectable. Sometimes I'm not so sure our business is either. Actually, when I went to college I wanted to be one of those men who detects fakes in art. I studied for a while, but the forgeries always fooled me. I hope I do better now."

Deanna smiled. From the look of the gallery and the house in Carmel, she felt sure he did.

"Tell me," he said abruptly, "how long have you been married?"

She was surprised at the suddenly personal question. He had asked her none so far. "Eighteen years. I was nineteen."

"That makes you. . . ." He went through the ritual on his fingers, and she laughed.

"A hundred and three, in November."

"No." He frowned. "Isn't it a hundred and two?"

"At least. What about you? Have you ever been married?"

"Once. Briefly." His eyes retreated from hers for a moment. "I'm afraid I wasn't very good at detecting fakes there either. She took me for a beautiful ride, and I had a wonderful time. And then it was over." He smiled and met her glance again.

"No children?"

"None. That's the only thing I've regretted. I would have liked to have had a son."

"So would I."

There was a hint of wistfulness in her voice that made him watch her as he said, "But you have a lovely daughter."

"I also had two boys. They both died right after they were born." It was a weighty piece of information to pass across a dinner table to a relative stranger, but he only watched her eyes. He saw there what he needed to know.

"I'm sorry."

"So was I. And then, stupidly, it was a sort of blow when Pilar was born. In French families baby girls are not greeted with applause."

"You wanted applause?" He looked amused.

"At least." She smiled back at last. "And a brass band. And a parade."

"One can hardly blame you. She was the third?" he asked. Deanna nodded. "Are you very close?" He imagined they would be and was surprised to hear they were not.

"Not just now, but we will be again. For the moment she is terribly torn between being American and French. That kind of thing can be hard."

"So can being fifteen." He remembered with horror his sister at the same age. "Does she look like you?" He hadn't been able to tell from the distant glimpses in Deanna's paintings.

"Not at all. She is the image of her father. She's a very pretty girl."

"So is her mother."

For a moment Deanna said nothing, then she smiled. "Thank you, sir."

The conversation drifted back then to art. He stayed away from painful and personal subjects, but sometimes she wondered if he was even listening. He seemed to be watching her all the time and saying other things with his eyes. It was midnight when at last they were encouraged to leave.

"I had a marvelous evening." She smiled at him happily as he drew up alongside the parked Jaguar.

"So did I." He said nothing more. As she started her car, he backed away with a wave. She saw him in her rearview mirror, walking back to his own car, his hands in his pockets and his head pensively bowed.

She was already in bed, with the lights out, when the telephone rang. But the rapid whir of the lines told her it was long distance.

"Deanna?" It was Marc.

"Hello, darling. Where are you?"

"In Rome. At the Hassler, if you need me. Are you all right?" But the connection was poor. It was very hard to hear.

"I'm fine. Why are you in Rome?"

"What? I can't hear you. . . ."

"I said why are you in Rome?"

"I'm here on business. For Salco. But I'll see Pilar this weekend."

"Give her my love." She was sitting up in the dark and shouting to make herself heard.

"I can't hear you!"

"I said give her my love."

"Good. Fine. I will. Do you need money?"

"No, I'm fine." For a moment all she heard was static and gibberish again. "I love you." For some reason she needed to tell him that and to hear him say the same. She needed a bond to him, but he seemed an interminable distance away.

"I love you, Marc!" And for no reason she could understand, she found that there were tears in her eyes. She wanted him to hear her, she wanted to hear herself. "I love you!"

"What?"

And then they were cut off.

She quickly dialed the overseas operator and asked her for Rome. But it took another twenty-five minutes to put through her call. The operator at the Hassler answered with a rapid, "*Pronto*," and Deanna asked for Signore Duras. They rang his room. No answer. In Rome, it was already ten o'clock in the morning. "We are sorry. Signore Duras has gone out."

She lay back in the dark and thought of her evening with Ben.

7

Marc-Edouard Duras walked along the Via Vèneto in Rome, glancing into shop windows and occasionally casting an admiring glance at a pretty girl wandering past. It was a brilliantly sunny day, and the women were wearing T-shirts with narrow straps, white skirts that clung to shapely legs, and sandals that bared red enameled toes. He smiled to himself as he walked, the briefcase under his arm. It didn't make sense really, this brief sojourn in Italy, but after all, why not? And he had promised. . . . *Promised*. Sometimes he wondered how he could promise so easily. But he did.

He paused for a moment, an aristocratic figure in an impeccably tailored gray suit, waiting for the machine-gun spurt of Roman traffic to hurtle past him, casting itself hurly-burly in all directions, sending pedestrians scurrying in flight. He smiled as he watched an old woman wave a parasol and then make an obscene gesture. *Ecco, signora.* He bowed slightly to her from the opposite side of the street, and she made the same gesture to him. He laughed, glanced at his watch, and hurried to a table in a café. Beneath a brightly striped umbrella he could take refuge from the sun and continue to admire the energy and ecstasy that were the very essence of Rome. *Roma*—it was a magical city. Perhaps the promise had been worth keeping after all. For an instant, but only that, the abortive conversation with Deanna crept into his mind. It had been almost impossible to hear her, and he was relieved. There were times when he simply couldn't deal with her, couldn't reach out to her, couldn't bear to imagine the pain in those eyes or hear the loneliness in her voice. He knew it was there, but it was sometimes more than he could handle. He could cope with it in San Francisco, in the context of his ordinary routine, but not when he was in the throes of a professional crisis abroad, or when he was at home in France, or . . . here, in Rome. He shook his head slowly, as though to brush away the memory of her voice, and found himself gazing longingly up the street. He couldn't think of Deanna now. Couldn't. No. Not now. His mind was already a thousand miles away from her as his eyes sifted through the crowd: a pretty blonde, a tall brunette, two very Roman-looking men in light linen suits with thick dark hair, a tall Florentine-looking woman, like something in a Renaissance painting, and then he saw her. Striding gaily down the street with her own inimitable gait, the endless legs seeming to dance across the sidewalk as a brilliant turquoise skirt caressed her thighs. She wore the palest mauve silk shirt, delicate sandals, and a huge straw hat that almost hid her eyes. Almost. But not quite. Nothing could hide those eyes, or the sapphire lights that seemed to change with her every mood. They changed from the brilliance of fire to the mystery of the deep blue sea. A rich chestnut mane swept her shoulders.

"*Alors, chéri.*" She stopped only inches from him, and sensuous lips offered a smile for his eyes alone. "I'm sorry I'm late. I stopped to look at those silly bracelets again." He stood to greet her, and for once the chill reserve of Marc-Edouard Duras was clearly shattered. He wore the face of a boy, and one who was very much in love. Her name was Chantal Martin, and she had been a model at Dior. Their top model, in fact, for six-and-a-half years.

"Did you buy the bracelets?" His eyes caressed her neck, and as she shook her head, the chestnut hair danced beneath the hat he had bought her only that morning. It was frivolous, but delightful. And so was she. "Well?"

Her eyes laughed into his. She shook her head again. "No, again I didn't buy them." Unexpectedly, she tossed a small package into his lap. "I bought you that instead." She sat back, waiting for him to open it.

"*Tu me gâtes, petite sotte.*" You spoil me, silly little one.

"And you don't spoil me?" Without waiting for an answer, she signaled for a waiter. "*Senta! . . . Cameriere! . . .*" He approached instantly, with a look of pleasure, and she ordered a Campari and soda. "And you?"

"Inviting me to drinks, too?" She never waited for him to take matters in hand. Chantal liked to run her own show.

"Oh, shut up. What'll you have?"

"Scotch." She ordered it the way he liked it, and he watched her eyes for a long moment as they sat beneath the umbrella. The beginnings of the lunchtime crowd swirled colorfully around them. "Will you always be this independent, my love?"

"Always. Now open your gift."

"You're impossible." But that was precisely what had always fascinated him about her. She was impossible. And he loved it. Like a wild mare running free on the plains of Camargue. They had gone there together once, the land of the French cowboys and the beautiful, wild, white horses. He had always thought of her that way after that. Untamed, just a fraction out of reach, yet more or less his. More or less. He liked to think it was more rather than less. And it had been that way between them for five years.

She was twenty-nine now. She had been twenty-four when they met. It was the first summer that Deanna had refused to join him in France. He had felt odd to spend a summer without her; it had been awkward to explain to his family, insisting that she hadn't felt well enough to travel that year. No one believed it, but they had only said so behind his back, wondering if she were leaving Marc-Edouard or merely had a lover in the States. They would never have understood the truth—that she hated them, that she felt ill at ease, that she had wanted to stay at home, to be alone, to paint, because she detested sharing Marc with them, detested the way he was when he was with them, and detested even more watching the way Pilar became like them. It had been a shock for Marc-Edouard when she refused to come, a shock that left him wondering what it would mean now that she would no longer spend the summers with his family in France. He had decided to send her something beautiful, along with a letter asking her to change her mind. Remembering the eighteen-year-old wistful beauty who had sat in his office that day so long ago, he had gone to Dior.

He sat through the entire collection, making notes, watching the models, carefully studying the clothes, trying to decide which ones were most her style, but his attention had incessantly wandered from the outfits to the models, and in particular, one spectacular girl. She had been dazzling, and she had moved in a way that spoke only to him. She was a genius at what she did, whirling, turning, beckoning—to him alone, it seemed—and he had sat breathless in his seat. At the end of the show he had asked to see her, feeling uncomfortable for a moment, but barely longer. When she walked out to meet him in a starkly narrow, black jer-

sey dress, her auburn hair swept up on her lovely head, those remarkable blue eyes alternately clawing and caressing, he had
wanted to seize her and watch her melt in his embrace. He was a
rational man, a man of power and control, and he had never felt
that way before. It frightened him and fascinated him, and Chantal seemed very much aware of the power she had. She wielded it
gracefully, but with crushing force.

And instead of buying Deanna a dress, Marc had bought Chantal a drink, and another, and another. They had finished with
champagne at the bar of the hotel George V, and then much to
his own astonishment, he heard himself ask her if she would let
him take a room. But she had only giggled and gently touched his
face with one long, delicate hand.

"Ah, *non, mon amour, pas encore.*" Not yet.

Then when? He had wanted to shout the words at her, but he
hadn't. Instead he had courted her, cajoled her, showered her with
gifts, until at last she acquiesced, demurely, shyly, in just the way
that turned his heart and soul and flesh to fire beneath her touch.
They had spent the weekend in an apartment he had borrowed
from a friend, in the posh surroundings of the Avenue Foch, with
a miraculously romantic bedroom, and a balcony looking out on
gently whispering trees.

He would remember for a lifetime every sound and smell and
moment of that weekend. He had known then that he would
never have enough of Mademoiselle Chantal Martin. She had
woven herself like thread beneath his skin, and he would never be
quite comfortable again except with her. She drained him and
enchanted him, and made him almost mad with a desire he had
never felt before. Elusive, exotic, exquisite Chantal. It had gone
on for five years. In Paris, and Athens, and Rome. Wherever he
went in Europe, he took her and of course presented her in hotels
and restaurants and shops as "Madame Duras." They had both
grown used to it over the years. It was simply a part of his life
now, and hers. A part of which his partner, Jim Sullivan, was
acutely aware, and his wife, thank heaven, was not. Deanna would
never know. There was no reason to tell her. It took nothing away
from her, he told himself. She had San Francisco and her own little world. He had Chantal, and a much wider one. He had everything he wanted. As long as he had Chantal. He only prayed that

it would go on for a lifetime. But that was a promise Chantal would never make.

"*Alors, mon amour,* your present, your present, opcn it!" Her eyes teased and his heart soared. He pulled open the box. It was the diver's watch he had admired that morning, saying it would be fun to have for their trips to the beach and his stays in Cap d'Antibes.

"My God, you're mad! Chantal!" It had been monstrously expensive, but she waved his objections away with a disinterested hand. She could afford it now that she was no longer at Dior. Three years before she had retired from the runway and opened her own modeling agency. She wouldn't let him set her up in an apartment in Paris to do nothing except her hair and nails and wait for him. She refused to be dependent on anyone, least of all him. It irritated him sometimes, and frightened him as well. She didn't need him, she only loved him, but at least of that he was sure. No matter what she did when he was in the States, she loved him. He was certain of it. And the perfection of their time together cemented that belief.

"Do you like it?" She eyed him coyly over her Campari.

"I adore it." He dropped his voice, "But I love you more."

"Do you, m'lord?" She arched an eyebrow, and he felt a rising at his crotch.

"Do you require proof?"

"Perhaps. What did you have in mind?" She eyed him evilly from beneath her hat.

"I was planning to suggest lunch out in the country somewhere, but perhaps. . . ." His smile matched hers.

"Room service, darling?"

"An excellent idea." He waved to the *cameriere* and quickly paid their bill.

She stood up languidly, letting her body sway gently against his for a tantalizing instant, then began to weave her way through the crowded tables, casting a glance at him over her shoulder now and then. He could hardly wait to get her home. He wanted to run back to the hotel, holding fast to her hand, but she walked at her own pace, in her own style, knowing that she had Marc-Edouard Duras precisely where she wanted him. He watched her, amused. In a very few moments he would have her precisely whcrc he wanted her. In his arms, in bed.

In their room he began unbuttoning her blouse with alarming speed, and she brushed him away playfully, making him wait before she'd let him reveal what he was so hungry for. She fondled him with one hand and nipped gently at his neck, until at last he found the button to her skirt and it dropped to the floor, leaving her in transparent pink lace. He almost tore at the blouse now. In a moment she stood naked in front of him as he softly moaned. She undressed him, quickly and expertly, and they fell together on the bed. Each time they made love was better than the time before, and ever reminiscent of the first. It left him sated, yet still hungry, eager to know that they would soon be joined again.

She rolled over in bed, lying on one elbow, her hair tousled but still beautiful. She watched him silently, smiling. Her voice was a husky whisper near his ear as her fingers played slowly across his chest and down toward his stomach. "I love you, you know."

He looked at her intently, his eyes searching hers. "I love you too, Chantal. Too much perhaps. But I do." It was a remarkable admission for a man like Marc-Edouard Duras. No one who knew him would have believed it. Least of all Deanna.

Chantal smiled and then lay back with her eyes closed for a moment, and there was concern in his eyes. "Are you all right?"

"Of course."

"You'd lie to me, though. I know it. Tell me seriously. Are you all right, Chantal?" A look of almost frantic worry crossed his face. She smiled.

"I'm fine."

"You took your insulin properly today?" He was all fatherly concern now, the passion of the moment before forgotten.

"Yes, I took it. Stop worrying. Want to try your new watch in the bathtub?"

"Now?"

"Why not?" She smiled happily at him, and for once he felt totally at peace. "Or did you have something else in mind?"

"I always have something else in mind. But you're tired."

"Never too tired for you, *mon amour*." And he was never too tired for her. The years between them vanished as he made love to her again.

It was three o'clock in the afternoon when they lay quietly side by side again. "Well, we've taken care of this afternoon." She smiled mischievously at him, and he grinned in answer.

"You had other plans?"

"Absolutely none."

"Want to do some more shopping?" He loved to indulge her, to spoil her, to be with her, admire her, drink her in. Her perfume, her movements, her every breath excited him. And she knew it.

"I could probably be lured back to the shops."

"Good." The trip to Rome had been for her anyway. He was going to have to work hard that summer, and Athens would be dull for her. He knew how she loved Rome. And he always made a point of bringing her. Just to please her. Besides, he was going to have to leave her for the weekend.

"What's wrong?" She had been watching him very closely.

"Nothing. Why?"

"You looked worried for a moment."

"Not worried." But it was best to get it over with. "Just unhappy. I'm going to have to leave you for a couple of days."

"Oh?" Her eyes iced over like a winter frost.

"I have to stop off in Antibes to visit my mother and Pilar before we go to Greece."

She sat up in bed and looked at him with annoyance. "And what do you plan to do with me?"

"Don't make it sound like that, darling. I can't help it. You know that."

"Don't you think Pilar is old enough to withstand the shock of knowing about me? Or do you still find me so unpresentable? I'm no longer the little mannequin from Dior, you know. I run the biggest modeling agency in Paris." But she also knew that in his world that didn't count.

"That's not the point. And no, I don't think she's old enough." In what concerned Pilar he was oddly stubborn. It irritated Chantal a great deal.

"And your mother?"

"That's impossible."

"I see." She threw her long legs over the side of the bed and stalked across the room, grabbing a cigarette on her way, turning to look at him angrily only when she had reached the window at the opposite side. "I'm getting a little bored with being dumped in out-of-the-way places while you visit your family, Marc-Edouard."

"I'd hardly call Saint-Tropez an 'out-of-the-way place.'" He was beginning to look annoyed, and his tone showed none of the passion of the hours before.

"Where did you have in mind this time?"

"I thought maybe San Remo."

"How convenient. Well, I won't go."

"Would you rather stay here?"

"No."

"Do we have to go through this again, Chantal? It's getting very tedious. What's more, I don't understand. Why has this suddenly become an issue between us, when for five years you have found it perfectly acceptable to spend time on the Riviera without me?"

"Would you like to know why?" Suddenly her eyes blazed. "Because I'm almost thirty years old, and I'm still playing the same games I was playing with you five years ago. And I'm just a little tired of it. We play make-believe games of 'Monsieur and Madame Duras' halfway around the world, but in the places that matter—Paris, San Francisco, Antibes—I have to hide and slink around and disappear. Well, I'm sick of it. You want an exclusive arrangement. You expect me to sit in Paris and hold my breath for half the year, and then come out of moth balls at your command. I'm not going to do that anymore, Marc-Edouard. At least not for much longer." She stopped, and he stared at her, stunned. He didn't dare ask if she were serious. For a terrible instant, he knew that she was.

"What do you expect me to do about it?"

"I don't know yet. But I've been giving it a lot of thought lately. The Americans have a perfect expression, I believe: 'Shit or get off the pot.'"

"I don't find that amusing."

"I don't find San Remo amusing."

Christ! It was useless. A small sigh escaped him, and he ran a hand through his hair. "Chantal, I can't take you to Antibes."

"You *won't* take me to Antibes. There's a difference."

And what's more, she had added San Francisco to the list of her complaints. That startling bit of information hadn't escaped him either. She had never even wanted to go to the States before.

"May I ask what brought all this on? It can't just be your thirtieth birthday. That's still four months away."

She paused, her back to him, as she looked silently out the window, and then slowly she turned to face him again. "Someone else just asked me to marry him."

Time seemed to stand still. Marc-Edouard stared at her in horror.

8

"Deanna?" The phone had rung before she'd gotten out of bed. It was Ben.

"Yes."

She sounded sleepy, and he smiled. "I'm sorry. Did I wake you?"

"More or less."

"What a very diplomatic answer! I'm calling to bug you a little more. I figure that sooner or later I'll wear down your resistance and you'll sign with the gallery just to get me off your back. How about lunch?"

"Now?" She was still half asleep and turned toward the clock wondering how late she had slept, but Ben was laughing at her again.

"No, not at eight o'clock in the morning. How about twelve or one? In Sausalito?"

"What's there?"

"Sunshine. A condition we're not always blessed with on this side of the bridge. Have I sold you?"

"More or less." She laughed into the phone. What the hell was he doing, calling her at eight o'clock in the morning? And why lunch so soon? They had had dinner the night before, and lunch in her studio the day before that. She was beginning to wonder if she had found a new friend, an ardent potential dealer for her work, or something else. She wondered if it were wise to see him again quite so soon.

"Yes, it is."

"What is?" She was confused.

"You're wondering if it's a good idea to have lunch with me. It is."

"You're impossible."

"Then we'll have lunch in the city."

"No, Sausalito sounds nice." She had accepted without thinking further and found herself smiling at the ceiling as she spoke into the phone. "I'm an easy sale at this hour of the day. No defenses yet, no coffee."

"Good. Then how about signing with the gallery before coffee tomorrow?"

"I may hang up on you, Ben." She was laughing, and it felt wonderful to start the day off with laughter. She hadn't done that in years.

"Don't hang up on me till we settle lunch. Do you want me to pick you up around noon?"

"That'll do." What'll do? What was she doing having lunch with this man? But she liked him. And lunch in Sausalito sounded like fun.

"Wear your jeans."

"O.K., see you at noon."

He pulled up in front of her house at exactly 12:02. He was wearing a turtleneck sweater and jeans, and when she climbed into the car, she saw that there was a basket on the seat, draped in a red-and-white cloth. The neck of a bottle poked its way out at one side. Ben opened the door for her and put the basket on the backseat.

"Good morning, madam." He smiled broadly as she slid in beside him. "I thought maybe we'd have a picnic instead. O.K.?"

"Very much so." Or was it? Should she be having a picnic with this man? The head of Madame Duras told her no, while the heart that was Deanna's wanted an afternoon in the sun. But surely there were other things she could do, and she had the terrace outside her studio if she really wanted sun.

Ben glanced at her as he started the car and saw the faint pucker between her brows. "Do we have a problem?"

"No." She said it softly as he pulled away from the curb. She found herself wondering if Margaret had seen them.

He amused her with stories about some of the gallery's more colorful artists as they drove across the splendor of the Golden

Gate Bridge. He fell silent then for a moment. They were both looking out at the view.

"Pretty, isn't it?" he asked. She nodded with a smile. "May I ask you an odd sort of question?"

She looked surprised for a moment. "Why not?"

"How is it that you and your husband live here, instead of France? From what I know of the French they don't, as a rule, like living very far from home. Except under duress."

She laughed. What he had said was true. "There's a lot of business to be done here. And Marc isn't here that much anyway; he travels most of the time."

"Lonely for you." It was a statement, not a question.

"I'm used to it."

He wasn't quite sure he believed her. "What do you do when you're alone?"

They spoke in unison with a burst of laughter: "Paint."

"That's what I thought."

"What ever made you come down to Carmel?" He seemed to be riddled with questions. So far they were all easy to answer.

"Kim. She insisted that I needed to get away."

"Was she right?" He glanced over at her as he took the turnoff that led into the military preserve on the other side of the bridge. "Did you need to get away?"

"I suppose I did. I'd forgotten how lovely Carmel is. I hadn't been there in years. Do you go every weekend?" She wanted to turn the questions back to him. She didn't really like talking to him about Marc.

"I go whenever I can. It's never often enough."

She noticed then that they had taken a narrow country road and were driving past deserted bunkers and military buildings. "Ben, what is this?" She looked around herself with curiosity. They might have stumbled onto a stage set for a movie depicting the years after a war. The barracks on either side of the road were crumbling and boarded up, and there were wild flowers and weeds climbing onto the road.

"It's an old army post from the last war. For some reason they hang onto it, though it's empty now. There's a beautiful beach down here at the end. I come here sometimes, just to think." He looked over at her with a smile, and once again she was aware of how comfortable it was just to be with him. He had all the makings of a good friend. They fell into an easy silence as he drove the rest of the way.

"It's eerie, isn't it? It's so pretty and there's no one here." His was the only car there when they stopped just before they reached the beach. She hadn't seen another car since he'd turned off the main road.

"There never is. And I've never told a soul about it. I like coming here by myself."

"Do you do that sort of thing often? Like walk on the beach in Carmel by yourself?" she asked. He nodded, reaching over for the basket in the backseat. He was looking very closely at her.

"I never thought I'd see you again after that night on the beach."

"Neither did I. It was strange, walking along, talking to you about art. I felt as though we'd known each other for years."

"So did I, but I thought it was because you looked so much like the Wyeth." She smiled and lowered her eyes. "I wasn't quite sure what to say the next day when I found you in my den. I didn't know whether or not to acknowledge that we'd met."

"What made you decide not to?" She looked back into his eyes with a very small smile.

"The ring on your left hand. I thought it might be awkward for you if I did."

It was like him, Deanna realized, perceptive and thoughtful. She saw him frown a little, and sit back in his seat.

"Would it be awkward for you if people knew we were having lunch?" he asked.

"I don't see why." But there was more bravado than truth in her face, and he saw it.

"What would your husband say, Deanna?"

The words were unbearably soft, and she wanted to tell him that she didn't give a damn, but she did. The bitch of it was that she did care. A lot.

"I don't know. The question has never come up. I don't have lunch with men very often."

"What about art dealers who want to show your work?" Ben smiled at her. They had not moved from the car.

"No, least of all with art dealers. I never have lunch with them."

"Why not?"

She took a deep breath and looked him in the eye. "My husband does not approve of my work. He thinks it's a nice hobby, a pastime, but 'artists are hippies and fools.'"

"Well, that certainly takes care of Gauguin and Manet." He thought for a moment. When he spoke, she felt as though his eyes were burning straight into her soul. "Doesn't that hurt? Doesn't it force you to deny an essential part of yourself?"

"Not really. I still paint." But they both knew that her denial was a lie. She had been forced to give up something she wanted very much. "I suppose marriage is a kind of exchange," she went on. "Everyone compromises something." But what did Marc compromise? What had he given up? She looked pensive and sad, and Ben looked away.

"Maybe that's what I had all wrong when I got married. I forgot the compromises."

"Were you very demanding?" Deanna watched him with surprise.

"Maybe I was. It was so long ago, it's hard to be sure. I wanted her to be what I had always thought she was. . . ." His voice drifted off.

"And what was that?"

"Oh"—he looked up with a wry little smile—"faithful, honest, pleasant, in love with me. The usual stuff." They both laughed then, and he grabbed the picnic basket and helped Deanna out of the car. He had brought a blanket too and spread it out carefully for her on the sand.

"Good God, did you make this lunch?" She looked at the goodies he was pulling out of the basket. There was crab salad, pâté, French bread, a little box of pastries, and more wine. There was also a smaller basket filled with fruit and richly sprinkled with cherries. She reached for a cluster and hung it over her right ear.

"You look lovely in cherries, Deanna, but have you tried grapes?" He handed her a small bunch. She laughed and draped them over her left ear. "You look as though you should be climbing out of a horn of plenty . . . it's all very *Fête Champêtre*."

"Isn't it though?" She leaned back, looking up at the sky with a broad smile. She felt terribly young and irrepressibly happy. It was easy being with him.

"Ready to eat?" He looked down at her, a bowl of crab salad in one hand. She looked startlingly beautiful, reclining easily on the

blanket with the fruit peeking through her dark hair. Seeing his
smile, she remembered the cherries and the grapes. She pulled
them away from her ears and sat up on one elbow.

"To tell you the truth, I'm ravenous."

"Good. I like women with healthy appetites."

"And what else? What else do you like?" It wasn't an appropriate question, but she didn't care. She wanted to be his friend.
She wanted to know more, and to share.

"Oh, let's see . . . I like women who dance . . . women who
type . . . women who can read—and write! Women who paint
. . . women with green eyes." He stopped, staring down at her
again. "And you?" His voice was barely audible.

"What kind of women do I like?" She laughed at him.

"Oh, shut up. Here, have something to eat." He handed her the
loaf of French bread and the pâté, and she broke off the heel and
slathered it handsomely with the delicate meat.

It was a perfect afternoon; the sun was high in the sky and
there was a gentle breeze as the water lapped softly at the beach.
Now and then a bird would fly by. Behind them the deserted
buildings stood staring sightlessly. It was a world of their own.

"You know"—she glanced around and then back at him—
"sometimes I wish I painted things like this."

"Why don't you?"

"You mean like Wyeth?" She smiled at him. "It's not me. We
each do what we do, very differently." He nodded, waiting for her
to say more. "Ben, do you paint?"

He shook his head with a rueful grin. "Not really. I used to try.
But I'm afraid it's my lot in life to sell art and not to make it. I
did create one piece of art though." He looked dreamy again as he
stared out at the bay. The summer wind played with his hair.

"What was it?"

"I built a house. A small one, but it was damn pretty. I built it
myself with a friend."

"How amazing!" She was impressed. "Where?"

"In New England. I was living in New York then. It was a
surprise for my wife."

"Did she love it?"

He shook his head and turned to look at the bay again. "No.
She never saw it. She left three days before I was going to take her
up to see it for the first time." Deanna sat in silence for a mo-

ment, stunned. They had both had their disappointments in life.

"What did you do with it?"

"Sold it. I hung onto it for a while, but it was never much fun. It always hurt a little too much. And then I moved out here. And bought the house in Carmel." He looked over at Deanna, his eyes soft and sad. "But it was nice to know I could do it. I don't think I ever felt as good as the day I finished that house. What a feeling! It really was an accomplishment."

She smiled softly, listening. "I know," she said, after a moment. "I felt that way when I had Pilar. Even though she wasn't a son."

"Does that really matter so much?" He seemed annoyed.

"It did then. It meant a great deal to Marc, to have a boy. But I don't think he really cares anymore. He adores her."

"I think I'd rather have a daughter than a son," Ben said. Deanna looked surprised. "Why?"

"They're easier to love. You don't have to get hung up with images and macho and all that crap that doesn't mean anything. You can just love them." He looked as though he regretted not having a child, and she found herself wondering if he'd ever remarry.

"No, I won't." He wasn't looking at her when he said it.

"Won't what?" She was confused. He had a way of answering questions she hadn't asked. Except in her own head.

"Get married again."

"You're incredible. Why not?" She was still amazed that he had known what she was thinking.

"There's no point. I have what I need. And now I'm too busy with the galleries. It wouldn't be fair, unless it were someone as involved in them as I. I was less entranced by my business ten years ago. Now I'm in it up to my neck."

"But you want children. Don't you?" She had understood that much.

"I also want an estate outside Vienna. I can live without that too. And what about you?"

"I already have a child. Do you mean do I want more?" She didn't understand.

"No, or maybe that too, but do you think you'll ever remarry?" He looked at her openly, with his deep, green eyes.

"But I am. Married, I mean."

"Happily, Deanna?"

The question was painful and direct. She started to say yes, then stopped. "Sometimes. I accept what I've got."

"Why?"

"Because he and I have a history behind us." She found herself not wanting to say Marc's name to Ben. "You can't replace that, or deny it, or run out on it. We have a past."

"A good one?"

"At times. Once I understood the rules of the game." She was being brutally honest, even with herself.

"Which were?" His voice was so unbearably soft, it made her want to reach out to him and not talk about Marc. But Ben was her friend now. And she had a right to no more than that. Only his friendship. It was just as well that they were speaking of Marc. "What were the rules?"

She sighed and then shrugged. "A lot of 'Thou shalt nots'. Thou shalt not defy the wishes of thy husband, thou shalt not ask too many questions, thou shalt not want a life of your own, least of all as a painter. . . . But he was very good to me once. My father left me stranded and penniless and scared when he died. Marc bailed me out. I don't think I wanted quite as much bailing as he gave me, but he did. He gave me comforts and a home, a family and stability, and eventually he gave me Pilar." She had not mentioned love.

"Was it all worth it? Is it now?"

She tried to smile. "I guess so. I've stuck around; I like what I've got."

"Do you love him?"

The smile faded slowly. She nodded.

"I'm sorry, Deanna. I shouldn't have asked."

"Why not? We're friends."

"Yes." He smiled at her again. "We are. Want to go for a walk on the beach?" He was on his feet, his arm extended to help her up. Their hands touched briefly before he turned and made rapid strides toward the shore, beckoning to her to catch up. She walked slowly, thinking of what they had said. At least everything was clear, and she did love Marc. At least now she wouldn't get into trouble with Ben. For a moment or two she had feared it; there was something about him that she liked very much.

He handed her seashells and walked in the water up to his knees, having discarded his sandals hours before. He looked like a tall, happy boy playing in the surf, and she smiled as she watched him.

"Want to race?" He looked at her mischievously as he came back to her side, and she accepted the challenge with amusement. If Pilar could see her mother now, racing with a man on the beach, as though they were children. But she felt like a girl, pounding along the damp sand, breathless and wind-tousled. She stopped at last, laughing and out of breath, shaking her head as he thundered past.

"Give up?" He shouted the words back to her. When she nodded, he loped back across the beach and came to a halt next to where she had sunk down on the sand. The sun had set off glints of red in her dark hair. He let himself down next to her, and they sat together, looking out to sea and catching their breath. After a moment she looked up at him, knowing what she would see: those sea-colored eyes, waiting for hers.

"Deanna. . . ." He waited an interminable time, looking at her, and then leaned slowly toward her, whispering the words into the windswept darkness of her hair. "Oh, Deanna, I love you. . . ."

As though he couldn't stop himself, he felt his arms go around her and his mouth close gently on hers, but her arms were as quickly around him and her mouth as hungry as his own. They sat there for a long time, holding each other and touching each other's faces, gazing into each other's eyes, with no more words between them than those he had spoken first. They didn't need words; they had each other in a world where time had stopped. It was Ben who pulled away at last, saying nothing, only standing up, quietly, slowly, reaching a hand out for hers. Together, hand in hand, they walked back down the beach.

They didn't speak again until they were back in the car. Ben sat there for a time, looking troubled.

"I should tell you I'm sorry, Deanna, but I'm not."

"Neither am I." She sounded as though she were in shock. "But I don't understand it."

"Maybe we don't have to. We can still be friends." He looked at her then with an attempt at a smile, but there was none in her eyes, only the glimmer of something haunted.

"I don't feel betrayed. At least not by you." She wanted him to know that much.

"By yourself?"

"Perhaps. I think I just don't understand."

"You don't have to. You were very clear about your life when we talked about it before. There's nothing for you to understand, or explain." His voice was so unbearably gentle. "We can forget. I'm sure we will."

But she didn't want to, and that was what astonished her most. She didn't want to forget at all.

"Did you mean what you said?" She meant his "I love you," but she could see that he understood. "I feel that way too. It's really a little crazy."

"Isn't it just!" He laughed aloud this time and gently kissed her cheek. "Maybe it's even very crazy. But however we feel, I won't destroy your life. You have what you need, and you don't need me rocking your boat now. I suspect that it's taken you the last eighteen years to come to terms with that life." It was true, and she knew it. "I promise, Deanna. I won't hurt you."

"But what will we do?" She felt like a child, lost in his arms.

"Nothing. We'll be big kids, both of us. And good friends. Does that sound all right to you?"

"I suppose it has to." But there was relief in her voice too, as well as regret. She didn't want to cheat on Marc. It meant a lot to her to be faithful.

He started the car, and they drove slowly home, saying little on the way back. It was a day she would not quickly forget. It seemed an eternity before they stopped at her house.

"Will you come to lunch in my studio now and then?" She sounded so forlorn that it made his pain more acute, but he smiled.

"Anytime. I'll call you sometime soon."

She nodded and slipped out of the car. She heard him drive away before she had a chance to look back.

She walked slowly up the stairs to her bedroom, and lay down on the bed; then, glancing at the phone, she saw a message from Marc. Margaret had taken the call that afternoon. She cringed as she read it. PLEASE CALL MR. DURAS. She didn't want to call now, didn't want to hear him. Not now. But she knew she had to. She had to force herself back to her life and away from the dream on the beach.

It took her half an hour to steel herself to make the call. At last, she dialed the overseas operator for Rome and asked for Marc's room at the Hassler.

This time he was in.

"Marc? It's me."

"Yes. Hello." He sounded strange and cold.

"Deanna." She thought for a moment that he didn't understand who it was. Then she realized the time. It was two A.M. in Rome. He had undoubtedly been fast asleep.

"Yes, yes, I know. I was asleep."

"I'm sorry. We were cut off the last time we talked, and Margaret left a message. I thought perhaps it was important." But suddenly she felt awkward with him. He didn't sound as though he'd been asleep.

"Right. Where were you?" God, why did he sound so cold? Why now? She needed a reason to hang on. A reason not to fall in love with Ben. A reason to stay faithful.

"I was out. Shopping." She hated the lie, but what could she tell him? I was kissing Ben Thompson on the beach? "Is everything all right in Rome?"

"Fine. Look"—he seemed to hesitate for a moment—"I'll call you back."

"When?" She had to know. She needed to hear him, needed to keep his voice in her head. Surely that would dull the pain of what she couldn't have. "When will you call me?"

"Tomorrow. This weekend. I'll call, don't worry. D'accord?"

"Yes, all right, fine." But she was cut to the quick by his tone. "I love you." The words were a tentative plea. He didn't seem to hear it.

"So do I. Ciao." And then, without saying more, he hung up, as Deanna sat staring blindly at the phone.

Deanna ate alone in her studio that night, then stood for half an hour on the little tiled terrace, watching the sun set over the bay. She could have seen it with Ben, if she hadn't sent him away. Why had she? So she could feel virtuous when she called Marc halfway around the world? She felt tears slide down her cheeks. When she heard the doorbell ring, she jumped. She decided not to answer, and then wondered if it might be Kim, coming to see how she was. Kim would have recognized the lights in the studio and known she was hiding. She wiped the tears away with the tail of her shirt and ran barefoot down the back stairs. She didn't even think to ask who it was, she simply opened the door, looking like a tired, rumpled little girl, in jeans and bare feet, with her hair falling into her eyes. She looked up, expecting to see Kim and stood back in surprise when she saw who it was. It was Ben.

"Is this a bad time?" he asked. She shook her head. "Can we talk?" He looked as troubled as she felt, and he was quick to come inside when she nodded yes.

"Come up to the studio. I was up there."

"Working?" He searched her eyes, and she shook her head.

"Thinking."

"Me too."

She closed the door softly behind them. He followed her up the stairs, and she motioned him to her favorite chair. "Coffee, or wine?"

"Neither, thanks." He looked suddenly very nervous, as though he wondered why he had come. Then he sat back in the chair, closed his eyes, and ran a hand through his hair. "This is crazy, I shouldn't have come."

"I'm glad you did."

"In that case"—he opened his eyes and smiled tentatively at her —"so am I. Deanna, I—I know this is crazy . . . but dammit I love you. And I feel like an irrational kid. I shouldn't even be here. I have absolutely nothing intelligent to say, except what I told you today on the beach." His voice dropped to a whisper and he lowered his eyes. "Just that I love you."

The room was very still for a long moment as she watched him, her eyes filling with tears. He heard her sigh. "I love you too."

"You know what I came here to tell you?" he asked. "That I'll accept anything. A moment, an evening, a summer. I won't stand in your way after that. I'll let go. But I can't bear to see us lose what we might have." He looked at her then. Her face was wet with tears that dripped slowly onto her paint-splattered shirt, but she was smiling at him and holding out a hand. He took it firmly in his and pulled her toward him. "Doesn't that sound crazy to you?"

"Yes. Very. And at the end of the summer?"

"We let go."

"And what if we can't?"

"We'll just have to. I will because I know it will be for your peace of mind. What about you?"

"I suppose I could too." Her arms went around him. "I don't care what happens then, I just love you."

He was smiling broadly as he held her close. It was what he had wanted to hear. He felt suddenly free and excited and alive.

"Will you come home with me, Deanna? My place is a mess, but I want to share it with you, show you my treasures. I want to show you the things I care about, give you my life, show you my galleries and how they work. I want to walk on the beach in Carmel with you, I want to . . . oh, Deanna, darling, darling, I love you!"

They were both laughing now as he swept her into his arms and carried her down the stairs. For a moment Deanna was grateful that it was Margaret's night off, but she didn't dare think for longer than that. Only a moment, which was more thought than she spent on Marc. She was Ben's now. Ben's for the summer.

9

"Good morning." She heard Ben's voice softly in her ear. She opened one eye. The room was unfamiliar. She was staring at a pale-yellow wall. Someone had thrown wide the shutters on the large windows that looked out at the bay, and sun streamed into the room. There were trees just outside his window, and she could hear birds singing. It was a splendid, hot summer day, more like September than June.

Deanna let her eyes wander across the pale-yellow wall, and quickly she was entranced by a watercolor of a beach, and then by a smaller pastel, and an oil. The art work was all very subtle and sunny, not unlike Ben himself. She propped herself up on one elbow with a yawn and a stretch and a smile. He was looking down at her with the face of new love.

"I've been waiting for you for an hour. I thought you'd never get up!" He suddenly sounded less like a lover than a small boy, and she laughed.

"I think I was a trifle tired." She smiled again and slid back into the sheets, with one hand on his thigh. It had been a long, delicious night in his arms, and they hadn't fallen asleep until dawn.

"Is that a complaint?"

"Uh-uh." She let her lips drift up his leg and then stop at his hip, where she kissed the pale, tender white skin where a small vein throbbed. "Good morning, my love." She smiled at the life she saw stirring, and Ben pulled her gently back into his arms.

"Have I told you yet this morning how much I love you?" He was looking tenderly into her eyes, and there was something in his face she had dreamed of and painted but never seen. It was a kind of passion, a kind of unfettered love. It was something that she had long ago longed for and ceased to believe could exist. "I love you, Deanna . . . I love you. . . ." His words melted away on her lips as he kissed her for the first time that morning and let his body slide slowly over hers. She protested faintly but with laughter and squirms as he pressed her close to him. "You have an objection?" He looked amused and surprised; he didn't look as though he would be swayed by whatever she said.

"I haven't even brushed my teeth! Or combed my hair . . . or. . . ." Her words kept fading, swept away by his kisses, as she giggled and ran her hands through his uncombed hair. "Ben . . . I have to . . ."

"No, you don't. I love you like this." He seemed sure.

"But I . . ."

"Shhh. . . ."

"Ben!" But this time she forgot about her teeth and her hair; she was too happy right where she was, swept away, adrift on a sea of delight as his whole body seemed to enter her soul.

"Sleepy, darling?" His voice was a whisper when they finally spoke. Almost two hours had passed, and she was curled happily in his arms, one leg braided between his.

"Mm-hmm . . . Ben?"

"Yes?" His voice was so soft on the warm, summer morning.

"I love you." Hers was almost the voice of a child.

"I love you, too. Now go to sleep."

And she did, for another two hours. When she opened her eyes, he was standing at the foot of the bed, dressed and holding a tray. She woke up in surprise. He was wearing a businesslike, striped blue suit. "What are you doing?" Confused, she sat up in bed and ran a hand through her hair. Suddenly she felt very naked and unkempt, as the sweet smell of their lovemaking drifted up from the bed. "How long have I slept?"

"Not very long. I'd look like that too except I have a luncheon at the gallery. I canceled one yesterday and if I cancel this one too, Sally will quit. But I won't be gone long." He placed the tray on her knees as she sat back against the pillows in the large double bed. "I hope that'll do." There were croissants, fruit, café au lait, and one carefully poached egg. "I wasn't sure what you like for breakfast." He looked very young again as he smiled.

Deanna looked at the breakfast in astonishment and then at him. What could she say? He had appeared in her life on a beach in Carmel, and now he was making her poached eggs and croissants for breakfast and apologizing for not knowing what she liked. They had made love all through the night and for most of the morning; he had told her he loved her, and she him; she didn't even feel guilty for waking up in his bed and not her own—the bed she had shared for eighteen years with Marc. She didn't even give a damn about Marc this morning. She felt happy and young and in love, and all she wanted was what she had with Ben. She looked up at him with a rapturous smile and a sigh as she picked up a croissant.

"I warn you, sir, if you spoil me rotten, I will be unbearable in less than a week."

"No, you won't." He said it with certainty and amusement. Suddenly he seemed very grown-up once again.

"Yes, I will." She closed her eyes blissfully as she ate the roll. "I'll come to expect croissants every morning, and poached eggs, and café au lait. . . ." She opened her eyes again. They were very bright and very full of mischief. "I'll even expect you to stay home from the office every day, just so we can make love."

"No, you won't."

"Oh, no? Why won't I?"

"Because tomorrow it's your turn to make breakfast for me. This is a democracy, Deanna. We live here together; we take turns. We spoil *each other*. We make *each other* poached eggs."

He leaned down to kiss her one last time. "And I like mine fried."

"I'll make a note of that." She grinned at him.

He stood up. "I'll remind you."

"O.K." She went on eating her breakfast, perfectly happy and at ease. She felt as though they had lived together for months if not years. It did not seem strange at all to have him smile happily at her naked breasts as she sipped café au lait from a bright-yellow mug. Everything between them was comfortable and easy and real. It was a far cry from the formality and rituals in her own home. And she found that she liked Ben's way better. The yellow mug in her hand had a feel of solidity. It felt strong, not like the prissy blue-flowered Limoges from Marc's mother.

"What are you doing today?"

"I think first of all I'll take a bath." She wrinkled her nose, and they both laughed.

"I love you just like that."

"You're a piggy." She held her arms up to him though, and he kissed her again. When he pulled away, he rolled his eyes with regret.

"God, maybe I'll have to cancel that lunch after all."

"There's later. Or"—she started to ask him if they would see each other that night, but she could already see the answer in his eyes.

"No 'or,' Deanna. I'll be finished at the gallery at five. I thought we could go somewhere quiet for dinner. Maybe somewhere in Marin?"

"I'd love it." She sat back against the pillows with a broad smile, but she noticed that there was a shadow of concern in his eyes. "Something wrong?"

"Not for me. But I—I was wondering how you feel about—about going out. I don't want to create any difficult situations for you." He had to remind himself that she had another life. That she would never be entirely his. That she was on loan. Like a masterpiece from a foreign museum, not something he could own and keep on his gallery wall. It would make her infinitely more precious in the time that they'd share. "Won't it create a problem for you if we go out?" He looked at her very openly, his green eyes tender and wide.

"It doesn't have to. It will depend on what we do, where we go, how we behave. I think it could be all right." He nodded, saying nothing, and she held out a hand. He took it silently and sat down again on the bed.

"I don't want to do anything that will hurt you later."

"You won't. Now stop worrying. Everything will be fine."

"I mean it though, Deanna. I would hate it if you suffered for this afterward."

"Don't you think we both will?"

He looked up in surprise. "What do you mean?"

"I mean that this is going to be the most beautiful summer of my life, and hopefully yours. When it ends, when we both go back to our own lives, don't you think that we'll suffer?"

He nodded and looked down at the graceful hand he held tightly in his own. "Do you regret what we decided?"

Deanna threw back her head and laughed a silvery laugh before kissing him tenderly on the cheek. "Not for a moment." And then she grew serious again. "But I think we'd be crazy if we expected not to suffer later. If it's worth a damn, if it's beautiful, if we really care . . . then we will. We'll have to accept that."

"I do. For myself. But—"

"But what? You don't want me to hurt too? You don't want me to feel it? Or to love you? Don't be crazy, Ben. It's worth it."

"I understand that. I agree. But I also want to be discreet. I don't want to create problems for you with Marc." She almost cringed at the sound of his name. Ben leaned toward her again, kissed her quickly, then stood. "I think we've said enough for one morning." He hated to think of what would happen at the end of the summer, but it was hard to believe that time would come. Their moments together had just begun. "Where will you be at five?" He looked at her over his shoulder from the door. "Here?"

She shook her head. "I'd better go home."

"Shall I pick you up there?" He looked dubious for a moment. "I'll meet you here."

He nodded, smiled, and was gone. She heard the little German car drive away a moment later, as she walked around the room, and then sat naked on the edge of the bed and crossed one leg. She was smiling to herself. She wanted to sing. She felt wonderful, and she was in love. What a lovely man he was, how gentle and how careful and how wise. And he amused her too; he loved to laugh, loved to tell silly stories and endless funny tales. He had

spent hours the previous night telling her stories of his youth,
showing her albums of photographs of himself as a child, and his
parents and sister and their friends, many of them famous artists
and actors and playwrights and writers. The albums still lay
spread out on the floor.

He had a comfortable little house, very different from the cottage in Carmel. The place in Carmel was larger and wore the
same bland, sandy colors as the beach, whites, beiges, grays, dust-
colored woods, and soft off-white·wools. The city house was a tiny
"bijou" nestled high on Telegraph Hill and crammed full of paintings and books. There were two deep, red-leather couches in a living room walled with handsomely bound volumes, mostly about
art. The walls were a soft beige that enhanced the two paintings
he'd hung; the floors were of old burnished wood, and the rug was
Oriental but not as fine as the ones Marc had brought back for
her years before from Iran. Ben's little home was not a show-
place; it was warm and lovely and a place he clearly liked to be, to
spend evenings with his artists or his friends. There was an often
used fireplace with brass andirons he had found in France and a
bass fiddle propped up in one corner. He had a small piano and a
guitar, a handsome, old English desk and a bronze bust of
Cézanne. Throughout, there was a kind of friendly scramble, a
kind of elegant wear and tear. Some of the objects were of value,
but most were only of value to him and the people who loved
him. The living room was very Ben, as was the pretty little yellow
bedroom that looked east over the bay, and that was as bright as
the morning sun. It boasted a tiny terrace filled with an array of
bright flowering plants, and two comfortable, faded canvas chairs.
Other than that there was a kitchen and one extra room, in which
Ben housed his work—a few rare paintings, many files, another
desk. The additional room allowed him to work at home, and like
his car, was useful but not luxurious. As Deanna looked around,
she realized again that he was an odd mixture of comfort and
style, and he always seemed to happily marry the two in a way
that was uniquely his. Deanna slipped into his blue-and-black silk
bathrobe and wandered out onto the terrace. She sat down on one
of the faded canvas chairs. It had once been a bright parrot
green, now sun-bleached to a very pale lime. She stretched her legs
out for a moment, turning her face to the sun and thinking of
him, wondering where he was—already at the gallery? Having

lunch? Signing checks with Sally? Talking to Gustave? She liked the way he led his life, what he did, how he handled the people around him—how he handled her. She found that she even liked the idea of taking turns making breakfast—a democracy, he'd called it. It was just a very pleasant way to live. She let the robe fall slightly open, and smiled as she felt the bright warmth of the sun. In a while she would go home to her studio and paint. But not yet. She was too happy sitting in the sun like a cat, thinking of Ben.

"Grazie Signore . . . Signora Duras." The concierge at the Hassler bowed formally to Chantal and Marc as they checked out of the hotel and Marc endowed him with a more than healthy tip. A car was already waiting for them outside the hotel. Their bags had been stowed in the trunk, and the driver waited to take them to the airport.

Chantal was strangely quiet as they rode to the airport. At last Marc pulled his gaze from the windows and allowed himself to seek out her eyes.

"You're sure that's what you want to do?"

"Absolutely."

But it worried him. She had never been this obstinate before. She had insisted that she was not going to hide in San Remo or some other town on the Riviera. She wanted to go back to Paris and wait for him there, while he visited his family in Cap d'Antibes. So that she could steal a weekend with her lover, the man who had asked her to marry him? The implied threat had not been lost on Marc. He felt a surge of murderous jealousy.

"Just what exactly are you planning to do with yourself all weekend?" There was a decided edge to his voice, but she returned his gaze evenly as the car raced through the traffic.

"I'll go into the office. I can't leave everything on Marie-Ange's shoulders. It's bad enough that whenever we travel I have to dump everything in her lap. As long as I have the time, I might as well go in and see what's happening there."

"I'm impressed by your devotion to your business. That's new, isn't it?" It was rare for him to be sarcastic with Chantal.

But her tone matched his. "No, it's not. You're just not around to see it very often. What exactly did you think I was going to do?"

"Your bit of news yesterday did not go unnoticed, Chantal."

"I said someone asked me. I did not say I accepted."

"How comforting. One would assume, however, that he didn't ask you on the basis of two luncheons and a tea party. I would assume that you know each other rather well."

Chantal didn't answer. She merely looked out the window, as secretly Marc-Edouard raged. Dammit, what did she expect of him? He couldn't be with her more than he already was, and he could hardly propose marriage. He had Deanna.

But Chantal's voice was oddly soft as she answered him. "Don't worry about it."

"Thank you." He sighed, and his shoulders seemed to sag as he took her hand. "I love you, darling. Please, please try to understand."

"I do try. More than you know."

"I know it's difficult for you. It is for me too. But at least don't establish a competition between you and Pilar and my mother. That just isn't fair. I need to see them too."

"Perhaps, so do I." There was something so sad in her voice that he didn't know what more to say. Had he been a less rational man, he might have decided to throw reason to the winds, and take her with him, but he simply couldn't.

"Darling, I'm sorry." Gently, he slipped an arm around her shoulders, and pulled her closer to him, and there was no resistance. "I'll try to think this thing out. All right?" She nodded and said nothing, but a tear hovered on the end of her lashes, and he felt something tear at his heart. "It's only for a few days, I'll be home on Sunday night, and we can have dinner at Maxim's, before we leave for Athens."

"When are we leaving?"

"Monday or Tuesday."

She nodded again. He held her close all the way to the airport.

Deanna turned her key in the door and stopped for a moment, listening for Margaret. There was no one at home. It was still Margaret's day off. Could it be? Hadn't weeks passed? Or months or even years? Had she only gone with Ben the night before to make love with him for the very first time? Had it only been eighteen hours since she'd left the house? Her heart pounded as she closed the door behind her. It had been so peaceful at his place as she bathed and got dressed. She had watched two little birds play on the terrace, and she had listened to one of his records while she made the bed. She'd grabbed a plum from a large basket of fruit in the kitchen as she left, feeling as though she had lived there for years, as though it were hers as well as his. Now, suddenly, she was here again. In Marc's house, in the home of Monsieur and Madame Duras. She glanced at a photograph of them in a silver frame, taken during their first summer in Cap d'Antibes. Could that have been her? Standing awkwardly with a glass of white wine in her hand, while Marc chatted with his mother beneath her gigantic straw hat. How awkward she felt again just looking at it, how awkward she felt in this room. She stood at the entrance to the pale-green silk living room with the Aubusson rug, thinking that just looking at it made her feel cold. But this was her home. This was where she belonged, not in that tiny house on the hill where she had just spent the night with a strange man. What on earth was she doing?

She slipped her feet out of her sandals, walked barefoot into the chilly green room and sat down carefully on the couch. What had she done? She had cheated on Marc for the first time in eighteen years, and it had all seemed so natural, so normal. For one entire night it was as though she didn't even know Marc, as though she were married to Ben. She reached for a small photograph of Pilar in another silver frame and saw that her hand was shaking. Pilar was in tennis clothes; the photograph had been taken in the South of France. Deanna stared at it almost blindly. She didn't even hear the persistent ringing of the bell. It was two or three minutes before she realized that there was someone at the door. She jumped up, startled, and put down the photograph of Pilar. Her mind raced as she walked to the door. Who was it? Who knew? And what if it was Ben? She didn't feel ready to see him now. It was wrong what they had done. She had to tell him, she had to stop, now before it was too late, before her orderly life came apart at the seams . . . before. . . .

"Who is it?"

A voice informed her that there was a package. Reluctantly, she opened the door and saw the delivery boy. "But I didn't order. . . ." Then she knew. They were flowers from Ben. For a moment she wanted to turn them away, send them back, pretend that the night before hadn't happened and never would again. Instead, she held out her arms and took the bundle inside, where she pulled off the card and held it for a moment before reading what it said:

Hurry home, my darling. I'll meet you at five.

I love you,

Ben

I love you, Ben. Her eyes ran over the words and filled with tears. *I love you, Ben.* It was already too late. She loved him too.

She ran upstairs to her room and packed a small bag. Then she went to the studio. That's all she would take. Just one or two canvases, some paints, she'd make do for a while. She didn't have to stay for more than a few days. That was all.

She left a number for Margaret and explained that she was staying with a friend. By five-thirty she was back at his house. She parked the Jaguar half a block away and walked hesitantly toward the door. What in hell was she doing? But he'd heard her on the front steps. Before she rang, he opened the door with a bow and a smile and a sweep of one arm.

"Come in. I've been waiting for hours." He closed the door softly behind her. For a moment she stood there, her eyes tightly shut against tears. "Deanna? Are you all right, darling?" There was concern in his voice, but she nodded. Slowly, he put his arms around her. "Are you afraid?"

She opened her eyes and hesitantly nodded her head.

But Ben only smiled and held her very close as he whispered into her hair, "So am I."

10

"O.K., kid, off your ass. It's your turn." Ben poked her gently in the small of her back, and Deanna groaned.

"It is not. I made breakfast yesterday." She smiled into the pillow and hid her face.

"Do you know that I love you, even if you are a liar? I made breakfast yesterday and two days before that and for four days just before that. In fact I think you owe me three in a row."

"That's a lie!" She was giggling.

"The hell it is. I told you, this is a democracy!" He was laughing too and trying to turn the naked body he loved so that he could see her face.

"I don't like democracy!"

"Tough. I want coffee and French toast and eggs."

"What if I won't do it?"

"Then tonight you sleep on the terrace."

"I knew it. I should have brought Margaret."

"A ménage à trois? It sounds lovely. Can she cook?"

"Better than I can."

"Good. We'll have her move in today." He rolled over in bed with a satisfied smile. "Meanwhile, get off your dead ass and feed me."

"You're spoiled rotten."

"And I love it."

"You'll get fat." She sat on the edge of the bed looking at his far-from-overweight body. "Besides, eggs aren't good for you, they have carbohydrates or cholesterol or chromosomes or something, and. . . ." He pointed toward the kitchen, a mock scowl lining his face, and Deanna stood up. "I hate you."

"I know."

Laughing, she vanished into the kitchen. They had been together for two weeks—a moment; a lifetime. They shared the cooking and the chores. A funny little old lady came in twice a week to clean, but Ben liked doing things for himself, and Deanna found that she enjoyed sharing those things with him. They went marketing, cooked dinners, polished the brass, and pulled weeds from among the flowers on the terrace. She watched him pore over catalogues of upcoming auctions, and he watched her sketch, or work in pastels or oils. He was the first person she had allowed to see her work in progress. They read mystery books and watched television and went for drives; they walked on the beach once at midnight, and twice went down for the night to his house in Carmel. She went to another opening at his gallery and on a visit to a new artist, masquerading as his wife. It was as though nothing had come before and nothing would come after—they had only the time and the life that they shared.

Deanna set down the tray with his breakfast and the paper. "You know something? I like you. I really do."

"You sound surprised. Were you afraid democracy would wear you out?"

"Maybe." She sat down with a small, happy shrug. "I haven't taken care of myself or anyone else, in a practical way, in a long time. I'm responsible for everyone, but I don't think I've made breakfast in years. Or done any of the things that we've done."

"I don't like being dependent on other people, like maids. Basically, I like a very simple life."

She grinned to herself, remembering the three lavishly expensive paintings he had bought the day before in L.A., but she knew that what he was saying was true. Opulence wasn't his style. He had seen too much of it as a child, in the home of his grandparents and then his father. He was happier with the little house on the hill in San Francisco and the unpretentious cottage in Carmel.

He leaned over to kiss the tip of her nose, then sat back against his pillows again with the breakfast she had made still waiting on the tray. "I love you, Deanna." He was smiling wickedly. "Now when are you going to sign with the gallery?"

"Are you back at that again? *That* is what this is all about. You just want me to sign with the gallery. I knew it! I knew it!" She laughed as he ducked the pillow she aimed at his head. "The things some people will do to sign new artists!"

"Well? Did it work?"

"Of course not! You'll have to do better than that!"

"Better?" He looked at her ominously and put aside the breakfast tray. "What exactly do you mean by 'better,' why I. . . ." He closed his mouth over hers and reached for her body with his hands. "Better . . . ?" They were both laughing now. It was half an hour later before they had untangled themselves and caught their breath. "Well, was that *better?*" Ben asked.

"Much."

"Good." He looked up at her happily from where he lay on the bed. "Now will you sign?"

"Well. . . ." She lay her head on his chest and looked at him with a small yawn. "Maybe if you'd just run through that again . . ."

"Deanna!" He rolled over and covered her body with his own, holding her throat menacingly in both hands. "I want you to sign with me!" His voice boomed.

She smiled sweetly, "O.K."

"What?" He sat up, a look of astonishment on his face.

"I said O.K. O.K.?"

"Did you mean it?"

"Yes. Do you still want me? For the gallery, I mean." She grinned, and looked at him questioningly. Maybe it had been only a game all along.

But he was looking at her as though she were crazy. "Of course I still want you, you lunatic! You're the best new artist I've gotten my hands on in fifteen years!"

She rolled over again and looked at him with a feline little smile. "And just whom have you 'gotten your hands on' in the last fifteen years?"

"You know what I mean. I mean like Gustave." They both laughed at the thought. "Are you serious, Deanna? Will you sign?" She nodded. "You don't have to, you know. I love you even if you never let me show your work."

"I know. But I've been watching you work for weeks, and I can't stand it. I want to be part of it too. I want my own show."

He laughed. "Your own, eh? No other artists. All right, you've got it. When?"

"Whenever it works for you."

"I'll check the calendar with Sally. Maybe in a few weeks." He dug into his breakfast with a broad smile. He looked as though she had just given birth to his son.

"Should I make you something else?" She was watching him devour the ice-cold French toast.

"All you have to do is bring me your paintings and let me show them. From now on I'll make breakfast. Every day. No . . . five times a week. You do weekends. How's that?"

"Wonderful. I knew there were benefits to giving in." She pulled the covers back to her chin. "Ben? Do you think I'm doing the right thing?"

He knew what was coming. The doubts were written all over her face. But he was not going to let her back away. "Shut up. If you start that, we'll do the show next week. You're good enough. You're terrific. You're fabulous. For God's sake, Deanna, you're the best young artist in this town, probably in L.A. too. Just shut up and let me do the show. All right?"

"All right."

For a time she was very quiet, thinking about Marc. How could she tell him she had finally decided to show? Or did he even have to know? He had told her years ago to put her dreams about art away, that Madame Duras could not be some kind of "hippie painter." But she wasn't, dammit, and what right did he have to . . .

"What are you thinking?" Ben was still watching her.

"Nothing much." She smiled. "I was just thinking about the show."

"Are you sure? You looked as though you were about to be beaten up."

She sighed, then looked at him again. "I felt as though I was. I was trying to think of . . . of what to tell Marc."

"Do you have to?" Ben sounded momentarily strained.

"I probably should. I suppose it sounds crazy to you now, but I don't want to be dishonest with him. No more than I have to."

"It does sound crazy, but I understand what you mean. He won't be pleased about a show, will he?"

"No, he won't. But I think I ought to tell him."

"And if he says no?" Ben looked hurt and Deanna lowered her eyes.

"He won't."

But they both knew he would.

Marc quietly let himself into the apartment. It was the second weekend he had gone away without Chantal. But his weekends in the South of France with his family were sacred. She had always understood that before. Why was she giving him problems about it now? She had barely been speaking to him on Friday when he had left. He set his bag down in the hall and looked around. She wasn't home. But it was already after nine o'clock. Where the hell was she? Out? Out with whom? He sighed a long tired sigh as he sat down on the couch. He glanced around. She hadn't left him a note. He looked at his watch again, and this time he reached for the phone. It would be noon in San Francisco, a good time to report to Deanna about Pilar. He dialed the call direct and waited for the phone to ring. He hadn't spoken to her in a week. He had been too busy to call, and the one time he had, Margaret had told him she was out.

"Hello?" Deanna answered the phone breathlessly as she came

up the studio stairs. Ben had just dropped her off. She had promised to come home and pick out twenty-five of her favorite paintings. That would keep her busy for days. "Yes?" She still hadn't caught her breath and at first she hadn't even noticed the whir of a long distance call.

"Deanna?"

"Marc!" She stared at the phone in astonishment, as though he were a ghost from the past.

"You needn't sound that surprised. It hasn't been that long since we've spoken."

"No, no, I'm sorry. I just . . . I was thinking of something else."

"Is anything wrong?"

"No, of course not. How's Pilar?" She sounded vague to him as though she were at a loss for what to say. "Have you seen her lately?"

"Just today. I just got back from Antibes. She's fine. She sends you her love." It was a lie, but one he told often. "And my mother sends her love too."

Deanna smiled at this last. "Pilar's all right?" Suddenly, speaking to Marc again reminded her of her duties. With Ben, she only thought of him and herself. She thought of her paintings and his galleries, their nights together, their good times. She was a woman again, a girl. But Marc's voice returned her to her role as mother. It was as though for a time she had forgotten.

"Yes, Pilar is fine."

"She didn't buy the motorcycle, did she?"

There was a long moment of silence. Too long.

"Deanna . . ."

"Marc, did she?" Deanna's voice rose. "Dammit, she did! I know it."

"It's not really a motorcycle, Deanna. It's more, more a. . . ." He looked for the words, but he was tired, and where the hell was Chantal? It was nine forty-five. "Really, you have no need to worry. She'll be fine. I saw her drive it. She is extremely careful. Mother wouldn't allow her to ride it if she were not."

"Your mother doesn't see her drive it away from the house. She has no more control over her than I do, or you. Marc, I told you explicitly. . . ." Tears began to sting her eyes. She had lost to them again. She always lost. And this time it was something dangerous, something that might. . . . "Goddammit, Marc, why don't you ever listen to me?"

"Calm yourself. She'll be fine. What have you been up to?"

There wasn't a damn thing she could do. And she knew it. The subject of Pilar and the motorcycle was closed. "Not much." Deanna's voice was like ice.

"I called once; you were out."

"I've started painting in a studio."

"Can't you work at home?" Marc sounded irritated and confused.

Deanna closed her eyes. "I found a place where it's easier for me to work." Her heart started to race as she thought of Ben. What if Marc could read her mind? What if he knew? What if someone had seen them together? What if . . .

"With both of us gone, I can't understand why you don't paint at home. And what is this sudden new frenzy for your work?"

"What 'frenzy'? I'm painting as much as ever."

"Deanna, I really don't understand." But the tone in which he said the words suddenly hit her like a slap in the face.

"I enjoy my work." She was goading him and she knew it.

"I don't really think you need call it 'work.'" He sighed into the phone and looked at his watch.

"I call it work because it is. I'm having a show at a gallery next month." Her voice rang with defiance, and she felt her heart race faster and faster. He didn't answer.

Then: "You're what?"

"Having a show at a gallery."

"I see." There was a nasty tone of amusement in his voice, and for a moment she hated him. "We're having a bohemian summer are we? Well, maybe it will do you good."

"Maybe it will." *Bastard . . . he never understood!*

"Is it necessary to prove your point by having a show? Why not dispense with that? You can work in your other studio, and let it go at that."

Thank you, Daddy. "The show is important to me."

"Then it can wait. We'll discuss it when I get back."

"Marc. . . ." *I'm in love with another man. . . .* "I'm going to do the show."

"Fine. Just let it wait till the fall."

"Why? So you can talk me out of it when you come home?"

"I won't do that. We'll talk about it then."

"It won't wait. I've already waited too long."

"You know, darling, you're too old for tantrums and too young for menopause. I think you're being very unreasonable."

She wanted to hit him, except that for a moment she also wanted to laugh. It was a ridiculous conversation, and she realized that she sounded a great deal like Pilar. She laughed and shook her head. "Maybe you're right. Tell you what: You win your case in Athens; I'll do what I need to do with my art, and I'll see you in the fall."

"Is that your way of telling me to mind my own business?"

"Maybe so." She was suddenly braver than she had been in years. "Maybe we both just have to do what we need to do right now." *Oh God, what are you doing? You're telling him. . . .* She held her breath.

"Well, in any case, you need to listen to your husband, and your husband needs to go to bed, so why don't we just relax about all this for a while? We'll talk again in a few days. All right? Meanwhile, no art show. *C'est compris? Capisce?* Understood?"

She wanted to grit her teeth. She wasn't a child, and he was always the same. Pilar got the motorcycle, Deanna did not get the art show, and we'll all discuss it "when I have time." His way, always *his* way. But not anymore. "I understand, Marc, but I don't agree."

"You don't have a choice."

It wasn't like him to be so obvious. Deanna realized that he must be very tired. He must have noticed it too. "Never mind," he said. "I'm sorry. We'll talk another time."

"Fine." She stood silently in her studio, waiting, wondering what he would say.

He said, *"Bonsoir."*

And he was gone. Good night. And this time she hadn't bothered to tell him she loved him. "No art show." The words rang in her head. No art show. She sighed heavily and sank into her chair. What if she defied him? What if she had the show anyway? Could she do that to him? To herself? Was she brave enough to just go ahead and do what she wanted? Why not? He was away. And she had Ben. But it wasn't for Ben. It was for herself. She looked around the room for a long moment, knowing that her lifetime was facing those walls, hidden on canvases no one had seen and would never see unless she did what she knew she had to do now. Marc couldn't stop her, and Ben couldn't make her do it. She had to do it now. Had to. For herself.

As Marc set down the phone, he looked at his watch again. It was almost ten, and the call to Deanna had done nothing to soothe his nerves. Dammit. He had told her about the motorcycle, and he hadn't meant to. And her bloody art show. Why the hell didn't she give up on that nonsense? And where the hell was Chantal? Jealousy was beginning to gnaw at his insides again as he poured himself a Scotch. When he heard the bell, he went to the door and opened it an inch. It was the little old man from next door. Monsieur Moutier. He was sweet, Chantal said, and he was taken care of by a daughter and a maid. He too had once been a lawyer, but now he was eighty years old. He had a soft spot for Chantal. Once he had sent her flowers.

"*Oui?*" Marc looked at him questioningly, wondering if the old man was ill. Why would he come to their door at this hour? "Is something wrong?"

"I . . . no. I . . . *je regrette.* I wanted to ask you the same thing. How is mademoiselle?"

"Very well, thank you, except that as far as I can see she's a little bit late getting home." He smiled at the elderly gentleman wearing the black smoking jacket and needlepoint slippers doubtless made by his daughter. "Would you like to come in?" Marc stepped aside, wanting to get back to his Scotch, but the old man shook his head.

"No, no. . . ." He looked sorrowfully at Marc. He understood only too well. The man who always traveled, who was never there. He had been that way too. His wife had died, and he had learned too late. "She is not late, monsieur. They took her to the hospital last night." He gazed at Marc as the shock registered on his face.

"Chantal? My God! Where?"

"The American Hospital, monsieur. She was in some kind of shock. The ambulance driver said—"

"Oh, my God!" Marc glanced at the old man in terror and then ran inside to grab his jacket from a chair. He returned instantly and slammed the door to the apartment, as the old man stepped aside. "I have to go." Oh, my God. . . . Oh, Chantal. . . . Oh, no. . . . Then she wasn't out with another man. Having raced down the stairs, his heart hammering in his chest, Marc ran into the street and hailed a cab.

11

The taxi pulled up at 92 Boulevard Victor Hugo in Neuilly in the quiet outskirts of Paris. Marc thrust some franc notes into the driver's hand and raced inside. It was well past visiting hours, but he walked purposefully toward the information desk and inquired for Mademoiselle Chantal Martin. Room 401, admitted with insulin shock, present condition satisfactory. She can go home in two days. Marc stared at the nurse, dismayed. Without discussing the matter further, he took the elevator to the fourth floor. A nurse sat sternly at her station and observed him as he disembarked from the elevator.

"*Oui,* monsieur?"

"Mademoiselle Martin." He tried to sound commanding but he felt suddenly frightened. How had it happened and why? He felt a sudden surge of guilt for having gone to Antibes. "I must see her."

The nurse shook her head. "Tomorrow."

"Is she asleep?"

"You may see her tomorrow."

"Please. I—I came all the way from—" He was about to say the South of France, then had a better idea. He flipped open his wallet. "From San Francisco, in the United States. I caught the first plane after I heard." There was a long pause.

"Very well. Two minutes. And then you go. You are . . . her father?" Marc only shook his head. It was the final blow.

The nurse led him to a room not far away. Inside, a dim light burned. She left Marc-Edouard at the door. He hesitated for a moment on the threshold before stepping softly inside.

"Chantal?" His voice was a whisper in the dark room. She was lying in her bed, looking very pale and very young. In her arm there was an intravenous tube, attached to an ominous-looking bottle. "Darling. . . ." He approached, wondering what he had done. He had taken on this girl and only given her half his life. He had to hide her from his mother, his child, his wife, sometimes even from himself. What right did he have to do this to her? His eyes were too bright as he stood at her side and gently took her free hand. "Darling, what happened?" A sixth sense had already told him that the insulin shock was no accident. Chantal had the kind of diabetes one didn't fool around with. But as long as she took her insulin, ate well, slept enough, and didn't get pregnant, she'd be all right.

Her eyes closed and tears filtered through her lashes. "*Je m'excuse*. I'm so sorry. . . ." Then after a pause: "I stopped taking my insulin."

"On purpose?" As he watched her nod, he felt as though someone had delivered a blow to his heart. "Oh, my God. Chantal, darling . . . how could you?" He watched her in sudden terror. What if she had died? What if . . . ? He couldn't bear losing her, couldn't bear it. Suddenly, the full force of it struck home. He reached for her unencumbered hand and pressed it hard. "Don't ever, ever do that again!" His voice rose desperately. "Do you hear me?" She nodded again. And then there were tears pouring down his face as well. He sat down at her side. "I would die without you. Don't you know that?"

There was no answer in her eyes. No, she didn't know it. But it was true. He himself knew it for the first time. Now there were two of them. Deanna and Chantal. Two of them he owed a lifetime to, and he was only one man. He couldn't live with himself if he put Deanna out of his life. And he couldn't live without Chantal. The weight of it struck him like an axe. He saw her watching him. He was almost gray. "I love you, Chantal. Please, please don't ever do anything like this again. Promise me!" He squeezed harder on the delicate hand.

"I promise." It was a whisper in the sudden electricity of the room. Fighting the sobs that were rising in his chest, Marc-Edouard folded her gently into his arms.

By the end of the day, Deanna had chosen eleven paintings. It was going to be hard work selecting the rest. She set the eleven to one side and then walked back to the main part of the house. She was still thinking of her talk with Marc. She wondered if she would have defied him about the show if he hadn't let Pilar buy the motorcycle. It was strange how those things worked. Their marriage was filled with petty revenges. She walked up the stairs to her bedroom and peered into the closet. What would she need? Another bathrobe, some jeans, the champagne-colored suede skirt that she was sure Ben would like. What was she doing here, in Marc's bedroom planning her life with another man? Was she being menopausal or childish, as he'd suggested, or merely crazy? The phone rang as she stared into her closet, wondering. She didn't even feel guilty anymore, except when she talked to Marc. The rest of the time she felt as though she belonged with Ben. The phone rang again and again. There was no one she wanted to talk to. She felt as though she had already moved out. But reluctantly, she picked it up.

"Hello?"

"Can I come get you? Are you ready to come home?" It was Ben. And it was only four-thirty.

"So early?" She smiled into the phone.

"You want some more time to work?" As though her work mattered, as though it were important, as though he understood.

But she shook her head. "Nope. I'm all through. I picked out eleven today. For the show."

Her voice was strong, and he smiled. "I'm so proud of you I can hardly stand it. I told Sally today, about the show. We're going to run a beautiful ad."

Oh, Jesus, not an ad. What about Kim? She felt as though she were gasping for air when she spoke again. "Do you have to do an ad?"

"You let me handle my business, and you handle yours. Speaking of which, I'd like to handle. . . ." His voice was very soft in the phone, and Deanna blushed.

"Stop that!'

"Why?"

"Because you're in your office, and I'm—I'm here."

"Well, if that's all that's stopping you, let's both get the hell out of those repressive places. I'll pick you up in ten minutes. Are you ready?"

"Desperately." She couldn't wait to get out of the house. Every moment she spent in it was oppressive.

"Desperate enough to go all the way to Carmel?"

"I'd love it." Then: "What about your housekeeper?"

"Mrs. Meacham? She'll be off." It was disagreeable to be hiding like that, but he knew Deanna felt that she had no choice. She still wasn't free. "Anyway, never mind Mrs. Meacham. I'll pick you up in ten minutes. And by the way, Deanna," he paused while she waited, wondering what he would say; he sounded very solemn. Then his voice dropped again, and she almost could see him smile. "I love you."

She smiled happily and closed her eyes. "So do I."

The weekend in Carmel was heavenly. The Fourth of July. They spent all three days wandering on the beach, lying in the sun, looking for shells, and collecting driftwood, and once or twice braving the still-icy ocean for a quick swim.

She was already smiling to herself as he lay down next to her on the blanket, shivering from the sea. She had been soaking up the sun and improving her deep-honey tan.

"What are you smiling about, sleeping beauty?" His body was cool and damp next to hers, and his skin felt delicious as she turned and ran her fingers down his arm.

"I was just thinking that this is all rather like a honeymoon. Or a very good marriage."

"I wouldn't know. I've never had either one."

"Didn't you have a honeymoon?"

"Not really. We spent it in New York. She was an actress and she was in something off Broadway, so we spent a night at the Plaza in New York. When the play folded, we went up to New England."

"Did the play have a long run?" She looked admiring, with her big, innocent, green eyes. Ben smiled.

"Three days." They both laughed, and Ben moved onto his side, so he could look at Deanna. "Were you happy with Marc before I came along?"

"I thought I was. Sometimes. Sometimes I was terribly lonely. We don't have a relationship like this. In a way we're not really friends. We love each other, but . . . it's very different." She remembered their last conversation when he had told her not to show her work. He was still the voice of authority. "He doesn't respect me the way you do—my work, my time, my ideas. But he needs me. He cares. In his own way he loves me."

"And you love him?" His eyes searched her face. She didn't answer immediately.

"I thought we weren't going to talk about things like that. This is *our* summer." There was reproach in her voice.

"But it's also *our* life. There are some things I need to know." He was strangely serious.

"You already know them, Ben."

"What are you saying?"

"That he's my husband."

"That you won't leave him?"

"I don't know. Do you have to ask me that now?" Her eyes held an autumnal sorrow. "Can't we just have what we know we can have, and then—"

"And then, what?"

"I don't know yet, Ben."

"And I promised I wouldn't ask. But I find that increasingly difficult."

"Believe it or not, so do I. My mind drifts to the end of the summer, and I ask myself questions I can't answer. I keep hoping for an act of God, a miracle, something that will take the answers out of our hands."

"So do I." He smiled at her then and leaned over to kiss her lips again and again. "So do I."

12

"Ben?" He smiled to himself as Deanna's voice reached him from his spare room. It was late on a Sunday night, and they were just back from another weekend in Carmel.

"What? Need some help?" All he heard was a shout and a gurgle of laughter. She had been in there for over an hour. He climbed out of bed and went to see what was going on. As he opened the door to the spare room, in which he often worked, she was staggering to hold up a tenuously piled stack of canvases which had started to slide off a mountain of boxes propped against the wall.

"Help! It's an avalanche." She peeked out at him, a small paint brush clenched in her teeth, and both arms held aloft, trying to keep the pile of paintings from crashing to the floor. "I came in here to sign a few that I noticed I had forgotten to sign, and. . . ." She shoved the paintings aside as he lifted them from her arms. Then, his hands still filled with the mountain of her work, he bent his head to kiss the tip of her nose.

"Take the paintbrush out of your mouth."

"What?" She looked at him with an expression of absent-minded pleasure. She was still thinking about two of the paintings she knew she had to sign.

"I said"—he put the paintings carefully aside, and reached for the brush with one hand—"take that thing out of your mouth."

"Why? This way I have my hands free to look for. . . ." But he silenced her almost immediately with a kiss.

"That's why, you dummy. Now, are you coming to bed?" He pulled her close to him, and she nestled against him with a smile.

"In a minute. Can I just finish this?"

"I don't see why not." He sat down in the comfortable old chair at his desk and watched her ferret through the stack again looking for unsigned canvases. "Are you as excited as I am, madam, about the show?" It was only four days away. Thursday. He was finally going to launch her into the art world. She should have been showing for years. He looked at her with pleasure and pride, as she stuck the end of the brush through her hair to free her hands once again. There was a huge smile on her face. It not only played with her mouth, it danced in her eyes.

"Excited? Are you kidding? I'm half crazy. I haven't slept in days."

He suspected it was true. Every night when they went to bed, he looked sleepily into her eyes after their hours of lovemaking, and the last thing he remembered was always that smile. And suddenly in the mornings she was wide awake now. She jumped up and got him breakfast, then disappeared into the spare room where she had put all her work. She had brought her treasures to him, to keep until the show. She didn't even want them in the gallery until the day before the opening.

Now she signed the last one and turned to him with a grin. "I don't know if I'll make it till Thursday night."

"You will." He glowed as he watched her. What a beautiful woman she was. She seemed even prettier lately, her face had a soft, luminous beauty, and her eyes a kind of passionate fire. There was a tenderness and a burning about her all at once, like a velvet flame. And their time together had a magic about it, like nothing he had ever known. The little cottage in Carmel fairly hummed with her presence, filling the rooms with flowers, bringing back huge pieces of driftwood which they lay against as they toasted their feet near the fire on "their" dune just outside. She filled his dreams and his arms and his days. He could no longer imagine a life without her.

"What are you thinking?" She tilted her head to one side, and leaned against the stack of her paintings.

"About how much I love you."

"Oh." She smiled, and her eyes softened as she looked into his eyes. "I think about that a lot."

"About how much I love you?" He smiled and so did she.

"Yes. And about how much I love you. What did I ever do before you came along?"

"You lived excessively well and never made your own breakfast."

"It sounds awful." She walked toward him, and he pulled her down onto his lap.

"That's just because you're excited about the show and you can't sleep. Wait another month, or two. . . ." He paused painfully; he had been about to say a "year," but they didn't have a year. Only another five or six weeks. "You'll get tired of making breakfast. You'll see."

She wanted to see. She wanted to see for a lifetime, not a month. "I'll never get tired of this." She buried her face in his chest, feeling warm and safe like a child. They were both brown from their weekend in Carmel, and her feet were still sandy as they brushed along the floor. "You know what I think?"

"What?" He closed his eyes and smelled the fresh scent of her hair.

"That we're very lucky. What more could we have?"

A future, but he didn't say it. He opened his eyes and looked at her as she sat in his lap. "Don't you ever want another child?"

"At my age?" She looked stunned. "Good Lord, Pilar is almost sixteen years old."

"What does that have to do with anything? And what do you mean 'at your age'? Lots of women have babies in their thirties."

"But I'm thirty-seven. That's crazy."

He shook his head. Deanna was looking somewhat stunned. "It's not too old for a man, why should it be too old for a woman?"

"That, my darling, is very different indeed. And you know it yourself."

"I do not. I'd love to have our child. Or even two. And I don't think you're too old."

A *baby? Now?* She looked at him in astonishment, but he was perfectly serious. His arms were still around her.

"Do you mean it?"

"I do." For a long moment he watched her eyes and wasn't sure what he saw. Confusion, amazement, and also sorrow and pain. "Or are you not supposed to have any more children, Deanna?" He had never asked. There was no reason to. She shook her head.

"No, there's no reason why I can't, but . . . I don't think I could go through it again. Pilar was a gift after the two boys. I don't think I'd want to do it again."

"Do they know why those things happened?"

"Just flukes, they said. Two inexplicable tragedies. The odds of that happening twice in one family are minute . . . but it did."

"Then it wouldn't again." He sounded determined, and Deanna pulled away.

"Are you trying to talk me into having a baby?" Her eyes were very large and her face very still.

"I don't know. Maybe I am. It sounds like it, doesn't it?" He smiled and hung his head. Then he looked up. "Do you think that's what I was doing?"

She nodded, suddenly very serious. "Don't."

"Why not?"

"I'm too old." *And I already have a child. And a husband.*

"That is the only reason I categorically will not accept! That's nonsense!" He sounded almost angry this time, and she wondered why. What did it matter whether or not she was too old for a child?

"Yes, I am. I'm almost forty years old. And even this is pretty crazy. I feel like a kid again. I'm acting like I'm seventeen, not thirty-seven."

"And what's wrong with that?" He searched her eyes, and she surrendered.

"Absolutely nothing. I love it."

"Good. Then come to bed." He picked her up in his arms and deposited her in the next room, on his large comfortable bed. The quilt was rumpled from where they had lain when they came back from Carmel, and there was only one small light on in the room. The soft colors looked warm and pretty, and the big vase of daisies she had picked Friday afternoon on the terrace gave the bedroom a country air. She did something special to his house, she gave it a flavor that he had longed for, for years. He had never really known what was missing, but now that he had her, he knew. What had been missing was Deanna, with her green eyes and dark hair piled onto her head, with her bare legs peeking out of his bed, or sitting cross-legged with her sketch pads on his deck surrounded by the flowers. Deanna, with her stack of paintings and her paintbrushes stuck into all his coffee cups, with the shirts that she "borrowed" and splattered with paint, and with the countless thoughtful gestures—the ties she had cleaned, the suits she put away, the little presents she bought, the books she brought him that she knew he would love, the laughter and the teasing and the soft eyes that always understood. She had drifted into his life like a dream. And he never wanted to wake up. Not without Deanna at his side.

"Ben?" Her voice was very small next to him in the dark.

"What, love?"

"What if I get bad reviews?" She sounded like a frightened child, and he wanted to laugh, but he didn't. He knew how great her fear was.

"You won't." He put his arms around her again, beneath the quilt. It had been a present from an artist's wife to his mother, years ago, in New York. "The reviews will be wonderful. I promise."

"How do you know?"

"I know because you're very, very good." He kissed her neck

and trembled at the feel of her naked flesh against his legs. "And because I love you so much."

"You're silly."

"I beg your pardon?" He looked at her with a grin. "I tell you I love you, and you think I'm silly. Listen here, you. . . ." He pulled her closer and covered her mouth with his, as they disappeared in unison beneath the quilt.

She woke at six the next morning and instantly disappeared into the spare room. She had remembered a painting that shouldn't be there. Then she thought of another that was probably not in the right frame. After coffee she remembered two more without signatures, and so it went for the remaining four days. She was in a frenzy of nervousness over the show. Through it all Ben smiled and loved and cajoled. He took her to dinner, dragged her to a movie, made her join him at the beach; he forced her to go swimming, kept her up late at night making love. On Thursday he took her out to lunch.

"I don't want to hear it." He held up a hand.

"But, Ben, what if—"

"No. Not a word about the show until tomorrow."

"But . . ."

"No!" He put his finger to her lips, and she moved it aside with a fresh burst of worry. But he only laughed. "How is the wine?"

"What wine?" She looked around, distracted, and he pointed to her glass.

"The wine you're not drinking. How is it?"

"I don't know, and what I wanted to ask you is . . ."

He put both fingers in his ears, and she started to laugh at him. "Ben! Stop it!"

"What?" He smiled happily at her across the table. She was laughing.

"Listen to me! I wanted to ask you something about tonight!"

He started to hum gently, his fingers still in his ears. Deanna couldn't stop laughing. "You're horrible and I hate you!"

"No, you don't. You can't keep your hands off me, and you want to drag me away with you so you can attack me. Right?"

"Actually, now that you mention it. . . ." She grinned and took a sip of her wine, and they teased throughout lunch. He had taken the afternoon off. The paintings were all hung to perfection for Deanna's show. Sally was in control at the gallery, and he thought it a good idea to stay with Deanna, before she changed her mind or came apart at the seams. And he had a surprise for her that afternoon. He looked at his watch as they walked back to the car after lunch.

"Deanna, do you mind if I stop at Saks?"

"Now?" She looked surprised. "No, that's all right."

"It won't take me long." He parked in front of the store with an abstracted smile. "Want to come in?"

"No, I'll wait."

"Sure?" He didn't push; he knew she didn't want to be alone today, not even for a short time.

"All right. I'll come." It had been an easy sale, and he walked happily beside her into the store. "What do you have to do?"

"Pick up a dress." He said it with absolute self-confidence and complete nonchalance.

"A dress?"

"For Sally. She said she wouldn't have time. So I told her I'd get it and bring it to the gallery tonight in time for her to change. By the way, what are you wearing?" She had been so busy with her signatures and her frames that he wasn't even sure she'd given it any thought.

"I don't know. I thought I'd wear my black dress." She had brought two or three dinner dresses from the house. They were hanging in his closet, along with her jeans, her paint-splattered shirts, several pairs of gabardine slacks, and half a dozen turtle-neck cashmere sweaters. He liked the way her clothes looked next to his.

"Why don't you wear the green dress?"

"Too dressy." She was ten thousand miles away when she spoke. "Listen, do you know which critics are coming?" Her eyes rushed into his.

"I don't think it's too dressy." He looked amused.

"Did you hear what I asked you?" Distress was creeping into her voice.

"No. Now, what about the green dress?"

"Screw the green dress, I wanted to ask you—" He kissed her hard on the mouth and left her breathless as they got off the elevator on the second floor. "Ben!" But there had been no one around to see what he'd done. "Will you listen to me?"

"No." He was already greeting the saleswoman. She brought the dress out. "Perfect." He smiled at her again and looked at Deanna. "What do you think?"

"Hm?" She was hopelessly vague, but her attention was suddenly arrested by the dress. It was an almost mauve, heather-blue wool with a high neck, long sleeves, and no back. And it had a beautifully cut matching coat. "That is pretty, isn't it? Is that Sally's dress?" She took a step forward to touch the thin wool. It was a French fabric and French design and must have cost her a fortune. "That's a beauty." The saleswoman and Ben exchanged a smile of the eyes. "Maybe I should wear the green after all."

"I don't think so. Why don't you just wear that?" He had a look of innocence which totally confused Deanna.

"Wear Sally's dress? Don't be silly."

"You could lend her your green."

"Darling, I love you, but I think you're quite mad." She smiled at the saleswoman and started to walk away, but Ben gently took her arm and whispered in her ear.

"I think you're crazy too, now go try on your new dress."

She looked at him in astonishment. "Are you kidding?" He shook his head. "It's for me?"

He nodded with a satisfied smile. "Do you like it?"

"I . . . oh, Ben, I can't. It's gorgeous!" She turned to look at it again, and her eyes grew wide. It was exquisite, but probably also monstrously expensive. And Ben had done that for her? The man who drove an anonymous German car, and would rather eat spaghetti than caviar? The man who took pride in not having a maid but only a cleaning lady once or twice a week, when his grandfather had lived surrounded by an army of servants, and his father had retired to a palazzo near Rome? This man had bought her that dress? It was the sort of thing she would have hesitated even to charge to Marc. "Good Lord!"

"Shut up and go try it. I want to see!"

She did, and he saw. It was perfect. The cut, the style, the color. She looked regal, coming toward him, the coat draped over her arm. Her tan set off the rich heather-blue, and her bare back and shoulders were perfectly sculpted into the dress. "What'll you wear with it?"

"Diamond earrings and black silk sandals. And my hair up."

"Oh, God, I can't stand it." He grinned with such pleasure that even the saleswoman laughed.

When she put it on that night, he was sitting on the bed. They smiled at each other, and he zipped up what there was to zip in the back. She clipped the diamond earrings on her ears and smoothed her hair up high on her head. She looked perfect, and for a moment it took his breath away. Then, with a smile, he gently took off the diamond earrings.

"What are you doing?"

"Taking these off."

She looked puzzled. "Why? Don't you like them?" Maybe it was because they had been a present from Marc. "I don't have any others here that would do."

"Never mind." He reached into his pocket and took out a little blue silk bag. He opened it and took out two large and very beautiful pearls. There was a tiny diamond beneath each pearl, and the earrings looked very old and fine. "I want you to wear these."

"Oh, Ben." Deanna looked at them with astonishment, then raised her eyes to his. "What have you done?" The dress, the earrings, the show. He was giving her so much. Everything. . . .

"The earrings were my grandmother's. I want you to have them, Deanna. This is a very special night." There were tears in her eyes when she looked up at him again. Tenderly, he took her face in his hands. "I want this to be the most beautiful night of your life. This is the beginning of your life in the art world, Deanna. And I want everyone to know just how good you are." There was more love welling up in his eyes than she had ever seen, and her heart trembled as she put her arms around him.

"You are so good to me."

"We're good to each other, and that's a very special gift."

"I can't keep the earrings." She couldn't. Not unless she stayed with Ben. But in another month she would have to go back to Marc.

"Yes, you can keep the earrings. I want you to have them. No matter what."

He understood. He always understood. And somehow it made things worse. The tears spilled over and ran sadly down her face. Sobs began to shake her shoulders.

"Darling, don't."

"Oh, Ben . . . I can't leave you."

"You don't have to. Not yet. Let's just enjoy what we have."

He hadn't sounded that philosophical since the beginning, and she wondered if finally he had accepted what would have to be. "I love you." Her voice was strained. She clung to him, and he closed his eyes.

"I love you too. Now, how about going to this opening of yours?"

He pulled away to look at her, and she nodded. Gently, he took one of the earrings and clipped it to her ear. And then, stopping at her mouth for a kiss, he clipped on the other. "You look exquisite. And I'm so proud that this opening is yours."

"I keep thinking I'm going to wake up, and it all will have been a dream. I'll wake up on the beach in Carmel, feeling like Rip Van Winkle, and Kim will still be waiting for me at the hotel. But every time I feel that way, I look around, and you're real." She looked at him in astonished delight, and he laughed.

"Very much so." He laughed again as he slipped a hand into her dress. "And I would very much like to prove it to you, my darling. But I'm afraid we don't have time." He held out an arm to her with a small bow. "Shall we?"

She took his arm. "But of course."

"Are you ready?" They had just pulled up in front of the gallery.

"Oh, God, no!" Her arms went out to him, and her eyes were wide, but he held her close for only a moment, then swept her inside. There was a photographer waiting, and there were already a considerable number of guests. The art critics were there in force, and she even saw Kim, developing a cozy relationship with one of the gentlemen of the press. Sally hovered near, agog at the beautiful heather-blue dress.

All in all the evening was a smash. The gallery sold seven of her paintings. For a moment she felt as though she were parting with old friends. She didn't want to give up her paintings, but Ben teased her about it as he introduced her to the admirers of her work. Ben was wonderful with her: he was always nearby, yet never too close, supportive but not obvious. He was Benjamin Thompson III, gallery owner extraordinaire. No one would have known about their affair. He was as discreet as he had been that first morning with Kim, and Deanna knew she had nothing to fear. For a moment that day she had been afraid of what Marc might hear. One never knew who came to these shows, who would see, or what they would guess. But no one guessed anything that night, not even Kim, who had sent a huge bouquet of flowers to the house. She felt personally responsible for the match between Deanna and Ben—from a professional standpoint, of course, as she was not aware of any other. She had wondered, though, if Deanna had told Marc of the opening. But later in the evening Deanna told Kim that she had.

"What did he say?"

"Not very much. But he wasn't pleased."

"He'll get over it."

"I suppose he will." But Deanna had not said more on the subject. She didn't tell Kim that Marc had forbidden her to have the show and hung up on her in the end. He had told her it was vulgar and pushy, but for the first time in their marriage she had stood her ground. It was too important to her for her to give in this time. *He* hadn't given in to her wishes about Pilar and the motorcycle. Why should she give in about her art?

"My heavens, what are you frowning about, darling?" Ben spoke softly, so no one else would hear, and Deanna drifted back from her own thoughts.

"Nothing. I'm sorry. I . . . it's just . . . so much has happened."

"You can say that again. Sally just sold two more of your paintings." He looked as happy as a boy, and Deanna wanted to throw her arms around him in a hug. Instead, she just caressed him with her eyes. "Can I interest you in a celebration dinner?"

"Only if it's pizza." She grinned at him, knowing his preferences.

"Not this time, madam. The real thing."

"Hamburgers?"

"Go to hell." Without further ceremony, he put an arm around her shoulders and kissed her cheek.

It was not an inappropriate thing for a gallery owner to do on the night of an artist's first success, but as Kim watched them she suddenly found herself wondering if there was something more. Deanna had just whispered something in Ben's ear, in answer to which, Kim had heard him say with a gentle smile, "I'm glad you liked them." Deanna had touched the pearls at her ears and happily walked away. As Kim watched, an idea came to her for the very first time.

13

"O.K. I'm ready. Tell me the truth." Deanna sat in the bed in the yellow bedroom with her eyes closed, her hands clenched, a pillow held over her head.

"You look like you're waiting for the earthquake." Ben looked at her and laughed. He was perched on the bed, next to her, the paper in his hand. "What would you like me to read to you, darling? The stock market? The comics? Oh, I know!"

"Will you read it to me, dammit. I can't stand it another minute more." She gritted her teeth, and he laughed again, turning to the reviews of her show. But he already knew what he would read. He had been in the business for too long to be very surprised. He generally knew what was in store. And as he glanced over the article, he knew he had been right again.

"O.K., now? Are you ready?"

"Benjamin! Read it dammit!" She said it through tensely clenched teeth and looked terrified as he started to read.

". . . a luminous, delicate style that shows not only years of study and devotion to her work, but the kind of talent we too seldom see. . . ." His voice droned on as her eyes flew wide and she pulled the pillow away from her head.

"You made that up!" She grabbed for the paper. He held it out of her reach and went on reading, until he had come to the end of the piece.

"I don't believe it." She looked as though she were in shock. "It can't be."

"Why not? You're good. I told you that. I know it, they know it, the people who bought your paintings know it. Everyone knows it except you, you big, silly, dopey, humble. . . ." He had reached out for her and was tickling her.

"Stop it! I'm famous! You can't tickle me now!" But she was giggling too hard to stop him. "Stop it! I'm a star!"

"Yeah? And who made you a star? Who told you that you had to have a show? Who begged you? Who wanted to show your work the first time he saw it? Huh? Tell me, tell me." They were both laughing now, and she was tangled into his arms, her pale pink silk nightgown creeping up toward her waist. He stopped for a moment, and looked at her, lying in his arms. She had never looked as beautiful, as delicate, and he wanted to hold her that way forever. He wanted to stop time.

"What's the matter, darling?" She had seen the look in his eyes and was watching him warily. "Is something wrong?"

"On the contrary. You are incredibly beautiful."

"And entirely yours." She slid her body onto his and smiled happily at him as she settled her mouth on his for a long tender kiss. In less than a minute the pink silk nightgown lay on the floor. It was noon before they climbed out of bed. Deanna yawned sleepily as she stood at the door to the terrace, still naked, with her hair falling down her back like an ebony stream. He watched her from the bed, wanting her to stay there forever.

"You know, I think you're destroying my career." He kept his eyes on her as she turned to him again. She looked so fragile and so young. Her looks belied the toughness he knew lay within. There was a certain steel in her, or she would never have survived the loneliness of her years with Marc.

"Why am I destroying your career? I thought I was going to make you a fortune with my brilliant paintings." She looked imperiously over her shoulder.

"You would if I'd ever go to the office. It's a good thing I told Sally not to expect me in today. Do you know I've never done anything like this in my life?" But he didn't look unhappy with his new life-style as he wrapped himself in a towel, threw her his robe, and followed her out onto the terrace where they sat comfortably in the two green canvas chairs. "You make me lazy and happy and horny and young."

"Which is precisely what you do to me." She leaned toward him and they kissed. "I feel about twenty-one. Maybe twenty-two."

"Good. Then let's get married and have twelve kids."

She glanced at him again, and for a moment she almost thought he was serious. "That would certainly give us some fresh problems to think about. Wouldn't it?" She tried to keep her tone light. She didn't want to talk about that with him again. She couldn't. It wasn't right. Instead, she asked, "What are we doing this weekend?"

She held her face up to the sun and closed her eyes contentedly. It was lovely being with him, living with him, going to Carmel and staying in town, waking up in the morning and falling asleep at night beside him. She felt as though they had been together for the last hundred years, not merely seven weeks. Was it already that? Had their lives soldered together that quickly? It was remarkable how much had happened and how rapidly.

"Do you want to go down to Carmel, or are you tired of that?"

"I'll never be tired of that. It is the most perfect, peaceful place to be."

"I'm glad." He reached over and took her hand. "That's how I feel too. But I keep thinking that you might like to do something more exotic."

"Like what?" She was amused at the idea. Athens? She forced her mind back from thoughts of Marc.

"I don't know. We could go down to Beverly Hills. I haven't been down there in weeks." He usually went just for the day and was back in time for dinner. "Or one of these days we could even go to New York." He was never very far from his work—other galleries, other dealers, auctions, artists. In his own way, his passion for his profession wasn't so different from Marc's. The differences were that he included her and that it was a passion which she shared as well. "In any case, my darling, what is your pleasure this weekend?"

"I told you. Carmel." She opened her eyes with a warm, happy smile.

"Then Carmel it is."

"And that reminds me. . . ." She put her head back with a frown. "There are some things I want to pick up at the house." She hadn't been there in days. Now and then she wondered what Margaret must be thinking. She had explained that she was working in a friend's studio and that it was easier to sleep there most of the time. But her occasional morning stops at the house to

rumple her bed after Margaret had had the night off wouldn't
fool anyone, least of all a woman who had worked for her for
years. But what could she say? I'm in love with another man? So
she simply kept her peace and avoided the old woman's wily, blue
eyes.

It was two in the afternoon when Ben dropped her a block
from the house. She wanted to look at the mail and sign a few
checks. She had to pay Margaret and leave her more money for
food, not that she ever ate at home anymore. Her heart and her
stomach all lived somewhere else. She didn't even work in her
own studio anymore. She did all her painting at Ben's, including
the painting she had been working on secretly, whenever he
wasn't at home.

Deanna let herself in and called out to see if anyone was home.
But Margaret wasn't there. Why should she be? Deanna never
was, and there was little to do. There was the usual stack of bills
and uninteresting invitations, no letter from Pilar, and nothing
from Marc. He didn't write to her. He called. There was no mail
for him either. Whenever he was away, Dominique came to the
house three times a week and collected his mail to send by pouch,
along with official papers.

She walked slowly up to her room, the mail in one hand and
the other holding the banister, and stopped at the head of the
stairs. It was depressing to be back here. It was like being forced
to give up a dream, to grow old again, away from the man who
talked about marriage and twelve kids. She smiled to herself at
the thought and sighed when she heard the phone. She decided
not to answer it, but then wondered if it might be Ben, stopping
at a pay phone while he waited. It was as though no one else
existed anymore, only the two of them. She couldn't imagine that
it would be anyone but him.

"Yes?" There was a smile in her voice when she answered.

"*Allo?*" Oh, *Jesus*, it was Marc. "*Allo?*"

"Marc?"

She was buying time.

"Obviously. And I'd like you to explain this nonsense about the
show. Dominique just called me."

"How convenient."

"I told you what I thought. And what you've done is in very
poor taste." He sounded livid.

"On the contrary, I can assure you it was all in very good taste."

"That, my dear, is debatable. You know perfectly well I forbade you to have the show. And the publicity! For God's sake, Deanna, it makes you sound like some sort of hippie."

"It most certainly does not." Her back stiffened at the thought. "The reviews made me sound like a serious artist. And it could just be that I am."

"I thought we had resolved that quite a while ago."

"Maybe you did, but I didn't." Damn him. He didn't understand. He never had.

"I see. In any case, I hope this gala new you isn't planning to indulge in conspicuous events like this everyday."

"Hardly. I'll be lucky if I show every five years."

"In that case, I'm sorry I missed this one."

"No, you're not." She was furious now and she would not play his game.

"I beg your pardon?"

"I said you're not sorry you weren't here. I'm sick and tired of your hypocrisy. How dare you belittle my work."

"Deanna?" He was shocked.

"I'm sorry, I. . . ." *God, what was happening?* She couldn't keep her stuffing inside anymore. It was as though she had to let everything out. "I don't know, Marc. . . . I think I'm tired."

"I think you must be. Was this a bad time to call?" His voice dripped sarcasm and ice. He didn't like her attitude at all. She should have been made to go to Cap d'Antibes for the summer.

"No. I was just leaving for Carmel."

"Again?"

"Yes. With Kim." *Oh, God, not again.* She hated lying to him. "It's not as though I have a lot to do, you know, when you're gone." She knew that would keep him at bay.

"Well, it won't be for much longer."

"How long?" She closed her eyes and held her breath. *Make it long, oh, please, don't let him come home. . . .*

"About a month."

Deanna nodded silently. She and Ben had one month left. That was all.

They sped off on the familiar road to Carmel half an hour later. Deanna was unusually quiet as they drove. Ben glanced at her, beautiful and troubled with the breeze whipping through her hair.

"Anything wrong?" he asked. She shook her head. "Bad news at home just now?"

"No." After a long hesitation, she looked at the countryside speeding past and spoke again. "He called."

"How was it?" *Did you ask for a divorce . . . ?*

"As usual. It made me angry. He was furious about the show. His secretary called Paris especially to tell him."

"Does it matter?" he asked. She shrugged. "Do you still care so much if you make him angry?"

She turned to look at him then. "In some ways he's like my father. Marc has been my authority figure for years."

"Are you afraid of him?"

"I never thought so, but perhaps I am. I just thought I respected him. But . . . oh, who knows. . . ."

"What's the worst thing he could do to you?"

"Leave me—or that's what I used to think."

"And you don't feel that way anymore?"

She shook her head. "No." In an odd way, she almost wished he would leave her. It would make everything so simple, but then of course there would be Pilar. Pilar would never forgive her. Deanna's brows knit, and Ben touched her hand.

"Don't worry so much. It'll all work out."

"I wish I knew how. Ben, I—I don't know what to do." She did. But she didn't want to do it. Lose him, or leave Marc. "And . . . I also have an obligation to Pilar."

"Yes, and an obligation to yourself. Your first obligation is to yourself, your second to your child. After that, it's all up to you."

Deanna nodded, saying nothing for a while. She looked less troubled than she had at first. "It's strange. I forget he exists most of the time. For eighteen years he has been the hub of my life, and suddenly in a month and a half it's as though he's gone and I've never known him. I feel like someone new. But he does exist, Ben. He calls and he's real and he expects me to talk to him, and somehow I can't."

"Then don't talk to him for now."

Jesus, he doesn't understand. And God, don't let him get possessive. Please, not yet. . . .

But Ben went on, "Why don't you just relax and enjoy what is. Later you can worry about what will be."

"And that's what you do, is it?" She slid a hand onto his neck and kissed his cheek. She had seen the worry in his face, the fear in his eyes, the concern when he thought she wasn't looking. "You don't worry at all, do you?"

"Me?" He shook his head, with a look of such assurance that she laughed.

"You're lying. You're as worried as I am. So don't make me any speeches. I used to think you were so cool that it never got to you. Well, I know better now."

"Oh, yeah?" He looked at her, laughter and bravado mingled in his eyes. But he was terrified about what would happen in the fall. It was the one thing he could not bring himself to face.

"Well, at least he said he wouldn't be home for a month."

"A month?"

Deanna nodded silently, and they drove on.

14

"Come on, sleepyhead. Get up. It's almost ten." She opened one eye, groaned at him, and turned over. He patted her behind, then leaned over her with a kiss. "Come on. You have an appointment with a prospective buyer today. You have to be at the gallery by eleven."

"And what about you?" She spoke to him from the depths of her pillow.

"I'm going now. Darling, will you get up?"

"No."

He sat down again next to her. "Deanna, are you all right?" She had been frequently exhausted in the last two weeks since the show.

"I'm fine." But she didn't feel it. Her head was heavy, and her body felt dipped in cement. It was so much easier to stay in bed, to sleep the day away, and drowse.

"How come you're so tired these days?" He was looking down at her with considerable concern.

"I think it must be old age."

"Apparently. I just hope success won't prove to be too much for you, because it looks like you might just turn out to be very successful." He chatted with her over his shoulder as he went out to the kitchen. "Do you want toast?"

The idea did not appeal to her. She shook her head as she closed her eyes again and buried her head in the pillow. "No, thanks!" But he reappeared a moment later with coffee, and for the first time in years that did not appeal to her either.

"Deanna? Are you really all right?"

"I'm fine. I'm just tired." And sick with apprehension about Marc's return. It had to be that. It was draining her to the core, thinking about him, and Pilar. It was stupid letting them spoil these last weeks with Ben, but she couldn't help it. "Really, darling, I'm all right. You don't need to worry." She smiled brightly at him and took a sip of the coffee, but as the warm fumes rose into her face she almost gagged. She turned visibly pale and set down the cup.

"You are sick!" It was an accusation filled with fear.

"I'm not, so stop it. I'm fine, I'm wonderful, I'm healthy, and I adore you." She reached out her arms for him with a bright smile, and he held her close. He didn't want anything to happen to her, he was suddenly terrified of losing her. He thought about it ten thousand times a day. She could get sick, have an accident, drown in the surf at Carmel; she could die in a fire. . . . *She could go back to Marc.*

"Who is this buyer we're meeting with today?"

"His name is Junot. He's either Swiss or French, I'm not sure which."

French? Maybe he knew Marc. But before she could speak, Ben already had the answer.

"No. He just got to town this week, and he liked your work when he walked past the gallery. Nice and simple. O.K.?"

"Perfect, you mind reader."

"Good. Then I'll see you there at eleven." He looked at her again, forcing a smile. He waved as he closed the door. They both had it now, and he knew it. The clutches. She had nightmares and held him desperately tight as they fell asleep, and now this exhaustion and malaise. They were both suffering the same terrors, wondering what the end of the summer would bring, and already fearing their loss. They had two more weeks. Maybe even three if Marc were delayed. He was bringing Pilar home with him. But what then? Neither of them had any of the answers. Not yet. And the miracle they both wanted had not yet occurred.

Deanna was at the gallery promptly at eleven, wearing a cream-colored silk suit with an ivory silk blouse. Her shoes and bag were in the same vanilla colors. She wore her mother's pearls and the earrings Ben had given her just before her show. The prospective buyer, Monsieur Junot, looked awed. He made all the appropriate gestures, offers, and radiated charm. He bought not one of her paintings, but two of her best. She and Ben shook hands gleefully after he left. The sale had totaled almost eight thousand dollars, nearly half of which would, of course, go to Ben. He took the standard dealer's 40 per cent. Some dealers even took fifty. But she had still done handsomely in the past weeks. Since the show she had made almost twelve thousand dollars.

"What'll you do with it all?" Ben watched her in amusement. She was gazing happily at the check.

"Be independent," she said suddenly, remembering what Marc had said before he left. That that was why she still painted, so she could be independent if she ever had to be again. Maybe he was right. It wasn't the only reason, certainly, but the feeling that she now had something of her own made her feel brand new.

"Want to prove your independence and take me to lunch?" Ben was looking at her with an admiring gaze, but though she looked remarkably pretty, he could still see in her eyes that she was not quite herself. "How about it? Lunch?" He was dying to go out with her, to be with her, to take her home, to be alone with her, to enjoy every minute they still had. It was becoming an obsession. But she was shaking her head.

"I'd love to. But I can't. I'm having lunch with Kim."

"Damn. All right, I won't ask you to break it. But when I leave here at five today, madam, you're all mine."

"Yes, sir." She looked up at him with pleasure.

"Promise?"

"That'll be an easy promise to keep."

"All right, then."

He walked her to the door of the gallery, bestowed a small gentlemanly kiss on her cheek, and watched as she crossed the street to the Jaguar. What an elegant woman she was. And she was his. He smiled with pride as he went back inside.

"So, how's my favorite artist today? The new Mary Cassatt." Kim had on a broad smile as Deanna slipped into her seat. They met, as usual, at Trader Vic's. Deanna hadn't been there in almost two months.

"Would you believe we just sold two more paintings this morning?"

"I believe it. Thank God Thompson knew when to push. I never thought I'd see the day you'd give in." But she also knew that a lot of it had to do with Marc's absence. Deanna would never have agreed to the show, if Marc had been there to squelch it. "Anyway, I'm delighted you did, and it's about time." Kim signaled to the waiter and ordered champagne, despite Deanna's laughter and protests. "Why not? We've barely seen each other since Carmel for chrissake. And we have a lot to celebrate."

Deanna laughed to herself. More than Kim knew.

"So, other than the fact that you're now a famous artist, what's new?" Kim's eyes searched hers, but Deanna only smiled. "You look like the cat that swallowed the canary."

"I don't know why."

"Bull! I think that maybe I know why." She had seen it that night at Deanna's opening, but at first she hadn't been sure. "Well, are you going to tell me, or am I going to die of suspense?"

"You mean I have a choice?"

"Never mind that. Come on, Deanna, be nice . . . tell me."

Kim was playing but Deanna was suddenly serious. "It sounds as though you already know. Jesus, I hope it's not that obvious."

"It's not. I just suddenly began to wonder, that night. At the opening. But I don't think anyone else would have known." Their eyes met at last, and Deanna was silent for a time.

"He's incredibly special, Kim. And I love him. Very much."

Kim let out a slow sigh and waited. "He seems like a very nice man. Is it serious?" she asked. Deanna nodded, and Kim sipped her champagne.

"I'd like to say I don't know. But I do know." Her eyes filled with tears. "I have to go back to Marc. Ben knows it too. I can't start all over again, Kim. I can't. I'm too old. I'm almost forty, and . . ." her voice was barely a whisper, "I have a life with Marc. I've always loved him. And . . . and there's Pilar. . . ." But Deanna couldn't go on. Her eyes were brimming, and she had to blow her nose.

Kim wanted to put her arms around her and come up with a magical solution. They both knew there was none.

"There's no other way?" Deanna shook her head. "How does Ben feel?"

Deanna took a deep breath. "As panic stricken as I. But I just can't walk out and start all over again. I can't. . . ." She sounded desperate as she whispered at Kim. "I'm too old."

"If that's all that's stopping you, you know damn well you're not. Hell, women remake their lives at sixty when their husbands die. At thirty-seven, you'd be crazy to throw something away you really want."

"But it's not right. And I *am* too old, dammit, Kim. He wants children for God's sake, and I have a daughter who's almost grown."

"All the more reason. Pilar will be gone. If you want more children, now's the time."

"You're as crazy as he is." Deanna tried to smile, but it was not an easy subject. She felt as though the next two weeks were already vanishing beneath her eyes.

"Are you happy with Ben, Deanna?"

"I've never been as happy in my life. And I can't understand it. I've lived with Marc for almost twenty years; we know each other, and suddenly. . . . Oh, God, Kim, I can barely remember what Marc looks like, how he sounds. It's as though my whole life is with Ben. At first I felt guilty; I thought I was horrible for doing what I did. Now I don't even feel badly. I just love him."

"And you think you'll be able to give that up?" Kim looked at her with sorrow for what she knew was happening to her friend.

"I don't know. Maybe we can still see each other. Maybe . . . Kim, I just don't know."

Neither did Kim, but she suspected that Ben Thompson wouldn't put up with sharing her for very long. He didn't seem like that kind of man.

"Will you tell Marc?"

Deanna shook her head. "Never. He would never understand. He'd be heartbroken. I—we'll just have to see. Ben has to go to

New York in September for a few weeks. That'll give me time to see how things stand."

"If I can do anything, Deanna . . . if you need a shoulder or a hand—I'm always there for you, babe. I hope you know that."

"I do."

The two exchanged a smile and went on to other things, but long after Kim left her, she was haunted by Deanna's face, and what she had seen.

And when she had left Kim, Deanna had slowly driven home. She had to check the mail and pay her bills. She wasn't meeting Ben again till five. They'd go some place quiet for dinner, and then maybe for a walk, or to a movie, do the kind of things people did who didn't have children, or pressures, or too little time. She wanted to spend these two weeks as they had spent the two months before, simply, quietly—together. It was what Ben wanted too.

"Mrs. Duras?" Margaret was waiting for her as she turned her key in the door. She was wearing a look of tension which, at first, Deanna did not understand.

"Margaret? Are you all right?" She thought the older woman looked pale. As she reached the hall table, she realized that the housekeeper was still staring. "Margaret? Is something wrong?" Her voice was more insistent this time, and she looked long and hard at the woman in the dark blue uniform. Could she know about Ben? Had she seen them? "What is it?"

"There have been two calls . . ." Margaret trailed off, not knowing what more to say. She wasn't really sure. She had no right to worry Mrs. Duras but she had had a feeling.

"From Mister Duras?" Deanna stood up very straight.

"From Madame Duras, his mother."

"What did she say?" There was a frown in Deanna's eyes now. "Was anything wrong?"

"I don't know. She only spoke to the operator in Paris. But she wants you to call back. Right away."

"In Paris? You mean Antibes." To Margaret, Deanna knew, it was one and the same. The housekeeper shook her head emphatically.

"No. It was Paris. They left a number." Margaret ferreted the message from the pile and handed it to Deanna. She was right. It was Paris. It was the number of the house on the rue François

Premier. Something was wrong. Perhaps the old lady was ill and wanted Pilar sent home early. Marc! Something had happened to Marc! A thousand catastrophes leaped into her head as she ran up the stairs to the bedroom phone. It would be just after midnight in Paris. Too late? Should she wait until morning?

The overseas operator put the call through quickly, and the familiar purring of the French phone was instantly in her ears. For years it had sounded to her like a busy signal, but now she was used to it and she knew. "It may take them a minute to answer, I'm awfully sorry."

"That's quite all right." The operator sounded Californian and unhurried and Deanna smiled. Then she heard her mother-in-law's voice on the line.

"Allo? Oui?"

"Mamie?" The term of affection had never come easily to Deanna. After nearly twenty years she was still tempted to call her mother-in-law Madame Duras. "Mamie?" It was not a very good connection, but Deanna could hear, and she raised her own voice to make herself heard. Madame Duras sounded neither sleepy, nor pleasant. She never did. "It's Deanna. I'm awfully sorry to call so late, but I thought that . . ."

"Deanna, il faut que tu viennes." Oh, Jesus, not in French, with a connection like that! But the older woman went on in a rush of French. Deanna could barely hear.

"Wait, wait. I can't hear you. I don't understand. Please say it in English. Is something wrong?"

"Yes." The word was a long mournful wail, and then there was silence while Deanna waited. What had happened? It was Marc. She knew it! "Pilar. . . . She had . . . an accident . . . on the moto—"

Deanna felt her heart stop. "Pilar?" She was shouting into the phone now, and she didn't hear Margaret come into the room. "Pilar?" The connection was fading, and she shouted louder. "Mamie? Can you hear me? What happened?"

"Her head . . . her legs . . ."

"Oh, God! Is she all right?" The tears were pouring down her face and she was desperately trying to control her voice. "Mamie? Is she all right?"

"Paralysées. Les jambes. Her legs . . . paralyzed. And her head. . . . We don't know."

"Where is she?" Deanna was shrieking.

"At the American Hospital." The old woman was sobbing now. "Have you called Marc?"

"We can't find him. He's in Greece. His *société* is trying to locate him. They think he will be here tomorrow. Oh, please, Deanna . . . you will come?"

"Tonight. Right now." Her whole arm was trembling as she looked at her watch. It was ten minutes to four. She knew there was a flight at seven-thirty. Marc took it all the time. With the time difference, she would be there at four-thirty Paris time, the next day. "I'll be there . . . in the afternoon . . . I'll go directly to the hospital. Who is her doctor?" She hastily scribbled his name. "How can I reach him?" Madame Duras gave her his home number.

"Oh, Deanna. The poor child. . . . I told Marc that the *moto* was too big for a child. Why didn't he listen? I told him. . . ."

So did I. "*Mamie*, is anyone with her?" It was the first thing that had come to her mind. Her baby was alone in a hospital in Paris.

"We have nurses, of course." That sounded more like the Madame Duras Deanna knew.

"No one else?" There was horror in her voice.

"It is after midnight here."

"I don't want her alone."

"Very well. I'll send Angéline down now, and I shall go in the morning." Angéline, the oldest maid on the face of the earth. Angéline. How could she?

"I'll be there as soon as I can. Tell her I love her. Good-bye, *Mamie*. I'll see you tomorrow."

Desperate, Deanna flashed the operator. "Doctor Hubert Kirschmann, person to person. It's an emergency."

But *Docteur* Kirschmann was not answering his calls. And a call to the American Hospital did not yield a great deal more. Although still critical, Mademoiselle Duras was resting comfortably, she was conscious, and there was a possibility that they might operate in the morning. It was too soon to tell. She had been flown in from Cannes only that evening, and if Madame would be good enough to call the *docteur* in the morning. . . . Oh, go to hell. Pilar was not able to take phone calls, and there was nothing more Deanna could do. Except get on a plane.

She sat very still for a moment, fighting back tears, holding her head in her hands, until a sudden sob escaped her, wrenching its way free from her heart. "Pilar . . . my baby. Oh, my God!" The blue uniform was around her then, and Margaret's comforting arms held her tightly.

"Is it very bad?" Her voice was a whisper in the too silent room.

"I don't know. They say her legs are paralyzed, and there's something wrong with her head. But I couldn't get intelligent answers from anyone. I'm going to take the next plane."

"I'll pack a bag."

Deanna nodded and tried to marshal her thoughts. She had to call Ben. And Dominique. Instinctively, her fingers dialed Dominique at the office. The voice she disliked was quick to answer the phone. "Where is Monsieur Duras?"

"I have no idea."

"The hell you don't. Our daughter just had an accident, and they can't find him. Where is he?"

"I . . . Madame Duras, I'm very sorry. . . . I'll do my best to locate him by morning and have him call you."

"I'm leaving for Paris tonight. Just tell him to be there. And call his mother. Pilar is at the American Hospital in Paris. And for God's sake, do me a favor, will you please, Dominique, and find him?" Her voice trembled on the words.

"I'll do my best. And I'm really very sorry. Is it serious?"

"We don't know."

She called the airline and the bank. She glanced at what Margaret had put in her bag and quickly dialed Ben before he left the gallery. She had an hour before she had to leave for the airport. He was quick to come on the line.

"I have to leave town tonight."

"What did you do this afternoon? Rob a bank?" His voice was full of mischief and laughter; he was looking forward to the evening ahead. But he was quick to sense that something was wrong.

"Pilar had an accident. Oh, Ben. . . ." And then the tears came, sobbing, aching, frightened, and angry at Marc for letting her have the bike.

"Take it easy, darling. I'll be right there. Is it all right if I come to the house?"

"Yes."

Margaret opened the door to him seven minutes later. Deanna

was waiting in her room. She was still wearing the suit she had worn at lunch and the earrings Ben had given her. She was wearing those to France. He looked at her quickly as he walked in, and took her into his arms. "It's all right, baby, it's all right. She'll be all right."

She told him then about the paralyzed legs.

"That could just be a temporary reaction from the fall. You don't know the details yet. It may not be nearly as bad as it sounds. Do you want something to drink?" She was dangerously pale, but she shook her head. All he saw was her face and the heartbreak written there. She began to cry again and took refuge once more in his arms.

"I've been thinking such awful things."

"Don't. You don't know. You just have to hang in till you get there." He looked at her again with a question. "Do you want me to come?"

She sighed and gave him a glimmer of a smile. "Yes. But you can't. I love you for asking though. Thank you."

"If you need me, call, and I'll come. Promise?" he asked. She nodded.

"Will you call Kim and tell her where I've gone? I just tried to reach her and she's out."

"She won't find it suspicious if I tell her?" He looked worried, but he was worried about Deanna, not Kim.

"No." Deanna smiled. "I told her about us today at lunch. She had already guessed, don't ask me how. At the opening. But she thinks you're a very special man. I think she's right." She reached out to him again and held him close. It would be the last time for a while that she could do that, hold him and be his. "I wanted a chance to go home again . . . just to be there . . . it gives me so much peace." She meant his house, not her own, but he understood.

"You'll be home again soon."

"Promise?" Her eyes found his.

"Promise. Now come on, we'd better go. Do you have everything you need?" he asked. She nodded and closed her eyes again. For just a fraction of a moment she had been dizzy. "Are you all right?"

"I'm fine." She followed him down the stairs and hugged Margaret as she left. They had an hour to get to the airport. Forty-five minutes later she would be on the plane. Twelve hours after that, she'd be in Paris—with her baby. Pilar.

During the drive to the airport Deanna found herself silently praying that she'd find her alive.

15

"*Quoi? Oh, mon Dieu!* Dominique, are you sure?"

"Absolutely. I also spoke to your mother. And the doctor."

"What's his name?" She passed the information on to Marc as he gestured frantically for a pen. Chantal handed him hers. "When did they operate?"

"This morning, Paris time. Three hours ago, I believe. She's a little better, they think, but she hadn't yet regained consciousness. They're mainly worried about her skull, and . . . and her legs."

The tears had started to pour slowly down Marc-Edouard's cheeks as he listened to Dominique. "I'll send a wire. I'll be there tonight." He flashed the concierge. His orders were terse. "This is Duras. Get me on a plane. Paris. Immediately." He hung up and wiped his face, looking strangely at Chantal.

"It's Pilar?" she asked. He nodded. "Is it very bad?" She sat down on the couch next to him and took his hands.

"They don't know. They don't know. . . ." He couldn't bring himself to say the words, or to tell her that the motorcycle had been a gift from him, as the sobs began to convulse him.

Deanna got off the plane at Charles de Gaulle Airport in a cloud of exhaustion, terror, and nausea. She had spent the night staring straight ahead and clenching her hands. She called the hospital from the airport, but there was no news. Deanna hailed a taxi just outside the airport and sat silently as they sped along. She had given the driver the address of the American Hospital and told him only, "*Aussi vite que possible.*"

In true Gallic style, he took her at her word. The trees at the roadside were barely more than a green blur in the corners of

Deanna's eyes as she stared straight ahead of her, watching the driver's maneuvers as he lunged and careened past every obstacle in sight. She could feel every pulse in her body, every throb of her heart . . . hurry . . . hurry . . . *VITE!* It seemed hours before they reached the Boulevard Victor Hugo and screeched to a halt in front of the big double doors. Deanna reached quickly into her wallet for the francs she had exchanged from dollars at the airport. Without thinking she handed him a hundred francs, and flung open the door.

"*Votre monnaie?*" He looked at her questioningly, and she shook her head. She didn't give a damn about the change. Her lips were a tight, narrow line lost somewhere in the ivory agony of her face. He had understood from the first, when she had given him the address of the American Hospital. He had known. "Your husband?"

"*Non. Ma fille.*" Once again her eyes filled with tears.

The driver nodded in sympathetic chagrin. "*Désolée.*" He picked her small brown-leather valise off the seat and opened his door. He stood there for a moment, holding it, looking at her, wanting to say something more. He had a daughter too, and he could see the pain in Deanna's eyes. His wife had looked like that once, when they had almost lost their son. He silently handed the bag to Deanna. Her eyes held his for only a fraction of a second, then she turned and strode rapidly into the hospital.

There was a sour-looking matron sitting at a desk.

"*Oui, Madame?*"

"Pilar Duras. Her room number?" *Oh, God, just her room number, please. Don't let them tell me . . . don't . . .*

"Four-twenty-five." Deanna wanted to let out a long anguished sigh. Instead, she only nodded curtly and followed the sign. There were two men and a woman on the elevator, going to other floors. They had the look of businesslike Europeans, maybe they were friends of patients, maybe husbands or wives, but none of them looked particularly shaken or upset. Deanna watched them enviously as she waited for her floor. The long, fear-filled plane ride was taking its toll. It had been a long sleepless night, and her thoughts had ricocheted from Pilar to Ben. What if she had let him come with her? She found herself longing for his arms, his warmth, his comfort, his support, and the gentleness of his words.

The elevator doors opened on four, and hesitantly she stepped out. There was a bustle of nurses, and in a few sedate little cliques she noticed elderly distinguished men; doctors. But suddenly, Deanna felt lost. She was six thousand miles from home, looking for a daughter who could even be dead. Suddenly, she wasn't even sure if she could speak French anymore, or if she would ever find Pilar in that maze. Tears stung her eyes. She fought off a wave of dizziness and nausea, then slowly made her way to the desk.

"I'm looking for Pilar Duras. I'm her mother." She didn't even try it in French. She just couldn't. She only prayed that someone would understand. Most of the nurses were French, but someone would speak English. Someone would know . . . someone would make it all better—would take her to Pilar, would show her that she wasn't really that badly hurt. . . .

"Duras?" The nurse seemed troubled as she looked up at Deanna, and then frowned at a chart. Everything inside Deanna turned first to jelly, then to stone. "Oh, yes." She met Deanna's eyes and nodded, wondering suddenly if the desperately pale woman trembling in front of her was ill. "Madame Duras?"

"Yes." Deanna couldn't manage more than a whisper. Suddenly every moment of the trip had caught up with her. She just couldn't anymore. She even found herself wishing for Marc.

"Madame Duras, are you all right?" The young woman in the white uniform had a heavy accent but her English was fluent. Deanna only stared at her. Even she wasn't quite sure. She felt very odd, as though she might faint.

"I have to . . . I think. . . . May I sit down?" She looked around vaguely, and then watched in fascination while everything around her first turned gray, then shrank. It was like watching a slowly fading screen on a disgruntled television, as slowly . . . slowly . . . the picture just faded away. At last, all she heard was a hum. Then she felt a hand on her arm.

"Madame Duras? Madame Duras?" It was the same girl's voice, and Deanna felt herself smile. She had such a pleasant young voice . . . such a pleasant. . . . Deanna felt unbearably sleepy. All she wanted to do was drift away, but the hand kept tugging at her arm. Suddenly, there was something cool on her neck, and then her head. The picture returned to the screen. A dozen faces surrounded her, all looking down. She started to sit up, but a hand immediately restrained her, and two young men spoke urgently to each other in French. They wanted to transfer her to emergency, but Deanna rapidly shook her head.

"No, no, I'm fine. Really. I've just had a very long flight from San Francisco, and I haven't eaten all day. Really, I'm just terribly tired and. . . ." The tears welled up in her eyes again. She tried to will them away. Dammit, why did they want to take her to emergency? "I have to see my daughter. Pilar . . . Pilar Duras."

The words seemed to stop them. The two young men stared at her, then nodded. They had understood. In a moment, with a hand at each elbow, she was on her feet, while a young nurse helped her straighten her skirt. Someone brought a chair, and the first nurse brought her a glass of water. A moment later the crowd had dispersed. Only the young nurse and the older one remained.

"I'm awfully sorry," Deanna said.

"Of course not. You are very tired. You have had a long trip. We understand. In a moment we will take you to see Pilar." The two nurses exchanged a glance, and the older one nodded almost imperceptibly.

"Thank you." Deanna took another sip of water and handed back the glass. "Is Doctor Kirschmann here?" The nurse shook her head.

"He left earlier this afternoon. He was with Pilar all night. They performed surgery, you know."

"On her legs?" Deanna felt herself trembling again.

"No. Her head."

"Is she all right?"

There was an endless pause. "She is better. Come, you will see for yourself." She stood aside to help her up, but Deanna was steady now and furious with herself for the time she had just wasted.

She was led down a long peach-colored hall and stopped at last at a white door. The nurse looked long and hard at Deanna, then slowly opened the door. Deanna took a few steps inside and felt the air freeze in her lungs. It was as though she could no longer breathe.

Pilar was wrapped in bandages, and covered with machinery and tubes. There was a severe-looking nurse sitting quietly in one corner, and at least three monitors were feeding out mysterious reports. Pilar herself was barely visible through the bandages, and her face was badly distorted by the various tubes.

But this time Deanna did not faint. She dropped the valise where she stood and advanced into the room with a firm step and a smile, as the nurse who had brought her in watched. She exchanged glances with the nurse on duty in the room. The woman approached, but Deanna didn't notice. She continued to make her way toward the bed, praying for strength and fighting back tears with a heartbreaking smile.

"Hi, baby, it's Mommy." There was a soft groan from the bed, and the eyes of her child followed her steps. It was easy to see that Pilar knew her and understood. "Everything's going to be just fine. Just fine. . . ." She stood next to the bed and reached for Pilar's one undamaged hand, and gently, almost so lightly as not to touch her, she took the hand in both of hers, lifted it to her lips, and kissed the fingers of her little girl. "It's all right, my darling, you're going to be fine."

There was a gruesome sound from the girl in the bed.

"Shh . . . you can talk to me later. Not now." Deanna's voice was barely more than a whisper, but it was firm.

Pilar shook her head. "I . . ."

"Shhh. . . ." Deanna looked distressed, but Pilar's eyes were too full of words.

"Is it something you want?" Now Deanna watched, but there was no answer in the eyes. Deanna glanced at the nurse. Could she be in pain? The nurse approached, and together they watched and waited as Pilar tried again.

"Gl . . . ad . . . youuu . . . came." It was a threadlike, fragile whisper from the bed, but it filled Deanna's heart with passion and tears. Her eyes filled. She forced herself to smile while she went on holding Pilar's hand.

"I'm glad I came too. Now don't talk, baby. Please. We can talk later. We'll have a lot to say."

This time Pilar only nodded yes, and then at last, closed her eyes for a while. The nurse told Deanna when they stepped into the hall that except for when they operated and she had been given an anesthetic, Pilar had been awake the entire time, as though she were waiting for someone, for something, and now it was easy to see why.

"Your being here will make an enormous difference, you know, Madame Duras." Pilar's nurse spoke impeccable English and looked terribly crisp. Deanna was relieved at her words. Pilar *had* been waiting for her. She still cared. It was stupid that at a time like this that should matter, but it did. She had feared that even in direst circumstances, Pilar might still reject her. But she had not. Or had she really been waiting for Marc? It didn't matter. Deanna walked softly back inside the room and sat down.

It was more than two hours before Pilar woke, and she only lay there watching her mother, her gaze never leaving Deanna's face. At last after their eyes had seemed to hold for hours, she thought she saw Pilar smile. Deanna approached the bed again and gently took the girl's hand once again.

"I love you, darling. And you're doing just fine. Why don't you try to get some more sleep?"

But her eyes said no. They stayed open again for an hour, watching, only watching, staring into her mother's face, as though drinking it in, as though she were reaching out with the words she couldn't find the strength to say. It was another hour before she spoke again.

"Doggie. . . ." Deanna looked puzzled, and Pilar tried again. "Did . . . you . . . bring my . . . doggie?" This time Deanna could not stop herself from crying. Doggie, the treasure of the years when she'd still been a child. Doggie, so old and dirty and bedraggled, and finally retired to a remote shelf somewhere in the house. Deanna had never been able to throw it out. Doggie brought back too many memories of Pilar as a child. Now Deanna watched her, wondering if she still knew where she was, or if she had drifted back to some distant place, to childhood, and Doggie.

"He's waiting for you at home."

Pilar nodded with a tiny smile. "O.K. . . ." The word was feather soft on her lips as she drifted back to sleep.

Doggie. It brought Deanna back a dozen years as she sat in the narrow chair and let her own thoughts wander back to when Pilar had been three, and four, and five, and nine . . . and then too soon twelve, and now almost sixteen. She had been so sweet when she was little, so tiny and graceful, the little girl with the golden curls and blue eyes. The delicious things she had said; the dances she sometimes had done for her parents when she played; the tea parties she'd held for her dolls; the stories she'd written, the poems, the plays; the blouse she had made Deanna one year for her birthday from two chartreuse kitchen towels . . . and Deanna had worn it, very seriously, to church.

"Madame Duras?" Deanna was jolted back from a great distance at the sound of the unfamiliar female voice. She looked around, startled, and saw a new nurse.

"Yes?"

"Do you not wish to rest? We can make you a bed in the next room." Her face was very gentle, and the eyes were wise and old. She patted Deanna's arm with her hand. "You have been here for a very long time."

"What time is it now?" Deanna felt as though she had been living in a dream for hours.

"Nearly eleven."

It was two P.M. in San Francisco. She had been away from home for less than twenty-four hours, but it felt more like years. She stood up and stretched.

"How is she?" Deanna looked intensely at the bed.

The kindly nurse hesitated for a moment. "The same."

"When is the doctor coming back?" And why the hell hadn't he been there in the five hours that Deanna had been at Pilar's side? And where was Marc, dammit? Wasn't he coming? He'd whip these morons into shape and then things would start to move. Deanna glared at the monitors, irritated at the hieroglyphics they wrote.

"The doctor will be back in a few hours. You could get a little rest. You could even go home for the night. We have given Mademoiselle another injection. She will sleep now for quite a while."

Deanna didn't want to leave, but it seemed as though it might be time to put in her appearance at her mother-in-law's house. She could find out if they had located Marc and see what was happening with this doctor. Who was he? And where? And what did he have to say? The only thing Deanna knew now was that Pilar was critical. Deanna felt desperately helpless, sitting there for hours, waiting for an explanation, or a sign, something to herald encouragement or good news . . . someone to tell her it was nothing. But that would have been difficult to believe.

"Madame?" The nurse watched her sorrowfully.

Deanna looked almost as wan as Pilar as she picked up her bag. "I'll leave a number where I can be reached, and I'll be back soon. How long do you think she'll sleep?"

"At least four hours, perhaps even five or six. But she will not be awake before three. And I promise . . . if there is a problem, or if she wakes and wants you, I will call."

Deanna nodded and jotted down Marc's mother's number. She looked agonizingly into the nurse's eyes. "Call me immediately if . . . I should come." She couldn't bring herself to say more but the nurse understood. She clipped Deanna's number to the chart and smiled into Deanna's very tired eyes.

"I will call. But you must get some sleep."

Deanna could never remember feeling so tired in her life, but the last thing she planned to do was sleep. She had to call Ben. Talk to the doctor. Find out about Marc. Her mind raced and she felt dizzy again. She steadied herself against the wall, but this time she did not faint. She merely stood for a long moment, looking at Pilar. Then, with eyes flooded with tears, she left the room, her suitcase in one hand, her coat over her arm, and her heart dragging behind her.

She found a taxi at a stand across the street from the hospital and sank back into the seat with a sigh so loud it was almost a groan. Every inch of her was tired and painful and sore, every fiber in her body was tense and exhausted, and her mind never seemed to stop its constant whirring: Pilar as a baby . . . Pilar last year . . . Pilar at seven . . . Pilar in her room. In school. At the airport. With a new hairdo. Her first stockings. A red bow. It was a never ceasing film she had been watching all day, sometimes with the sound track, sometimes without, but it was a vision she couldn't escape, even as the cab sped through Paris to the rue François Premier.

It was an elegant neighborhood, conveniently located near Christian Dior. The street was as pretty as any in Paris, quite close to the Champs Élysées. When she was younger, Deanna had often escaped in the afternoon to look at the shops and have an espresso at a café before returning to the austerity of life at her mother-in-law's, but now all thought of those days slipped from her mind. She rode blindly along, exhaustion enveloping her like a blanket drenched in ether.

The driver was smoking a Gauloise *papier maïs* and singing an old song. He was too happy to notice the gloom in the backseat, and when he stopped at the address, his eyes met Deanna's with a lure and a smile. She didn't notice. She simply handed him the money and got out. The driver only shrugged and drove away as she plodded toward the door. It had not gone unnoticed that her mother-in-law had not been at the hospital all evening. The nurse said she had been with Pilar for two hours in the morning. Two hours? That was all? And left her in that appalling condition all alone? It proved everything Deanna had always thought. Madame Duras had no heart.

She rang the doorbell with two quick, sharp jabs, and the heavy wooden outer door swung open before her. She stepped over the high threshold and closed the door behind her, making her way quickly to the tiny elegant cage. She always felt as though there ought to be a canary in that elevator and not people, but today her thoughts were far from flip as she pressed the button for the seventh floor. It was the penthouse; Madame Duras owned the entire floor.

A faceless maid in a uniform was waiting at the door, when Deanna stepped out. "*Oui, Madame?*" She looked Deanna over with displeasure, if not disdain.

"*Je suis Madame Duras.*" Deanna's accent had never been worse, and she didn't give a damn.

"*Ah, bon.* Madame is waiting in the salon." How sweet. Pouring tea? Deanna felt her teeth grind as she marched behind the maid toward the living room. Nothing was unusual, nothing was out of place. No one would have believed that Madame Edouard Duras's granddaughter lay, possibly dying, in a hospital two miles away. Everything appeared to be in perfect order, including Madame Duras, as the maid escorted Deanna into the room. Her mother-in-law was wearing dark green silk and an impeccable coiffure, her step was firm as she walked toward Deanna with an extended hand. Only her eyes betrayed her concern. She shook hands with Deanna and kissed her on both cheeks, looking with dismay at the expression on her daughter-in-law's face.

"You've just come?" Her eyes glanced immediate dismissal to the maid, who instantly fled.

"No. I've been with Pilar all evening. And I've yet to see the doctor." Deanna pulled off her jacket and almost fell into a chair.

"You look very tired." The older woman watched her with a face set in stone. Only the wily, old eyes suggested that someone did indeed live behind the granite of her face.

"Whether or not I'm tired is beside the point. Who the hell is this Kirschmann and where is he?"

"He is a surgeon and he is known all over France. He was with Pilar until late this afternoon, and he will see her again in a few hours. Deanna"—she hesitated, then said more gently—"there is simply nothing more he can do. At least not for the moment."

"Why not?"

"Now we must wait. She must get her strength. She must . . . live." Her expression showed pain at the word, and Deanna ran a hand across her eyes. "Would you like something to eat?"

Deanna shook her head. "Just a shower and a little rest. And"— she looked up with an expression of agony in her face—"I'm sorry to just march in like this. I haven't said any of the appropriate things like 'good to see you,' 'how are you,' but Mamie, I'm sorry, I just can't."

"I understand."

Did she? Deanna wondered. But what did it matter now if she did or not.

"I do think you should eat, my dear," Madame Duras was saying. "You look very pale."

She felt very pale too, but she simply wasn't hungry. She couldn't have eaten, no matter what. Not tonight. Not after seeing Pilar limp and broken in that bed, asking for Doggie, and too weak to hold her mother's hand.

"I'll just shower and change and get back. It's liable to be a long night. By the way, have you heard from Marc?" Her brows knit as she asked. Her mother-in-law nodded.

"He'll be here in an hour."

An hour. . . . One hour. After more than two months, Deanna felt nothing inside except what she felt for Pilar.

"He's coming in from Athens. He's very upset."

"As well he might be." Deanna looked his mother straight in the eye. "He bought her the motorcycle. I begged him not to."

Madame Duras instantly bridled. "Deanna, he cannot be blamed. I'm sure he feels quite badly enough."

"I'm sure he does." She looked away, then stood up. "He'll be landing in an hour?"

"Yes. Will you go to meet him?"

Deanna started to say no, but something inside her wavered. She was thinking of Pilar, and how the child looked . . . how it would be for Marc walking in, as she had, and seeing her for the first time. It seemed cruel to let him walk into that alone. Pilar

was his baby, his treasure, his child. She was also Deanna's, but to
Marc, Pilar was almost a goddess. She couldn't let him face it as
she had. She had to meet him at the plane.

"Do you have his flight number?" His mother nodded. "Then
I'll go. I'll just wash my face. I won't bother to change. Can you
call a taxi?"

"Certainly." The elder Madame Duras looked pleased. "I'll be
more than happy to. Fleurette will make a sandwich for you."
Fleurette, little flower. The name of the immensely rotund cook
Madame Duras employed had always struck Deanna funny, but
not tonight. Nothing was funny anymore. She nodded curtly at
her mother-in-law and hurried down the hall. She was just about
to turn into the guest room when she noticed the painting in a
dark passage. Left there, unwanted, unloved, unadmired, forgotten. It was the portrait of herself and Pilar. Madame Duras had
never been very fond of it. Now, without thinking further,
Deanna decided that this time she'd take it home, where it
belonged.

In the familiar guest room, she looked around. Everything was
a polite shade of sandy beige, in damask or silk, and the furniture
was all Louis XV. It was a room that had always seemed cold to
Deanna, even when she had slept in it on her honeymoon with
Marc. She ran a comb through her hair and tried to make herself
think of Marc. What would it be like to see him again? To see his
face, touch his hand . . . after Ben. Why was it that Ben seemed
more real to her now, or was he only a dream? Had she once more
been swallowed alive by this beige-silk world, never to return? She
wanted desperately to call Ben but she didn't have time. She had
to get to the airport in time to catch Marc as he left the gate from
the plane, or she'd miss him entirely. She wondered if there were
any way to leave a message that she was coming, but she knew
from experience that such messages always went astray. A man
with a thin, thready voice would stand in a corner of the airport
whispering to himself, "Monsieur Duras . . . Monsieur Duras," as
Marc marched unknowingly by. And if he did get it, it might
frighten him too badly about Pilar. She could at least spare him
that.

The maid knocked on the guest-room door and told her the taxi
was waiting. As she spoke the words, she handed Deanna a small

package. Two ham sandwiches and part of a chicken. Perhaps Monsieur would be hungry too. Hungry? Jesus, who could eat?

Unlike the earlier ride from the airport which had seemed interminable, this one seemed much too short. She found herself nodding slowly off to sleep in the backseat as they raced along into the night, her thoughts jumping in disjointed confusion from Pilar to Ben to Marc. It seemed only moments later, that the cab screeched to a halt.

"*Voilà.*"

She muttered an absentminded "*merci*" to the driver, paid the fare and a handsome tip, and hurried inside, smoothing her skirt again as she ran. She was beginning to feel as though she hadn't changed her clothes in a week, but she didn't really care how she looked, she had too many other things on her mind. She glanced at the big board that listed the flight numbers and the gates and started out at a run in the direction of the gate from which she knew he'd come. The flight had just landed. It would be only a minute or two before the passengers would deplane. She had just enough time to make it. First-class passengers always debarked first, and Marc always traveled first class.

She darted in and out between other travelers, almost stumbling over someone's bags. But she reached the area just as the first passengers were coming through customs, and with a sigh backed off into a corner to watch. For a mad moment she wanted to surprise him, to show him that she cared, despite her betrayal of the summer. But even in this ghastly time of agony over Pilar, she wanted to hold out something to Marc, to make it easier for him. She would simply walk up beside him with a touch of the hand and a smile. She could still do that for him, she could give him a moment of pleasure in the midst of so much pain. She pulled her jacket closer around her and looked down at the cravat on her ivory silk shirt. Seven or eight people had already walked past her, but there was still no sign of Marc.

Then suddenly she saw him, tall and thin and narrow and neat, impeccably orderly and well tailored, even after the flight. She noticed with surprise that he looked less distraught than she had feared. Obviously, he did not yet understand how serious things were, or maybe. . . . And then, as she took a step from her hiding place, Deanna felt her heart stop.

He was turning, with a slow, soft smile, the smile that called her *Diane* and not Deanna. She saw him reach out and take a young woman's hand. She was yawning sleepily, and he let his hand drift to her shoulder as he pulled her close. The woman said something and patted his arm. Deanna watched them in speechless stupefaction, wondering who the girl was, but not even really caring. What she had seen was the missing piece in the puzzle, the answer to so many years of questions in her life. This was no casual acquaintance, no girl he had picked up on the flight. This was someone he was comfortable with, familiar with, someone he knew well. The way they walked and spoke and moved and shared told Deanna everything.

She stood riveted to the floor in the corner, with her hand raised in horror to her barely open mouth, and watched them walking away from her down the concourse until she could no longer see them. Then, her head down, running, seeing no one, and wanting desperately not to be seen, she ran toward the exit and hailed a cab.

16

Feeling panic-stricken and out of breath, Deanna gave the cab driver the address of the hospital. She lay her head back against the seat and closed her eyes. She could hear her heart pounding in her ears. All she wanted was to get away, to put as many miles between herself and the airport as she could. There was a momentary feeling of madness, of being swept along by a wave, of having walked into someone else's bedroom and found him undressed, of having discovered what she had never been meant to see. But had she? Was it truly that? What if it was only a woman with whom he had shared the ride on the plane? What if her assumptions were crazy, her conclusions insane? No, there was more to it than that. She had known it the moment she had seen them. In her heart of hearts, she had simply known. But who was she? And how long had it been happening? A week? A month? A year? Was that what had happened this summer or was it something more? Much, much more . . . ?

"*Voilà*, Madame." The driver turned to her with a backward glance at his meter. Deanna could barely hear. Her mind was running in fourteen directions at once. During the whole agonizing ride from the airport she hadn't thought even once of Ben. It didn't occur to her that she had done the same, all she knew was that she had seen her husband with another woman, and she still cared. Very much. She was blinded by the surprise and the pain.

"Madame?" The driver stared at her as she looked again at the meter, glassy-eyed, vague.

"*Je m'excuse*." She quickly handed him the money and got out, looking around. She was back at the hospital, but how had she gotten there? When had she told him that address? She had planned to go back to the apartment to collect her wits, but instead she had come here. It was just as well. Marc would be going home to drop off his things and see his mother, and then would finally come to Pilar. Deanna had bought a little more time. She was not yet ready to see him. Every time she thought of him, standing there, she saw the pretty young head leaning close to his, her hand on his arm, their eyes linked as he slipped an arm around her shoulders. And she looked so damn young. Deanna's eyes filled with tears as she pushed her way through the heavy glass doors and back into the hospital lobby. She took a deep breath. It already had a familiar smell. Without thinking, she felt her hand push the elevator button for the fourth floor. She had become a robot, an automated body without a mind: she could feel herself functioning, but she couldn't understand it. All she could think of was that face, next to Marc's. And he had looked so happy, so young. . . .

"You'll be all right?" Marc looked at her with tired eyes as he picked up his coat. Chantal was lying on the bed.

"I will be fine. You have enough to think about without worrying about me." But she knew that he hated it when she was tired. The doctor had warned him after her brush with death that she mustn't wear herself out. Ever since, Marc had been treating her like an overprotective papa with a delicate child. He wanted her to get lots of rest, eat well, and take care of herself so that the diabetes would never get out of hand and the dire possibilities the doctor had warned them of would never occur. "Will *you* be all right?" She held her arms out to him. She hated to see him go, hated to know how little she could do for him. But she knew that she couldn't go to the hospital with him. Deanna would be there. It was one thing to insist upon being taken to Cap d'Antibes, to make a stand when everything was well, but it would have been madness for her to go with him now. This wasn't the time. Chantal understood that. Her timing had always been excellent. "Will you call me and tell me how she is?" There was real concern in her eyes, and Marc was instantly grateful.

"As soon as I know anything. I promise. And darling. . . ." He sat down and held her close. "Thank you. I—I couldn't have made the trip without you. This has been the most difficult night of my life."

"She'll be all right, Marc-Edouard. I promise you." He held her very tightly. When he pulled away, he wiped his eyes and cleared his throat.

"*J'espère.*" I hope.

"*Oui, oui. Je le sais.*"

But how could she know it? How did she know? And what if she were wrong?

"I'll be back later for my bag."

"You'll wake me if I'm asleep?" It was a kittenish smile that lurked in her eyes, and he laughed.

"*On verra.*" But he had already left her, his mind was somewhere else. They had only gotten in from the airport ten minutes before, but already he felt as though he had lingered too long. He slipped into his raincoat.

"Marc-Edouard!" He stopped and turned at the sound of her voice. He was already at the door.

"*N'oublie pas que je t'aime. . . .*" Don't forget that I love you.

"*Moi aussi!*" The door closed soundlessly on his words.

He drove Chantal's tiny Renault to the hospital and parked down the street. He should have taken a taxi, but he didn't want to waste another moment. He wanted to be there. At her side. Seeing what had happened. Trying to understand. Coming back on the flight, he had run it over and over and over in his mind. The why and the how and the when, none of it making any sense. There were moments when it seemed as though nothing had happened, as though they were just going back to Paris as always after his business meetings in Greece . . . and then suddenly it would all come crystal clear again and he would remember Pilar. He would never have been able to keep himself together on the flight back had it not been for Chantal.

The lobby was quiet. Dominique had already given him Pilar's room number when they spoke on the phone, and he himself had succeeded in getting through to Dr. Kirschmann before he left Athens. It had been too soon to know anything. The damage to her skull was considerable, to her legs perhaps permanent; her spleen had been ruptured, one kidney bruised. She was, all in all, a very sick girl.

Marc felt his chest go tight as he entered the elevator and pressed four. His mind was a blank as the elevator ascended. Then, with a whir, the doors opened and he stepped out. He felt lost for a moment, powerless and afraid, as he glanced around him, wondering where to find his child. He saw the head nurse at the desk and somberly approached her.

"Pilar Duras?" The nurse began to give him directions to the room. He held up a hand. "*D'abord*, how is she?"

"Critical, monsieur." The nurse's eyes were grave.

"But any better than she has been?" In answer: only a shake of the head. "And Dr. Kirschmann? He's here?"

"He was and he has left again. He'll be back in a while. He's keeping a very close watch on the situation. She is completely monitored. . . . We're doing all that we can."

This time Marc only nodded. He cleared his throat and dabbed at his eyes with his handkerchief as he marched purposefully down the hall. He had to pull himself together, show Pilar that everything would be all right, he would make her better, he would give her his strength. Chantal was forgotten, all that he had in his mind was his little girl.

The door was ajar, and he glanced inside. The room seemed to be filled with machines. There were two nurses, one in a sterile, green operating-room suit and the other in white. Their eyes searched his face. Soundlessly, he stepped inside.

"I am her father." The whispered words had a ring of authority, and they both nodded as his eyes swept the room. He instantly found her, dwarfed by the bed and the tubes and the monitors that jumped with precision at her every breath. For a moment he

felt a chill seize him as he looked at her face. She was a very pale
gray and she looked like no one he knew, until he stepped closer
and recognized the distorted features of his child. The tubes and
the pain and the bandages had almost totally changed her, but it
was his Pilar. He watched her for a long moment as she lay there
with her eyes closed, and on silent feet he came nearer and ever so
delicately reached out and touched her hand. The hand stirred
only slightly. She opened her eyes. But there was no smile, and
only the faintest look of recognition.

"Pilar, *ma chérie, c'est Papa.*" He had to fight back tears. He
said nothing more, he only stood there, staring at her, holding her
hand, and watching until once again she closed the brilliant blue
eyes. He felt as though all the air in the room had been sucked
away, it was so difficult to think and see and breathe. How could
this happen? How? And to his child? He felt his knees tremble,
and for a moment he thought he would be sick, but he went on
standing, watching, and touching the pale little hand. Even her
nails were a strange mottled color, she was barely getting enough
air. But he stood there, and he stood there, never moving, never
speaking, only watching his child.

Silently, from her seat in the corner, Deanna watched him. She
had said nothing when he entered the room, and he hadn't seen
her, concealed as she was by the mammoth machines.

It was almost twenty minutes later when at last he found the
familiar face and those eyes . . . watching him with a look of despair. He looked surprised when he saw her, as though he didn't
understand. Why had she said nothing? Why did she just sit
there? When had she come? Or was it simply that she was in
shock? She looked ravaged, almost as pale as Pilar.

"Deanna. . . ." It was the merest whisper.

Her eyes never left his face. "Hello, Marc."

He nodded and let his gaze drift back to Pilar. "When did you
get here?"

"At five o'clock."

"You've been here all night?"

"Yes."

"Any change?"

There was silence. Marc looked at her again, the question repeated in his eyes.

"She seems to be a little worse. I went out for a little while, earlier . . . I had to . . . I went to your mother's house to drop off my bag. I was only gone for about two hours, and . . . and when I came back, she seemed to be having a great deal of trouble breathing. Kirschmann was here then. He said that if she's not better in a few hours, they'll want to operate again." She sighed and lowered her eyes. It was as though she had lost them both in those two hours. Pilar and Marc.

"I just got in."

Liar. You didn't. You got in two hours ago. Where did you go? But Deanna said nothing at all.

They stayed that way for almost an hour, until finally the nurse asked them to step outside, just for a few minutes; there were some dressings that had to be changed. Slowly Deanna stood up and left the room. Marc had hung back for a moment, reluctant to leave his child. Deanna's mind wandered back to the scene at the airport. It was suddenly all so strange. She hadn't seen him in two months, yet they had barely said hello. She couldn't play the game of the happy reunion. Suddenly it was too late. But he wasn't playing it either, or perhaps he was just too distraught over Pilar.

She wandered down the hall, solemnly, her head bowed, thinking of bits of prayers she had known as a child. She had no time now to waste on Marc; all her energies had to be spent on Pilar. She heard his steps just behind her, but she didn't turn; she merely kept walking, foot after foot after foot, down the hall until she reached the end, and stood staring blankly out a window with only a view of a nearby wall. She could see him standing behind her as she gazed at the reflection in the glass.

"Deanna, can I help?" He sounded tired, subdued. She shook her head slowly. "I don't know what to say." His voice caught as he began to cry. "I was wrong to give her the . . . to. . . ."

"It doesn't matter now. You did it. It's done. It could have happened in any of ten thousand ways. She had an accident, Marc. What difference does it make now whose fault the accident was, who gave her the motorcycle, who. . . ." Deanna's own voice was shaky.

"*Mon Dieu*. . . ." She watched him drop his face into his hands and then she saw him straighten and heard him take a deep breath. "My God, if only she'll come out of it all right. What if she can't walk?"

"Then we'll teach her to live the best way she can. That's what we owe her now. Our love, our help, our support, in whatever she has to face. . . ." *If only we get that chance.* For the first time in almost twenty years, Deanna felt a hideous wave of terror. . . . *What if?*

Deanna felt his hands on her shoulders, then he turned her slowly around. His eyes were the eyes of Pilar, and his face was that of a very old, tired man.

"Will you ever forgive me?"

"For what?" Her voice was distant and cold.

"For this. For what I've done to our child. For not listening to you when I should have. For—"

"I came to pick you up at the airport tonight, Marc."

Something in her eyes told him that she had died, and he felt something inside him freeze. "You must have just missed me." But there was a question in his voice. He searched her face.

"No. I left. I . . . it explained a great deal to me, Marc. I should have known. A long time ago. But I didn't." She smiled a tiny smile, then shrugged. "I suppose I've been a fool. And may I congratulate you. She looks not only pretty, but young." There was bitterness as well as sorrow in her voice.

"Deanna," the hands on her shoulders tightened, "you're coming to some very strange conclusions. I don't think you understand." But it all sounded lame. He was too tired and upset to come up with a worthwhile story. He felt his life coming down around his ears. "It was a nerve-racking flight, and this has been an incredible day, you know that yourself. The young lady and I began to talk and really—"

"Marc, stop. I don't want to hear it." She simply knew. That was all. And she didn't want reassurances in the form of lies. "Please. Not tonight."

"Deanna. . . ." But he couldn't go on. Another time he might have been able to, but not then. He simply couldn't concoct an appropriate tale. "Please." He turned away then; he couldn't look at the pain in her eyes. "It really isn't what you think." But he hated himself for the words. It was what she thought, every bit of it. And now he felt traitorous, denying Chantal. Whichever way he turned, he was damned now. "It isn't."

"It is, Marc. It was as clear as day. Nothing you could tell me now would change that. Nothing would take away what I saw, what I felt, what I knew." It had been like an arrow, straight to her heart. "You must have thought me very stupid for all these years."

"What makes you think it has been years?" *Dammit,* how did she know?

"The way you moved together, the way you walked, the way she looked at you. It's difficult to achieve that kind of ease in a very short time. You looked more married with her than you ever did with me." But suddenly she wondered. Hadn't she looked just as married with Ben? And in a very short time. Still, as she had ridden back from the airport that evening, she had known—the absences, the distance, the constant trips, the phone number in Paris that appeared too often on their bill, the few odd stories that had never quite fit. And tonight, the look in his eyes. If it hadn't been that girl, it had been someone. For years. She was sure.

"What do you want me to say?" He faced her again.

"Nothing. There is nothing left to say."

"Are you telling me it's over? That you'd leave me because you saw me at the airport with a girl? But that's insane. Deanna, you're mad."

"Am I? Are we so happy together? Do you enjoy my company, Marc? Do you long to come home when you're away? Or is it that we have a deep and meaningful relationship, that we respect each other's needs and virtues and feelings? Maybe it's that we're so blissfully happy with each other, after all these years—"

"Maybe it's that I still love you." As he said it, his eyes filled with tears, and she turned her head.

"It doesn't matter if you do." It was too late now. They had each gone their separate ways.

"What are you saying, Deanna?" He was suddenly gray.

"I'm not entirely sure. First let's get through this with Pilar. After that we can talk about us."

"We'll make it. I know we will." He looked at her with determination, and she felt fatigue wash over her like a wave of cement.

"What makes you think so? Why should we make it?"

"Because I want to." But he didn't sound totally sure.

"Really? Why? Because you like having a wife as well as a mistress? I can hardly blame you. That must be a very cozy arrange-

ment. Where does she live, Marc? Over here? That must work out
perfectly." And that was why he hadn't wanted her to join him on
the trip to Greece.

"Deanna, stop it!" He reached out and grabbed her arm, but
she pulled away.

"Leave me alone." For the first time in her life, she hated him,
what he was, what he did to her, and all that he didn't understand, and for one painful, blinding moment she found herself
longing for Ben. But was Marc really so bad? Was she any
different, any better? Her mind was in a whirl. "I don't want to
discuss this with you tonight. We have enough on our minds. We
can discuss it when Pilar is out of the woods."

He nodded, relieved. He needed time. He had to think. He'd
find the right words to say. He would set things right.

Almost at that instant the nurse beckoned to them both from
down the hall, and their own problems were forgotten as they hurried toward her.

"Is there any change?" Marc was the first to ask.

"No. But she's awake. And she's asking for both of you. Why
don't you talk to her a little, but be careful not to wear her out.
She needs the little strength that she has."

Deanna noticed a subtle change in Pilar as they entered the
room. Her color was no better, but her eyes seemed more alive.
They seemed to wander nervously from one face to another, looking for someone, searching, darting here and there.

"Hello, sweetheart. We're right here. Papa's here now too."
Deanna stood very close to her and ever so gently stroked her
hand. When she closed her eyes, she could imagine that Pilar was
still a very small child.

"That . . . feels . . . nice. . . ." Pilar's gaze drifted to her father and she tried to smile, but her breathing was labored and she
closed her eyes from time to time. "Hi, Papa. . . . How . . . was
. . . Greece?" She seemed much more aware of current events
than she had been earlier, and suddenly she also seemed more rest-
less. "I'm . . . thirsty. . . ."

Deanna glanced at the nurse, who shook her head and made a
sign with her finger: "No."

"Water?"

"In a little while, sweetheart." Deanna went on talking in a
soothing voice while Marc stood near her, agonized. He seemed to

have lost his power to speak, and Deanna could see from his full eyes and trembling lip that he was waging a constant battle with tears.

"*Ça va?*" At last he had spoken, and again Pilar tried to smile. She nodded gently. "*Ça va.*" But how could anything be O.K. in the condition that she was in? Then, as though she understood what he was going through, she looked pointedly at him and fought to find the words. "I . . . was going . . . much too fast. . . . My fault, Papa . . . not yours. . . ." She closed her eyes and squeezed Deanna's hand. "I'm sorry."

The tears now ran freely down Marc's face. Quietly he turned away. Pilar's eyes remained closed.

"Don't worry, darling. It doesn't matter whose fault. But your mother was right." He glanced at Deanna.

"Mommy. . . ?" Her voice seemed to be growing weaker.

"Shh. Don't talk. . . ."

"Remember the little playhouse I used to have . . . in the garden? I keep dreaming . . . of that . . . and my little dog. Augustin."

He had been a funny little terrier, Deanna remembered, who had been replaced by a pug, and then a cat, and then a bird, until finally there were no more pets. Marc-Edouard did not like animals in his house.

"Where . . . did you send . . . Augustin?" They had given him to a family in the country.

"He went to the country. I think he was very happy." Deanna pattered on, but now her eyes sought Marc's. What did this mean? Was she better or worse? She was reminded suddenly of the tiny baby boy who had moved so much in her arms in the few hours before he died. Philippe-Edouard. Was this the same, or was this a sign that she was improving? Neither of them knew.

"Mommy? . . . could I have . . . Augustin back? . . . You ask Papa. . . ." It was the voice of the child now. Deanna closed her eyes and took a quick breath.

"I'll talk to Papa."

Marc's eyes were suddenly filled with fear. He looked at Pilar, and then Deanna. "We'll get you a dog, *chérie*. . . . You'll see. A wonderful little dog with floppy ears and a very waggly tail." He was looking for anything he could find in his head, just to find the words to put in his mouth.

"But I want . . . Augustin." The voice was plaintive now, and the nurse signaled them away. Pilar had drifted off again and she didn't notice them leaving the room.

This time they paced up and down the hall, at first saying nothing. Without thinking, Deanna reached for Marc's hand. "When the hell is Kirschmann coming back?"

"They said soon. Do you think she's worse?"

Deanna nodded. "She seems nervous, fidgety, anxious."

"But she's talking. That might be a hopeful sign."

"Maybe it is," Deanna said. But there was terror in both their hearts. As they paced the hall, his arm slipped around her shoulders, and she didn't fight him away. Suddenly she needed him there, as he needed her. He was the only person who understood, who could share what she felt, who *knew*.

"Marc?" He looked at her with anguished eyes, but she only shook her head. Tears poured down her face, and silently he took her into his arms. He had nothing to say, no words of comfort, only his tears to add to hers.

They walked the long hall again, end to end, seven or eight more times, and finally sat down on two straight-backed chairs. Deanna's eyes were glazed with fatigue. She stared at the hem of her much creased cream skirt.

"Do you remember when she was five and we got her that dog?" She smiled to herself as she remembered. They had hidden the little puppy in a boot and left him in Pilar's closet, ordering her to immediately open the door and pick up her clothes. And there he had been, peeking out of the boot. Pilar had squealed with delight.

Marc smiled to himself too, with the memory. "I will always remember her face."

"So will I." Deanna looked up at him, smiling through her tears and reached for his handkerchief to blow her nose. It was strange. Only an hour before they'd been fighting and she'd been hinting at divorce. But it didn't matter now. Their marriage was no longer what mattered, only their child. Whatever pain had passed between them, they still shared Pilar. At that precise moment Marc was the only person who had any idea what she felt, and she was the only living soul who shared his terror with him. It was as if they held each other very tightly and didn't let go, and kept moving, and kept talking and hoping and praying . . . then

Pilar would still be there, she couldn't die. Deanna looked up at Marc again, and he patted her hand.

"Try to relax."

She sighed again and put a hand over her eyes, but before she could speak, the nurse was at their side.

"Doctor Kirschmann would like to see you. He's in with her now."

They leaped to their feet and almost ran to the room, where he stood at the foot of the bed, alternately watching the girl and the machines. It seemed hours before they walked out to the hall.

"*Docteur?*" Marc was the first to speak.

He looked grieved. "I want to give her a little more time. If things aren't looking better in an hour, we'll take her back to the operating room and see what we can do."

"What do you think?" Marc wanted words from him, promises, guarantees.

"I don't know. She's holding on. I can't tell you more than that." He could have told them how good her chances were, but they weren't, so he didn't volunteer the odds. "Do you want to sit with her for a while?"

"Yes." Deanna spoke first and reclaimed her post near Pilar's head. Marc joined her.

They stood there like that for almost an hour, while Pilar slept, making strange sounds, now and then stirring, and seeming to fight for breath. Marc rested one hand on the bed, feeling the little frail body near him, his eyes never leaving her face. Deanna held her hand and waited. For something . . . for hope. The hour was almost over when at last she woke.

"Thirsty. . . ."

"In a little while, darling." Deanna's words were a gentle whisper caressed by a smile. She touched the girl's forehead with an infinitely light hand. "In a while, my love. Now sleep. Mommy and Papa are here, darling. Sleep . . . you're going to feel so much better, very soon."

And then Pilar smiled. It was a real smile, despite the tubes, and it tore at Marc's and Deanna's hearts.

"I feel . . . better . . . now."

"I'm glad, *chérie*. And you'll feel much better tomorrow. Mommy is right." Marc's voice was as soft as a summer breeze. Once again Pilar smiled and closed her eyes.

It was only a moment later when the doctor stepped back in and nodded for them to go out.

He whispered to them as they left. "We'll prepare her for surgery now. You can step back in in just a moment." He turned, and they went outside. Deanna felt breathless now too, as though like Pilar she had to fight for air. The hallway was at the same time too cold and too stuffy, and she had to hold onto Marc for support. It was four o'clock in the morning, and neither of them had slept in two days.

"She said she felt better." Marc held out the slim hope and Deanna nodded. "I thought her color was a little better too."

Deanna was about to say something but Dr. Kirschmann reappeared, coming down the length of the hall.

"*Merde*. He ought to be spending his time with Pilar, dammit. Not looking for us." Marc began to walk toward him, but Deanna stopped. She already knew and clutched Marc's arm. She knew, and she could walk no further. The world had just ended. Pilar was dead.

17

The sun was just coming up as they left the hospital. It had taken more than an hour to sign the papers and make the arrangements. Marc had decided that he wanted the funeral held in France. Deanna didn't care. One of her babies was buried in California, the other in France. It didn't matter to her now. And she suspected that Pilar herself would have preferred it. Doctor Kirschmann had been sympathetic and kind. There had been nothing for him to do. She had been much too far gone when they brought her in from the South of France. The blow to her head had been too severe, and he marveled only that she hadn't died in the moments after the accident. "Ahh . . . motorcycles!" he said as Marc visibly cringed.

They had been offered coffee, which they had refused, and finally they were through. Marc took her arm and guided her gently toward the street. She felt as though her brain had ceased to function within the last hour. She couldn't think, couldn't move, couldn't even feel. She had gone through all the formalities mechanically, but she felt as though she too had died.

Marc walked her to the little blue Renault and unlocked the door.

"Whose car is this?" It was a strange question to ask on a morning like that, but her eyes stared at him almost blindly as she spoke.

"It doesn't matter, get in. Let's go home." He had never felt so tired, or so lost, or alone. All his hopes had been dashed, all his joys, all his dreams. It didn't even matter to him now that he had Deanna, and Chantal. He had lost Pilar. The tears rolled slowly down his face again as he started the car, and this time he let them flow unchecked. He didn't care.

In her seat Deanna put her head back and closed her eyes, feeling a knot in her chest and a lump in her throat. There was a lifetime of crying lodged there, but for the moment it wouldn't come out.

They drove slowly through Paris, as street cleaners swept and the sun shone too brightly on the pavement. It should have been a day of rain and heavy mist, but it wasn't, and the bright sun made the horror seem a lie. How could she be gone on a day like this? But she was . . . she was—gone. The thought kept running through Marc-Edouard's head—gone—while Deanna stared unseeingly out of the window.

The maid was already at the door when they reached the Duras apartment, still draped in her bathrobe. She had heard the elevator and come running to know. Marc-Edouard's face said it all. Silently she began to cry.

"Shall I wake Madame?"

Marc shook his head. There was no point waking her now. The bad news could wait.

"Some coffee, monsieur?"

This time he nodded and softly closed the door as Deanna stood by, feeling lost. He looked at her for a moment, wiped his eyes, and held out a hand. Without saying more, she took it, and they walked slowly to their room.

The shades were drawn, the shutters were closed, the bed was turned down, but somehow Deanna did not want to go to bed.

She couldn't face it, couldn't bear lying there and thinking, couldn't bear knowing that Pilar was dead. Marc-Edouard sank into a chair and put his face in his hands. Slowly the sobs came again. Deanna went to him and held his shoulders in her hands, but there was nothing more she could do. At last he cried himself out, and she helped him to the bed.

"You should try to sleep." She whispered it to him as she had to Pilar.

"And you?" His voice was hoarse when he spoke.

"I will. Later. Didn't you bring a bag?" She looked around the room in surprise. None of his things was there.

"I'll get it later." He closed his eyes. Picking up his bag meant seeing Chantal. He would have to tell her about Pilar. As he would have to tell his mother. And their friends. He couldn't bear it. Telling them would make it real. The tears seeped out of the corners of his eyes again. Finally, he drifted to sleep.

Only Deanna drank the coffee when it came. She took her cup to the salon, where she sat alone, looking out over the rooftops of Paris, thinking of her child. She felt peaceful as she sat there, thinking, looking at the gilt-edged morning sky. Pilar had been so many things, and not often easy in recent years, but eventually she would have grown up. They would have been friends. . . . *Would have been.* It was hard to imagine. She felt as though Pilar were right there, nearby, and in no way lost. It was inconceivable to her that they would no longer talk, or laugh, or argue, that Pilar would no longer fling that long golden hair like a mane, or flash those blue eyes to get whatever she might want, that Deanna's slippers would no longer be borrowed, her lipstick wouldn't be gone, her favorite robe wouldn't disappear along with her best coat. . . . As she thought of it, the tears finally came in great waves. She knew, finally, that Pilar was no more.

"Deanna?" It was the old woman, standing in the center of the room, looking like a statue in an icy-blue robe. "Pilar?"

Deanna shook her head and closed her eyes. Madame Duras steadied herself on a chair.

"Oh, my God. Oh, *bon Dieu . . . bon Dieu.*" And then, looking around, tears rolling down her cheeks: "Where is Marc?"

"Asleep, I think. In bed." Her mother-in-law nodded and silently left the room. There was nothing she could say, but

Deanna hated her once more for not even trying. It was her loss too, but she owed Deanna the words at least.

On tiptoe Deanna walked back to their room. She was afraid to wake Marc and she opened the door very quietly. He was still sleeping, snoring softly. This time, as she watched him, he no longer looked young. His whole face seemed to sag with grief and even in sleep Deanna could see that he wasn't at peace.

She sat for a time, watching him, wondering what would happen, what they would do. A great deal had changed in a day. Pilar. The woman she had seen him with at the airport. She realized now that was probably where he had gotten the car and where he had left his bag. She wanted to hate him for it, but now she didn't care. She suddenly realized she had to call Ben. A glance at Marc's watch told her that it was past eight-thirty. It would be midnight in San Francisco. He might still be up, and she had to call him now, while she could.

She ran a hand over her hair, put her jacket on again, and grabbed her handbag. She would make the call half a block away at the post office where Parisian residents without telephones made their calls. She didn't want his number on her mother-in-law's bill.

She felt numb as she rode downstairs in the tiny elevator and then walked the half block to the *poste*. She could not move her feet quickly and she couldn't slow her steps either; she just kept moving at the same pace, like a machine, until she reached the post office phone booth and closed the door.

The number rang only twice, and the connection had been rapidly made. She felt herself tremble as she waited, and then she heard his voice. He sounded sleepy, and she realized then that he had already been in bed.

"Ben?"

"Deanna? Darling, are you all right?"

"I. . . ." And then the words stopped. She couldn't say more.

"Deanna?"

She was trembling violently, still unable to speak.

"Oh, darling . . . is it . . . ? How bad is she? I've been thinking of you every minute, ever since you left." The only sound Deanna made in answer was a short convulsed sob. "Deanna! Please, sweetheart, try to calm down and talk to me." But sud-

denly a ripple of fear raced up his back. "My God, is she . . .
Deanna?" His voice was suddenly very soft.

"Oh, Ben, she died this morning." For another endless moment
she couldn't speak after she said the words.

"Oh, God, no. Darling, are you alone? Where are you?"

"In the post office."

"Oh, for God's sake, what are you doing there?"

"I wanted to call you."

"Did . . . is he in Paris too?"

"Yes." She tried to catch her breath again. "He got here last
night."

"I'm so sorry. For both of you."

She sobbed again. With Ben she could let herself go, she could
reach out to him and show him how badly she needed him. With
Marc she always kept up a front. She had to live what he expected, be what he thought she should be.

"Do you want me to come over? I could take the first plane out
in the morning."

And do what? she wondered. It was too late for Pilar. "I'd love
you to, but it doesn't make much sense. I'll be home in a couple
of days."

"Are you sure? I don't want to be a problem, but I'll come over
right away if it'll help. Would it?"

"Very much." She smiled through her tears. "But it's better not
to."

"And . . . everything else?" He tried not to sound concerned or
upset.

"I don't know. We'll have to talk."

He knew she was talking about Marc. "Well, don't worry about
all that now. Just get through this, and then we can worry about
the rest. Is it . . . are you going to have it here?"

"The funeral?" She wanted to die when she said the word. Her
hand shook terribly. She tightened her grip on the phone. "No,
Marc wants it here. It doesn't matter. I think Pilar probably
would have preferred it too. In any case I'll be home in two or
three days."

"I wish I could spare you all that."

"It . . ." but she couldn't go on for a moment ". . . doesn't
matter. I'll be all right." But would she? She wasn't so sure. She
had never felt this shaky in her life.

"Well, remember, if you need me I'll come. I won't go any-where for the next few days without leaving a number, so you can always reach me. O.K.?"

"O.K." She tried to smile as she said it, but the effort made her cry more. "Can you . . . could you call . . ."

"Kim?"

"Yes." It was a sad little croak.

"I'll call right away. Now I want you to go home and get some rest. Darling, you can't keep pushing. You have to rest. Go get some sleep. And as soon as you come home, we'll go to Carmel. No matter what. I don't care what happens after that, but you're coming to Carmel with me. We'll walk on the beach, and we'll be together."

She was sobbing violently now. They would never be together again. She'd never walk on that beach again, or any other. She would be trapped in this nightmare forever, alone.

"Deanna, listen to me," Ben was saying. "Will you think of Carmel through all this, and try to remember that I love you?"

She nodded sadly, still unable to get out the words.

"My love, I'm with you every moment. Be strong, my darling. I love you."

"I love you too." But her voice was only a whisper as she hung up the phone, then walked to the counter and paid the woman at the desk for the phone call—and passed out cold on the floor.

18

"Where on earth have you been?" Marc was sitting in the living room looking rumpled and haggard when she returned. "You were gone for hours." It was an accusation. He was staring at her, red-eyed, over a cup of coffee. She looked scarcely better, in fact considerably worse. "Where were you?"

"I went for a walk. I'm sorry. I needed some air." She put her handbag down on a chair. "How is your mother?"

"You can imagine. I called the doctor half an hour ago, and he gave her a shot. She probably won't wake up until noon."

For a moment Deanna envied her. What an easy way out. She didn't voice the thought. Instead, she asked, "And you?"

"We have a lot to do today." He looked at her mournfully and then noticed the smudges on her skirt. "What happened? Did you fall?"

She nodded and looked away. "I must have been tired. I stumbled. It's nothing."

He came to her then and put an arm around her. "You should really go to bed."

"I will. But what about the arrangements?"

"I'll take care of it. You don't have to do anything."

"But I want to. . . ." She suddenly felt out of control again, as though she never had any say.

"No. I want you to get some sleep." He led her to the bedroom and sat her on the bed. "Shall I call the doctor for you?" She shook her head, then lay down, looking up at him with heartbroken eyes that tore at him. "Deanna . . ."

"What about your friend?"

He stood up and turned away. "Never mind that."

"Maybe now isn't the time, but sooner or later we'll have to talk about it."

"Perhaps not."

"What does that mean?" She stared at him very hard. He turned to face her.

"It means that it's not your affair. And that I will do my best to settle it."

"Permanently?"

He seemed to hesitate a long time, and then he quietly nodded, his eyes never leaving hers. "Yes."

Chantal heard his key turn in the lock as she climbed out of the shower. She hadn't dared call the house on the rue François Premier, and her last anonymous call to the hospital had brought only the information that Pilar was the same. She had intended to call again as soon as she had coffee, but Marc-Edouard arrived first, looking as though he hadn't slept all night. Chantal looked up and smiled from the bathroom doorway. The pale yellow towel was drying her leg.

"*Bonjour, mon chéri.* How's Pilar?" She stood up with a serious expression, holding the towel in one hand. There was something in his eyes that suddenly frightened her. He closed them and covered them for a moment with one hand. It seemed a very long time before he looked at her again.

"She—she's gone. At four o'clock this morning." He sat down heavily in a chair in the living room, and Chantal came to him quickly, pulling a pale pink robe off a hook on the bathroom wall.

"Oh, Marc-Edouard . . . oh, darling, I'm so sorry." She knelt beside him and pulled him gently into her arms, encircling his shoulders and holding him tight like a child. "*Oh, mon pauvre chéri*, Marc-Edouard. *Quelle horreur. . . .*"

This time he didn't cry, he only sat with his eyes closed, feeling relieved to be there.

She wanted to ask him if something else was wrong. It was an insanely stupid question, given what had happened that morning, but he seemed odd to her, different, strange. Perhaps it was only exhaustion and the shock. She let go of him only long enough to pour him a cup of coffee, and then sat down again at his feet, her body curled on the white rug, the pink bathrobe concealing only the essentials and leaving long silky legs bare. He was staring at her as she lit a cigarette. "Is there anything I can do?"

He shook his head. "Chantal, Deanna saw us last night. She came to the airport to pick me up, and she saw us both get off the plane. And she knew. Everything. Women are uncanny that way. She said she knew by the way we moved that we had known each other for a long time."

"She must be a very intelligent woman." Chantal studied him, wondering what he would say next.

"She is, in her own quiet way."

"And? What did she say?"

"Not too much. Yet. Too much has been happening, but she's an American. She doesn't take this kind of thing well. None of them do. They believe in eternal fidelity, the perfect marriage, husbands who wash the dishes, children who wash the car, and everyone goes to church together on Sunday and lives happily ever after until they're all a hundred and nine." He sounded bitter and tired.

"And you? Do you believe that?"

"It's a nice dream anyway. But not very real. You know that as well as I do."

"*Alors*, what do we do? Or, more exactly, what do you do?" She didn't want to ask, "her or me," but it amounted to that and they both knew it.

"It's too soon to know, Chantal. Look at what has just happened. And she is in terrible condition; it's all bottled up inside."

"It's still fresh."

He nodded agreement and looked away. He had come here to say good-bye to Chantal, to end it, to explain that he couldn't do this to Deanna—they had just lost their only child. But as he looked at her, as he sat next to her, all he wanted was to reach out and pull her into his arms, to run his hands over her body, to hold her close, now and forever, again and again. How could he let go of what he loved and needed so much?

"What are you thinking about, Marc-Edouard?" She could see the look of torment on his face.

"About you." He said it very softly, looking down at his hands.

"In what way?"

"I was thinking," he looked up into her eyes again, "that I love you, and that right now I want more than anything to make love to you."

She sat watching him for a long moment, then she stood up and held out a hand. He took it and followed her silently into the bedroom. She smiled as he slipped the pink robe off her shoulders.

"Chantal, you will never know how much I love you."

For the next two hours he showed her in every way he knew how.

19

The funeral was brief and formal and agonizing. Deanna wore a plain black woolen dress and a little black hat with a veil. Marc's mother was dressed all in black with black stockings. Marc himself wore a dark suit and black tie. It was all done in the most formal of French traditions in a pretty little church in the *seizième arrondissement,* and the "Ave Maria" was sung by the parish-school choir. It was heartbreaking, as the children's voices soared over the notes, and Deanna desperately tried not to hear. But there was no avoiding any of it. Marc had done it all *à la française* —the service, the music, the eulogy, the little country cemetery with yet another priest, and then the gathering of friends and relatives at the house. It was an all-day enterprise, with endless rounds of handshaking and regrets, explanations and shared sorrows. To some it was undoubtedly a relief to mourn that way, to Deanna it was not. Once more she felt that Pilar had been stolen from her, only now it really didn't matter anymore. This was the very last time. She even called Ben collect from the house.

"I'm sorry. I won't stay on long. I just needed to talk to you. I'm at the house."

"Are you holding up?"

"I don't know. I think I'm numb. It's all like a circus. I even had to fight them about an open coffin. Thank God, at least that battle I won."

He didn't like the sound of her voice. She sounded nervous, tired, and strained. But it was hardly surprising under the circumstances. "When are you coming back?"

"Sometime in the next two days, I hope. But I'm not sure. We'll discuss it tonight."

"Just send me a wire when you know."

She heaved a small sigh. "I will. I guess I'd better get back to the ghoulish festivities now."

"I love you, Deanna."

"So do I." She was afraid to say the words, lest someone walk into the room, but she knew he'd understand.

She went back to the fifty or sixty guests who were milling around her mother-in-law's rooms, chatting, gossiping, discussing Pilar, consoling Marc. Deanna had never felt as much a stranger as now. It seemed hours since she had seen Marc. He found her at last in the kitchen, staring out a window, at a wall.

"Deanna? What are you doing out here?"

"Nothing." Her big sorrowful eyes looked into his. He was actually looking better. And day by day she seemed to look worse. She wasn't feeling well either, but she hadn't mentioned that to Marc, or the fact that she had fainted twice in the past four days. "I'm just out here catching my breath."

"I'm sorry it's been such a long day. My mother wouldn't have understood if we'd done it differently."

"I know. I understand."

Suddenly, looking at him, she realized that he understood too, and that he could see what a toll it was taking on her. "Marc, when are we going home?"

"To San Francisco?" he asked. She nodded. "I don't know. I haven't given it any thought. Are you in a hurry?"

"I just want to get back. It's . . . harder for me here."

"*Bon.* But I have work I must complete here. I need at least another two weeks."

Oh, God, no. She couldn't survive two more weeks there under her mother-in-law's roof—and without Ben. "There's no reason why I should stay, is there?"

"What do you mean? You want to go home alone?" He looked distressed. "I don't want you to do that. I want you to go home with me." He had already thought about it. It would be too hard for her to face the house alone: Pilar's room, all her things. He didn't want that. She'd have to wait for him.

"I can't wait two weeks." She looked frantic at the idea, and he noticed again how exhausted and overwrought she was.

"Let's just see."

"Marc, I have to go home." Her voice trembled as it rose.

"All right. But first, would you do something for me?"

"What?" She looked at him strangely. What did he want? All she wanted was to get away.

"Will you go away with me for two days? Anywhere, for a weekend. Someplace quiet, where we both can rest. We need to talk. We haven't been able to here, and I don't want you to go back until we do talk. Quietly. Alone. Will you do that for me?"

She waited for a long moment and looked at him. "I don't know."

"Please. It's all I ask. Only that. Two days, and then you can go."

She turned away to stare out at the rooftops again. She was thinking of Ben and Carmel. But she had no right to rush home to him just to make herself feel better. She owed something to their marriage, even if it was only two days. She turned to look at Marc and slowly nodded. "All right. I'll go."

20

"*Merde alors!* What do you expect of me? My daughter dies three days ago, and you want me to announce to Deanna that I want a divorce? Doesn't that seem a little hasty to you, Chantal? And has it occurred to you that you're taking unfair advantage of this situation?" He felt torn between two women, two worlds. Once again he felt an odd kind of pressure from Chantal, a kind of emotional blackmail that told him there would be tragedy if Chantal suffered a loss. Both women wanted him to make a choice, a painful choice. He'd realized that all the more this week. Deanna seemed as though she would be only too happy to leave him right now. She had yet to forgive him for what she had seen at the airport the night of Pilar's death. But he didn't want to lose Deanna. She was his wife, he needed her, he respected her, he was used to her. And she was his last link to Pilar. Leaving Deanna would be like leaving home. But he couldn't give up Chantal either—she was his excitement, his passion, his joy. He looked at Chantal now with exasperation and ran a hand through his hair. "Can't you understand? It's too soon!"

"It's been five years. And now she knows. And maybe it isn't too soon. Maybe it's the best time right now."

"For whom? For you? Dammit, Chantal, just be a little bit patient. Let me sort things out."

"And how long will that take? Another five years, while you live there and I live here? You were supposed to go back in two weeks, and then what? What about me? I sit here waiting for two months until you return? *Et alors?* I was twenty-five when we met, now I'm nearly thirty. And then I'll be thirty-five, and thirty-seven and forty-five. Time passes quickly. Especially like this. It goes much, much too fast."

He knew that was true, but he was simply not in the mood. "Look, could we just put this away for a while? Out of simple decency, I'd like to let the woman recover from the loss of her daughter before I destroy her life." For a moment he hated Chantal. Because he did care, because he didn't want to lose her—and because that gave her the upper hand.

And she knew it. "What makes you think your leaving her would destroy her life? Maybe she has a lover."

"Deanna? Don't be ridiculous. In fact I think you're being absurd about this whole thing. I'm going away for the weekend. We have a lot of things to discuss. I'll talk to her, I'll see how things are. And in a while I'll make the right move."

"What move is that?"

He sighed imperceptibly and suddenly felt very old. It had come to this. "The one you want."

But as he hailed a cab two hours later to go back to his mother's apartment where Deanna was waiting, he found himself wondering. Why did Chantal have to pull this on him? First the arguments over Cap d'Antibes, then that terrible night he had returned to find her gone—perhaps forever—when she had stopped taking her insulin. And now this. But why? Why now? For an odd reason he did not understand, it made him want to rush back to Deanna and protect her from a world that was about to be very cruel.

They left for the country in the morning. Deanna was strangely quiet as they drove out of town. She sat lost in her own thoughts. He had wanted to take her some place neutral, where there wouldn't be a cascade of memories of Pilar. They both had enough of that to deal with at his mother's house. A friend had offered his country house, near Dreux.

He glanced over at Deanna distractedly and then shifted his concentration back to the road, but he found himself thinking of Chantal again. He had spoken to her that morning before they left:

"Will you tell her this weekend?"

"I don't know. I'll have to see. If I drive her to a nervous breakdown, it won't do any of us any good." But Chantal had sounded petulant and childish. Suddenly, after so many years of patience, she was getting out of hand. Still she had been the mainstay of his life for the past five years. He couldn't give her up. But could he so easily give up Deanna? He glanced over at her again. Her eyes were still closed and she hadn't said a word. Did he love her? He had always thought so, but after the summer with Chantal he wasn't as sure. It was impossible to know, to figure it out, to understand—and damn Chantal for pushing him now. He had promised Deanna only two days ago that he would end the relationship with Chantal, and now he had made the same promise to his mistress about Deanna.

"Is it very far?" Deanna's eyes fluttered open, but she did not move her head. She felt weighed down by the same exhaustion that had plagued her for days.

"No. It's about an hour. And it's a pretty house. I haven't stayed there since I was a boy, but it was always lovely." He smiled at her. There were circles under her eyes. "You know, you look awfully tired."

"I know. Maybe this weekend I'll get some rest."

"Didn't you get some sleeping pills from my mother's doctor?" He had told her to the last time the man had come to the house.

She shook her head. "I'll work it out for myself." He made a face and for the first time, she smiled.

They arrived before she spoke again. It was indeed a beautiful place, an old stone house of considerable grandeur and proportion, almost in the style of a château, surrounded by magnificently manicured gardens. In the distance were fruit orchards that stretched for miles.

"It's pretty, isn't it?" He said it tentatively, and their eyes met.

"Very. Thank you for arranging this." Then as he reached for the bags, she spoke again, barely audibly. "I'm glad we came."

"So am I." He looked at her very cautiously, and they both smiled.

He carried the bags into the house and set them down in the main hall. The furniture was mostly English and French Provincial, and everything in the rooms was faithful to the seventeenth century when the house had been built. Deanna wandered down the long halls, looking at the beautifully inlaid floors and glancing out the tall windows into the gardens. She stopped at last at the end of the corridor, in a solarium filled with plants and comfortable chairs. She sat down in one and stared silently out at the grounds. It was a while before she heard Marc's footsteps echoing down the hall.

"Deanna?"

"I'm in here."

He entered the room and stood in the doorway for a while, looking outside and occasionally glancing at his wife.

"*C'est joli, non?*" He spoke absentmindedly, and her eyes reached up to his. "It's pretty."

She nodded. "I understood. Marc?" She didn't want to ask, but she had to. And she knew he wouldn't be pleased. "How's your friend?"

For a long time he didn't answer. "I don't know what you mean."

"Yes, you do." She felt nausea rise in her as she searched his eyes. "How have you decided to handle it?"

"Don't you think it's a little too soon to discuss it? We just got out of the car."

She smiled at him. "How French. What did you have in mind, darling? That we spend the weekend being charming and then discuss it on the way home Sunday night?"

"That was not why I brought you here. We both needed to get away."

She nodded again, her eyes filling with tears. "Yes. We did." Her mind immediately sped back to Pilar. "But we have to talk about this too. You know, I suddenly wonder why we've stayed married." She looked up at him again. He came into the room and slowly sat down.

"Are you mad?"

"Maybe I am." She looked for her handkerchief and blew her nose.

"Deanna, please. . . ." He glanced at her, then looked away.

"What? You want to pretend that nothing has happened? Marc, we can't." Too much had happened over the summer. She had had Ben, and now she knew Marc had someone too. Only in Marc's case, it probably had gone on for years.

"But this is not something for you to worry about now."

"What better time? We're both already in such pain, we might as well lance the whole boil. If we don't, it'll go on throbbing and hurting forever, while we try to make believe it's not there."

"Have you been so unhappy for so long?"

She nodded slowly, turning to look outside. She was thinking of Ben. "I never realized until this summer how terribly lonely I've been, how constantly alone . . . how little we do together, how little we've shared. How little you understand what I want."

"And what is it you want?" His voice was very low and soft.

"Your time, your affection. Laughter. Walks on the beach. . . ." She said the last without thinking and then turned her head toward him in surprise. "I want you to care about my work, because it's important to me. I want to be with you, Marc. Not all by myself at home. What do you think will happen now, with Pilar gone? You'll travel for months, and what will I do? Sit there and wait?" The very thought of that existence made her tremble inside. "I can't do it anymore. I don't want to."

"Then what do you suggest?" He wanted her to say it, wanted her to ask for the divorce.

"I don't know. We could call it a day, or if we decide to stay married, then things would have to be different, especially now." Jesus, what was she doing? If she stayed with him, she couldn't have Ben. But this was her husband, the man she had lived with for eighteen years.

"You're telling me you want to travel with me?" He looked annoyed.

"Why not? She travels with you, doesn't she?" Deanna had finally figured that out. "Why couldn't I?"

"Because . . . because it's unreasonable. And impractical. And —and expensive." And because then he couldn't take Chantal.

"Expensive?" Deanna raised an eyebrow with a small, vicious smile. "My, my. Does she pay her own way?"

"Deanna! I will not discuss this with you!"

"Then why did we come here?" Her eyes were fierce in the narrow white face.

"We came here to rest." They were the words of a monarch, her king. The subject was now closed.

"I see. Then all we have to do is get through the weekend, be polite, and go back to Paris pretending nothing happened. You go back to your little friend, and in two weeks we go back to the States and go on as always. And just how long will you stay there this time, Marc? Three weeks? A month? Six weeks? And then you'll be gone again, and for how long, and with whom, while I sit all alone in that goddamn museum we live in, waiting for you to come back. Alone again dammit. Alone!"

"That's not true."

"Yes it is, and you know it. And what I'm telling you now is that I've had enough. As far as I'm concerned, those days are over." She stood up suddenly then and was about to leave the room, but when she got to her feet, she felt faint. She stopped for a moment, looking down and holding on to her chair.

He watched her, at first saying nothing, then with concern in his eyes. "Is something wrong?"

"No. Nothing." She straightened herself and glared at him from where she stood. "I'm just very tired."

"Then go and rest. I'll show you our room." He gently took her elbow until he was sure that she was steady on her feet, then led the way down the long hall to the other end of the house. They had taken over the master bedroom, a splendid suite done in silks the color of raspberries and cream. "Why don't you lie down for a while, Deanna." She was looking steadily worse. "I'll take a walk."

"And then what?" She looked up at him miserably from the bed. "Then what do we do? I can't do this anymore, Marc. I can't play the game."

He was tempted to say "What game?" to deny it all. He said nothing, and Deanna went on, looking directly into his eyes as she spoke. They looked troubled and a little too full.

"I want to know what you feel, what you think, what you're going to do. What's going to be different for me, other than the fact that we no longer have Pilar. I want to know if you're going to go on seeing your mistress. I want to know all the things you think it's rude to say. Say them now, Marc. I need to know."

He nodded silently and walked to the other side of the room, looking out the window toward the gently rolling hills. "It's not easy for me to talk about those kinds of things."

"I know." Her voice was very soft. "Half the time we've been married, I've never been sure if you loved me."

"I always did." He spoke without turning around, and all she could see was his back. "I always will love you, Deanna."

She felt tears sting her eyes. "Why?" She could barely say the word. "Why do you love me? Because I'm your wife? Out of habit? Or because you really care?" But he didn't answer, he only turned to her with a look of intense pain on his face.

"Must we do this? Now . . . so soon after Pilar's . . . death?"

Deanna didn't speak. His whole face had trembled as he spoke of Pilar. "Deanna, I—I just can't."

Without another word he strode out of the room, and she next saw him, with his head bent, walking in the garden. Her eyes filled with tears again as she watched him. The past few days felt like the end of her life. For a moment she didn't even think of Ben. Only Marc.

He did not return to the house for an hour, and when he did, he found her asleep. There was still a look of exhaustion around the black-circled eyes. For the first time in years, she was wearing no makeup, and in contrast to the raspberry silk bedspread he thought her face looked almost green. He wandered back into the main hallway and into a study beyond. For a moment he sat there, staring at the phone. And then, as though he had to, he started to dial.

She answered on the third ring. "Marc-Edouard?"

"*Oui.*" He paused. "How are you?" What if Deanna woke up? Why had he called her?

"You sound odd. Is something wrong?"

"No, no. I'm just very tired. We both are."

"That's understandable. Have you talked?" She was relentless. It was a side of Chantal he had never known.

"Not really. Only a little."

"I suppose it's not easy." He could hear her sigh.

"No, it's not." He paused. There were footsteps in the hall. "Look, I'll call you back."

"When?"

"Later." And then: "I love you."

"Good, darling, so do I."

He hung up with a trembling hand as the footsteps approached. But it was only the caretaker, come to see that they were comfortably settled. Satisfied, the man went away, and Marc sank slowly into a chair. It would never work. He couldn't keep up the charade forever. Calling Chantal, pacifying Deanna, flying back and forth between California and France, hiding and excusing, and showering them both with guilt-inspired gifts. Deanna was right. It had been almost impossible for years. Of course Deanna hadn't known then, but now that she did, it made everything different. It made him feel so much worse. He closed his eyes, and his mind went immediately back to Pilar, to the last time he had seen her.

They had walked on the beach. She had teased him and he had laughed, and he had made her promise to be careful with the motorcycle. Again, she had laughed. . . . The tears flooded his throat again, and suddenly the room was filled with the sound of his sobs. He didn't even hear Deanna come in, catlike, on stockinged feet. She went to him slowly and held his shivering shoulders in her arms.

"It's all right, Marc. I'm here." There were tears on her face as well, and he could feel the warm wetness through his shirt as she rested her cheek on his back. "It's all right."

"If you only knew how I loved Pilar. . . . Why did I do it? Buy her that damned machine! I should have known."

"It doesn't matter now. It was meant to be. You can't do this to yourself for the rest of your life."

"But why?" His words shook with pain as he turned to look at his wife. "Why her? Why us? We already lost two boys, and now the only child we had. Deanna, how can you bear it?"

She squeezed her eyes shut. "We don't have any choice. I thought—I thought I would die myself when the two babies died. . . . I thought I couldn't go on another day. Each day I just wanted to give up, to hide in a corner. But I didn't. I went on . . . somehow. In part, because of you. In part, because of myself. And then we had Pilar, and I forgot that kind of pain. I thought —I thought I'd never feel that way again. But now I remember what it's like. Only this time it's so much worse." She lowered her head, and he reached out and took her in his arms.

"I know. If you knew how I wish now that we had had those sons. We have—we have no more children." Deanna nodded silently, feeling more than ever the pain of his words. "I would do anything to—to have her back."

They sat there for a long time, holding each other. At last they went outside for a walk. It was dinnertime when they came back.

"Do you want to go into the village to eat?" He looked at her with an expression of grief and fatigue, but she shook her head.

"Why don't I make something here? Is there any food?"

"The caretaker said his wife left us some bread and cheese and eggs."

"How about that?" He nodded indifferently. She took off the sweater she had worn on their walk, set it on a large Louis XIV chair, and headed for the kitchen.

She was back in twenty minutes with scrambled eggs, toast and Brie, and two cups of steaming black coffee. She wondered if they'd feel better after they ate, if it really made any difference. All week long, people had told them to eat, as though that would help. But she didn't care anymore if she ever ate. She had made the dinner for Marc and because it gave them something to do. Neither of them seemed to want to talk, although there should have been a great deal to say.

They ate in silence. After the meal they drifted apart, she to the long halls and galleries to study the collection of paintings, Marc to the library. At eleven o'clock they went to bed in silence, and in the morning he got out of bed as soon as she stirred. It was eleven before either of them spoke. Deanna had just gotten up and was feeling queasy as she sat on a dressing-room chair.

"Ça ne va pas?" He looked at her with a frown of worry.

"No, no. I'm fine."

"You don't look it. Should I get you some coffee?" The very idea made her sick. She shook her head almost in desperation.

"No, really. Thanks."

"Do you think something is wrong? You haven't looked well in days."

She tried to smile, but it was a futile attempt. "I hate to say this, darling, but neither have you."

He only shrugged. "You don't suppose you have an ulcer, Deanna?" She had had one after the death of their first little boy, but it had never recurred. She shook her head.

"I don't have any pain. I'm just exhausted all the time, and now and then I feel sick. It's just fatigue," she went on, forcing a smile. "It's no wonder. Neither of us has had much sleep. We're both fighting staggering time changes, long trips, the shock. . . . I suppose it's a wonder we're still on our feet. I'm sure it's nothing."

But Marc wasn't sure he agreed. He saw her sway for a moment when she stood up. Emotions could do strange things to one. It made him think of Chantal again as Deanna disappeared into the shower. He wanted to call her again, but she wanted reports, she wanted to hear news, and he had none to give her, except that he was spending a weekend with his wife—and they both felt like hell.

In the shower Deanna stood with her face turned up and the water racing down her back. She was thinking of Ben. In San

Francisco it was two in the morning; he would still be asleep. She could see his face so clearly in his bed, the dark hair tousled, one hand on his chest, the other resting somewhere on her. . . . No, he was probably in Carmel, and she found herself thinking of their weekends there. How different it was from these days with Marc. It was as though she and Marc had nothing left to say. All they had was the past.

She turned the shower off at last and stood thinking for a moment, looking out the open windows into the garden as she dried herself with thick raspberry-colored towels. This house was a far cry from Carmel. A château in France, and a cottage in Carmel. Raspberry silks, and comfortable old wools. She thought of the cozy plaid blanket on Ben's country bed as she caught a glimpse of the ruffled silk bedspread in the other room. It was like the contrast between her two lives. There, the simple, easy reality of life with Ben in his "democracy" where they took turns making breakfast and putting the garbage outside the back door; and here, only the eternal empty splendor of her life with Marc. She ran a brush through her hair and let out a long sigh.

In the bedroom beyond, Marc was reading the paper with a frown. "Will you join me in church?" He looked over the paper as she emerged from the bathroom, her robe firmly closed, and stood in front of the wardrobe. She nodded and pulled out a black skirt and a sweater. They were both wearing formal *deuil*, the solid black mourning still common in France. The only things she omitted were the black stockings, which her mother-in-law wore.

Deanna looked strangely plain in the unalleviated black, with her dark hair pulled severely into a bun at the nape of her neck. Once again she wore no makeup. It was as though she no longer cared.

"You look terribly pale."

"It's just the contrast with all this black."

"Are you sure?" He stared at her for a moment before they left the house, but she only smiled. He acted as though he was afraid she were dying, but maybe he was afraid of that too. They had both lost so much.

They drove in silence to the tiny country church of Sainte Isabelle. Deanna slipped quietly into the pew at Marc's side. The church, tiny and pretty and warm, was filled with peasants, and a few weekenders like them, down from Paris. She suddenly remembered that it was still summer, not quite the end of August. In the States it would soon be Labor Day, heralding the fall. Her sense of time had vanished in the past week. She could not keep her mind on the service. She thought of Carmel, and of Ben, of Marc, and then Pilar; she thought of long walks in the country as a child, and then she stared fixedly at the back of someone's head. It was stuffy in the small church, and the sermon droned on and on. Finally, gently, she touched Marc's arm. She began to whisper that she was too warm, but suddenly his face swam before her eyes, and everything went dark.

21

"Marc?" She reached out to him as he and another man carried her to the car.

"Quiet, darling, don't talk." His face was a pale, perspiring gray.

"Put me down. Really, I'm all right."

"Never mind that." He thanked the man who had helped him carry her to the car, and once more clarified their directions to the nearest hospital.

"What? Don't be crazy. I only fainted because it was so hot."

"It was not hot, it was quite cool. And I won't discuss it." He slammed the door on her side and got in behind the wheel.

"Marc, I will *not* go to the hospital." She put a hand on his arm. Her eyes implored him, but he shook his head. She was a pale, opaque kind of gray. He started the car.

"I'm not interested in what you will 'not' do." His face was set. He didn't want to go to a hospital again, didn't want to hear those sounds, or smell those odors around him. Never . . . never again. He felt his heart race. What if it were serious? What if she were very ill? What if. . . . He glanced at her again, trying to mask his fear, but she was looking away, staring out at the countryside. He glanced at her profile and then down at her shoulders, her hands, everything draped in so much black. Austere. It seemed symbolic of everything happening to them now, everything they said. Why could they not escape it? Why wasn't this simply a weekend in the country, from which they would return relaxed and happy to find Pilar with that dazzling smile on her face. He looked over at Deanna once more, and let out a sigh. The sound dragged her eyes back from the road.

"Don't be so silly, Marc. Really, I'm perfectly all right."

"*On verra.*" We'll see.

"Would you rather we just go back to Paris?" Her hand trembled as she rested it in his, and he looked sharply at her again. Paris—and Chantal. Yes, he wanted to go back. But first he had to know that Deanna was all right.

"We'll go back to Paris once you've seen a doctor." She was about to protest again, but a wave of dizziness swept over her. She put her head back on the seat. He looked at her nervously and stepped on the gas. She didn't argue, she didn't have the strength.

It was another ten minutes before they pulled up in front of a small efficient-looking building with the sign HÔPITAL SAINT GÉRARD. Without a word, Marc got out of the car and came quickly to her side, but when he held open the door, Deanna made no move to get out.

"Can you walk?" There was terror in his eyes again. What if this were the beginning of a stroke? Then what would he do? She'd be paralyzed and he'd have to stay with her always. But that was madness, he *wanted* to stay with Deanna, didn't he? His pulse raced as he helped her out of the car.

She was about to tell him again that she was all right. By now they both knew she was not. She took a deep breath and stood up with a tiny smile. She wanted to prove to him that she'd make it, that this was only nerves. For a moment, as they walked into the hospital, she felt better, and wondered why they had come. For a minute she even walked in her usual, smooth, easy strides. Then, as she was about to boast of it to Marc-Edouard, an old man was rolled past them on a gurney. He was ancient and wrinkled, foul smelling, his mouth open, his face slack. She reached a hand out to Marc and passed out on the floor.

He gave a shout and collected her in his arms. Two nurses and a man in a white coat came running. In less than a minute they had her on a table in a small, antiseptic-smelling room, and she was awake again. She looked around for a moment, confused. Then she saw Marc, standing horrified in the corner.

"I'm sorry, but that man. . . ."

"That's enough." Marc approached slowly, holding up one hand. "It wasn't the old man, or the temperature in the church." He stood next to her, very tall, very grim, and suddenly very old. "Let's find out what it was—what it *is*. D'accord?" She didn't answer as the doctor nodded to him, and he left.

He haunted the corridor, looking strangely out of place and glancing at the phone. Should he call her? Why shouldn't he? What difference did it make? Who would see? But he didn't feel like it now. His thoughts were with Deanna. She had been his wife for eighteen years. They had just lost their only child. And now, perhaps. . . . He couldn't bear the thought. He passed the phone once more, without even stopping this time.

It seemed hours before a young woman doctor came to find him.

And then he knew. And knew he could tell Deanna the truth. Or he could tell her a lie—a very small lie. He wondered if he owed it to her to tell her, to tell her that he *knew*—or if, instead, Deanna owed something to him.

22

Deanna sat up straight in her bed, looking paler than the whitewashed wall behind her head. "You're wrong. It's a lie!"

Marc was staring at her and wearing a very small smile. He was completely calm. "It most certainly is not. And six months from now, my darling, you'll have a very hard time convincing anyone of that, I'm afraid."

"But I can't be."

"And why not?" His eyes searched her face.

"I'm too old to be pregnant, for chrissake."

"At thirty-seven? Don't be absurd. You will probably be able to have a child anytime in the next fifteen years."

"But I'm too *old!*" She was shrieking it at him and she looked near tears. Why had they not told her first, given her time to absorb the shock before she had to face Marc? But no, that was not the way of things here, in France, where the patient was always the last to know anything. And she could well imagine the scene Marc would have made: a determined man, an *important* man who must be informed of Madame's condition first; he did not wish his wife to be upset, and they had just been through so much, such tragedy. . . .

"Darling, please don't be foolish," Marc was saying. He stood up and walked to the side of the bed, where he gently rested his hand on her head, and ran it slowly down the long silky black hair. "You're not too old at all. May I sit down?" he asked. She nodded, and he sat down on the edge of the bed.

"But . . . two months?" She looked at him with eyes filled with despair. She had wanted it to be Ben's. She had thought of it too, for the first time just before she fell asleep. It had dawned on her, and she had argued with the thought, but as she drifted off to sleep she suddenly wondered—the dizziness, the nausea, the constant desire for sleep. All she had been able to think of was Ben. She didn't want it to be Marc's. She looked at him now in disappointment and pain. Two months pregnant meant it was Marc's, not Ben's.

"It must have happened that last night before I left. *Un petit au revoir.*"

"That is not funny." Tears filled her eyes. She was far from pleased. Now he understood even more than she knew. But now he understood that there was not only another man, but someone she loved. It didn't matter. She would forget him. She had something important to do in the next months. She owed Marc his son. "I don't understand."

"Darling, don't be naive."

"I haven't gotten pregnant in years. Why now?"

"Sometimes that's how those things happen. In any case it makes no difference. We're getting a whole new chance—another family, a child."

"We've already had a child." She looked like a petulant little girl as she sat cross-legged in her hospital bed, wiping away tears with the palm of her hand. "I don't want any more children." *At least not yours.* Now she knew the truth too. If she had truly loved him, she would have wanted his baby. And she didn't. She wanted Ben's.

Marc was looking embarrassingly pleased and painfully patient. "It's normal to feel that way at first. All women do. But when it comes. . . . Remember Pilar?"

Deanna's eyes flashed into his. "Yes, I remember Pilar. And the others. I've done that, Marc. I won't do it again. For what? For more heartbreak, more pain? For you to not be there for another eighteen years? At my age, you expect me to bring up a child alone? And another half-breed, another half-American, all French? You want me to go through that again, competing with you for the allegiance of our child? Dammit, I won't do it!"

"You most certainly will." His voice was quiet and as solid as steel.

"I don't have to!" She was shouting at him now. "This isn't the dark ages! I can have an abortion if I want to!"

"No, you can not!"

"The hell I can't!"

"Deanna, I won't discuss this with you. You're upset." She was lying in her bed now, crying into the pillow. "Upset" was barely adequate for what she felt. "You'll get used to the idea. You'll be pleased."

"You mean I don't have a choice, is that it?" She glared at him. "What'll you do to me if I get rid of it? Divorce me?"

"Don't talk nonsense."

"Then don't push me around."

"I'm not pushing, I'm happy." He looked at her with a smile and held out his arms, but there was something different in his eyes. She didn't come to him. After a moment he took her hands and brought them one after the other to his lips. "I love you, Deanna. And I want our child. Our baby. Yours and mine."

She closed her eyes and almost cringed as he said it. She had been there before. But he said nothing; he only stood up and took her in his arms, then stroked her hair briefly. Then he pulled away. She watched him leave, looking pensive and distracted.

Alone in the dark, she cried for a while, wondering what she should do. This changed everything. Why hadn't she known? Why hadn't she guessed? She should have figured it out before, but she'd only missed it once, and she thought that was nerves, there had been the opening of the gallery, her constant lovemaking with Ben, then the news of Pilar, the trip. . . . She thought it was just a matter of a couple of weeks. But two months? How could that be? And Jesus, it meant she had been pregnant by Marc the whole time she had been with Ben. Allowing that baby to stay in her now was like denying everything she'd had with Ben and tearing out her heart. This baby was a confirmation of her marriage to Marc.

She lay awake in her bed all night long. The next morning Marc-Edouard checked her out of the hospital. They were driving straight back to Paris, his mother's, before he left the next day for Athens. "And this is it. I'll be gone for five or six days. After that, I'll have it all wrapped up in Greece. A week from now we'll leave Paris, go home, and stay there."

"What does that mean? I stay there, and you travel?"

"No. It means I stay there as much as I can."

"Five days a month? Five days a year? Something like that?" She stared out the window as she asked. She felt as though she had been condemned to a replay of her first eighteen years as his wife. "When will I see you, Marc? Twice a month for dinner, when you're in town, and don't have to have dinner somewhere else?"

"It won't be like that, Deanna. I promise."

"Why not? It always has been before."

"That was different. I've learned something now."

"Really? What?" She looked bitter as she watched him drive, but his voice was soft and sad when he spoke and he kept his eyes on the road.

"I've learned how short life can be, how quickly gone. We had learned that together before, twice, but I had forgotten. Now I know. I have been reminded again." Deanna hung her head and said nothing. But he knew he had hit his mark. "After Pilar, after the others, could you really have this one aborted?"

She was shocked that he had read her thoughts, and she didn't answer for a long time. "I'm not sure."

"*I'm* quite sure. It would destroy you." The tone of his voice frightened her. Maybe he did know. "The guilt, the emotional pain, you'd be finished. You'd never be able to think or live or love, or even paint again. I guarantee it." The very idea terrified her. And he was probably right. "You don't have the temperament to be that cold-blooded."

"In other words," she sighed, "I have no choice."

He didn't answer.

They were in bed at nine-thirty that night, and nothing more was said. He kissed her gently on the forehead as he left her in their room. He was taking a taxi to the airport.

"I'll call you every night." He looked concerned, but also undeniably pleased, and he no longer had that terrifying worry in his eyes, the only sorrow left there was what he felt for Pilar. "I promise, darling. I'll call every night." He repeated it, but she looked away.

"Will she let you?" He tried to ignore the remark, but she looked pointedly at him from the bed. "You heard me, Marc. I assume she's going with you. Am I right?"

"Don't be ridiculous. This is a business trip."

"And the last time wasn't?"

"You're just upset. Why don't we stop? I don't want to fight with you before I leave."

"Why not? Afraid I'll lose the baby?" For an insane moment she wanted to tell him that the baby wasn't his, but the worst of it was that if she was two months pregnant, it was.

"Deanna, I want you to rest while I'm gone." He looked at her with an air of fatherly tenderness, blew her a kiss, and softly closed the door.

She lay there for a while, listening to the sounds of her mother-in-law's house. So far no one knew. It was "their secret" as Marc called it.

When she awakened the next morning, the house was still. She lay in bed for a long time, thinking, wondering what to do. She could fly to San Francisco while Marc was in Greece, she could have an abortion and be free, but she recognized the truth of what he had said to her. Having an abortion would destroy her as much as it would him. She had suffered too much loss already. And what if he were right? If it were a gift of God? And what if . . . what if it were Ben's? A last ray of hope flickered and then died. Two months, he had said, and the young, shy-looking doctor had nodded her agreement. It couldn't have been Ben's.

So she would lie in this beige silk cocoon for a week, waiting for Marc to return, to take her home, so they could begin the same charade again. She felt panic rising in her at the thought, and suddenly all she wanted to do was to run away. She climbed out of bed, steadying herself for a moment against a wave of dizziness, then dressed quietly. She had to get out, to go for a walk, to think.

She turned into streets she barely knew and discovered gardens and squares and parks that delighted her. She sat on benches and smiled at passersby, funny little old ladies in lopsided hats, little old men playing chess, children babbling at their friends, and here and there a girl pushing a pram. A girl—they all looked twenty-one or -two, not thirty-seven. Deanna watched as she rested. The doctor had told her to take it easy, to go for walks, but stop and rest; to go out but come home and nap, not to skip meals, and not to stay up late, and in a few weeks she'd feel better. She already did. And as she walked around Paris, she stopped often, and thought. About Ben. She hadn't called him in days.

It was late afternoon when she finally stopped at a post office. She couldn't stay away any longer. She gave the woman the number and nodded at her, surprised, *"L'Amérique?"* It seemed aeons before she heard him, but it was less than a minute before he answered the phone. For him it was eight o'clock in the morning.

"Were you asleep?" Her voice sounded intense even across six thousand miles.

"Almost. I just woke up." Ben settled back in bed with a smile. "When are you coming home?"

She squeezed her eyes shut and fought back tears in answer. "Soon." *With Marc—and his baby.* She felt a sob lodge in her throat. "I miss you terribly." The tears started to roll, silently, down her face.

"Not as much as I miss you, darling." He listened, trying to hear. There was something she wasn't saying, something he didn't understand. "Are you all right?" He knew she would still be distraught over Pilar, but she sounded as though there was something more. "Are you? Answer me!"

She was saying nothing, only standing in the booth, in silence, in tears.

"Deanna? Darling? . . . Hello?" He listened intently. He was sure she was still there.

"I'm here." It was a sad little croak.

"Oh, darling. . . ." He frowned and then smiled. "How about if I come over? Any chance of that?"

"Not really."

"How about next weekend in Carmel? It's Labor Day weekend. Think you'll be back?"

It was light years away. She was about to say no, then stopped. Next weekend in Carmel. Why not? Marc would be in Greece. If she left tonight, they would have until the end of the weekend, and maybe even one more day before he got back. Together. In Carmel. And then it would be over, as they had foreseen. The end of the summer would have come. Her mind raced. "I'll be home tomorrow."

"You will? Oh, baby . . . what time?"

She made a rapid calculation in her head. "About six o'clock tomorrow morning. Your time." She stood in the booth, suddenly beaming through her tears.

"Are you sure?"

"I certainly am." She told him the airline. "I'll call you if I can't make that plane, but otherwise, count on it." And then as she laughed into the phone, she felt tears sting her eyes again. "I'm coming home, Ben." How long it seemed since she'd left. It had only been a week.

That night she left a note for her mother-in-law. She explained only that she had been called back to San Francisco, that she was sorry to leave in such a rush. And, incidentally, she had felt an irresistible need to reclaim her portrait of herself and Pilar. She was sure her mother-in-law would understand. She instructed the maid to tell Marc, when he called, that she was out. That was all. That would buy her a day at least. But there was nothing he could do. He had to finish up in Greece. She thought about it on the plane on the way home. Marc would leave her alone for a week. There was no reason why he should not. He would be annoyed that she had flown home from Paris, but that was all. She was free now. For one more week. It was all she could think of.

An hour before they landed she could hardly sit still in her seat. She felt like a very young girl. Even the occasional waves of nausea didn't dampen her mood. She would just sit very still for a few minutes and close her eyes, and the nausea would pass. She kept her mind on Ben.

She was one of the first off the plane in San Francisco, after it had seemed to drift down through the clouds, racing the sun as everything around it turned pink and gold. It had been a splendid morning, but even that wasn't enough to take her mind off Ben. He was all she could think of as the plane finally ground to a halt at the gate, and she waited impatiently to be released from her seat. She was already wearing a half-smile, as she shrugged on the black velvet jacket over white slacks and a white silk shirt. Her ivory face and ebony hair added to the portrait in black and white. She looked considerably paler than she had when she had left, and her eyes told a multitude of tales, but they danced and sang too as she inched her way toward the door.

Then she saw him, standing there, alone in the terminal at six A.M., waiting for her beyond the customs barrier, with a jacket slung over his arm and a smile on his face. They rushed toward each other as she came through the door, and she was instantly in his arms.

"Oh, Ben!" There were laughter and tears in her eyes, but he said nothing, he only held her close. It seemed an eternity before he pulled away.

"I worried about you terribly, Deanna. I'm so glad you're back."

"So am I."

He searched her eyes but wasn't quite sure what he saw. One thing he knew was there—pain, but more than that he couldn't tell. She only reached out to him and held him tightly.

"Shall we go home?"

She nodded, her eyes filled with tears again. Home. For a week.

23

"Are you feeling O.K.?" She was lying back in his bed, with her eyes closed and a small smile on her face. She had been back home for four hours, and in bed with him the whole time. It was only ten o'clock in the morning, but she hadn't slept all night on the flight from Paris. He wasn't quite sure if it was the effect of the long flight that he was seeing, or if the week of Pilar's death had taken an even greater toll than he'd thought. She had shown him the painting when she'd unpacked. "Deanna? Are you O.K.?" He was watching her when she opencd her eyes.

"I've never felt better in my life." Her smile told him she meant it. "When do we leave for Carmel?"

"Tomorrow. The day after. Whenever you want."

"Could we go today?"

There was a tiny thread of desperation woven in there somewhere, but he had not yet discovered where. It troubled him. "We might. I could see what I can work out with Sally. If she doesn't mind taking on the gallery single-handed while we're gone, then it'll be all right."

"I hope she can." It was softly spoken, but earnestly said.

"As bad as that?" he asked. She only nodded, and he understood. He went to make breakfast. "Tomorrow it's your turn." He sang it out to her from the kitchen, and she laughed as she walked across the room, naked, and stood in the doorway watching him. It didn't matter now if they made love with Marc-Edouard's child in her belly. They had been doing it all summer, and she didn't care. She wanted to make love to Ben. She would need that to remember. "Deanna?"

She smiled and cocked her head. "Yes, sir?"

"What's wrong? I mean other than the obvious . . . Pilar. Is there something else?"

She started to tell him that that was enough, but she couldn't lie to him.

"Some things came up while I was in France."

"Anything I should know about?" Like Marc, he was suspicious of her health, she just looked too frail. He eyed her carefully from where he stood.

Slowly, she shook her head. He didn't need to know about the baby. It would have been different if it had been his.

"What kind of things came up?" His eyes smiled a little as he asked, "Fried or scrambled?"

"Scrambled would be nice." The thought of fried eggs turned her green, but she could manage scrambled, as long as she didn't get too strong a whiff of his coffee. "No coffee."

"How come?" He looked shocked.

"I've given it up for Lent."

"I think you're six or seven months early."

Seven months . . . seven months. She pulled her mind away from the thought and smiled at his attempt at a joke.

"Maybe so."

"So? What's up?"

"Oh, I don't know." She came into the kitchen and put her arms around him, leaning into his back. "I don't know . . . I don't know. I just wish my life were a little bit simpler."

"And?" He turned in her grasp and faced her as they both stood naked in front of his kitchen stove.

"I love you, that's all." Dammit, why did it have to be now? Why did she have to tell him so soon? Her eyes filled with tears, but she forced herself to look at him. She owed him that. "And . . . things aren't going to work out as easily as I thought."

"Did you really think it would be easy?" His eyes never left hers.

She shook her head. "No. But easier than it is."

"And how is it?"

"I can't leave him, Ben." There. She had said it. Oh, God, she had told him. She looked at him for an endless time, tears filling her eyes.

"Why not?"

"I just can't. Not now." *And not even later, not once I've had his child. Call me in another eighteen years. . . .*

"Do you love him, Deanna?"

Once again, she shook her head. "I thought I did. I was sure of it. And I know I did once. I suppose I still love him in a way. He has given me something for eighteen years, in his own way. But it's—it's been over for years. I just didn't understand that until this summer. I understand it even better now, after this week." She paused for a breath, then went on. "There were even times, with you, when I wasn't sure if I should leave him or not. I didn't know. It seemed as though I had no right. And I also thought that maybe I still loved him."

"And you don't?"

"No." It was a small choking sob. Finally she looked away and wiped her face with her hands. "I only realized it a few days ago. Something happened . . . and I knew." *Because I don't want his baby, Ben, I want yours!*

"Then why are you staying with him? Because of Pilar?" He

was strangely calm as he spoke to her, almost like a father speaking to a child.

"That and other reasons. It doesn't matter why. I just am." She looked at him in agony again. "Do you want me to go?" But he only stared at her, then silently left the room. She heard him in the living room for a moment, and then heard him slam the bedroom door as hard as he could. She stood in the kitchen for a time, wondering, stunned. She knew she had to leave now. There would be no Carmel. But all her clothes were locked up with him, in his room. She had no choice except to stay until he came out. At last he did, an hour later. He stood in the doorway, looking red-eyed and distraught. For a moment she wasn't quite sure if he was insanely angry or simply upset.

"What exactly were you telling me, Deanna? That it's over?"

"I . . . no . . . I . . . oh, God!" For a moment she thought again that she might faint, but she couldn't, not now. She took two deep breaths and sat down on the edge of the couch, her long, slim, bare legs hanging gracefully to the floor. "I have a week."

"And then what?"

"I disappear."

"Into that lonely life again? Into a life by yourself? In that mausoleum you lived in, and without even Pilar now? How can you do that to yourself?" He looked tormented.

"Maybe it's just what I have to do, Ben."

"I don't understand." He was about to walk back into his bedroom, but he stopped, turning to face her. "Deanna, I told you . . . I said it could just be for the summer and . . . I'd understand. That was what I said. I have no right to change that now. Do I?"

"You have every right to be furious, or very, very hurt."

She saw tears well up in his eyes and felt them well up in her own, but he never wavered as he watched her.

"I'm both. But that's because I love you very much."

She nodded, but she could no longer speak. She only walked back into the circle of his arms. It seemed hours before either of them let go.

"Shall we go to Carmel today?" He was lying on his stomach, looking into her face. She had just awakened from a three-hour nap, and it was almost five. He had never gone to the gallery—he had explained that he'd be gone all week and Sally would have to hold her own. "What do you really want to do?"

"Be with you." She said it solemnly but with a small happy smile in her eyes.

"Anywhere?"

"Anywhere."

"Then let's go to Tahiti."

"I'd rather go to Carmel."

"Seriously?" He ran a finger down her thigh. She smiled.

"Seriously."

"O.K., then let's go. We can have dinner down there."

"Sure. It's two o'clock in the morning, Paris time. By the time we have dinner, I'll be ready for breakfast."

"Jesus. I wasn't thinking about that. Do you feel half dead?" She was looking very tired but she seemed to have more color now.

"No, I feel fine, and happy, and I love you."

"Not half as much as I love you." He took her face in his hands and pulled her closer. He wanted to kiss her, hold her, and touch her, and have all of her that he could for the few days they had left. Then he thought of something. "What about your work?"

"What about it?"

"Will we still work together at the gallery? Will we still represent you—will I?" He wanted her to be incensed, to answer "of course," but for a long moment she said nothing. Then he knew.

"I don't know. We'll have to see." But how could they? How could she go to see him at the gallery in a few months, when she would be swollen with Marc-Edouard's child?

"It's all right," he said. "Never mind."

But the look of pain in his eyes now was too much for her to bear. She burst into tears. She seemed to be doing that a lot.

"What's wrong, love?"

"You're going to think I'm like her—the fake, the girl you were married to."

He knelt on the floor at her side. "You're not a fake, Deanna. Nothing about you has ever been fake. We just undertook something difficult and now we have to live up to the deal. It's not easy, but it's honest. It's always been honest. I love you more than

I've ever loved anyone in my life. I want you to remember that always. If you ever want to come back, I will always be here for you. Always. Even when I'm ninety-three years old." He tried to make her smile, but he failed. "Shall we make another deal now?"

"What?" She was pouting as she looked up at him. She hated Marc-Edouard, and hated herself more. She should have an abortion. Anything so she could be with Ben. Or maybe he would accept Marc's child, if she told him the truth from the start. But she knew that she could never tell him. He would never understand.

"Come on, I want us to make another deal. I want us both to promise that we won't talk about it being 'just one more week.' Let's just live each day, love each day, enjoy every moment, and face that time when it comes. If we talk about only that, we'll spoil the time that we have. Is it a deal?" He took her face in his hands and kissed her gently on the mouth as her hair fell softly down around her face from the loose knot she had wound it into on the top of her head. "Deal?"

"Deal."

"O.K." He nodded solemnly, kissed her again, and left the room.

An hour later they left for Carmel, but it was difficult not to feel the pall. Things weren't the same as they had been before. It was almost over, and whether they said it or not, they both knew. It was much too near. The summer was coming to a bittersweet end.

24

"Ready, my darling?" It was midnight, on Monday night. Labor Day. It was over. Time to go home. She looked around the living room for the last time, then silently took his hand. The lights were already out, the woman on the beach in the Wyeth hid her face in the moonlight. For the last time Deanna glanced at her as she left the house. It was chilly, but there was a bright moon and a sky filled with stars.

"I love you." They were whispered words as she slid quietly into the car. He touched her face, then he kissed her.

"I love you too." They were both smiling, suddenly it was not a time to be sad. They had shared a bond of joy and peace and love like none other, and it was something no one could ever take away. It was theirs. For a lifetime. "Are you as happy as I am, Deanna?" he asked. She nodded, smiling. "I don't know why I feel so goddamn good, except that you make me happy, and you always will. No matter what."

"You do the same for me." *And you will.* She would cling to the memories in the long winter's night of her life with Marc. She would think of him when she held the baby, thinking that it could have been his. She wished that it had been; suddenly she wished that more than anything in her life.

"What are you thinking?"

They had started the drive back to San Francisco. They planned to be back by two in the morning. The next day they'd sleep late, and then after breakfast he'd take her home. Marc was due in that afternoon. Tuesday, at three. That was all his telegram had said. Margaret had read it to her on the phone when she called to make sure that all was well at the house. Tuesday, at three.

"I asked you what you were thinking."

"A minute ago I was thinking that I would have liked to have your son." She smiled into the night.

"And my daughter? Wouldn't you want her too?" They both smiled.

"How many children do you have in mind?"

"A nice even number. Maybe twelve." This time she laughed and leaned against his shoulder as he drove. She remembered the first time he had said that, the morning after her show. Would there ever be another morning like that one?

"I would have settled for two."

He hated the tenses she used. It told him what he didn't want to know. Or remember. Not tonight.

"Since when did you decide that you're not too old?"

"I still think I am, but . . . it's easy to dream."

"You'd look cute pregnant." This time she said nothing. "Tired?"

"Just a little."

She had been tired too often all week long. It was the strain, but still he didn't like the dark circles under her eyes, or the pallor of her face when she got up in the morning. But he was no longer to worry after today. This was his last chance. Miraculously, on the morrow, he was to stop.

"Now what are you thinking?" She looked earnestly up at him.

"Of you."

"That's all?" She tried to tease, but he wouldn't play.

"That's all."

"What about?"

"I was thinking how much I wanted our child."

She felt a sob make a fist in her throat and she turned her head away. "Ben, don't."

"I'm sorry." He pulled her closer, and they drove on.

"And what is that supposed to mean?" Chantal glared at Marc from across the room. He closed his suitcase and swung to the floor.

"It means exactly what it sounds like, Chantal. Come on, don't play games. I've been here for almost three months this summer, now I have to do some work over there."

"For how long?" She looked livid, and her eyes showed that she had been crying.

"I told you. I don't know. Now be a good girl, and let's go."

"*Non, tant pis.* I don't give a damn if you miss your plane. You're not going to leave me like that. What do you think I am? Stupid? You're just going back to her. Poor, poor little wife, all heartbroken because she lost her daughter, and now little darling husband is going to console her. *Alors non, merde!* What about me?" She advanced on him menacingly, and a muscle tightened in his jaw.

"I told you. She's sick."

"With what?"

"A number of things. It doesn't matter with what, Chantal. She just is."

"So you can't leave her now. Then when can you leave her?"

"Dammit, we've been over and over this for a week. Why do we have to do this when I have to catch a plane?"

"The hell with your plane. I won't let you leave me." Her voice had risen dangerously and her eyes were darting around the room. "You can't go! *Non*, Marc-Edouard, *non!*" She was in tears again. He sighed as he sat down.

"Chantal, *chérie*, please. I told you, it won't be for much longer. Please, darling. Try to understand. You've never been like this before. Why do you have to be so unreasonable now?"

"Because I've had it! I've had enough! Whatever happens, you stay married to her. Year after year after year after year. *Bien merde alors, j'en ai marre.* I'm fed up!"

"Must you be fed up right now?" He looked at his watch with despair. "I told you last night, if it looks as though it will be a long time, I'll have you come over. All right?"

"For how long?"

"Oh, Chantal!" He had the look of irritation he had previously worn only with Pilar. "*Voyons.* Let's see how it goes. You can stay in the States for a while, if you come over."

"How long is a while?" But she was beginning to play now, and he saw it, with an exasperated gleam in his eye.

"As long as my foot. Will that do? Now, let's go. I'll call you almost every day. I'll try to be back in a few weeks. And if not, you'll come over. Satisfied?"

"Almost."

"Almost?" He shouted the word, but she tilted her face up for a kiss, and he couldn't resist.

"*Toi, alors!*" He kissed her, and they both laughed as they raced back into the bedroom, teasing and touching and hungry again.

"I'll miss my plane, you know."

"So what? And afterwards let's have dinner at Maxim's."

One would have easily thought that she was the pregnant one, but they most emphatically knew she was not. They had once thought she was pregnant, and it had produced such an appalling scare because of her diabetes that they had decided never to take any chances again. They couldn't afford to. Her life was at stake. And she didn't really mind not getting pregnant, she had never been particularly anxious to have a child. Not even Marc's.

Ben stopped the car halfway down the street. "Here?"

She nodded, feeling as though the world were going to end. As though someone had announced the Apocalypse to them. They knew it was coming, they even knew when . . . but now what?

Where to go? What to do? How would she live every day without him? How could she exist without the moments they shared in Carmel? How could she not wake up in that yellow bedroom, figuring out if it was his turn to make breakfast or hers? She wondered, as she sat there, if it could even be done. She looked at him long and hard and then held him tightly in her arms. She didn't even care if anyone saw her. Let them. They would never see her hug him again. They would think it had been a mirage. She wondered for a moment if that was what she would think in years to come. Would it all seem like a dream?

Her words were a whisper in his ear. "Take good care. I love you. . . ."

"I love you too."

They clung to each other then, saying nothing. At last, he snapped open her door. "I don't want you to go, Deanna. But if you stay any longer, I won't be able to . . . to let you go." She saw that his eyes were too bright, and she felt her own fill with tears. She looked down into her lap, and then quickly up at him. She had to see him, had to know he was still there. Instantly her arms were around him again.

"Ben, I love you." She held tightly to him, then slowly peeled herself away and looked at him for a long, agonizing moment. "Can I tell you that these months have made my whole lifetime worthwhile?"

"You can." He smiled at her and kissed the tip of her nose. "And can I tell you to get the hell out of my car?" She looked at him in surprise. Then she laughed.

"You cannot."

"Well, I figure there's not going to be an easy way to do this so we might as well have a good laugh." And she did, and at the same time started to cry again.

"Jesus, I'm a mess."

"Yes, you are." He said it with an appreciative nod and a grin that gave way to a slightly sobered look in his eye. "And so am I. But frankly, my dear, I think we've got one hell of a lot of style." And then, with a lopsided grin, he bent to kiss her once more, looked at her very hard, and said, "Go."

She nodded, touched his face. With her hands clenched into tight fists she slid out of the car, looked at him for an interminable moment, turned, and walked away. As soon as she had turned her back, while she still fumbled in her bag for her keys, she heard him drive away. But she never turned, never looked, never saw, she simply buried him in her heart and walked back inside the house she would share for the rest of her life. With Marc.

25

"Good morning, darling. You slept well?" He looked down at her in bed.

"Did you miss your plane?" There was no mention of the past week, of the fact that she had literally run away from Paris.

"I did. Stupidly. I couldn't get a cab, there was a traffic jam, ten thousand tiny incidents, and I had to wait six hours for the next flight. How do you feel?"

"Decent."

"No more than that?"

She shrugged in answer. She felt like hell, and she wished she were dead. All she wanted was Ben. But not like this. Not with Marc-Edouard's baby.

"I want you to see the doctor today," Marc said. "Shall I have Dominique make an appointment for you, or do you want to do it yourself?"

"Either way."

Why so docile? He didn't like what he saw. She looked haggard and pale, nervous and unhappy, and yet indifferent to everything he said. "I want you to see him today," he repeated.

"Fine. Can I go by myself, or will you have Dominique take me?" Her eyes spat fire into his.

"Never mind that. You'll go today?"

"Count on it. And where are you going today, Athens or Rome?"

She walked past him into the bathroom and quietly closed the door. It was going to be a delightful eight months, Marc thought grimly. When the baby came a month later than Deanna expected, he was simply going to tell her it was overdue. That happened all the time, babies born three weeks late. He had thought about it all the way over on the plane.

He walked to the bathroom and spoke firmly at the closed door. "I'll be at my office if you need me. And be sure you see the doctor. Today. Understood?"

"Yes. Perfectly." She kept her voice steady so he wouldn't know she was crying. She couldn't go on like this. She couldn't live with it. It was too much. She had to leave him, to find her way back to Ben, with or without this damned child. But she had an idea. When she heard the front door slam, she emerged and went directly to the phone. The nurse told her he was busy but when she had the woman explain who was on the phone, he took the call.

"Deanna?" He sounded surprised. She rarely called anymore.

"Hi, Dr. Jones." Her voice sagged with relief just to hear him. He would help her. He always had before. "I have a problem. A very large problem. Can I come see you?" He could hear the urgency in her voice.

"What did you have in mind, Deanna? Today?"

"Will you hate me if I say yes?"

"I won't hate you, but I may tear out the little hair I've got left. Can it wait?"

"No. I'll go crazy."

"All right. Be here in an hour."

She was, and he settled back in the huge red-leather chair that she always thought of when she thought of him. "So?"

"I'm pregnant." His eyes didn't waver. Nothing moved in his face.

"How do you feel about it?"

"Awful. It's the wrong time . . . and everything about it is wrong."

"Marc feels that way too?"

What did he have to do with it? What did it matter? But she had to be honest. "No. He's pleased. But there are a thousand reasons why I think it's wrong. For one thing, I'm too old."

"Technically, you're not. But do you feel too old to cope with a small child?"

"It's not so much that, but . . . I'm just too old to go through it again. What if the baby dies, what if something like that happens again?"

"If that's what you're worrying about, you don't have to, and you know it. You know as well as I that the two incidents were totally unrelated, they were just tragic accidents. It won't happen again. But I think what you're telling me, Deanna, is that you just don't want this baby. Never mind the reasons. Or are there reasons you don't want to tell me?"

"I . . . yes. I—I don't want Marc's child."

For a moment the good doctor was stunned. "Any special reason, or is that a whim of the moment?"

"It's not a whim. I've been thinking of leaving him all summer."

"I see. Does he know?" he asked. She shook her head. "That does complicate things, doesn't it? But the baby is his?" He would never have asked her that ten years before, but now things were apparently different, and he asked with such kindness that she didn't mind.

"The baby is his." She hesitated and then went on. "Because I'm two months pregnant. If I were less pregnant, it wouldn't be his."

"How do you know that you are two months pregnant?"

"They told me in France."

"They could be wrong, but they probably aren't. Why don't you want the baby? Because it's Marc's?"

"Partially. And I don't want to be tied to him any more than I am. If I have the baby, I can't just get up and leave."

"Not very easily, but you could. But then what would you do?"

"Well, I can hardly go back to the other man with Marc's child."

"You could."

"No, doctor. I couldn't do that."

"No, but you don't have to stay with Marc because you're having his child. You could get out on your own."

"How?"

"You'd find a way if that was what you wanted."

"It isn't. I want . . . I want something else."

And then he knew.

"Before you tell me, let me ask you how your daughter fits into all of this. How would she feel, one way or the other, if you had another child?" But Deanna was looking somberly into her lap.

At last she looked up at him. "That doesn't matter anymore either. She died two weeks ago, in France."

For a moment everything stopped, and then he leaned forward and took her hand. "My God, Deanna. I'm so sorry."

"So are we."

"And even given that, you don't want another child?"

"Not like this. Not now. I just can't. I want an abortion. That's why I'm here."

"Do you think you could live with it? Afterwards, you know, there's no getting it back. It's almost always a situation that creates remorse, guilt, regret. You'll feel it for a very long time."

"In my body?"

"In your heart . . . in your mind. You have to want to get rid of it very badly, in order to feel comfortable about what you've done. What if there were a mistake in their diagnosis in France, and there was a chance that this were the other man's child? Would you still want the abortion?"

"I can't take the chance. I have to get rid of it in case it's Marc's. And there's no reason to think they made a mistake."

"People do. I sometimes do myself." He smiled benevolently at her, then frowned as he had another thought. "Given what just happened to Pilar, do you feel able to cope with this now?"

"I have to. Will you do it?"

"If it's what you want. But first I want to examine you and make sure I agree. Hell, maybe you're not even pregnant."

But she was. And he agreed, it was probably two months though it was always difficult to be precise so early in a pregnancy. It was just as well to do the operation quickly, Deanna seemed so determined on it.

"Tomorrow?" he asked her. "Come in at seven in the morning, and you can go home by five. Will you tell Marc?"

She shook her head. "I'll tell him I lost it."

"And then?"

"I don't know. I'll have to work that out."

"What if you decide to stay with Marc and have another child, but after this one you find you can no longer conceive? Then what, Deanna? Will you destroy yourself with guilt?"

"No. I can't imagine that happening, but if it does, I'll just have to live with it. And I will."

"You're quite sure?"

"Totally." She stood up, and he nodded and jotted down the address of the hospital where he wanted her to go. "Is it dangerous?" She hadn't even thought to ask until then. She didn't really care. She would just as soon die as be pregnant now with Marc's child.

But Dr. Jones shook his head and patted her arm. "No, it's not."

"Where are you going at this hour?" Marc picked up his head and glanced at her as she slid out of bed, annoyed at herself for having awakened him.

"To my studio. I can't sleep."

"You should stay in bed." But his eyes were already closed.

"I'll spend a lot of time in bed today." At least that much was the truth.

"All right." But he was sleeping again by the time she was dressed and he didn't see her go. She left him a note: She had gone out and would be back in the afternoon. He might be annoyed, but he would never know, and when she came home it would be too late. As she got into her car and started the motor, she looked down at her sandals and jeans. She had last worn them in Carmel with Ben. As she waited for the car to warm up, she found herself thinking of him again and looking up at the pale morning sky. The last time she had seen a sky like that, it had been with him. Then for no reason at all she remembered what the doctor had asked her: What if the baby were Ben's? But it couldn't be, how could it? Two months before, she had made love with Marc. But she had also met Ben at the end of June, it could have been his too. Why couldn't she be certain? Why couldn't she be only one month pregnant instead of two? "Damn." She said the word aloud as she put her foot on the gas and backed out into the street. But what if it were his child? Would she still want the abortion? She suddenly wanted to talk to him, to tell him, to ask him what he thought, but that was insane. She drove straight to the address, her mind beginning to swim.

She looked pale and drawn when she got there. Dr. Jones was already waiting. He was quiet and gentle, as always, and he touched Deanna's arm.

"You're sure?" he asked. She nodded, but there was something he didn't like in her eyes. "Let's go talk."

"No. Let's just do it."

"All right." He gave instructions to the nurse, and Deanna was led to a small room where she was told to change into a hospital gown.

"Where will they take me?"

"Down the hall. You'll be gone all day. You won't be back here all day." Suddenly for the first time she felt frightened. What if it hurt? If she died? If she hemorrhaged on the way home? If. . . . The nurse proceeded to explain the suction technique to Deanna, and she felt herself grow pale.

"Do you understand?"

"Yes." It was all Deanna could think to say. She suddenly, desperately, wanted Ben.

"Are you afraid?" The nurse tried to look gentle but didn't succeed.

"A little."

"Don't be. It's nothing. I've had three." *Jesus*, Deanna thought, *How wonderful. At a discount?*

Deanna sat in her little room, waiting. At last she was led down the hall and then put in a room, where they positioned her on a sterile table, her feet strapped into the stirrups. It was like the delivery rooms she'd been in when she'd had those two baby boys, and then finally Pilar. A delivery room—not an abortion room. She felt herself break into a sweat. They left her alone for almost half an hour. She lay there, with her feet up, fighting the urge to cry and reminding herself that it would be over soon. Over. Gone. They'd pull it out of her with that machine. She looked around her, wondering which piece of ominous looking machinery was The One, but they all looked equally terrifying. She felt her legs start to shake. It seemed hours before Dr. Jones came into the room, and she felt herself jump.

"Deanna, we're going to give you a shot to make you a little woozy, and a little more at ease."

"I don't want it." She tried to sit bolt upright, and struggled with her legs in the air.

"The shot? But it will be a great deal easier for you if you take it. Believe me. It's a lot harder like this." He looked immensely sympathetic, but she shook her head.

"I don't want it. Not the shot. The abortion. I can't. What if the baby is Ben's?" The thought had gnawed at her for the last hour, or was that only an excuse to keep it? She wasn't sure.

"Are you certain, Deanna? Or are you just afraid?"

"Both. Everything. . . . I don't know." Tears filled her eyes.

"What if the baby were just yours and no one else's? If there were no man involved. If you could just have the baby to yourself. Would you want it then?"

She raised her eyes to his and silently nodded.

He undid her legs. "Then go home, love, and work things out. You can have that baby all by yourself, if that's what you want. No one can take it away from you. It'll be all yours."

She found herself smiling at the thought.

Marc was in the shower when she got home, and she quietly went up to her studio and locked the door. What had she done? She had decided to keep the baby, and what the doctor had said was true. She could have the baby alone and just make it hers. She could, couldn't she? Or would the baby always be Marc's? *Just as Pilar had been.* Suddenly she knew she would never escape. The baby was Marc's. She didn't yet have the courage to have it alone. And what did it matter? She had already lost Ben.

26

"Good morning, Deanna." Marc glanced at her as he settled himself in his chair. The usual assortment of newspapers was properly displayed, the coffee was hot, and Deanna was eating an egg. "Hungry this morning?" It had been weeks since he'd seen her eat.

"Not very. Here, you can have my toast." She pushed the lacy, blue Limoges plate toward him on the table. The tablecloth that morning was also a delicate pale blue. It matched her mood.

Marc looked at her carefully as she played with her egg. "Are you still feeling ill?" She shrugged, then after a moment looked up.

"No."

"I think perhaps you ought to call the doctor."

"I'm seeing him anyway next week." It had been three weeks since she'd seen him last. Three weeks since she'd run away the morning she could have had the abortion. Three weeks since she'd seen Ben. And there had been no news. She knew there wouldn't be again. She'd run into him some day, somewhere, some place, and they'd chat for a moment like old friends. And that would be all. It was over. No matter how much either of them cared. She felt her whole body sag at the thought. The only thing she wanted to do was go back to bed.

"What are you doing today?" Marc looked vague but concerned.

"Nothing. I'll probably work in the studio for a while." But she wasn't working. She was just sitting, staring at the mountain of paintings that had been sent back from the gallery, despite Ben's initial protests. But she couldn't do it. She couldn't let him sell her work and not see him at all. And she didn't want him to see her pregnant that winter. She had had no choice. She had insisted to Sally that they be returned. Now they leaned against the walls of her studio, bleakly faced away, their mud-colored canvas backs staring at her blindly, except for the one portrait of her and Pilar, which she looked at for hours every day.

"Would you like to join me somewhere for lunch?" She heard the words as she walked away and turned to see him in his seat in the dining room, looking like a king. He was her king now, and she was his slave, all because of this unborn child that she was too cowardly to abort.

Again she shook her head. "No, thank you." She attempted a smile, but it was barely a ray of sunshine in winter, less than a glimmer on the snow. She didn't want to go to lunch with him. She didn't want to be with him, or be seen with him. What if Ben saw them together? She couldn't bear the thought. She only shook her head once more and walked softly to the little studio, where she hid.

She sat huddled there, clutching her knees, with tears pouring down her face. It seemed hours later when she heard the phone.

"Hi, kiddo, what are you up to?" It was Kim. Deanna sighed to herself and tried to dredge up a smile.

"Not much. I'm sitting here in my studio, thinking I ought to retire."

"Like hell. Not after the beautiful reviews for that show you had. How's Ben? Has he sold any more of your work?"

"No." Deanna tried not to let her voice betray what she felt. "He—he hasn't really had the chance."

"I guess not. But I'm sure that when he gets back from London, he will. Sally says he'll be there for another week."

"Oh. I didn't know. Marc got home three weeks ago, and we've been awfully busy." Kimberly found that hard to believe; with the recent death of Pilar she knew that they weren't going anywhere. At least that was what Deanna had told her the last time they spoke.

"Can I lure you away from your studio for lunch?"

"No, I . . . really . . . I can't."

Suddenly Kim didn't like what she heard. She heard a tremor of pain in Deanna's voice that frightened her, it was so raw. "Deanna?" But there was no answer; she had begun to cry. "Can I come by now?"

She was going to tell her no, she wanted to stop her, didn't want her to see, but she didn't have the strength.

"Deanna, did you hear me? I'm coming over. I'll be there in two minutes."

Deanna heard Kim on the studio steps before she could come downstairs. She didn't want her to see the rows of paintings lined up against the walls, but it was already too late. Kim knocked once and stepped inside, looking around in astonishment, not understanding what she saw. There must have been twenty or thirty paintings lined up against the walls.

"What is all this stuff?" She knew it couldn't be new work. As she pulled the paintings free of the others that hid them and saw familiar themes, she turned to Deanna with surprise in her eyes. "You've withdrawn from the gallery?" she asked. Deanna nodded. "But why? They did a beautiful show for you, the reviews were good. The last time I talked to Ben, he told me he'd sold almost half your canvases. Why?" And then she understood. "Because of Marc?"

Deanna sighed and sat down. "I just had to withdraw."

Kim sat down across from her, concern furrowing her brow.

Deanna looked godawful, wan and pale and drawn, but worse than that there was something tragic stamped in her eyes. "Deanna, I—I know how you must feel about Pilar. Or really I don't know, but I can imagine. But you can't destroy your whole life. Your career has to be separate from everything else."

"But it isn't. Because—because of Ben." The words were muffled by her hands and her tears.

Kim moved closer to Deanna and took her firmly in her arms. "Just let yourself go."

Without knowing why, Deanna did. She cried in Kim's arms for what felt like days, for the loss of Pilar, of Ben, and maybe even Marc. She knew she had lost him to his mistress. The only thing she had not lost was the baby that she didn't want. Kim said nothing to her, but let her spend her sorrow in her arms. It seemed hours before the sobs finally stopped, and Deanna looked up into Kim's face.

"Oh, Kim, I'm so sorry. I don't know what happened. I just . . ."

"For chrissake, don't apologize. You can't hold it all inside. You really can't. Do you want a cup of coffee?"

She shook her head but then brightened a little. "Maybe a cup of tea." Kim picked up the phone and rang the kitchen.

"And maybe afterward we could go for a walk. How does that sound?"

"What about you? Did you give up your job, or just take the day off to play shrink to me?" Deanna smiled through her red, watering eyes.

"Hell, if you can withdraw from the gallery, maybe I should just quit. It makes about as much sense."

"No, you're wrong. I was right to do what I did."

"But why? I just don't understand."

Deanna was about to tell her something to put her off. Instead, she simply looked at Kim. "I don't want to see Ben anymore."

"You've ended it with Ben?"

For a long moment everything stopped in the room as the two women looked into each other's eyes. Deanna nodded.

"You're going to stay with Marc?"

"I have to."

She sighed and brought in the tray Margaret had left outside the door. She handed Kim her coffee and sat down with her tea, taking a tentative sip before she squeezed her eyes tightly shut and finally spoke again. "Marc and I are having a child."

"What? Are you kidding?"

Deanna opened her eyes again. "I wish I were. I found out when I was in France. I passed out in some country church a few days after the funeral, and Marc insisted on taking me to the local hospital. He thought I had something terminal, but we were both so hysterical at that point, who knew? All they found out was that I was two months pregnant."

"That makes you how pregnant now?"

"Exactly three."

"You don't look it." Still looking shocked, Kim lowered her gaze to Deanna's still totally flat stomach zipped into jeans.

"I know I don't look it. I guess I'm just small this time, and I've been so nervous that I've been losing a lot of weight."

"Jesus. Does Ben know?"

Deanna shook her head. "I couldn't bring myself to tell him that. I was thinking of—of having it . . . aborted. And I tried. I had it all set up, but when they got me on the table I just couldn't. Not with two dead babies, and now Pilar. No matter how much I don't want this child, I just can't."

"And Marc?"

"He's ecstatic. He'll finally get his son. Or a replacement for Pilar."

"And you, Deanna?" Her voice was painfully soft.

"What do I get? Not much. I lose the one man I truly love, I get locked into a marriage that I've discovered has been dead for years, I have another baby who may or may not live—and if it does, it will be Marc's and he'll turn it against me again, make it two thousand percent French. God knows, Kim, I've been through it. But what are my choices, what can I do?"

"You could have it alone, if you want the kid. Ben might even want it, even if it isn't his."

"Marc would never let me go. He'll do everything in his power to stop me." It seemed a nebulous threat but she looked terrified by her own words. Kim watched the pain in her friend's eyes.

"But what could he do?"

"I don't know. Something. Anything. I feel as though I could never get away. If I tried to make it on my own, he'd do everything he could to stop me. And somehow he shakes my self-confidence, he convinces me that I can't."

"Tell me something, Deanna." Kim looked at her long and hard. "Are you painting these days?"

Deanna shook her head. "What's the point? I can't show." She gave a small useless shrug.

"You didn't show for twenty years and you painted anyway. Why did you stop now?"

"I don't know."

"Because Marc told you to? Because he thinks it's foolish, because he makes you and your artwork seem very small?" Kim's eyes were blazing now.

"I don't know, maybe. . . . He just makes everything seem so trivial and pointless."

"And Ben?"

Deanna's voice was suddenly very soft, and there was that light in her eyes again, the one Kim had so rarely seen. "It's very different with Ben."

"Don't you think he could love that baby?"

"I don't know." Deanna came back to reality and she looked long and hard at Kim. "I can't ask him. Do you realize that I was pregnant with Marc's child the whole time I was sleeping with him? Do you have any idea how outrageous that is?" Deanna looked for a moment as though she hated herself.

"Don't be so goddamn uptight for chrissake. You didn't know you were pregnant. Did you?"

"No. Of course not."

"You see? For God's sake, Deanna, it might even be Ben's!"

But Deanna was shaking her head. "No. There's a discrepancy of a month."

"Could they have made a mistake? You ought to know."

"Yes, I should, but it's a little hard to tell. I'm irregular. That makes things very confusing. I have to rely on their theories, not mine. And they say I got pregnant in mid to late June. It could still be Ben's . . . but it's not very likely."

Kim sat silently for a long time, watching her friend, before she asked the one question that seemed to matter to her. The rest really did not. "Deanna, do you want the baby? I mean, if none of this existed, if they both fell off the face of the earth, and there was just you, would you want this kid? Think about it for a second before you answer."

But she didn't have to. Dr. Jones had asked her the same thing. She looked up at Kim with a small tender light in her eyes. "The answer is yes. Yes, I'd want it. I'd want it to be my baby. Mine." She looked away with tears in her eyes. "And I could always tell myself it was Ben's."

Kim sighed and put down her cup. "Then for God's sake, Deanna, have it. Enjoy it. Love it. Be with it. Thrive with it . . . but have it alone. Leave Marc, so at least you can enjoy this child."

"I can't. I'm afraid."

"Of what?"

She hung her head as though in shame. "The bitch of it is that I don't know."

27

"I don't know, Kim. I don't like the layouts, and the whole look just isn't polished enough." Ben ran a hand through his hair and stared absently at the far wall. He had been impossible to deal with all morning, and Kim knew what was distracting him as she watched him.

"Maybe if you'd gotten some sleep last night after your flight from London you'd like them a little better." She tried to tease, but it was useless. He actually looked worse than Deanna had, and that wasn't easy.

"Don't be a smartass. You know the look I want."

"All right. We'll try again. Will you be here long enough to check them out in a couple of weeks, or are you running off again?" He had been doing a lot of that lately.

"I'm leaving for Paris next Tuesday. But I'll be back in a couple of weeks. I have to do something about my house."

"You're redoing it?"

"I'm moving."

"How come? I thought you liked it." Over the months that Kim had been handling the account, they had become friends. And his relationship with Deanna had forged an extra bond between them.

"I can't stand the place anymore." Suddenly she found his eyes boring into hers. "Have you seen her?" Silently Kim nodded. "How is she?"

"All right." *Heartbroken, lousy, like you are.*

"Good. I wish I could say the same. Kim, I—I don't know how to say it. I'm going nuts. I can't stand it. I've never felt like this. Not even when my wife left me. But it just doesn't make any sense. We had everything going for us. And I promised her. . . . I promised that it would be just for the summer, that I wouldn't pressure her. But, Jesus, Kim, she's burying herself with that man. I don't think he even loves her."

"If it's any consolation, I've never thought so either."

"It's not. She still decided to stay with him, no matter what you or I think. Is she happy? Is she painting?"

Kim wanted to lie to him, but she couldn't. "No. Neither one."

"Then why? Because of Pilar? It just doesn't make any sense to me. She could have asked me to wait, I would have. She could have stayed with him a while. I wouldn't have pushed her. What hold can he possibly have on her?"

"Relationships are funny that way. It's hard for outsiders to see that. I've known people who hated each other and stayed married for fifty years."

"Sounds delightful." But as he spoke to her, his face looked grim. "I'd call her, but I don't think I should."

"What about you, Ben? How are you doing?" Her voice was painfully gentle.

"I'm keeping busy. I don't have any choice. She didn't leave me any choice."

She wanted to tell him that he'd get over it, but it seemed cruel to her to say something like that. "Can I do anything to help?"

"Yeah. Help me kidnap her." He looked away again. "You know, I can't even stand looking at my Wyeth anymore, it looks so much like her." He sighed and stood up, as though to get away from his own thoughts. "I don't know what to do, Kim. I don't know what the hell to do."

"There's nothing you can do. I wish I could help."

"So do I. But you can't. Come on, I'll buy you lunch."

Kim put the ads for the gallery back in her briefcase and replaced it on the floor. It was agonizing to see him like that.

"You know, I find myself wishing I'd run into her. Every restaurant I go to, every store, even the post office, I find myself searching . . . as though if I look hard enough, I'll see her face."

"She doesn't go out much these days."

"Is she all right? She's not sick, is she?" Dumbly Kim shook her head, and he went on, "I suppose the only solution is to keep moving, traveling, running."

"You can't do that forever." She stood up and followed him to the door, as his eyes looked at her sadly from behind his private prison walls.

"I can try."

28

"What did the doctor say today?" Deanna was already in bed when Marc got home. "Everything fine?"

"He said for four months I'm awfully small, but he assumes it's just nerves and the weight I've lost. He wants me back in two weeks this time though, to make sure he can hear the baby's heart. He's still too little to hear, and Jones said he should have heard him today. Maybe in another two weeks." But Marc didn't look worried at any of the news. "How was your day?"

"Excessively tiresome. But we got a new case." He looked pleased.

"Where?"

"In Amsterdam. But I'll share it with Jim Sullivan." He looked down at her with a smile. "I told you I wouldn't be going away all the time. Have I been true to my word?"

"Absolutely." This time she smiled too. He had been home for two months, and he hadn't stirred. Not so much as a weekend trip to Paris. Not that it really mattered now. In some ways she'd have

been relieved, but he had told her that it was over with that girl.
"There's no reason for you not to take the case though. When
will it go to court?"

"Probably not till June. Well after the baby comes."

The baby. It still didn't seem real. Not to her. Only to Marc.

"Do you want something to eat? I'm going downstairs for a
snack." He looked back at her from the doorway, again with that
tender smile. All he could think of now was their child, and her
well-being, as it related to their son. Sometimes it touched her,
most of the time it annoyed her. She knew it had nothing to do
with her. It had to do with the baby. With his Heir.

"What are you going to eat, pickles and ice cream?"

"What would you prefer, Deanna? Caviar and champagne?
That can be arranged too."

"A few crackers will be fine."

"Most unexciting. I hope the baby has better taste."

"I'm sure it will."

He was back a few minutes later, with crackers for her and a
sandwich for himself.

"No strawberries, no pizza, no tacos?"

It was the first time he had seen her sense of humor in months.
But she had had a pleasant day. After her visit to the doctor, she
had gone to lunch with Kim. Kim was helping her to keep her
sanity, in these strange, lonely days. And Deanna could tell her
how much she missed Ben. She was still waiting for the hurt of
that to stop. So far, though, it had shown no sign of abating.

Marc was about to offer her a bite of his sandwich, when the
phone next to her rang. "Want me to get it? It's probably for
you."

"At this hour?" He looked at his watch, then nodded. It was
eight in the morning in Europe. It was very probably for him. He
sat down on the bed again, next to his wife. He hadn't seen her
this friendly in weeks. He smiled at her once more and picked up
the phone. "Hello?" There was the usual whir of lines from overseas, and he waited to hear which of his clients was in dire need.

"Marc-Edouard?" It was a voice frantic with desperation, and
he felt himself grow suddenly pale. Chantal. Deanna saw his back
stiffen slightly, and he turned away from her with a frown.

"Yes? What is it?" He had spoken to her only that morning.
Why was she calling him at home? He had already promised her

that he would be back in Europe within the next few weeks. He
was sure he could get away from Deanna just after Thanksgiving.
By then, he would have paid his dues. Two-and-a-half months at
her side, in the States. "Is something wrong?"

"Yes." She let out a long strangled sob, and he felt fear flit
through his heart. "I'm—I'm in the hospital again."

"Ah, *merde*." He closed his eyes, and Deanna watched him
frown. "Why this time? The same thing?"

"No. I got my insulin mixed up."

"You never mix it up." *Except on purpose*, he thought, remembering the night in the hospital and the panic he'd felt. "After all
these years, surely you must know. . . ." *Shit*. It was so awkward
sitting there, talking to her, with Deanna looking on. "But you're
all right?"

"I don't know." And then after a pause, "Oh, Marc-Edouard, I
need you. Can't you please come home?" Damn. How could he
discuss it with her here?

"I don't have the right papers here to apprise you of that situation. Can we discuss it tomorrow from my office?" He picked up
the phone and walked across the room to a chair. Deanna had
gone back to reading her book. The conversation sounded dull,
and Marc looked annoyed.

But Marc was finding the exchange anything but dull. Chantal
had given a small shriek at his suggestion of discussing it from his
office the next day.

"No! You can't keep putting me off!"

"I'm not putting you off. I simply don't know when I can."

"Then let me come to you. You promised before you left that if
you couldn't get away, I could come there. Why can't I?"

"I'll have to discuss it with you tomorrow, when I have the
files. Can you wait ten hours and I'll call you back?" There was
steel in his voice now. "Where can I reach you?" She gave him
the name of a private clinic, and he was grateful that this time at
least she was not at the American Hospital, he couldn't have
borne having to call her there. "I'll get back to you as soon as I
reach the office."

"If you don't, I'll just get on the next plane."

She was behaving like a spoiled child. And a dangerous one. He
didn't want any more trouble with Deanna. Not until after the
child. Then they would just have to see. But because of his own

nationality the child would be legally French, as well as American. And when in France it was under French jurisdiction. It would be his. If he chose to take his child into France, there would be nothing Deanna could do to get him out. Nothing. The thought of that would keep him afloat for the next seven months. When the baby was a month old, they'd take him to France to see his grandmother for the first time. Deanna would come of course, but then she could make her own choice. She could go or stay. But the baby would not leave the country again. If necessary, he would live with Marc's mother, and Marc would see to it that he spent more of his time there. That baby was his . . . as Pilar should have been totally—would have been if it hadn't been for Deanna. The thought of the new baby kept his mind off Pilar. This was going to be entirely his child. In the meantime he needed Deanna. He needed her healthy and happy until she delivered the child. And afterwards, he would be perfectly happy to stay married to her—if she wanted to stay with the baby in France. He had it all worked out—all of it. And now was not the time for Chantal to rock the boat.

"Marc-Edouard? Did you hear me? I said that if you didn't come over, I'd just get on the next plane."

"To where?" His tone was icy.

"San Francisco of course. Where do you think?"

"Let me make that decision. And I'll let you know. Tomorrow. Understood?"

"*D'accord*. And Marc-Edouard?"

"Yes?" He softened a little at the sound of her voice.

"I love you so much."

"I'm absolutely certain that is a reciprocal agreement." For a moment he almost smiled. "I'll talk to you in a few hours. Good night."

Marc put the phone down with a sigh. He didn't notice that Deanna was watching.

"Disgruntled clients?"

"Nothing I can't work out."

"Is there anything you can't work out?"

He smiled, watching her eyes. "I hope not, my dear. I sincerely hope not."

He was in bed half an hour later; Deanna lay awake at his side.

"Marc?"

"Yes?" The room was dark.

"Is something wrong?"

"No, of course not. What would be wrong?"

"I don't know. That call . . . should you be traveling more than you are?" But she knew the answer to that question.

"Yes. But I can manage as things are. I don't want to leave you alone."

"I'd be fine."

"Probably. But as long as I don't have to go anywhere, I won't."

"I appreciate it."

It was the first kind thought she'd had of him in months, and he closed his eyes for a moment as she touched the back of his hand. He wanted to take her hand, to hold it, to kiss her, to call her *Ma Diane,* but he couldn't anymore. Not anymore. Not now. Already, thoughts of Chantal were crowding his mind.

"Don't worry, Deanna. Everything will be all right." He patted her hand and turned his back to her on the very far side of the bed.

"What kind of madness is that, calling me at home in the middle of the night?" Marc-Edouard's voice raged at her over a continent and an ocean. "What if she had answered the phone?"

"So what dammit, she knows!"

No. She *knew.* Past tense, not present. "I don't give a damn what she knows, you have no right to do that, I've told you not to."

"I have a right to do whatever I want." But her voice wavered. Suddenly she was crying in his ear. "I can't, Marc-Edouard. I can't go on. Please, it's been more than two months."

"It's been exactly two days more than two months." But he was stalling. He knew that if he was not to lose her, something had to be done. It was going to be a difficult winter, running between them both.

"Please. . . ." She almost hated herself for begging him, but she needed him. She wanted to be with him. She didn't want to lose him again to his wife. Events were always conspiring against her, even to the death of Pilar, things that brought him and Deanna closer, moments when they needed each other. Now she needed him more and she wasn't going to lose. "Marc-Edouard?" The threat was back in her voice.

"Chantal, darling, can't you please hang on for a little while longer?"

"No. If you don't do something now, it's over. I can't go on like this anymore. It's driving me mad."

Oh, God, what was he going to do with her? "I'll come over next week."

"No, you won't. You'll find an excuse." Suddenly, her tone hardened again. "I was brought to the hospital by a friend, Marc-Edouard, a man. The one I mentioned to you this summer. If you don't let me come to you once and for all, I'll—"

"Don't threaten me, Chantal!" But something in her words and her tone made his heart turn over. "What are you telling me, that you'll marry this man?"

"Why not? You're married, why shouldn't I be as well?"

Christ. What if she meant it? If, like the suicide attempts, she actually went ahead and did it? "If you come over here," he said, "you can't just run all over town. You'd have to be extremely discreet. You'd get bored very quickly."

"Will you let me decide that?" She could tell that he was wavering, and at her end there was a small smile beginning to dawn on her face. "I'll be good, darling, I promise you."

And then he smiled too. "You are always good. Not even good —extraordinary. All right, you determined little blackmailer, you, I'll arrange the ticket today."

She gave a whoop of victory and joy. "When can I come?"

"How soon will they let you leave the hospital?"

"Tonight."

"Then come tomorrow." They were both smiling openly now. To hell with the complications, he was dying to see her. "And Chantal . . . ?"

"*Oui, mon amour?*" She was all innocence and power, like a nuclear missile wrapped in pink silk.

"*Je t'aime.*"

29

Chantal was the first person through customs, and as he watched her wend her way toward him, he felt a smile wipe itself all over his face. My God, she looked beautiful. She was draped in pale-champagne suede, with a huge lynx collar and matching hat. Her auburn hair peeked out at him, and the golden eyes seemed to dance as she ran to his side. He saw that, for a moment, she was going to kiss him, and then she remembered. Instead, they walked side by side, whispering, talking, laughing; they might as well have kissed and torn off each other's clothes. It was clear how happy they were to be together again. He had almost forgotten how incredibly appealing she was, how special. Reduced to their exchanges on the phone, he had almost forgotten how heady were her charms. He could barely keep his hands off her as they disappeared into his rented limousine. It was there at last that his hands touched her body, her face, that he pressed her close to him and drank her mouth with his own.

"Oh, God, you feel so good to me." He was almost breathless as he held her, and she smiled. Now she was in control again, and her power laughed at him from her eyes.

"Idiot, you'd have kept me away for a year."

"No, but I . . . things just got too bogged down."

She rolled her eyes and sighed. "It doesn't matter. It's over now. As long as we're together, I don't give a damn." For a moment he wondered how long she was planning to stay, but he didn't want to ask. He didn't want to speak to her at all, he just wanted to hold her and make love to her for the rest of his life.

The car pulled up outside the Huntington Hotel, and Marc helped her out. He had already checked her in and paid for ten days. They had nothing to do but disappear into her room. He had told his office he would be gone for the day.

"Marc?" She picked her head up sleepily in the dark and

smiled. It was well after two in the morning, and she'd been asleep for two hours.

"No, it's the President. Whom did you expect?"

"You. How come you're so late?" He hadn't even called, but she hadn't really been worried.

"Clients in from out of town. We had sequestered meetings all day. We didn't even go out for lunch." They had ordered room service instead, and he had made special arrangements to have dinner sent up from L'Etoile.

"It sounds very dull." She smiled in the dark and turned around in the bed.

"How do you feel?" He was getting undressed and he had his back to his wife. It was strange to come home to her now. He had almost stayed out for the night, but he had to prepare the stage for that. He had promised Chantal the weekend, and a few other days.

"I feel sleepy, thank you."

"Good. So do I." He slipped into their bed, touched her cheek, and kissed her somewhere on the top of her head. "*Bonne nuit.*" It was what he had said to Chantal when he left, except to her he had added, "*mon amour.*"

"I don't care," Chantal said, "I'm not leaving. And if you stop paying for the hotel, I'll pay for it myself or find an apartment. My visa says I can stay for six months."

"That's absurd." Marc glared at her from across the room. They had been arguing for an hour, and Chantal's delicate chin jutted toward him in petulant fury. "I told you. I'll be back in Paris in two weeks."

"For how long? Five days? A week? And then what? I don't see you for another two months. *Non! Non, non et non!* Either we stay together now, or it is finished. Forever! And that, Marc-Edouard Duras, is my last word. Make up your mind what you want. Either I stay here now, and we work out something together, or I go home. And we're through. *Finis! C'est compris?*" Her voice was a shriek in the elegant room. "But this game we have played is over for me. No more! I told you that before I came over. I don't understand why you want to stay married to her. You don't even have Pilar as an excuse now. But I don't give a damn. I'm not going to go on living without you forever. I just can't. No, I'm staying. Or—" she looked at him ominously "—I go for good."

"What about six months from now when your visa runs out? That is if I let you stay here." His mind was racing and he was thinking . . . six months. It could work. Chantal could go home then, and he'd follow in a few weeks. Then he'd establish Deanna and the baby on the rue François Premier with his mother. It might even make sense for him to spend most of his time there. He'd be commuting back and forth to the States, but Paris would be home base. "You know, Chantal," he said, "things might just work out after all. What if I were to tell you that I am thinking of moving my main residence back to Paris next year? I would still keep the office here, but instead of traveling from here to Paris all the time, I would do it the other way around, and live over there."

"With your wife?" She eyed him suspiciously. She wasn't sure what he had in mind.

"Not necessarily, Chantal. Not necessarily at all. I am planning a number of changes next year." He looked at her with the faint hint of a smile, and something in her eyes lit up too.

"You'd move back to Paris? Why?" She wanted to say "For me?" but she didn't quite dare.

"I have a number of reasons for moving back, and you're not least among them."

"You're serious?" She stood watching him and she liked what she saw.

"I am."

"And in the meantime?"

"I might just let you stay here." He wore a half-smile. Almost before the words were out of his mouth, she flew across the room and into his arms.

"Do you mean it?"

"Yes, my darling, I do."

30

Marc-Edouard parked his Jaguar at the corner and pulled the large plainly wrapped box off the seat. He had already sent her flowers, and they would have been awkward to carry down the street. The box was cumbersome, but discreet. He stopped at the narrow house tucked between the palaces on Nob Hill and pushed one of two buzzers. It was a quiet flat up a shallow flight of stairs. The floors were black-and-white marble, the fixtures all well-polished brass, and he waited in amusement as he heard her run to the door. They had rented it furnished from November until June. And they had found it in less than a week. She had been in it for exactly two days, but this would be their first dinner "at home."

He listened to her footsteps hastening toward him, and couldn't suppress a smile. It had been the right decision, even if she had forced his hand, but it would be good to have her there all winter. Spring. Deanna didn't keep him company anymore; she hid in the studio most of the time, not that she seemed to be working there. She just sat.

"*Alors!*" He pushed the buzzer again. Suddenly the door flew open and there she was, dazzling in a white chiffon caftan with silvery sandals on her feet.

"*Bonsoir*, monsieur." She curtsied low, then rose with a mischievous grin. The lights in the apartment were dim, and in the back room he saw a small round table set for dinner with flowers and candles.

"How pretty everything is!" He held her in one arm and looked around. It was all silver and candlelight; everything sparkled and shone. It was a pretty little apartment, owned by a decorator who was spending the winter with his lover in France. A perfect arrangement. He pulled her closer into his arms. "You are a beautiful woman, Chantal, *ma chérie*. And you smell heavenly too." She laughed. He had sent her a huge bottle of Joy the day before. It was delightful having her so nearby. He could run away from the office at lunch, meet her at night before he went home. He could stop by for coffee and a kiss in the morning or for love in the afternoon.

"What's in the box?" She was eyeing the large package with curious amusement. He slipped a hand slowly up her leg. "Stop that! What's in the box?" She was laughing, and he was running his hand up and down her bare legs.

"What box? I didn't bring anything in a box." He brought his mouth to the back of her knee, and then slowly upward, on the inside of her thigh. "I find you much more interesting, my love, than anonymous packages." And so did she. In minutes the caftan lay crumpled on the floor.

"*Merde!*" She jumped away from his arms, as they lay drowsing on the bed. They had been asleep there for almost half an hour. Marc-Edouard sat up in surprise.

"*Merde?* What do you mean?" He tried to look offended as he stretched his long naked body across the bed. He looked like a very long, very pale cat. But she was already halfway across the room.

"The turkey! I forgot!" She sped into the kitchen, and he lay back on the bed with a grin. But she was back in a minute, looking relieved.

"*Ça va?*"

"*Oui, oui.* I've been cooking him for almost six hours, but he still looks all right."

"They always do. They just taste like straw. And why, may I ask, after a mere three weeks in the States, have you already started cooking turkey?" He laughed at her as he sat up, and she came to sit next to him on the bed.

"I cooked it because tomorrow is Thanksgiving, and I am very thankful."

"Are you? For what?" He lay back again, as he tousled her thick auburn hair. It touched her shoulders now and delicately framed her face. "What are you so thankful for, pretty girl?"

"You. Living here. Coming to the States. *La vie est belle, mon amour.*"

"Is it? Then go open your package." He tried to conceal a smile.

"Oh, *toi alors!* You!" She ran into the other room and came back with the brown-paper wrapped box. "What is it?" She looked like a little girl at Christmas and he smiled. "*Qu-est-ce que c'est?*"

"Open it and see!" He was enjoying it now almost as much as she was as she tore off the brown paper and discovered a very plain-looking brown box. He was delighted at the ruses he had used. She sat staring at the box, afraid to open it, still enjoying the surprise.

"Is it something for the house?" Her eyes were enormous as they held his, but his gaze rapidly slipped down to the perfectly shaped breasts as she knelt, naked, next to him on the bed, clutching the large box.

"Go on, silly . . . *vas-y*. She pulled off the lid and burrowed into the tissue paper to discover what was there. Her hands shot backward as though she had touched flame and instantly flew to her mouth.

"Ah, *non!* Marc-Edouard!"

"*Oui*, mademoiselle?"

"Oh. . . ." Her hands burrowed back into the tissue, and her eyes grew even wider as slowly, carefully, with exquisite caution, she pulled it out. This time she gasped as she held it aloft, then ran her hand gently up and down the pelts. It was a very beautiful, bittersweet chocolate, Russian sable coat. "Oh, my God."

"Let's try it on." He took it from her and slipped it carefully over her shoulders. She shrugged herself into it and buttoned it to her chin. It was beautifully cut and it looked magnificent on her as it fell in sleek lines over her tiny waist and narrow hips.

"*Bon Dieu, chérie, que tu es belle.* How incredibly beautiful you are, Chantal. Oh, my dear!" He looked on in mingled awe and ecstasy as she twirled on one foot, the coat opening subtly to reveal a bare leg.

"I've never had anything like this." She looked stunned as she watched herself in the mirror and then back at him. "Marc-Edouard, it's such . . . such an unbelievable gift!"

"So are you." Without another word he left the room to get the bottle of champagne. He returned with the bottle and both glasses, set them down, and took her into his arms. "Shall we celebrate, my darling?"

With a golden smile she nodded and melted again into his arms.

"What's Marc doing tonight?"

"Business meetings, as usual." Deanna smiled at Kim. "He has clients here from Europe these days. I never see him." It was the first time she had actually let Kim drag her out to dinner. Between the death of Pilar and her pregnancy, Deanna had been nowhere for months. They had decided, as usual, on Trader Vic's. "Jesus, I hate to admit it, but it feels good to get out." And here she had no qualms about running into Ben. She knew he hated places like this.

"How do you feel?"

"Not bad. It's hard to believe I'm already almost five months." But it was finally beginning to show, just the merest of bulges in the A-shaped dress of black wool crepe.

"Do you want a shower?" Kim looked at her with a grin over the hors d'oeuvres.

"A baby shower?" Deanna asked. Kim nodded, and Deanna rolled her eyes. "Of course not. I'm too old for that. My God, Kimberly!"

"You are not. If you're not too old for a baby, you're not too old for a shower."

"Don't start me on that one!" But Deanna was looking at her with a wry smile. There was no anger or pain in her eyes tonight. Kim hadn't seen her looking this peaceful in weeks, and her sense of humor seemed to have returned. "What are you doing for Thanksgiving by the way? Anything special?"

"Nothing much. I'm having dinner with some friends. You?"

"The usual. Nothing." Deanna shrugged. "Marc will be working."

"Want to come with me?"

"No. I'll probably manage to drag him out to dinner somewhere. I always did with Pilar. A restaurant or a hotel, it's not what you'd call a real Thanksgiving, but it'll do. And at least we won't be stuck with turkey sandwiches for two weeks." But suddenly she found herself wondering what Ben was doing. Probably going to Carmel, or maybe he was still back East. She didn't want to ask Kim.

The conversation drifted on to other subjects then. It was ten-thirty when at last they stood up, a little tired, a lot full, and having spent a very pleasant evening without any strain.

"Can I lure you out for a drink?" Kim asked. But she didn't look as though she wanted to drag out the evening any longer. And Deanna was tired.

"Maybe another time. I hate to admit it, but I'm beat. I'm still at the stage when I'm tired all the time."

"When does that stop, or does it?"

"Usually almost exactly at four months, but this time it seems to have dragged on. I'm four and a half, and still sleepy all the time."

"So enjoy it and be glad you don't work." But she wasn't. She wished that she did. It would give her something to think of while she didn't paint. She still hadn't been able to start her work. Something stopped her every time she sat down. Her thoughts would shift instantly to Pilar or Ben, or she would find herself panicking about the baby. Hours would drift by while she did nothing but sit, staring blindly into space.

They brought Kim's little red MG up to the door. With a groan Deanna got in as Kim tipped the valet and slid behind the wheel.

"I'm going to have to give up driving with you in a couple of months." Her legs were cramped almost up to her chin and she laughed, as did Kim.

"Yeah, I guess you'd have a hell of a time getting into this thing with a belly." They both laughed again, and Kimberly drove off, turning left out of Cosmo Place and then left again, until she made a sharp right at Jones to avoid some construction blocking the street. "We might as well drive past Nob Hill." She glanced over at Deanna with a smile, and they sat together in silence. Deanna was longing for her bed.

They had stopped at a stop sign when she saw them. For a moment she marveled at how much the man looked like Marc, and then she realized with a start that it was he. She felt herself gasp. Kim looked sharply at her, then in the direction she was staring. It was Marc with an elegant woman draped in a magnificent, dark sable coat. They were wrapped in each other's arms. He looked like a much younger man, and she looked especially beautiful with her hair loose and full and a bright red dress peeking through the coat. She threw her head back and laughed, and Marc kissed her full on the mouth. Deanna stared.

As the woman pulled away, Deanna suddenly saw who she was. It was the girl from the airport—the one she had seen him with the night Pilar died. She suddenly felt as though all the air had been squeezed out of her until she had to gasp for breath. They climbed into his car. Deanna clutched Kimberly's arm.

"Drive, please. Let's go. I don't want him to see us . . . he'll think. . . ." She turned her head away from the window, wanting to see no more, and as though by reflex Kim stomped her foot on the gas. The car lurched forward, and they sped toward the bay as Deanna tried to settle her rapidly whirling mind. What did it mean? Why was the girl there? Was it . . . did it . . . had he . . . but she knew all the answers, as did Kim. They had sat there for five minutes, silent and staring, in the little red car. It was Kim who finally spoke first.

"Deanna, I—I'm sorry. Is there . . . shit! I don't know what to say." She glanced at Deanna. Even in the darkness she looked terrifyingly pale. "Do you want to come home with me for a while until you calm down?"

"You know what's very strange?" She turned to Kim with those huge, luminous green eyes. "I am calm. I feel as though everything has suddenly stopped. All the whirling and confusion and fear and despair . . . it's all over, it's gone." She stared out the window into the foggy night and she spoke to Kim without turning to see her face. "I think I know now what I'm going to do."

"What?" Kim felt worried about her friend. It had been one hell of a shock. She herself was still shaking.

"I'm going to leave him, Kim." For a moment Kimberly didn't respond, she only looked at Deanna's profile, sharply etched against the night. "I can't live like this for the rest of my life. And I think it's been like this for years. I saw him with her in Paris . . . the night Pilar . . . she came in with him from Athens. The joke of it is that when he came home in September, he swore it was over."

"Do you think it's serious?"

"I don't know. Maybe it doesn't matter. The trouble is"—she finally looked back at her friend—"there isn't enough in it for me. No matter what. I'm alone all the time. We don't share anything and we won't even share this child. He'll take it away from me,

just as he did Pilar. Why should I stay with him? Out of duty, out
of cowardice, out of some insane feeling of loyalty that I've
dragged with me over the years? For what? Did you see him tonight? He looked happy, Kim. He looked young. He hasn't looked
like that with me in almost eighteen years. I'm not even sure
anymore if he ever did. Maybe she's good for him. Maybe she can
give him something I never had. But whatever it is, that's his
problem. I'm getting out."

"Why don't you give it some thought." Kim spoke quietly and
looked at Deanna. "Maybe this isn't the right time. Maybe you
should wait until after the baby comes. Do you want to be alone
when you're pregnant?"

"Maybe you haven't noticed—I already am."

Kim agreed, but she was afraid of the look in Deanna's eyes.
She had never seen that burning determination there before. It
was frightening. Finally they came to a stop in front of her house.

"Do you want me to come in?" At least they knew that Marc
wouldn't be home. But Deanna shook her head.

"No. I want to be alone. I have to think."

"Will you talk to him tonight?"

She looked at Kimberly for a long time before she answered,
and this time Kim saw pain in her eyes. It did hurt. Somewhere
inside her she still cared. "Maybe not. He may not come home."

31

Alone in her bedroom, Deanna slowly pulled off the black dress
and stood staring at herself in the mirror. She was still pretty, and
in some ways still young. The skin on her face was supple and
taut, her neck had the graceful sweep of a swan, the eyes were
large, the eyelids didn't droop and the chin didn't sag, the
breasts were still firm, the legs thin, the hips small. There was no
real sign of age, and yet she looked at least ten years older than
that girl tonight. She had had the glow and the glamor and the excitement of a mistress. There was no fighting that. Was that what

he wanted then? Did that make the difference? Or was it something else? Was it that she was French, that she was one of his own . . . or maybe only that he loved her. Deanna wondered as she climbed into her robe. She wanted to ask him all those questions, wanted to hear all the answers from him—if he'd tell her, if he'd ever come home. She didn't want to wait all night long to ask him, she wanted to ask him now, but it had been clear that he and the girl were going out on the town. It might be daybreak before he came home, claiming that he had been involved in interminable negotiations and had had a sleepless night. She suddenly wondered how many of his stories had been lies, how long this had gone on. She lay her head back in the chair and closed her eyes against the soft lights. Why did he go on with the marriage, now that Pilar was gone? He'd had the perfect opportunity to leave Deanna in Paris, to tell her they were through. Why didn't he? Why had he stayed? Why did he want to hang on? And then suddenly she knew. The baby. That was what he wanted. A son.

She smiled to herself then. It was funny really. For the first time in their nearly twenty years together, she had the upper hand. She had the one thing he wanted. His son. Or even a daughter, now that Pilar was gone. But Marc wanted her child. It was mad really. He could have had a baby with that girl, since he appeared to hang on to her too. But for some reason he had not. It amused her. In a way she had him now. By the throat. She could leave him, or stay. She could make him pay. Maybe she could even force him to get rid of the girl. Or pretend to, as he had. He had let her think the affair was over, but it very clearly was not. With a sigh she sat up in the chair and opened her eyes. She had been living with her eyes closed for too many years. Silently she walked out of the room and down the stairs of the darkened house. She found herself in the living room, sitting in the dark and looking out at the lights on the bay. It would be strange not being there anymore, leaving this house—leaving him. It would be frightening to be alone, to have no one to take care of her, or the new child. It would all be terrifying and new. But it would be clean. It wouldn't be lonely in the same way. . . . It wouldn't be a lie. She sat there, alone, until dawn. Waiting for him. She had made up her mind.

It was just after five when she heard his key turn in the lock.

She walked softly to the door of the living room and stood there, a vision in white satin.

"*Bonsoir.*" She said it to him in French. "Or should I say *bonjour?*" The first light of day was streaking pink and orange into the sky over the mirror-flat bay. For once there was no fog. The first thing she saw about him was that he was drunk. Not disgustingly so, but enough.

"You're already up?" He tried to hold himself steady, but he pitched forward slightly and steadied himself on the back of a chair. He looked uncomfortable to have to be talking to her at all. "It's terribly early, Deanna."

"Or terribly late. Did you have a good time?"

"Of course not. Don't be absurd. We sat in the board room until four o'clock. And then we had drinks. To celebrate."

"How wonderful." Her voice was like ice. He stared at her, as if hoping to find the key. "What were you celebrating?"

"A new . . . deal." He almost said "coat," but caught himself just in time. "A fur trade arrangement with Russia." He looked pleased with himself and then smiled at his wife. Deanna did not smile back.

She looked like a statue. "It was a very beautiful coat." The words fell between them like rocks.

"What do you mean?"

"I think we both know perfectly well what I mean. I said it was a beautiful coat."

"You're not making sense." But his eyes seemed to waver from her gaze.

"I believe I am. I saw you tonight with your friend. I gather this is a lasting affair." She looked wooden as she stood there, and he spoke not at all. After a moment he turned away from Deanna and looked out at the bay.

"I could tell you that she was passing through." He turned to face her again. "But I won't. These have been difficult times for me. Pilar . . . worries with you. . . ."

"Does she live here now?" Deanna was relentless with those enormous green eyes. He shook his head. "No, she's only been here for a few weeks."

"How nice. Am I to accept this as part of my future, or will you eventually make a choice? I imagine she asks you the same questions. In fact right now I daresay the choice could be mine."

"It could." For a moment he seemed to be wavering again, then he stood up very straight. "But it won't be, Deanna. You and I have too much at stake."

"Really? What?" But she knew exactly what he meant. They had nothing at stake anymore though. After tonight the baby was hers. Not theirs. Hers.

"You know exactly what. Our child." He tried to look tender but he only glared. "That means everything to me. To us."

"Us? You know what, Marc, I don't even believe there is an 'us.' There is a you and a me, but there is no 'us.' Your only 'us' is with that girl. I could see that in your face tonight."

"I was drunk." For a moment desperation crept into his eyes. Deanna saw it, but she no longer cared.

"You were happy. You and I haven't been happy with each other in years. We cling to each other out of habit, out of fear, out of duty, out of pain. I was going to leave you the weekend after Pilar died. If I hadn't found out I was pregnant, I would have. And now that's exactly what I'm going to do."

"I won't let you. You'll starve!" He was angry now, and there was a vicious light suddenly in his eyes. She wasn't going to take away the one thing he cared about now—the child.

"I don't need you to survive." They were words of bravado, and they both knew it.

"What will you do to eat, my darling? Paint? Sell your little sketches to people on the street? Or go back to your own lover?"

"What lover?" Deanna felt as though she had been slapped.

"You think I don't know, you self-righteous, cheating bitch. You make me speeches about my . . . activities. . . ." He swayed slightly as he hurled the words at her head. "But you are hardly lily-white yourself."

She was suddenly pale. "What do you mean?"

"Exactly what you think I mean. I left for Athens and you obviously had a little fling. I don't know with whom and I don't care, because you're my wife and that's my child. I own you, both of you, do you understand?"

Everything inside her raged. "How dare you say that to me! How dare you! You may have owned me before, but you don't own me now and you never will, and you'll never own this child. I won't let you do what you did with Pilar."

He grinned at her evilly from the stairs. "You have no choice, my dear, the child is mine. . . . Mine, because I chose to accept it, to be its father, to keep you in spite of what you did. But don't you ever forget that I know. You're no better than I am, in spite of all your saintly airs. But remember," his eyes narrowed and he swayed again, "it is I who will keep your child from being a bastard. I'm giving him my name. Because I want him, and not because he's mine."

Deanna's voice was like measured ice. She stood immobile, watching Marc. "The baby isn't yours then, Marc?"

He bowed awkwardly at her and inclined his head. "Correct."

"How do you know?"

"Because the woman you resent so greatly is a diabetic, and if I'd gotten her pregnant it could have killed her. I had a vasectomy several years ago." He stared back at Deanna, satisfied with the disclosure, as Deanna steadied herself unthinkingly on the back of a chair.

"I see." There was a long silence between them. "Why are you telling me this now?"

"Because I'm tired of lies, and your miserable pathetic face, and your feeling put upon and used and abused by me. I have not abused you, madam. I have done you a favor. I have kept you, and your child, in spite of your appalling behavior. In spite of the fact that you're an adulteress. And now he's gone, and you have no one to turn to but me. You are mine."

"To do with as you choose, is that it, Marc?" Her eyes raged at him, but he was too drunk to see it.

"Precisely. And now I suggest that you take yourself and my son to bed, and I will take myself to bed. I will see you in the morning." He marched solemnly upstairs, totally unaware of the effect of his admission. Deanna had been freed.

32

The door to the back of the house, behind the kitchen, had been locked, and she had the key. She had called Kim and asked her to rent a car—a station wagon. She would explain later. She had had the grocery store deliver a dozen boxes. The equipment in her studio went easily into three. Her photographs and albums fit in five. The paintings were all neatly stacked next to the back stairs. Six suitcases waited to be packed. She picked up the phone and asked Margaret for her help. She would not do this alone. She had been working in her studio since six, and it was almost nine. She knew that Marc had probably already left the house. He didn't follow her to her studio after she left their room, and the silence in the house had been deafening. The end had come quietly, in silence. Now she could put away the past. In a dozen boxes and a few valises. She was leaving him everything else. It was all his. The furniture from France; the paintings; the rugs; and the silver, which had been his mother's, almost all of it sent from France. All that she had collected over the years was in her studio—art books, brushes, paints, a few trinkets, some bits and pieces that she liked but were worth nothing. She had her clothes. And the jewelry she would take too. She would sell it to eat, until she found a job. She was taking all her paintings, they meant nothing to him, and she could sell those too. All except the one of herself and Pilar. That was not a painting to sell, it was a treasure of a lifetime. The rest he could have. He could have it all.

She unlocked the door at the foot of the studio stairs and hesitantly made her way through the house. What if he was still there? If he was waiting? If he knew what she was going to do and how soon? But it didn't matter now. He couldn't stop her. He had told her what she needed to know last night. The baby wasn't his, it was Ben's. And he had known all along. But it didn't matter anymore. None of it did.

"Margaret, is . . . ?" She wasn't quite sure what to say.

"He left for the office at half past eight." Margaret's eyes were brimming with tears. "Mrs. Duras, you're not. . . . Oh, don't leave us, don't go. . . ."

It was the speech that should have been made by Marc, except that he already knew he had lost and he was too drunk the night before to follow through on his fears. He must have figured that if he slept it off and let her hide in her studio, he could come home with a handsome piece of jewelry, an apology, and a lie, and all would be well again. Not this time. Deanna put an arm around Margaret.

"I have to. But you'll come and see me."

"I will?" The old woman looked crushed; Deanna smiled at her through her own tears. She was crying for herself now, not for him.

The doorbell rang as they finished the second suitcase. Deanna jumped, startled, and for a moment Margaret looked like she might panic, but Deanna sped down the stairs and discovered that it was Kim.

"I got the biggest station wagon they had. It looks like a boat." She tried to smile but saw that Deanna was not in the mood. There were dark circles under her eyes, her hair was disheveled, and her eyes were rimmed with red. "Looks like it must have been a great night."

"The baby's not his." It was the first thing she could think of to say, and then suddenly she was smiling at Kim. "It's Ben's, and I'm so glad."

"Jesus H. Christ." For a moment, Kim didn't know whether to laugh or cry, but somehow she felt immensely relieved. Deanna was free. "Are you sure?"

"Absolutely."

"And you're leaving?"

"Yes. Now."

"I had a suspicion it was something like that. Because of the baby?" They were still standing at the door. Deanna started slowly toward the stairs.

"That and everything else. The other girl, the baby. It's not a marriage, Kim. And whatever it is or it isn't, it's over. I knew that for certain last night."

"Will you tell Ben?" But it was a dumb question. She knew that Deanna would. She knew it, until Deanna shook her head. "Are you kidding? Why not?"

"Why? So I can run from Marc's house to his? So he can take care of me too? I left him, Kim. I walked out. I went back to Marc and never told him I was having a child. What right do I have to call him now?" Her eyes looked too big in her face. Kim stared at her, trying to make sense of what was being said.

"But you're having his baby. What more right do you need?"

"I don't know. I just know I won't call."

"Then what the hell are you doing?" Kim grabbed her arm as she started up the stairs.

"Leaving here. I'll find an apartment and take care of myself."

"Oh, for chrissake, will you stop being so noble? How the hell will you eat?"

"Paint, work, sell my jewelry. . . . You'll see. Come on, I have to finish upstairs." Kim looked sober as she followed her up the stairs. She thought leaving Marc was the best idea Deanna had had yet but not calling Ben was insane.

Margaret had just finished packing the last bag. There was nothing left in the room except the things that belonged to Marc. The little trinkets and photographs, the tiny mementos, the jewel box, and the books . . . all were packed and gone. She stopped for only a moment on the threshold, then hurried down the stairs.

It took them twenty-five minutes to pack the car, with Margaret crying ceaselessly and Kim carrying all the heavy bags. Deanna carried only her paintings, which were light.

"Don't touch that!" Kim shouted at Deanna once, when she had been about to pick up a valise. "You're five months pregnant, you jackass." Deanna smiled.

"No, I'm not. Probably a lot more like four." Then they both grinned. Deanna had figured that out in the early morning as she cleaned all her paint brushes, wrapped them in newspaper, and put them away. He had told her that she had conceived at the end of June, which was when he'd left. But it was probably more like late July, when she was with Ben. That explained too why Dr. Jones hadn't heard the heartbeat until a month after he thought he should have and why she was so small. Also, why she was still so tired. She was probably almost exactly four months pregnant. "Oh, my God." She suddenly looked up at Kim. "Is today Thanksgiving?"

"It is."

"Why didn't you tell me?"

"I thought you knew."

"Aren't you supposed to be somewhere?"

"Not until later. We'll get you settled first. You can have a nap. And then we'll get dressed and have a turkey dinner."

"You're nuts. You act as though you've been planning for weeks to have me stay." The two women exchanged a smile as they stowed the last painting in the back of the car. "I'm going to stay at a hotel, you know." She said it firmly as she looked at the paintings and packages in the car.

"No, you're not." Kim was equally firm. "You're staying with me. Until you're ready to move out."

"We'll discuss it later. I want to go back inside for a minute and check."

"Is there any chance Marc might come back? It is a holiday after all."

But Deanna shook her head. "Not for him. He works on Thanksgiving." And then she smiled a half-smile and shook her head. "It isn't French." Kim nodded and got into the car as Deanna disappeared back into the house. Margaret was in the kitchen, and for a moment Deanna was alone. For the last time in what had been *her* house—except that it had never been. It had always been his. Maybe the little French girl in the fur coat would like it, maybe it would all mean something to her.

Deanna stood in the hall, looking through the living room, glancing at the portraits of Marc-Edouard's ancestors. It was amazing, after eighteen years she was leaving with almost as little as she'd brought when she had come. Some boxes, some canvases, her clothes. The clothes were more expensive now. The jewelry would keep her alive. The paintings were better, the art supplies finer. But it all still fit in one car. Eighteen years in as many boxes and bags. She sat down at her desk then and pulled a piece of paper out of a drawer. It was Wedgwood blue, trimmed in white, and the letterhead said MME. MARC-EDOUARD DURAS. She pulled out her pen, thought for a moment, and then wrote only a few words:

I loved you, darling.
   Good-bye.

She folded the sheet of paper, wiped a tear from her face with the back of one hand, and left the note stuck in the mirror in the hall. When she turned away, she saw Margaret watching her, the tears streaming from her eyes. Deanna said nothing, only went to her, held her tightly for a moment. Then, with tears streaming from her own eyes, she nodded and walked to the door. She said only one word as she left, and she said it so softly that Margaret could barely hear. She said it gently as she closed the door and smiled. "Adieu."

33

"Why won't you come?" Kim looked disappointed. "It's Thanksgiving, and I won't leave you alone."

"Yes, you will. I'm an uninvited guest, and an exhausted one at that. I can't, love. Honest. I'm just too goddamn tired. Leave me here, and I may even revive by tomorrow." But Kim wasn't sure of that either. The last twenty-four hours had taken their toll. Deanna looked exhausted and bleak. Kim had even gone so far as to call Dr. Jones from the kitchen phone, where Deanna wouldn't hear. She explained to him what had happened. His advice had been to just let Deanna be. Let her go at her own pace and do what she wanted. He felt sure that she'd be all right. On the strength of that Kim decided not to push.

"All right. But you're sure you won't be lonely."

"No, more likely I'll be asleep." She smiled tiredly at her friend and suppressed a yawn. "I don't think I'll miss Thanksgiving at all this year." The two women exchanged a smile, and Deanna was asleep before Kim left. Kim tiptoed out the door and quietly locked it.

The key turned in the lock around eleven that night, and for a moment he held his breath. It had been insane not to call, but he hadn't known what to say. What could he tell her? How could he take back what he'd said? He had wanted to buy her something pretty, something to buy her back, but all the stores had been closed. Thanksgiving. A day of thanks. He had spent half the day working at his desk, and the other half quietly with Chantal. She had known that something was wrong, but she was not quite sure what. He had clung to her in their lovemaking in a very odd way.

He opened the door and looked up. There was no light and no sound. She was obviously asleep. Her car had been in the garage. He didn't even see Margaret's light shining under her door down the hall. The entire house was still, and he put on only a small light as he hung up his coat. And then he saw the note paper, stuck into the frame of the mirror near the door. Was she out? Had she gone somewhere with a friend? He reached for the paper and held it, a sudden, odd feeling clutching at his heart. He stood there for a moment, as though waiting to hear her voice or her foot on the stairs. He looked up again and heard only silence, and then slowly he opened the folds of the paper at last. His eyes swam and his head pounded as he read it. 'I loved you, darling. Good-bye'. Why "loved?" Why in the past tense? But he knew. He had told her the one thing that she could never know. That the baby was not his. She knew now that he had lied to her about the baby, and about Chantal. . . . She knew about his other life. She had seen him with Chantal in Paris and again the other night. With feet like lead he tried to race up the stairs. He would find Deanna there. She would be asleep in their bed. All day he had ignored what had happened between them, hoping it would go away. Calling her would make it real. He couldn't. He didn't want to do that. Now all he had to do was run to the bed and he'd find her there, asleep.

But when he reached their room, he found it as he dreaded he would—empty. She was gone. Deanna was gone.

Marc-Edouard stood deathly still for a long moment, not knowing what to do. Then fighting back tears, he reached for the phone. He needed her. Desperately. She had to be there for him now. He knew she would be. He dialed, but when Chantal answered, she sounded strange.

"Chantal . . . I—I have to see you. . . . I'll be right there."

"Is something wrong?" She sounded distracted and in a hurry.

"Yes . . . no. . . . Just be there. I'm on my way over." She had wanted to tell him to hurry, but she hadn't known quite what to say, and she was still feeling awkward and looking a little bit confused when he arrived only moments later. But he saw nothing. He only took her quickly in his arms the moment she opened the door.

"Darling, what is it? You look ill."

"I am. . . . I don't know. . . . She's gone."

Poor man. Pilar again. Was he still so excessively haunted by that? But what had happened to trigger it so suddenly? "I know, my darling, but you have me." She held him close as they sat together on the couch.

"But the baby. . . ." And then he realized that he shouldn't have blurted it out.

"What baby?" Had he gone mad? She looked frightened as she pulled away from him.

"Nothing. . . . I'm upset. . . . It's Deanna. She's gone."

"For good? She left you?" He nodded numbly, and Chantal grinned.

"I'd say that's cause for celebration, not despair." Without thinking further, she rose from the couch and went out to the kitchen to find one of the bottles of champagne Marc had left with her only a few days before. She returned with the bottle and two glasses, and then stopped as she saw the agony on Marc's face. "Are you that unhappy then?"

"I don't know. I'm stunned. I said some things . . . I shouldn't have. . . . I—I overplayed my hand."

Chantal stared at him with chilly eyes. "I didn't realize you were that anxious to keep her. Now what? You fight to get her back?" As he watched her, he slowly shook his head. He couldn't get Deanna back and he knew it. While trying to tie her to him forever, he had told her the one thing that had severed her from him. The baby wasn't his. "By the way"—Chantal paused only for a moment—"what was that business you just mentioned about a baby?" He said nothing, he only stared at something she could not see. The death of hope. "Was she pregnant, Marc?" Her words were like a vise at his throat, and silently he nodded.

"Did she know it wasn't yours?"

"Not until last night."

"I see. And that was why you stayed with her until now—for a child that wasn't even yours. . . ." Her voice drifted away like a kind of distant death knell, disappointment filling her heart as well. "I didn't realize it meant that much to you."

"It doesn't." He lied to her and tried to take her in his arms.

"Yes, it does." The champagne stood unopened. They looked at each other in despair. "Yes, in fact, it does."

"We can adopt a child," Marc said. Slowly Chantal nodded. She knew that she would have to if it meant that much to him, but she didn't want children. She never had.

"Yes, I suppose we can." And then with sudden recollection, she glanced at her watch. "What are you going to do now?"

"Marry you." He tried to smile as he said it, but the words felt like lead in his mouth. "If that's what you still want."

"It is." She sounded solemn, but there was a filament of worry lurking in her eyes. "But I didn't mean that, darling. I meant to-night."

"I don't know. Can I stay here?" The idea of going back to his own home was unbearable to him, and it was too soon to take Chantal there, to sleep in the bed Deanna had vacated only the night before. She had slept in the studio after his disclosure.

"Why don't we go out to dinner?"

"Now?" He looked at her, shocked. "I'm hardly in the mood. A lot has changed for me in the past few hours, and no matter how much I love you, I need to adjust." For a moment he wondered if he had made a mistake coming to Chantal so quickly, before he had absorbed the shock. She seemed to understand nothing of what he was feeling. "Couldn't we just eat here?"

"No. I want to go out." She said it nervously now, as though she were in a hurry, and he noticed suddenly that she was wearing a black silk dress, as though she had been planning to go to dinner anyway.

"Were you going somewhere when I called?" He looked as though he didn't understand.

"I just thought I'd go out somewhere for dinner."

"Alone?" He looked shocked.

"Obviously." She laughed at him, but it had a tinsel ring, and before she had said more, the doorbell rang. She looked rapidly at Marc-Edouard and then hurried toward the door. "I'll be right back."

From where he sat on the couch, his view of the doorway was obscured, but he heard her open the door and step outside, and then suddenly something inside him raged. He strode across the room, following her path, and reached the almost-closed door where he could hear her speaking softly on the other side. He pulled it sharply open and heard her gasp as she jumped slightly aside. She was speaking to his partner, Jim Sullivan, who looked somewhat shocked to be facing Marc.

"Am I interrupting you, or would you care to step inside?" He was looking at his partner, but his words were addressed to both of them. Silently the trio walked into the apartment. Chantal closed the door.

"Darling, it's really. . . . Jim just thought I'd enjoy Thanksgiving dinner. I thought you would be . . . at home. . . ." Her face was taut with embarrassment, and her borrowed gaiety fooled no one.

"I see. How charming. Odd that neither of you mentioned it to me."

"I'm sorry, Marc." Jim looked at him soberly as they stood uncomfortably in the middle of the living room. "I don't think there's much more I can say." Marc-Edouard turned his back to him. Jim simply touched his shoulder, and a moment later Marc heard the sound of the front door close. He turned slowly to face Chantal.

"Is that what you've been doing?"

Her eyes were wide as she shook her head. "I've only had dinner with him a couple of times. I didn't really think you'd mind." But they both knew it was a lie.

"What do I say to you now?"

"That you forgive me. And I say to you that it will never happen again." She slipped herself quietly into his arms and held him close as he slowly bowed his head and felt the silk of her hair on his face. Tears hovered in his eyes as he held her, because he knew that it would happen again and again . . . and again.

34

Kimberly drove down the narrow streets of Sausalito and then into a small alley leading toward the bay. She glanced at the paper next to her on the seat and confirmed that she was going the right way. Another turn, another alley, a dead end, and then she was there. There was a tiny white-picket fence, a huge bush covered with daisies, and a little house hidden beyond. It was the gem Deanna had described, and Kimberly loved it on sight. Her arms were filled with packages, and she wrestled to reach the bell. A moment later Deanna pulled open the door.

Deanna was wearing jeans and red espadrilles and a full, red

sweater over a bright yellow blouse. Her hair was held up in a
knot, and there was a gentle smile for her friend in her eyes.

"Merry Christmas, madam. I'm so glad you could come!" She
held out her arms to Kim, and they hugged. "I only left you two
weeks ago, and I'm already homesick."

"Don't be. This is divine." Kim followed her inside and looked
around. Deanna had been working industriously, painting the
kitchen, cleaning the floors. In the corner there was a tiny Christmas tree with silvery balls and blinking lights. There were three
packages under the tree, and they were all marked KIM.

"Well, do you really like it?" Deanna looked like a little girl as
she grinned. For the first time in a long time she looked happy
and at peace. In only a few weeks she had found something of
herself. There was not a great deal of furniture in the bright little
front room, but what she had was comfortable and inviting.
There was wicker, freshly painted white, and a wonderful old
couch she had reupholstered in a soft blue. There were plants ev-
erywhere, and old bottles filled with flowers. Some of her favorite
paintings hung on the walls, and she had bought a wonderful,
richly patterned carpet. There were copper pots on the mantel-
piece and brass candlesticks on a little wooden dining table just
large enough for two, and the room had boasted a small bronze
chandelier of its own. She had made the curtains herself out of a
starched, lacy fabric she'd found in a trunk. She looked as though
she'd lived there for years. There was one tiny bedroom she'd endowed with a wonderful old print wallpaper in a warm, dusty rose,
and another tiny bedroom next to it, empty save for a bassinet
and a rocking horse, huddled near the door.

Kim looked around appreciatively and settled herself in a chair.
"I'm in love with it, Deanna. Can I stay?"

"For at least a year. But I think you'd find it has a few kinks.
The hot water comes and goes, the oven takes about a week to
warm up, the windows stick, the chimney smokes. . . ." She
grinned. "But I love it. Isn't it just like a little dollhouse?"

"Exactly. I like it much better than my place, which has absolutely no charm."

"Yours has more class. But this will do." No one would have
believed that a month before she'd been living in grandeur. She
seemed perfectly happy to be where she was. "Coffee?" she asked.

Kim nodded. Deanna disappeared, then returned with two steaming mugs.

"So what's new?" But the easel in the corner of the kitchen told her what she had been wondering. Deanna was already back at work.

"I'm painting again." She looked happy and proud.

"So I see. What are you going to do with them?"

"Sell them probably. I've already sold two or three. They paid for the furniture, the dishes, the sheets." Three paintings and the jade-and-diamond earrings. But she didn't explain that to Kim. And she didn't give a damn. There was nothing left that she wanted, except her child now. The rest didn't matter anymore. Not at all.

"Where are you selling them?" Kim looked at her with a purpose in mind, but Deanna saw her coming.

"Never mind that." She grinned and took a sip of her tea.

"Why don't you at least let him sell your paintings for chrissake? You don't have to see him." Kim had seen him only last week, and he looked like hell. She wanted to slip him Deanna's address, but she knew she couldn't. Deanna had to find her way back to him herself. If she ever did. Kim was beginning to doubt it. Deanna seemed happier by herself. "Why don't you at least call Ben about your work?"

"Don't be silly, Kim. What would that prove? I can't. And he'd probably spit in my eye if I called him and asked him to handle my work."

"I doubt that." But maybe she was right. He never asked Kim how she was anymore. It was a silent agreement between them. Neither of them spoke of Deanna. Kim understood. "What about Marc? Have you heard anything from him?"

Deanna shook her head. "I called him once after I spoke to my lawyer. He understands. There's no argument really."

"Do you think he'll marry that girl?"

Deanna sighed and then looked up with a smile. "Maybe. She's living with him at the house. But I think"—the smile slowly faded —"I think this has all been kind of a shock. A lot has happened to both of us this year."

For a moment Kim wondered if Deanna missed him; she looked as though she did. Maybe it was merely a question of habit. In any event she had certainly come a long way.

"How do you know he's living with that girl?" It seemed an unusually honest admission for Marc to have made.

"Margaret told me when I called one day to see how she was. Apparently she's quitting next month. It's probably just as well. He doesn't need any more reminders of me around there. We might as well all get a fresh start."

"Is that what you're doing?" Kim asked. Deanna nodded with another smile.

"It's not always easy, but I am. The house keeps me busy, and my work. I want to fix up the nursery next month. I found some adorable fabric. And I want to do some funny little Mother Goose people for the walls."

Kimberly smiled at her and they settled back for a nice cozy chat. It was after five o'clock when Deanna finally got up and turned on all the lights.

"Good Lord, we've been sitting here in the dark."

"And I really ought to get home. I still have to cross the bridge. Are you doing anything for Christmas, by the way?" But she was almost sure she was not.

Deanna shook her head. "This isn't really the year for that. I think I'll enjoy spending it quietly . . . here." Kim nodded and felt a pang of guilt.

"I'm going up to the mountains for some skiing. Want to come?"

Deanna laughed and pointed at her now swelling stomach. She was at last almost five months, and now the evidence tallied with the dates. She had a nice round little tummy under her blouse. She patted it with a warm smile and looked at Kim.

"I don't think I'll be doing much skiing this year."

"I know, but you could come up anyway."

"And freeze? No, I'd much rather be here."

"All right. But I'll leave you my number. You can call if you need me, you know."

"I know. I know." She scooped up Kim's presents then loaded them into her arms and looked warmly at the things Kim had left under her tree. "Merry Christmas, love. I hope it's a beautiful year."

Kim looked smilingly down at her friend's growing waistline and nodded. "It will be."

35

Christmas came and went without any of the splendor or ceremony of years gone by. There were no expensive peignoirs from Pilar, selected by her and charged to her father's account. There was no French perfume in crystal bottles, no diamond earrings, no fur. There were four presents from Kim, opened at midnight on the first Christmas Eve she had ever spent alone. She had been afraid of it at first, afraid of what it would be like to be alone, afraid that she wouldn't be able to stand the loneliness or the pain. But it wasn't lonely. And it was only a little bit sad. She found herself missing Marc and Pilar, because Christmas had always been theirs—the celebration, the noise, the ham or the goose or the turkey, Margaret in the kitchen, and mountains of boxes under the tree. It was the activity she missed, more than the riches; it was the faces she missed late at night. Pilar's young shining one, and Marc's in the days of long ago. There was no reaching back to them now though, they were irretrievably gone. It never occurred to her to call Marc, to hear his voice in the middle of the night. She drank hot chocolate and sat near her tree. But it did occur to her to call Ben. She guessed that he was in Carmel. Was he also alone?

In the distance, she could hear carolers wandering past, and she found herself humming "Silent Night" as she undressed. She was less tired than she had been in months, feeling better in fact than she had in a very long time. But life was much simpler now. Her only worry was financial, but she had even that under control. She had found a tiny gallery on Bridgewater that sold her work—for only a few hundred dollars each canvas—but it was enough money to pay the rent and buy whatever else she might need. She still had some money left from the jade-and-diamond earrings. And she had a safe-deposit box filled with jewelry she could sell in the next months. She would have to sell more when it came time for the baby, and eventually Marc would have to give her something after they went to court.

She smiled to herself as she slid into bed. "Merry Christmas, Baby." She patted her stomach and lay on her back and for a moment she fought back the thoughts of Pilar. Maybe it would be another girl. But this time how different it would be.

36

It was nine o'clock on a February morning. Ben sat in his office, looking at his new ads. He pressed a buzzer on his desk and waited for Sally to come into the room. When she did, she had an armful of papers, and he looked at her with a scowl.

"What do you think of this stuff, Sally? Does it work or not?"

"Yes." She hesitated as she looked. "But maybe it's a little too showy?"

He nodded emphatically and tossed them back on his desk. "That's exactly what I think. Get Kim Houghton on the phone. I have to see an artist in Sausalito at eleven. See if she'll meet me at the Sea Urchin around twelve-fifteen."

"In Sausalito?" Sally asked. He nodded distractedly, and she disappeared. It was almost ten o'clock when she popped her head in the door. "She'll meet you at the Sea Urchin at twelve-thirty, and she said bring the ads. She's got another bunch of possibilities to show you and she'll bring those too."

"Good." He looked up at her with a vague smile and sighed at the work on his desk. Sometimes it seemed endless. He had added four new artists to their roster that winter, but he wasn't really in love with their work. They had been the best of what he had seen, but they weren't wonderful, they weren't Deanna Duras. People still asked him about her, and he tried to explain. She had "retired." Another sigh escaped him as he plunged himself back into his work. He had done that since September, and it had almost worked. Almost. Except late at night and early in the morning. Now he understood how she must feel about Pilar. That feeling that you'll never touch someone again, or hold them, or hear them, never laugh with them, or be able to tell them a joke and see them smile. He stopped working for a moment and then chased the thoughts away. He was good at it now. He had had five months of practice.

He left the gallery at exactly ten-fifteen. That gave him time to cross the bridge, drive to Sausalito, and park. This at least was an artist he liked, a young man with a wonderful eye for color and a kind of magical flair, but his work was far more modern than Deanna's, and not nearly as good. He had never made the young man an offer, but he had decided that he finally would. Until then the young artist had been represented by a gallery near where he lived, a small cozy gallery in Sausalito that handled a mountain of very diverse work. Ben had first noticed the artist's paintings there, buried with some good and some bad, and he knew the young man was getting terrible payment for his work. A hundred and seventy-five was his top price. Ben would up the price to two thousand, right from the start. And he knew he could get it. The artist would be thrilled.

And he was. "Oh, my God. Wait till I tell Marie!" He grinned broadly and pumped Ben's hand. "My God. We might even be able to afford to eat something decent for a change." Ben laughed, amused, and they walked slowly to the door. It was a big airy studio in half of what had once been a barn. It was now surrounded by houses and ersatz Victoriana, but it was still a wonderful studio and a nice place to work. "By the way, whatever happened to that girl you handled last summer? Duras?"

"Handled." It was an interesting choice of words. But he didn't know. No one did. "We don't show her work anymore." Ben said it very calmly. He had said it a hundred times before.

"I know. But do you know who does?"

"No one. She retired." Ben had the speech down pat. But this time the young man shook his head.

"I don't think so. Are you sure?"

"Quite. She told me she was retiring when she withdrew her work." But something in the man's eyes bothered him. "Why?"

"I could swear I saw one of her pieces at the Seagull the other day. You know, the place that's been showing my work? I wasn't sure, and I didn't have time to ask, but it looked like it. It was a beautiful nude. And they were asking a ridiculous price for it."

"How much?"

"I heard someone say a hundred and sixty bucks. It's really a crime for a fine piece like that. You ought to take a look and see if it's her."

"I think I will." He looked at his watch. It was only eleven-thirty. He had enough time before his lunch with Kim.

The two men shook hands again. There was a profusion of thank you's and smiles. Ben slid into his car and drove a little too quickly down the narrow road. He knew exactly where the gallery was, and he left his car parked on the corner. He wanted to just stroll in and look around, but he didn't have to. Her painting was prominently displayed near the door. He could see it from where he stood, rooted to the spot on the street. It was indeed her canvas. The young man had been right.

He stood there for a moment, wondering what to do, trying to decide if he should go inside. He was about to walk away, but something drew him into the gallery. He had to get closer to the still life. He had seen her paint it. She had done it on their terrace in early July. Suddenly he felt pulled back into the summer.

"Yes, sir? May I help you?" She was a pretty blonde in sandals and jeans. She wore the usual uniform, T-shirt and pierced ears, her hair held up in the back with a wide leather thong.

"I was just looking at the painting over there." He pointed to Deanna's piece.

"It's a hundred and sixty. Done by a local artist."

"Local? To San Francisco, I suppose you mean."

"No. Sausalito." She was obviously confused, but there was no point arguing.

"Do you have any more of her work?" He was sure that they didn't. Much to his astonishment, the girl nodded.

"Yes, we do. I think we have two more."

As it turned out, there were three. One more from the summer, and two of her earlier works, none of them priced over two hundred dollars.

"How did you get these?" He found himself wondering if they had been stolen. If there had only been one, he might have suspected that someone who had bought one from him had been desperate to sell it, but that seemed unlikely, and it was obviously not possible since they seemed to have so much of her work.

The little blonde girl looked surprised by his question. "We have them on consignment from the artist."

"You do?" Now it was his turn to look stunned. "Why?"

"I'm sorry?" She didn't understand.

"I mean why here?"

"This is a very reputable gallery!" She looked unhappy at his remark, and he tried to cover his confusion with a smile.

"I'm sorry. I didn't mean that. I just . . . it's just that I know the artist, and I was surprised to see her work here. I thought she was away . . . abroad." He really didn't know what to say. On the spur of the moment he looked at the blonde girl with another smile. "Never mind. I'll take them."

"Which ones?" He was obviously crazy. Or maybe just stoned.

"All of them."

"All four?" Crazy, not stoned.

"Yes, that'll be fine."

"But that'll be almost eight hundred dollars."

"Fine. I'll write a check." The blonde girl nodded then and walked away. The manager checked with Ben's bank, and the check was good. Ten minutes later he walked away, and Deanna and the gallery were each four hundred dollars richer. He still wasn't sure why he'd bought them when he put them in his car. All he knew was that he had wanted to have her work. And the prices were insane. He didn't understand it. He would sell the four pieces in his gallery and turn the far larger profit over to her. As if she cared. . . . What was he trying to prove?

He was annoyed with himself as he parked in front of the Sea Urchin to meet Kim for their lunch. It had been a grandiose thing to do, buying all four of the paintings. When she found out, she'd probably be mad as hell. But something about the whole episode irked him. What did they mean, a "local" Sausalito artist?

Kim was waiting for him at a window table, enjoying the view of the city across the bay.

"Mind if I sit down?" She turned toward him, startled, then laughed.

"For a minute I thought you were a masher." She grinned up at him, and he smiled. He looked as pleasant as ever, as nicely put together, as well dressed in blazer, slacks and striped shirt, but she thought there was something troubled in his eyes.

"No such luck, Ms. Houghton, mashers are out of style. Or maybe they're all women these days."

"Now, now."

"Would you like a drink?" he asked. She nodded, and they

both ordered bloody marys. For a moment he looked out at the bay. "Kim?"

"Yes, I know. You're going to tell me you hate the ads. I don't love them either. But I've got some other ideas."

He shook his head and dragged his eyes back to hers. "Never mind that, though as a matter of fact you're right. We can talk about that later. I want to ask you something else." He paused for a long moment, and Kim waited, suddenly wondering if this was what she had seen in his eyes.

"What is it?" He looked so troubled, she wanted to reach out a hand.

"Deanna."

Kim's heart almost stopped. "Have you seen her?"

But he only shook his head again. "No. Have you?" Kim nodded in answer. "Is something wrong? I just found four of her paintings in a local gallery, and I don't understand. Why would she sell her work there? You know what they were selling them for? A hundred and sixty, one seventy-five. It's crazy, it doesn't make sense. And they said something about her being a local artist. Local to Sausalito. Now that really doesn't make sense. What the hell is going on?"

Kim sat looking at him for a moment, saying nothing. She wasn't sure what she could say. She had a date to visit Deanna that afternoon, right after lunch. She had been delighted with the excuse of having lunch in Sausalito. This way she could stop and see Deanna before heading back. But what could she say to Ben? How much could she tell him?

"Kim, please tell me. Do you know?" His eyes pleaded with her; they were filled with concern.

"Maybe someone else sold the paintings to the gallery after he bought them from her." She had to ask Deanna before she said anything to him. She had to. She owed that to Deanna, but she wanted to tell him now.

"No, that's not the case. The girl said they had them on consignment from her. But why? Why a gallery like that, and over here? Is she trying to sell them without her husband knowing? Is she in trouble? Does she need cash?" His eyes pleaded with Kim to speak, and she let out a long, troubled sigh.

"Oh, Ben. What can I say? A lot of things in Deanna's life have changed."

"But apparently not enough for her to call me."

"Maybe she will. In time. She is still very shaken up about Pilar." He nodded silently, and they didn't speak for a while. The last thing he wanted to discuss today was business. All he could think of was Deanna. He knew something was terribly wrong.

He looked up at Kim again, and she wanted to die from the look in his eyes. "Is she in some kind of trouble?" But Kim shook her head no.

"She's all right, Ben. She is. I think in some ways she's happy for the very first time." She wanted to tear her tongue out for saying it. Deanna had been even happier during the previous summer, but Kim wasn't sure how to alter what she had just said. "She's painting a lot."

"And she's happy." He looked at the bay and then at Kim. "With him. . . ." But suddenly Kim couldn't stand it anymore. She very slowly shook her head. "What do you mean?"

"He went back to France." Deanna had told her that just last month. Marc had finally gone back to his home.

"Permanently?" Ben looked stunned. Kim merely nodded. "And she stayed?" Kim nodded again, and now there was despair in his eyes. She hadn't called him. Marc was gone, and she hadn't called. But as he looked down into his drink, he felt Kim's hand gently touch his.

"Give her a chance, Ben. A lot of things have happened. I think it may take her a few more months to sort it all out."

"And she's living here? In Sausalito?" None of it made any sense. Why wasn't she living in their house? Had he just run off and left her? "Do you mean to tell me they're getting a divorce?"

She took a deep breath. "Yes. I do."

"Was it his doing, or hers? Kim, you have to tell me. I have a right to know."

"I'm the first person to agree with you, Ben." *But try telling her. . . .* "It was her doing, but he agreed. He really had no choice."

"How is she? Is she adjusting? Is she all right?"

"She's fine. She's living in a funny little house, working on some new paintings, getting ready—" And then she stopped; she had gone too far.

"Getting ready for what?" He was confused again, and Kimberly was driving him crazy. "For chrissake, Kim, is that lousy gallery giving her a show?" He was incensed. How dare they? Suddenly Kim laughed. She looked at him with a bright light in her eye.

"You know something? This is crazy. We're sitting here playing twenty questions about how Deanna is, when the one thing she needs is you." She pulled a pen out of her handbag and grabbed a piece of paper from among her ads. She jotted down the address and handed it to him. "Go. That's the address."

"Now?" He looked stunned as he took the piece of paper from her hand. "But what if . . . if she doesn't want to see me?"

"She will. But from now on it's up to you." She laughed. "And if she gives you any trouble, just punch her in the mouth." He grinned and looked at her again in confusion.

"What about our lunch?" All he wanted to do was get the hell out of there and go to find Deanna. He really didn't want to sit there a moment longer with Kim, but she knew it, and she smiled.

"Screw our lunch. We can talk about the ads some other time. Go." He bent to kiss her and squeezed her shoulder very hard.

"One day, Kim Houghton, I'll thank you. But right now"—he finally smiled back—"I've got to run. Tell me, do I break the door down or just climb down the chimney?"

"Throw a chair through the window. It works every time."

He was still smiling when he got to his car, and he was at the cul-de-sac five minutes after he left Kim. He glanced at the piece of paper again and quickly saw that it was the house hidden by the large daisy bushes and surrounded by the little picket fence. He wondered if she was at home. Maybe she wasn't in. He was frightened now. What would he say to her? What if she was angry that he'd come? He couldn't bear to have her do that to him now, after all the long months of dreams.

He got out of the car and walked slowly to the door. He could hear someone moving around inside, and there was a radio softly playing jazz. He rang the bell and then knocked. More quickly than he expected, her voice rang out from the back of the house.

"Hi, Kim, it's open. Come on in!" He opened his mouth to tell her it wasn't Kim, but he closed it as quickly. He didn't want her to know the truth until he was inside, until he saw her, just once, even for a moment. Just once more. He pushed the door open with one hand. He was standing in the bright, little front room, and there was no one there.

"Are you in?" She called out to him from the back. "I'm painting the other bedroom. I'll be right out."

He felt as though his guts were melting as he listened to her voice for the first time in five months. He simply stood in one spot and waited for her to come out. He wanted to say something to her, but he couldn't. He almost felt as though he didn't have the strength. But then she called out again. "Kim? Is that you?" This time he had to speak; he didn't want her to be frightened.

"No, Deanna. It's not." There was silence then, and he heard something drop. He stood there, silent, immobile, waiting. But no one came. Nothing happened. No one moved. And slowly he began to walk toward the back of the house. He didn't have far to go. A few steps and he was standing in the tiny bedroom doorway.

"Deanna?" She was standing there, one hand on a bassinet, leaning against the last unpainted wall. His eyes went to hers and he couldn't repress a smile. "I'm sorry, I. . . ." And then he saw, as her eyes grew wide and he saw her chin tremble. "My God, you're . . . Deanna. . . ." He didn't want to ask her, he didn't know what to say. When and how? And whose? And then not caring whose, he closed the gap between them and pulled her into his arms. That was why she was selling the paintings, why she was alone.

"It's ours, isn't it?" he asked. She nodded, tears spilling onto his shoulder. He held her tightly in his arms. "Why didn't you tell me? Why didn't you call?" He pulled away just enough so that he could see her face. She was smiling.

"I couldn't. I left you. I couldn't go back to you like that. I thought that maybe . . . after the baby. . . ."

"You're nuts, but I love you. Why after the baby? I want to be there with you, I want to . . . oh, Deanna, *it's ours!*" He pulled her back into his arms triumphantly, with laughter and tears.

"How the hell did you find me?" She laughed as she held him close and then sniffed. When he didn't answer, she knew. "Kim."

"Maybe so. Or maybe that atrocious little gallery that's selling your work. Deanna, how could you . . ." His voice trailed off, and she grinned.

"I had to."

"Not anymore."

"We'll see."

"You prefer Seagull to me?" He laughed at the thought, and she vehemently shook her head.

"I've just managed to do it all for myself though. I've gotten independent. I've made it. Do you realize what that means?"

"It means that you're wonderful and I adore you. Are you getting divorced?" He was holding her in his arms and gently touching her stomach. He jumped as the baby kicked. "Was that our kid?" The tears glazed his eyes again when she nodded yes.

"And yes, I'm also getting divorced. It will be final in May."

"And the baby?"

"Will be final in April."

"And in that case, you crazy, independent, mad woman, we will also be final in May."

"What does that mean?" But she was laughing now and so was he.

"Just what you think. And"—he looked around the room with a quizzical air—"pack your stuff, madam, I'm taking you home."

"Now? I haven't finished painting the baby's room. And—"

"And nothing, my darling. I'm taking you home."

"Right now?" She put down her paintbrush and grinned.

"Right now." He pulled her close to him again then and kissed her with all the longing of the past five months. "Deanna, I'll never be without you again. Never. Do you understand?" But she only nodded, smiling, and kissed him, as his hand traveled slowly to their child.